She should have grown up in a life of luxury and ease—instead, she was thrust into one of danger and deception...

Forced by her scheming mother to pretend that she was a boy, Vanessa Fordella becomes Van, the Dark Knight, in twelfth-century England. But when her now-dying mother demands that she leave behind her charade and marry, Van embarks on the most difficult journey of her life. And if her new husband ever finds out the truth...

After years of war, all he wants is peace and the simple life...

Peter Lawston, Lord Grayweist, hopes for a shy and controllable wife to run his castle and bear his children. What arrives, instead, is a hell cat, who doesn't know the first thing about being docile or obedient. There's something familiar about his unconventional wife, but Peter can't put his finger on it.

As Van struggles to let go of the knight she has been and become the wife she is expected to be, events unfold that threaten to destroy everything she holds dear, including her very life.

*The Dark L*ady is the first book in *The Dark Books* series. Visit Dawn at her website: http://www.dawnchandler.net/ to read chapter one of Book 2 of the series, *From Under a Dark Shadow*.

Her new life as a woman was hardest when innocents were in danger...

Peter watched her walk away, head high and determined. He was about to go after her, despite her objections when she placed two fingers into her mouth. The deafening whistle that issued forth stopped him in his tracks.

He registered the answering scream of a horse from the stables and the crash of wood that could only have been the stall gate. Not looking back at the screams of the stable hands, he kept his eyes glued to the tall woman as she grasped the hole where he now knew her dagger was kept.

Vanessa grasped the material and pulled. Peter heard the long tear as the skirt fell open completely on the side, baring her leg from thigh to ankle. During it all, she never broke her stride.

Peter called out as her huge destrier thundered past him, screamed for her to watch out. Beast began to slow until Vanessa whistled again. He regained his speed, tearing straight for her. Peter's breath caught in his throat as he knew he would not be able to save her.

She reached out a long arm, gripping the coarse waving mane as the animal thundered past, and smoothly swung herself onto his massive back.

Peter felt a jolt of fear as she wobbled slightly on the racing stallion, one creamy white leg glistening in the dim sunlight. Shadows played off the thick muscles as they rippled in her effort to stay on the unsaddled mount.

The men all stood with their mouths agape as their Lady rode toward the wall. For once Peter did not feel a twinge of jealousy. He fully understood their awe.

Vanessa leaned forward and ducked her head as if to avoid the wind. Her stallion rode straight for the wall. He did not slow or turn and then, to Peter's horror, he was too close to change course.

"She would not." Peter did not even realize he had spoken aloud until he felt a small hand on his. He looked down to see Amy's smile.

"Milord, she would, but she will be all right." She spoke with confidence.

Peter wished he could be as sure, but he wasn't.

He thought his heart would stop as Vanessa did what he had feared she would. He held in a scream as the massive animal bundled its legs underneath it, taking the jump smoothly. Leaning forward, she seemed one with the animal.

He had time to imagine her broken and bloody body lying beneath the horse, both dying.

KUDOS for *The Dark Lady*

The Dark Lady by Dawn Chandler is a wonderfully well-written historical romance. But it is also a great deal more than that. The Dark Lady is a tale of child abuse and a realistic look at the plight of women in medieval times. The story revolves around Vanessa Fordella, whose mother was forced to marry a man she didn't love. In her thirst for revenge, Patricia Fordella runs away with another man and takes one-year-old Vanessa with her. In order to hide her from her real father, Patricia makes Vanessa pretend to be a boy, the son on the man Patricia runs away with. The charade goes so far that Patricia actually sends Van to become a nobleman's squire. Van excels at this and when she saves the nobleman's life, the king makes her a knight...The story is well written, the plot strong, the research solid, and the characters extremely well done. – *Taylor Jones, reviewer*

The book is long, almost 180,000 words, and when I was first given it to review, I thought, surely they could have cut some of it. But as I read it, I discovered that there wasn't a scene I felt the book could realistically do without. This is not a book you can read in one sitting, but I believe it is worth the time it takes to read it. I don't usually care for sagas, but this one is so well done, I found myself so into the story that I didn't mind how long the book was. I loved reading about Vanessa as she struggled with all the things that encompassed being a woman, from the clothes she had to wear to the way she was allowed to ride a horse. I especially loved the scene where she decides if she has to wear the accursed dresses in order to be a woman, she will damned well learn how to move easily in them. And she practices for hours until she can move as easily in a dress as she could in pants. This one is a keeper, folks. – *Regan Murphy, reviewer*

Her new life as a woman was hardest when innocents were in danger...

Peter watched her walk away, head high and determined. He was about to go after her, despite her objections when she placed two fingers into her mouth. The deafening whistle that issued forth stopped him in his tracks.

He registered the answering scream of a horse from the stables and the crash of wood that could only have been the stall gate. Not looking back at the screams of the stable hands, he kept his eyes glued to the tall woman as she grasped the hole where he now knew her dagger was kept.

Vanessa grasped the material and pulled. Peter heard the long tear as the skirt fell open completely on the side, baring her leg from thigh to ankle. During it all, she never broke her stride.

Peter called out as her huge destrier thundered past him, screamed for her to watch out. Beast began to slow until Vanessa whistled again. He regained his speed, tearing straight for her. Peter's breath caught in his throat as he knew he would not be able to save her.

She reached out a long arm, gripping the coarse waving mane as the animal thundered past, and smoothly swung herself onto his massive back.

Peter felt a jolt of fear as she wobbled slightly on the racing stallion, one creamy white leg glistening in the dim sunlight. Shadows played off the thick muscles as they rippled in her effort to stay on the unsaddled mount.

The men all stood with their mouths agape as their Lady rode toward the wall. For once Peter did not feel a twinge of jealousy. He fully understood their awe.

Vanessa leaned forward and ducked her head as if to avoid the wind. Her stallion rode straight for the wall. He did not slow or turn and then, to Peter's horror, he was too close to change course.

"She would not." Peter did not even realize he had spoken aloud until he felt a small hand on his. He looked down to see Amy's smile.

"Milord, she would, but she will be all right." She spoke with confidence.

Peter wished he could be as sure, but he wasn't.

He thought his heart would stop as Vanessa did what he had feared she would. He held in a scream as the massive animal bundled its legs underneath it, taking the jump smoothly. Leaning forward, she seemed one with the animal.

He had time to imagine her broken and bloody body lying beneath the horse, both dying.

KUDOS for *The Dark Lady*

The Dark Lady by Dawn Chandler is a wonderfully well-written historical romance. But it is also a great deal more than that. The Dark Lady is a tale of child abuse and a realistic look at the plight of women in medieval times. The story revolves around Vanessa Fordella, whose mother was forced to marry a man she didn't love. In her thirst for revenge, Patricia Fordella runs away with another man and takes one-year-old Vanessa with her. In order to hide her from her real father, Patricia makes Vanessa pretend to be a boy, the son on the man Patricia runs away with. The charade goes so far that Patricia actually sends Van to become a nobleman's squire. Van excels at this and when she saves the nobleman's life, the king makes her a knight...The story is well written, the plot strong, the research solid, and the characters extremely well done. – *Taylor Jones, reviewer*

The book is long, almost 180,000 words, and when I was first given it to review, I thought, surely they could have cut some of it. But as I read it, I discovered that there wasn't a scene I felt the book could realistically do without. This is not a book you can read in one sitting, but I believe it is worth the time it takes to read it. I don't usually care for sagas, but this one is so well done, I found myself so into the story that I didn't mind how long the book was. I loved reading about Vanessa as she struggled with all the things that encompassed being a woman, from the clothes she had to wear to the way she was allowed to ride a horse. I especially loved the scene where she decides if she has to wear the accursed dresses in order to be a woman, she will damned well learn how to move easily in them. And she practices for hours until she can move as easily in a dress as she could in pants. This one is a keeper, folks. – *Regan Murphy, reviewer*

THE DARK LADY

Dawn Chandler

A BLACK OPAL BOOKS PUBLICATION

Black Opal Books

BECAUSE SOME STORIES JUST HAVE TO BE TOLD

GENRE: HISTORICAL ROMANCE/STEAMY ROMANCE

This is a work of fiction. Names, places, characters and incidents are either the product of the author's imagination or are used fictitiously, and any resemblance to any actual persons, living or dead, businesses, organizations, events or locales is entirely coincidental. All trademarks, service marks, registered trademarks, and registered service marks are the property of their respective owners and are used herein for identification purposes only. The publisher does not have any control over or assume any responsibility for author or third-party websites or their contents.

Published by Black Opal Books http://www.blackopalbooks.com

DEDICATION

To my loving husband, for helping me to believe in myself and for showing me that anything is possible and every dream achievable when you have someone to stand beside you.

To my children who spent much of their childhood listening to me say...just wait till I finish this chapter.

To my mother, who has always stood behind my dreams and supported me.

Thank you all for your loving support.

CHAPTER 1

England April, 1155:

Lightning crackled across the midnight sky illuminating the battle that raged around Peter Lawston. He took in the scene in that split second of brightness. The screams of his warriors paled beneath the sounds of thunder and the raging wind. Rain ran in rivers from Peter's drenched hair, blurring his vision and flooding into his mouth as he barked out orders. Worry constricted his chest as his men struggled against the enemy.

Eolian's attack had been swift and brutal, but Peter's men had been ready. The army riding with Knight Eolian had been terrorizing the neighboring holds and lands for months. burning fields, raping women, and killing anyone who stood up to them.

Following the path of destruction left by Eolian had been simple and Peter had pushed his men hard to get ahead of them. He then set up camp in their path and waited.

He did not have long to wait.

That morning, with dawn still hours away, the cries of battle had broken the silence that blanketed the land. At first torches had sufficed to light the way, now only the biggest of bon fires survived the deluge that befell them. Everything was drenched and the battle sounds fell short in the walls of water that cascaded down.

A blur of movement beside him drew Peter's attention and he tightened his grip on his mace. He tensed in anticipation as a warrior raced toward him, a broadsword held high above his head.

There was no time for fear, just a steady rush of awareness and energy. His body tingled with power. Mud flew from beneath the warrior's pounding feet and caked the fur of his leggings. Peter raised his mace and braced himself. He swung. Blood flew and the man fell.

The sodden ground sucked at Peter's feet as another man came at him. He waited and then swung his mace hard. There was the crunching of bone and the man fell. Man after man pierced the darkness, charging forward. When no one came to Peter he went to them.

The exhilaration of battle was short lived. Peter's adrenaline was quickly wearing off, leaving him feeling drained and empty as he fought his way through the muck. His mind was becoming just as weary of this life as his body was. He was too old for this.

He stopped in the ankle deep mud, trying to ignore the cold that crept through his muscles and invaded his bones. The battered and broken bodies of his enemy lay glistening with sweat and rain as the tenacious flames covered them with flickering light. Peter shook his head. Pity tightened his chest. These men would no longer feel the warmth of the glowing fire. Its welcoming heat caressed them, but was wasted.

Not long ago, Peter had enjoyed his role as leader of the army, but now what he thought of was the families of these men. No matter what these men had done, they had wives and children who would never see them again. Where once Peter had felt elation at victory, there was now only a painful sadness for the ones who were lost and the families who were left behind. At nine and twenty it was time to think of his own life and future, or more importantly the future of Castle Grayweist.

Rain hissed into the fire and steam swirled around him. In the mist that caressed his face he saw his father before him. Peter was once again standing at the crackling fireplace in the library, trying to convince his father that everything would be all right...

His father's face wrinkled in worry as he paced in front of the large oak desk. "What am I going to do if you do not return? If you die my name will end. You are all I have to show that I was ever here." Gesturing to the shelves of books and the expensive furniture that adorned the large room, he shook his head in frustration. "All I have built, all of this, will mean nothing without you. You are my future." His face relaxed as he stopped before Peter. Gripping his hand, he smiled softly. "Please come home safe."

A deep breath did little to calm Peter's emotions. "Father, everything will work out and I will be coming home." He could hear the strain within his own voice. Heat from the crackling fireplace behind him made him think of the cold and wet nights that were in store for him. He rolled his shoulders and closed his eyes. "I will be fine, I always am."

"Make this your last battle." His father's voice cracked with emotion. "I want to see you settled down with a wife and children who you love and cherish. I want to see my name go on but more, I want you to have a good life and to be loved and happy."

Lost in thoughts that had no business on the battle ground, Peter was drawn abruptly back into the Hell that surrounded him as pain exploded through his shoulder. The warm comfort of the library vanished as the long blade of a dagger cut violently into the small area that his chest plate failed to cover. Peter lost his footing as the man, wide as the boulders that surrounded them, first twisted and then ripped the dagger from his mangled shoulder.

Peter's mace slipped from his fingers and was lost in the sludge. The mud splashed around him as he fell. His helm slipped from his head. He threw his arms up to defend himself against the beast of a man who leaned in for the fatal blow. He wondered irrationally why this man was fighting with just a dagger as he reached for his own.

Peter's dagger never cleared its sheath as the man's log of a foot came down, crushing his wrist. This man was going to kill him. His father had been right to worry. He would not be going home.

That thought had just begun to form when a shadowy figure parted from the darkness and lunged at the man. The giant was knocked off balance as the man collided with him, forcing him off of Peter's arm. The crushing pain disappeared as he was freed. He slid closer to the bonfire. Heat penetrated through his armor and a warm trickle of blood ran down his arm and side.

Rain and fire fought their own battle behind him, hissing and crackling, creating a mist that enveloped everything around them. Peter could hear nothing but the sounds of the fire and the booming thunder. He never took his eyes off the two figures in the mist before him. The man that had saved him circled the enemy with not so much as a dagger in his hand.

His rescuer was tall and wide through the shoulders, but the massive man was a head taller and had at least a hundred pounds on the smaller man. Peter tried to identify him, but only caught a glimpse of shimmering chain mail and armor before he disappeared behind the larger man.

As the two circled, his rescuer came back into sight and his hairless face came into view. Lit by the fire it was obvious that he could be no more than fifteen. Shock rippled through Peter as he realized he wasn't a man. He was just a boy.

Peter struggled to get to his feet, knowing this boy didn't stand a chance against the larger, more experienced warrior. The pain and loss of blood made him weak. He managed to get one knee under him before his vision blurred and the world spun around him. The slick mud gave way and he fell back.

The boy grinned as he continued to circle through the swirling fog like a vulture who knows that death is imminent. The boy's grin only widened as the large man began to yell at him, getting angry enough that his voice was audible over the winds and the fire. He told him that his mother was a whore and that he was a bastard. He told him he was in the land of men now and he would die without ever seeing a woman naked.

The boy just laughed, yelling loudly, "I had seen more of a naked woman's body by the time I was ten than you have yet to see. One has been filling my bedding every night for many years now." Amazingly, no fear was shown, no hesitation evident.

A tight band of worry wrapped itself around Peter's chest and re-fused to let go. He knew it was going to end badly and he didn't want to see this boy die for him. He cupped his hand around his mouth and shouted for help, but he knew it was useless.

Reason stood that if he couldn't hear them over the blaring sounds of war and nature they would not be able to hear him either. Still, this kid had no business on the battleground. Peter could not just lay here with the cold seeping into his bones and do nothing. Struggling to his knees, he fought a surge of nausea as the world wavered around him.

The huge man lunged at the boy. The young kid waited until the big man was off balance and then he jerked to the left, not to avoid the man, but to ram a wide shoulder into his side. The man growled as he teetered to the opposite side. As his arms pin-wheeled for balance, he lashed out with the dagger.

The boy jerked back as the blade sliced across his bared cheek, lay-ing him open from his ear to the corner of his mouth. Blood welled, and then flowed freely covering the front of his armor before the rain washed it away.

As the big man tried to catch his balance, the boy slipped in behind him. He gave his wide backside a kick, sending the outraged man face first into the mud with a great splash. The man was surprisingly agile for his girth and took no time getting to his feet and charging the boy. The boy laughed.

Laughed! Peter could not believe the gall of the kid. Once again the kid waited until the last moment. Peter's breath caught in his throat as the enemy got within grasping distance. The giant made a final lunge at the motionless kid. Relief washed over Peter as the boy dove out of the way. Hidden behind the kid was one of Peter's men.

Richard Devenroe instantly brought his sword up. The big beast had no chance of stopping and ran full force into the long blade.

The whole act became clear even to his pain-clouded mind, and it had been an act. Dangerous, but all to a purpose. It had been devised to distract the man. To anger him to a boiling rage, one that would cloud his thoughts and make him careless. It had worked flawlessly, minus the heavy gash in the cheek.

The boy shrugged off Richard, who was trying to check his rapidly bleeding cheek, and rushed to Peter's side. Richard followed behind, a look of irritation on his face that made Peter want to laugh, if only he had the strength. Right on Richard's heels were several of Peter's men. Their concerned faces faded and disappeared as Peter's vision spun. He shut his eyes tightly.

Pain washed over him as he was dragged roughly to his feet. An arm slipped around his shoulder, supporting him. Opening his eyes, he saw the kid. The boy urged him forward, but his feet dragged through the mud, his legs not wanting to cooperate. The world around him swayed and he was forced to allow the boy to take his full weight.

A blurry lean-to appeared before him. Its opening faced the fire allowing in light and needed warmth. He bit his lip, staying a moan of pain as they placed him into the small shelter. He closed his eyes to keep the world from spinning. It didn't work.

Listening to the noises around him, Peter could feel the comforting warmth of the fire seeping through him. He growled deeply, opening his eyes as he was moved around. The boy shifted him slightly to remove his armor. Pain rushed through his shoulder, but the heavy weight of the metal seemed not to be of any bother to the young man. Peter ground his teeth together as he was moved again from side to side. Finally he was bared to his dingy white tunic.

Taking a deep breath, he prepared himself for the boy to remove it as well. Instead the boy used a dagger to start a cut in the material. Then grasping the jagged edges of the shirt in blood-stained, dirt-encrusted hands, he jerked the tattered remains away from the mangled shoulder. Peter closed his eyes against another onslaught of pain.

He sucked in a breath and jerked his eyes open as pressure was put onto the wound. The boy looked over his shoulder at Richard. "Go get the doctor. If he does not want to come, and come now, you have my permission to get him here at your enjoyment." The voice came out in a growl, an order too full of self-assurance to come from a mere page. No, he was a squire, no doubt. The kid had battle under his belt. Instinct and experience told Peter that the trick with the monster of a warrior who had almost killed him was just the beginning of his cunning.

Peter closed his eyes and his breathing became shallow. Numbness was beginning to overtake his mind. His thoughts were getting slower. He could feel it. He tried to concentrate on the boy's voice above him, but his mind felt heavy and sluggish.

The voice that had been gravelly and deep at first had changed—softened, like a gentle breeze across his heart. He was confused at his thoughts. His mind was hazy. Delirium was obviously setting in. A groan slipped from beneath his numb lips.

The sweet, concerned voice caressed him, washing over him like a warm caress. "Are you with me? Can you focus on my face? Come on, talk to me. Open your eyes. I need to know you are going to be all right." The gentle voice was like a melody to his war-ravaged ears, a loving voice that brought forth images of that life his father had spoken of. Of children to hold and to love, not just some faceless heir to be his future, but a child to be his life.

He opened his eyes to the young boy's blurry face. The light from the fire pierced into him, cutting through him like a dagger. He shut his eyes again with a moan.

"Come on, focus. You are going to be all right." There was fear in that soft voice that told him he was cared for. That he was needed. "Look me in the eye." The worry that he heard enveloped him in warmth in a way no fire ever could. He could almost picture the mother of those children who would hold him at night when he was cold, as he was now. She would be beautiful, dark, and exotic.

When he opened his eyes once again the boy was gone and in his place was the beautiful, yet blurry, face of a girl. "Are you all right?" she asked sweetly as she leaned close to him.

"I am here with you." Concern filled him as he spotted the large gash on her cheek, oddly in the same spot as the lad's injury. He shook his head to clear it. Confusion swirled through his weary mind. Peter lifted his hand and ran his fingers along the uninjured cheekbone as blood dripped onto his injured shoulder. "Your face. You are hurt. You must have it looked at."

The face swirled in and out of focus and the boy was there once again. Peter closed his eyes tightly and shook his head. "I will. You first, I can wait," the soft voice told him.

When Peter opened his eyes once again, she was smiling down at him. Her face was still blurred, but he knew it was her from her melodious voice.

"You have such dark eyes, almost black. One could get lost in them." Peter continued to stroke the smooth cheek above him, sliding trembling fingers down the warm and inviting skin gently cupping the soft and shapely chin before starting again. He squinted in an effort to keep the world focused as he looked deeply into those black eyes and thought of his future. "You are so beautiful."

Full lips parted in a sweet tinkling laugh, like water rippling over stones. "I will forgive you that since you have lost so much blood. Your thoughts must be scrambled and your vision faulty." A wide, beautiful smile took the sting from the words.

A deep trembling breath caused the world to shimmer and the image of the boy was once again before him.

Peter pulled his hand away in confusion. "Quite. I have lost a great amount." His arm dropped as darkness swallowed him.

CHAPTER 2

Sounds of anger invaded the peaceful cocoon of darkness that shrouded Peter. He blinked several times to adjust to the brilliant sunlight that poured through the flaps of the tent. The irate voice that had penetrated his sleep was coming from the boy. He stood stiffly, with his back to Peter.

The rough growl was back in his voice, if it had ever been gone. "Aye, that is right, I am still here and I will be the next time you come."

The boy stood at least six foot tall, hands on narrow hips, covered by a large wrinkled tunic that fell past the tops of his thigh high black leather boots. The armor and mail were gone from Peter's young rescuer and were now stacked in the corner of the tent. Peter glanced back at the bright sunlit opening and concern filled his chest as he considered how long he had slept. It was dangerous for his army to remain in one place for long.

"I am not leaving his side 'til he wakens," The boy growled. Peter shifted his head to see who the boy was challenging. Pain shot through his shoulder so he contented himself with glancing around the crowded tent.

Three men stood with the boy between Peter and whoever the kid was arguing with: Telpher Constaire, his brown hair standing on end and in disarray; Grant Hestlay, Peter's right hand man, his lanky frame stiff and unmoving; and Richard Devenroe, one of his higher ranked knights, as well as his good friend.

Richard stood motionless, his arms folded before him, his short sword still in the scabbard at his thick waist. Peter looked from Richard's stern profile to the side of the boy's face. Now stitched, it still looked brutal, damaged more than necessary by waiting to have it looked at.

As his gaze roamed across the jagged line of stitching a quick memory of the woman he had spoken with that night flashed across his vision.

God, had he really stroked the boy's cheek? Had he really said those things? He prayed it had all been a dream.

"You will move aside." The familiar voice of the doctor came from beyond Richard and the boy. Peter tilted his head until he could see the massive man. He was red faced in anger. His dark brown hair brushed the top of the tent. Dr. Jonas Cobb towered over everyone Peter knew, which was one of the reasons he had never seen anyone stand up to him before now.

"He will die if you do not let me help him," Cobb growled. "He will not awaken until I have bled him You will be responsible." The doctor raised one thick fist in the air. The boy didn't move, but Richard edged a little closer to him.

Peter smiled at his friend's protective nature.

"Nay, you are wrong. I allowed you, without opposition, to help him. You stopped his bleeding." The boy gestured to Peter, but not one of the men looked at him. "You stitched him up and gave him medicine to help him heal. You now propose…" he shook his head in frustration and took a stiff step forward. "After all the good you have done, after all the blood he has already lost—" The boy's gruff voice trembled slightly, but whether it was anger or worry Peter could not tell. "Now you think to bleed him and you have the stupidity to call it helping him."

The boy tried to take another step forward, but Richard grasped one arm and Grant the other. They pulled him back, but his tirade never ceased. "Do you know how many men I have seen die because doctors bled them? I will not allow it to happen again, not with this man." His gravelly voice cracked in passionate anger.

Peter shared his anger. He had seen many men die from that same injustice and had stood toe to toe with surgeons himself to protect them.

"Are you accusing me of killing men?" The doctor lunged at him.

Peter was about to call out when the lad shoved hard against the doctor's barrel chest, retreating a step as the doctor stumbled back. By the time the massive man recovered his balance the tall squire had pulled the short sword from Richard's scabbard. A quick step forward found the doctor facing the steady blade.

Standing tall, legs spread wide for balance, the young man held the sword steadily in one hand. "I will stay by his side until he can speak for himself and if you want to change this then you can move me. But if you are thinking you will find help in this with any of the men, you are sorely wrong." To prove this point all three men with him took a step forward, situating themselves in between Peter and Jonas Cobb.

Peter didn't think he had ever felt so important and respected. His chest swelled with pride to see them beside the arrogant squire, all four heads held high.

The doctor's face was almost purple with anger as he shifted from foot to foot. "The king will have your head for this. Do you not know who this man is that you are jeopardizing?"

"Nay. As a matter of course, I did not stop to inquire about his identity when I decided he was in danger. So nay, I knew not who he was. At the moment it was not all that important."

Peter leaned to the side to get a better view, but it was useless.

"As to my head—" The boy tapped himself on the top of the head for emphasis. "Well, I gave my loyalty to the king, and if he wants my head he can have it. I have risked my neck for this man once already and once more should not be too much to ask." The sword never faltered, never trembled, just pointed accusingly at the doctor's wide chest. "I did not risk my life and that of my good friend to have you bleed him to death."

Jonas stopped shifting and stood straight and tall, looking down at the arrogant boy. Peter watched his face tightened in resolve. "You cannot stop me. You will be responsible for his death, then I will see to it the king has your head for it." He leaned forward slightly, preparing to attack.

"We shall see." Every head turned at the sound of Peter's weak, trembling voice. Clearing his throat he attempted to sound more in charge and less like the invalid he felt like. "As I see it, he is responsible not for my death, but for my life." His throat was dry and raw and speaking was difficult. He coughed gently, but water would have to wait. "I will not be bled. Not now, not ever."

The sword arm dropped as the boy turned. He handed the weapon back to Richard without even a glance. His gaze remained locked on Peter's face.

The three men and the boy surrounded the mat where Peter lay. The fearless lad stood at Peter's feet, his face motionless. Peter shook his head in wonder. "Have you really been here with me all night? You have not left me?"

"I have been with you all night, all day, and the night again. It is now working on the mid meal of the day, my lord." The anger was gone from his voice, but the deep gravel was still present. "You must be famished." Without waiting for an answer the young man motioned to Telpher, who immediately rushed from the tent. To Peter's amazement, he did so without even looking to Peter for approval.

"You will stay for a while longer yet?" Peter asked the boy.

"If you wish it, my lord." There was a softness hidden beneath the boy's gruff mannerisms. A softness that brought fleeting images of the phantom woman from the night before.

Peter took a shaky breath and turned his attention to the doctor. Cobb stood stiffly, still red faced in anger, but no longer looking like he was ready to pounce. "I feel weak, due to loss of blood and hunger," Peter said. He swallowed what felt like sawdust for air and continued. "I feel a terrible thirst, but other than that I feel...alive. My shoulder hurts like the Devil. If you need to examine me, you may."

Cobb raised his dark brows and pursed his lips, making him look somewhat like a fish. He grunted and folded his arms across his chest but made no attempt to approach. "I need not see you now that you are awake. I will send something for the pain." With a small jerky bow, he stomped loudly out of the tent.

Peter looked at the ring of worried faces that gazed down upon him. A feeling of contentment flowed through his heart. He took a deep breath and flinched at the pain that splintered through his wound and down his side. He laid his head back and closed his eyes.

Opening them to see the billowing tent above him made it apparent that the rain had stopped. "I was moved?" The sun looked to have found its way out once again and he could feel the warmth radiating through the tent and lifting his spirits.

"Nay, the boy here refused to allow you to be moved, so the tent was built around you."

Peter turned to Hestlay. The tall red headed man, who had been by Peter's side for twelve years, spoke with respect.

"You looked surprised when Telpher took orders from the boy."

Peter nodded, looking toward the lad. The boy stood at attention but held a bemused grin on his face. He looked from Peter to Hestlay without saying a word.

Hestlay gave an amused snort, drawing Peter's attention back to him. "The upstart has been giving orders since you were hurt. Only one man argued, and he got a broken nose for it."

Peter turned to scowl at the lad. The grin only widened on the boy's face. He looked proud of what he had done. Peter took a deep breath and cocked his head, looking closely at the boy.

Was he familiar? Peter had to know him since he was a squire in his army, but he had seen so many young faces come and go over the years. He tried to spend time with each and every one of them, but they came and went so quickly that some of the faces blurred and faded. It saddened Peter, but there were too many young recruits and not enough time.

"You really don't know who I am? I could just be a lowly warrior?"

Indignation swam through the boy's dark eyes. He puffed out his chest and jerked his shoulders back. His spine was so stiff Peter thought he could hear it creaking. He clenched his fists. "I, sir, am a lowly warrior. All of the men I have fought beside for the last three years, and all the ones I have served under for the four years before that were the same." His voice, thick with anger, resounded throughout the tent. Peter watched his face and movements trying to remember where he had seen him before. "These were men that I greatly respected," the boy continued. "Men I would have risked all for, just as I did for you." He took a jerky step toward Peter.

Peter held up his good arm. "Easy. I meant no offense."

The boy had honor in his heart. Respect for this rash and arrogant boy nudged at him.

The young boy shifted on his feet, fists held tight at his sides, but he held his ground. Peter could sense the anger still alive within him. "Tell me this then, boy." Peter looked at the lad. Arrogance and pride dripped from him as he stood unafraid.

Overconfidence would get him, Peter knew. He had been the same way when he was fifteen. "You put yourself in danger. You risked your life and it didn't matter if I was king or foot soldier. Why would you do it? Do you not believe your life as important as theirs, or as mine?"

The boy's face relaxed into an easy grin. He shook his head and gave a short bark of laughter that sounded nothing like the soft, comforting laugh from the angel of Peter's pain induced delusion. Nonetheless he had to push away the insistent images that plagued him.

With a lop-sided, devil-may-care half-grin the boy said, "Nay, 'tis not like that. When I saw you, or see any situation where someone is in trouble, something I feel needs to be changed, I act. It is my body that takes action." The boy's dark eyes glimmered with amusement. "I don't think of myself, not until after I have acted. Until I have already done something stupid. Devenroe here—" The boy jerked his head toward Richard. His face wrinkled and he winced in apparent pain, opening his mouth slightly and working his jaw back and forth. Then with a grin, he opened his eyes and continued as if nothing had happened. "The fact that Devenroe will not allow me to forget that I did something stupid, for days afterwards does not help any either."

Peter looked to Richard. Devenroe stood by Peter's side, arms crossed and a grin on his face as he watched the boy speak. "My brain usually doesn't make an appearance until I have modified the problem," the boy continued. "I have always been mocked that I believe myself the master of every situation. I received several good beatings, while still a page, for giving orders to those above me."

Peter jerked his gaze back to the boy. *Beatings*? He remembered him now, and realized he did indeed know him. Peter had had several run-ins with him while the boy was still a page at his father's castle. As he remembered the boy was always arrogant.

Van? He thought the name was right. He had been Richard's squire for the last three years. Squires and pages were kept separate from the men, so it wasn't surprising that Peter hadn't seen him.

As to the boy's beatings, he himself had administered one of them. He had saved Van from some bullies, turned to leave and Van had attacked him. Peter had tried to just hold him off at first, but the boy would not stop. Van had taken the beating well and if Peter remembered correctly had been happier, almost satisfied, after it had happened. Peter could only assume it had been Van's wounded pride that had caused him to act. Perhaps it had been embarrassment that someone had stepped in to save him. He knew there was a lot of competition among the pages at the castle.

Van should know him. He may not have recognized him in the dark and the rain, but he should remember him now. Peter thought he was hiding that knowledge on purpose. To make a point and to show that it didn't matter what station or ranking you had, everyone was important. Peter fought a grin, knowing he would have done the same thing in Van's place.

Peter tried to pull himself up on the makeshift pallet, keeping his good arm under him and his injured one close to his side. Instantly Grant Hestlay and Van were assisting him. Once sitting he continued. "I think it is about time for introductions—"

A blare of a horn cut Peter off. The king glided through the flap of the tent. Peter struggled to rise as the others took their knee. "Nay, there will be none of that in here. Rise, except for you, Sir Lawston. You stay where you are. Rest, you will need your strength." The king looked down at Peter, causing him to shift uncomfortably under his gaze. Injured or not, Peter felt he should be on his feet.

"I do not want to interrupt. Did I hear something of introductions? Pray let us continue." The king gestured to the kneeling squire.

The boy rose shakily to his feet and the others followed suit. With a slight tremble in his voice he turned and gestured to Richard. "Your Majesty, it is my honor to present to you Sir Richard Devenroe, a great knight, a man of honor and duty." Peter heard the loyalty and respect in the boy's speech as he spoke of Richard.

King Henry smiled at Devenroe. "My pleasure." The king cocked his head slightly and raised his brow at the boy. "And you?"

He took several deep breaths that trembled through his frame. His hands were shaking slightly. "I am Van Burgess, your majesty."

"No great praise for yourself, yet you are the one who saved Lord Peter, my champion, the Dragon Knight, are you not?"

The king's voice held great esteem as he spoke of Peter. Pride swelled within Peter's heart and warmed his weary spirit.

Around the crowded tent the men stood at attention as the King spoke to the young man.

"Aye, but I did not act alone." The boy shifted, head bowed slightly. He seemed uncomfortable with the praise and attention. "I could not have accomplished it without Richard's help." He pointed to Richard and shifted once again.

"From the stories that I have heard you do not do yourself justice. I have also heard that you were unaware of who he was when you rescued him." Peter watched as the king's gaze slid over Van Burgess. Peter could almost feel the king sizing the nervous boy up. Henry's forehead wrinkled as he closely watched the lad's reaction.

"Not at the time, Your Majesty. I had seen one of our warriors fall to the enemy and I just reacted. I did not realize who it was until I had him in the tent and was putting pressure on his wound."

The king and lad both shifted their gazes to Peter. Peter then glanced beside him and caught the eye of Grant Hestlay. He decided that he didn't like being the center of attention any more than Van appeared to.

Van turned his gaze back to the King. "It was then I was close enough to see through the mud on his face, sire."

"So you knew who he was when you argued with the doctor?"

The boy nodded his head and said that he did.

Henry smiled at Peter before returning his attention to Van. "Even knowing who he was, you were willing to argue with the doctor as to his care? What if he would have died?"

Peter watched Van's face closely. This was the question he had been wondering about since the boy had first flown out of the shadows to save him.

"Most would not face adversity for someone else," the king continued.

"If he would have died, I would have willingly lost my head, knowing I had done the right thing. As to facing adversity…" He shrugged his shoulders. "He had done the same for me. I could do no less." With that he turned to Peter. "I cry your pardon if I have spoken out of place, my lord. I also want to thank you for allowing me to be a squire under your man. I am forever indebted to you, my lord, for all you have done for me."

Peter listened as Van spoke softly and respectfully, straining each word to accent it with quiet dignity. The part of the obedient and acquiescent subject was so out of place for the boy that Peter could not control the laugh that erupted.

He grabbed his bandaged shoulder as pain rippled through his freshly stitched-up wound. He swallowed hard, his raw throat screaming for water and relief. Getting quick control of the laughter, he took a deep breath to relax his muscles and to allow the cool air to sooth his angry throat.

Van Burgess, foregoing all his respectful talk, yelled for the young man who had just poked his head through the opening of the tent. "Did that doctor give you his potion?" At his nod Van impatiently waved him in. Telpher Constaire kept his head down as he entered with his tray of food and medicine. The king smiled and shook his head softly as he watched Van giving orders.

Van dropped to his knees, pushing away Peter's hand that still held the injured shoulder muscle, as he spoke over his shoulder to Telpher. "Go see to more food, His Majesty has traveled some distance. Hurry."

Telpher bowed to the king in mid-step as he rushed from the tent. King Henry's grin twitched slightly.

Peter just shook his head at the King as Van turned his attention back to the bandaged shoulder and began to scold him. "You have to be careful. I do not need to have that doctor back in here blaming me if you tear out your stitches. Now, here." Van held the water bag up to Peter's lips and gave him no other choice but to drink. The cold water was like heaven on his tattered throat. Sweet relief swept through him and he almost forgot about the pain in his shoulder.

Van held the bag for him to drink, but only allowed him a few sips at a time. Even knowing this was the best course of action, Peter had to force himself not to grab the bag and drink his fill. He knew his dehydrated stomach would expel the water as soon as it went in if he did.

Peter looked into the boy's dark, black eyes to help control the urge to gulp the sweet, cold water. Van leaned in a little closer, too close for Peter's still weary mind to focus clearly. His vision dimmed and the concerned face above him blurred, bringing back the fantasy of the beautiful woman. He knew it wasn't real. He knew it was just the boy, but it took an effort not to touch that cheek to see if it was as smooth and as warm as he imagined.

Realizing what he was thinking, he jerked his head back, trying to focus on the boy, trying desperately to dispel the illusion of the fictitious woman. Peter closed his eyes against the ripping pain the sudden movement caused. He barely noticed the cold water that splashed across his bare chest. Van gasped and pulled the blanket up to dry him.

Opening his eyes, Peter saw the concern on the faces circling him. He just smiled and shook his head. After all, what was he supposed to say? He couldn't very well tell them he was losing his mind. He had never looked at another man the way he was looking at this boy, and the fact that it was the imaginary woman and her seductive voice that he wanted didn't make him feel any better.

Food was quickly brought and Telpher disappeared from the tent once again. Van laid the water bag beside Peter and rose, facing the King. "Your Majesty. Shall I take my leave now to allow you to speak with your champion?" With a slight bow Van made a step for the flap. He appeared anxious to be gone.

"Stay. You were the one who saved me, you deserve to be here," Peter said, his voice weak. He hated feeling weak and helpless.

King Henry reached out and touched Van's shoulder. "Everyone shall sit and eat. You will stay at my side."

Peter smiled when Van glanced nervously at him. Everyone situated themselves around Peter and the King.

King Henry shook his head and took a large chunk of bread. "It is a shame that Eolian has escaped once more."

Peter grunted and took a small bite of his own bread, but the crusty bread only enhanced his thirst so he dropped the remainder. "We will get him, Your Majesty." He took a small drink of the cool water and let his mind wander to Eolian and his army.

Eolian had trained Peter when Peter had joined the armies. Peter had never trusted him, believing him to be loyal to the former king, King Stephen. When King Henry had learned of a plot to overthrow the crown, Peter had shared his concerns with the king and had taken Eolian's place as the King's Champion.

King Henry had just begun a campaign to recover the lands bartered away by the former King Stephen. These battles played a major role in the hostilities that now plagued the kingdom. Advocates of Stephen, as well as those who had received those lands, had been causing trouble for the new crown. Having been king for less than six months, King Henry was relying heavily on those loyal to Empress Matilda.

The conflicts between Stephen and Matilda had been long and gruesome. Loyalties to both sides still rode deeply. This made Peter's job extremely dangerous, but he was confident that he would capture Eolian.

"I think that will take time. His army took a heavy blow in the attack and it will take time for him to begin a new campaign. I believe it will take us time to find him once again, but I am sure he will not just give up." The king shook his head. "But we can hold out hope that he will disappear for good."

After the small meal, King Henry turned his full attention to Van. He stared silently at him, then smiled in a determined way, and shook his head again. "Yes indeed." Peter waited for him to continue, but he only said, "Help Peter outside," as he rose and moved toward the front of the tent.

Peter looked at the king in confusion. He wondered what King Henry was planning. Why did he want him outside? Peter was confident the King knew what he was doing and he trusted him but still, he liked to know what was going on around him. He raised a questioning brow at the King. The King just smiled and walked out of the tent. He had obviously come to some conclusion, but he didn't seem to be interested in letting them in on it.

Peter looked at the others who just shrugged and shook their heads. Pain seized his shoulder as Richard Devenroe and Grant Hestlay helped him to his feet. Careful of his injury, they assisted him out of the tent. Peter could hear Van right behind him grumbling under his breath.

Peter took a deep breath, squinting against the bright sunlight that prodded at his tired eyes. He wanted to go back to sleep, for at least a month. He wanted all this to be done, and he wanted to be home in his nice soft bed.

Van ceased his grumblings and took a spot next to Richard. It was obvious to Peter that the boy didn't like him being moved. Nonetheless, he kept his tongue still, but it was clearly taking a physical effort to do so. Van trudged along with a scowl on his face. Peter noticed the expressions on the faces of the men supporting him. Both struggled to suppress grins as they watched the boy nearly shaking in his effort to control himself.

Peter looked back to Van who was now looking at him. Van opened his mouth just to snap it closed again. Then he took a deep breath, clenched his fists, and looked away, grumbling something too quiet for Peter to hear.

Devenroe leaned over to whisper quietly to him. "You know, my lord, I am amazed to see him contain himself so well, even in front of the King." Peter felt his lips twitch as he struggled not to grin. He knew the lad wanted him to take the medicine the doctor had provided, but it would put him to sleep, and that would not be good with King Henry there.

The beautiful meadow that they had first taken camp in was now a ransacked and demolished mess of torn up grass and flowers. Ruts and deep holes, from the warriors and their horses, made walking on trembling legs difficult for Peter.

Out in front of all the men, the King's man blew once again on the horn. All stopped to look at the men standing with the King. Peter allowed his two good friends to sit him on a low boulder, in the warm sun. When all of Peter's men, as well as the men the King had brought, were circled around them, the King motioned to Van.

The King's face held a serious expression as he addressed the brave boy. "Van Burgess, will you please stand before me."

Van approached the King on shaky legs, head bowed. He appeared nervous and that surprised Peter. Why was this arrogant and self-assured boy so nervous around the King? Why was he so reluctant to be questioned or to be the center of attention? It almost appeared to Peter that the boy was hiding something. Peter took a deep breath deciding that more than likely the boy was just unaccustomed to all the fuss.

Peter's head was beginning to ache and he knew it would soon be a blaring headache. He took deep breaths and, concentrating on the King and Van, tried to ignore the throb that was becoming insistent.

The King's loud voice boomed across the torn up field, but he never took his eyes from the boy. "All who have gathered here will be witness to great deeds today."

Henry's bellowing voice tore through Peter's head like a stampede of sheep—prodding and gouging as they ripped through the soft tissue of his mind. Henry paused, but his words still echoed dimly in Peter's mind. He clenched his teeth against the pain as the king's voice once again filled the air.

"Van Burgess, for your bravery on the field of battle; for your selfless act to save another, with no regards to your safety or to personal gain; for your personal stand to protect your beliefs in the face of opposition I am here to acknowledge you—kneel."

Van dropped to one knee and bowed his head. He was sitting so still that between the black clothes and the deep black hair, he looked like a small dark boulder. The King took the sword offered to him by the soldier beside him. The shiny metal of the newly made sword touched each of Van's shoulders as the King said the words that made him a knight.

Peter's pride swelled within him as he listened to the familiar words. Richard cleared his throat beside him. Peter caught sight of the pride and emotion in Richard's face. With a grin Peter watched the King speak the final words of the creed. "Now rise. Rise as Sir Burgess, the Dark Knight."

The boy swayed. Peter thought he would fall, but somehow he managed to keep his feet.

"I have need of you to the west of here, Dark Knight." The king spoke seriously as his men began to gather up their horses. "You will take half of the army I have brought with me. They were brought here for the man who saved the Dragon Knight. For a man of great bravery and unselfish courage."

Once again the boy swayed, but he managed to keep his feet and to accept the sword the King offered. Van gave a grateful smile to the king and dropped once again to his knee to show his loyalty. "Get ready, you leave now." King Henry turned to leave as Van rose to his feet.

Van turned to Peter with a wide smile. "Thank you for everything, my lord." He looked to Richard, nodding his head before walking away. Richard rose and followed him. Peter watched curiously as they stopped not far off and began to talk.

Turning to Grant, he smiled. "Go in my bag and get my dagger."

"Yes, my lord."

Grant walked away to do what was requested and Peter turned his attention back to Richard and the newly knighted Dark Knight. Peter shook his head. He was too young to be a knight. The king must have decided on this course of action before knowing how young the boy was.

The two men seemed to come to some sort of conclusion and Richard walked back toward Peter. The boy headed over to the men now under his command, men who were close to twice his age.

"The men may not take well to a boy so young being in charge of them," Peter said as Richard reached him.

"No, they may not." Peter heard him take a shaky breath and looked up into Richard's nervous face as he continued. "That is something I want to talk to you about."

His good friend of ten years took another deep breath and continued rapidly. "Van has asked me to accompany him. It will be a step up in rank and commission for me. And although I don't want to leave your army, or lose your friendship, I think it will be a good step forward for me and the boy needs someone he can trust to help look out for him."

Peter didn't want to see him go, but he knew it was best for both Richard and Van. He held his hand up to get Richard to stop talking, to at least take a breath. "It is fine. I agree with you. You will never lose my friendship and you will always have a place in my army. If ever you decide to return to me, your spot will always be here for you."

Peter looked over to the boy coming their way. "And you are right. He is going to need all the help you can give him. Protect him well."

Grant returned with the dagger, handing it to Peter. He slid it behind him right before the boy reached them. Van smiled nervously at Peter. "I just wanted to thank you again for all you have done for me, now and in the past. It has been an honor to serve under you." He glanced at Hestlay and grinned. "Keep that doctor from bleeding him and make sure he stays down to heal."

Returning the smile, Hestlay nodded.

Peter smiled sadly. He carefully watched Van's face and said, "Well, Hestlay we are losing Richard. He is accompanying The Dark Knight."

Van turned a grateful and relieved look to Richard Devenroe.

"Did you think I would say no?" Peter asked him.

"No, my lord." Van's relief said otherwise as he turned back to Peter. "Thank you once again, but we must take our leave now."

"Burgess, wait. I have something for you." Peter only had one thing that was personal to him, something that held meaning. He wanted to show his gratitude for the danger the lad had faced to save his life, not just with the warrior but with the doctor as well.

Struggling to his feet, Peter brushed off the hands that tried to help him. He handed the dagger, jewel encrusted hilt first, to the gaping boy. The emeralds and rubies inlaid in the handle sparkled in the afternoon sun. The weapon had been a birthday gift from a friend of his father's. He thought Lord Matthew Fordella would have approved.

"My Lord, I cannot…"

Peter knew he was thinking to turn down the gift. He could see in his eyes that he wanted it, but would still deny it. Everyone also knew that it was disrespectful to turn down a gift from another warrior.

Van struggled with himself before coming to a decision. "Thank you, my lord."

Peter was shaken by the gratitude in the boy's trembling voice, by the emotion he saw sparkling deep within his bottomless black eyes. Peter wanted to speak to the boy about the night he was injured. Wanted to apologize for his behavior, but instead he watched him walk away.

Peter sent up a silent prayer as Richard and Van walked away from him. He prayed for them to be safe, for Van to have the opportunity to grow into a good man. He prayed for a quick end to the wars and a safe trip home for all the warriors involved in it.

☗☗☗

The dark, black eyes, filled with caring and concern, once more hovered over Peter. The blurry face of the woman swirled in and out of his vision and her sweet, hypnotizing voice sang to him. Enticing him as it had that night, singing her sweet siren song of home and family. He could feel the heat of her skin over and over as he ran his fingers along the smooth cheek. He could feel her blood dripping down into his shoulder, becoming one with his own.

Jerking his eyes open in the darkness, Peter took a ragged breath. He tried to pretend it was just a dream about a woman, but he could not.

His shoulder ached softly but not enough to convince him to roll over and take more of the bitter concoction the doctor had sent.

Closing his eyes, he lay in the quiet darkness and tried to dispel the lingering whispers of the phantom voice.

CHAPTER 3

England June 1158:

Daniel Farnsworth crouched deep within the bushes, trying to ignore the pricks and scratches as the jagged thorns dug into his weathered skin and pulled at what little gray hair he had left. He had watched the battle rage around him for most of the day. Fear raced through his heart as he huddled in his cold, damp hiding place. He was too old for this. If a sword did not kill him, his old heart might. His muscles were tight and pain settled deep in his bones.

The reason he was here ran through his weary mind for the thousandth time since he had agreed to deliver the message. He had consented to this trip because he desperately needed the money this job would pay. His wife had worked at the dress shop for many years but was now sick and unable to work. Now his only concern was what would happen to his wife if he did not come home at all.

His beautiful wife of thirty two years had pleaded with him not to come here. He had explained to her that Van Burgess had spent his childhood in their village of Junket, that he knew him, and would not harm him. She had reminded him several times that Van had always been unstable of temper and had grown into a dangerous knight since he had left. She had told him the money was not worth it and had begged him to stay home. He had not listened, but she was right. Money was worth nothing to a dead man.

Daniel's body shook violently—not only from fear, but from an immense chill that seemed to radiate from his very soul to envelope him. He watched men fall atop one another onto the blood-soaked ground until his innards were in turmoil and his mind numb. The heavy swords clanged so loudly he could feel them vibrate through the ground itself.

Taking a slow breath, he watched the man his message was meant for. The Dark Knight wielded his sword with deadly accuracy. A victorious guttural cry burst forth from the dark figure as man upon man fell to his weapon.

The Dark Knight's reputation preceded him and Daniel knew he was not a man to be trifled with. It was well known that he murdered men, raped women, and found joy in all that he pillaged and plundered.

The battle cries rose into a booming thunder. Daniel flinched as more fear raced through him. The enemy retreated and The Dark Knight's army took chase.

Daniel did not know how long he had crouched there in his cold damp hole, but he could not bring himself to leave the safety of concealment. Through the dense branches of the red berried bush he could see the knight standing proud in the misty late afternoon air. The eerie silence that draped itself over the now calm meadow was worse on Daniel's frayed nerves than the sounds of battle had been.

He closed his eyes and thought of the stories he had heard of the Dark Knight. The Dark Knight's heroics and his mischief were widely told among the commoners. According to the tales, he had killed more men than one could count. His temper was short and he answered with his fists more often than not, but that did not come as a surprise to Daniel. Van Burgess had always been that way. He had always been proud and arrogant.

Daniel took a deep, shaky breath. The smells of decaying vegetation and moist dirt filled his lungs. He swallowed hard and forced down a cough that threatened to burst loose and give away his position. He opened his eyes and watched as the fierce knight's penetrating gaze scanned the countryside. He could clearly see Van's nostrils quiver and flare as he seemed to scent the air for danger.

He ran his trembling, dirt-encrusted finger along the slightly rough surface of the rolled parchment. He knew he had lost his mind to have come here to deliver this message. If it was bad news, he did not want to face the Dark Knight's anger.

The darkly-clad and menacing figure walked slowly toward his hiding place. Daniel crouched lower into the soft and spongy ground, holding his breath to keep as still as possible.

His gaze was drawn to the flickering motion of the Dark Knight's pennant. It hung proudly upon a staff that had been embedded into the earth behind the tethered war horses. It fluttered gently in the breeze, an emblem of a rearing stallion, appearing for only a moment before it disappeared again into the waving folds of black cloth.

A shadow fell upon him, drawing his gaze back to Van, who now blocked the sun from his view. The fearsome knight was clad all in black. The only color to break the monotony was the silver destrier on his helm, one that matched the emblem on his pennant.

Sweat ran down Daniel's face and stung his eyes as he watched the Dark Knight stop not more than ten feet away. He took a slow deep breath and could smell the blood on the knight's heavy metal chest plate.

He thought to run. Forget the money promised him with a return message. He could say he never found the man and give back the money already given. His life was worth more than a small sack of coin.

He had left the money with his wife, along with a promise that he would hurry home, and he had sealed that promise with a kiss. He could almost smell his wife's sweet-scented soap on her warm soft skin, taste her lips beneath his.

Rough hands grabbed him from behind, jerking him from his concealment and the fantasy of his wife. Daniel screamed as he was catapulted through the brush covering, the thorns tearing at his face and hands as he fought for purchase. He landed only a few steps from the dark figure's booted feet.

Dirt stinging his eyes and terror freezing his thoughts, he fought to regain his footing. The knight spun toward him, drawing his large, blood-stained sword as he did so. Daniel's heart skipped a beat as his blood chilled. He dropped back to his knees in terror. Knowing he was about to die, he began to yell as he waved the message before him. "I am a messenger, please. I am a messenger, please." Over and over he pleaded, his heart thudding in his heaving chest.

"Bloody hell, shut up!" The menacing growl of the figure before him quickly shut his lips. The Dark Knight stalked the short distance between them, his black eyes drilling into Daniel's very soul.

"Are you quite done?" Van growled in irritation.

Daniel's eyes clenched as tightly shut as his lips were. He did not open either as he dropped his head to his chest. He cowered in the mud, the stained parchment trembling in his outstretched hand.

Van noticed that blood trickled from several scratches across the face and hands of the familiar messenger. There was only one person from Junket that would send a missive and the only reason that Van's mother ever made contact was because she wanted something. It was more than likely either money or repairs, but worry and concern still slithered around, refusing to be ignored.

Heavy boots splashed through the mud and Van looked up dismissing the messenger and his missive for the time being. There was no time to deal with either. Not just yet anyway, not with Eolian and his men still somewhere nearby.

Van glanced at Richard in concern. Richard nodded that all was clear, but anxiety was etched on his face. Van quickly scanned the area for the remaining scouts as the other men-at-arms began to circle.

Nervous tension twisted Van's stomach as the scouts returned. Each came back to camp with a nod to show that all was clear. None returned with prisoners, which was not a good sign.

Eolian and his army had escaped, once again. Anger boiled inside Van, bubbling like a cauldron until its poisoned waves spilled over the top. In a fit of rage, Van cursed loudly, turned, and kicked the blood soaked body of an enemy.

Taking a slow, calming breath he dispatched the guards and gazed after the men as they took up their posts around the perimeter of the camp. With knowledge that all was secure, Van turned back to the kneeling man who had still not moved. "How long have you been watching?"

The messenger remained immobilized, his arm outstretched and the message extended.

"Messenger?" Still nothing. Van peered closely at the old man. "Farnsworth, how long have you been watching?"

"Several hours, sir." The raspy voice was a bare whisper.

Van watched as the parchment trembled and shook in the old man's withered hand and understood that his fear was not from the battle he had just witnessed nor was it just the fear of him. It was from the message that he held as far from his body as possible.

With an amused grin, Van pulled off the black helm and shivered as the soft cool breeze drew goose flesh to overheated skin. "Rise and look at me."

The messenger rose shakily to his feet, held the message out, and looked in wide-eyed shock at the figure before him.

Van knew what the messenger saw. He saw a tall boy who looked all of eighteen. Van's smooth and defined cheek only added to the illusion of youth. The only thing that marred the baby face was the long jagged scar that had been earned three years before. If not for the wicked scar and the dirt and encrusted blood, Van would look effeminate. Not that anyone would dare say that to his face.

Van felt the same nagging anger that always surfaced when coming face to face with that shocked look. The expression in those wrinkled eyes said clearly that Van's lie would soon fail to be credible.

Van, short for Vanessa, had lived the lie all her life.

Van's father, wanting a son, had been enraged when she was born a girl and had vowed to kill her. Her mother had spoken of it often, telling her that she must always pretend to be a male or else her father would find her and finish what he had vowed to do the day she was born.

She had kept the secret all her life and had never strayed from the lie, but it had gotten to the point where very soon she would no longer be able to pull it off.

Worry grew within her as she considered her options. She could not stay as a knight, this she knew. She would never grow a beard and she was lucky that her woman's cycle had not been noticed.

Pain gripped her heart as she realized that she really only had one choice. She had to leave before she was caught in her deceptions. She hated being put in this position. She was angry with her father for wanting to kill her and with her mother for forcing her into this life. Mostly she was angry because she loved her life as a knight and was loath to let it go.

Richard cleared his throat gently beside her. Van looked into the concerned eyes of her friend. She raised one black brow at him and grinned.

Richard shook his head and groaned. He knew that look. Van was angry and when he was angry that made Richard nervous. Van turned back to the elderly man and jerked the message from his hand.

Farnsworth, who looked about ready to fall from fatigue and fear, screamed as the parchment was ripped away from him. The Dark Knight said, in the most arrogant voice Richard had ever heard him use, "Relax, I receive messages all the time and I assure you, very seldom do I have to kill a messenger."

The man teetered and would have fallen if Richard had not grasped the bone thin arm. Richard laughed a deep resonant sound to comfort the old man. "He is kidding you, my dear man. Come, we shall get you some water and some—" Richard looked at Van's ghost white face behind the unrolled parchment and his laughter died in his throat.

"Sir?" Richard had never seen that look on his friend's face. It was a mix of anger and concern, almost fear. Worry wormed its way through him as he stepped closer to his friend.

Van's helm went back over jet black hair that was pulled into the thick braid and wrapped full length with a black leather strap as it always was. There was no answer as the wide shouldered figure stalked toward the still saddled horses.

"Sir." Richard caught him in several strides and grabbed a mail clad arm. "Van. Where are you going?"

"I need to go. Take care of the men." Van looked agitated and nervous as he looked from the parchment to the horses. Richard had never seen his lord in such state. Indeed Van had only two emotions. Anger and calm. Richard was unsure of how to deal with this new emotion, but he did know that he could not allow his liege to ride off alone.

"Nay." Richard refused to release Van's arm even as Van pulled against his hand.

"Nay!" Anger flashed in the dark ebony eyes and Van gripped the hilt of his sword. Richard knew he was not used to being questioned, especially by a friend. Van was still in the habit of fighting for respect, of fighting just to survive with the men.

Richard had known the wild knight long enough not to be led into an argument. It was best with the arrogant and unsteady boy to be calm. If one raised their voice to Van, he jumped quickly into anger, but a calm argument would more than likely make him listen. "Nay. Look around you. You cannot go alone anywhere. Not with the night closing in. Not a lone rider."

The Dark Knight took in the surroundings and the men who lay dead. He shook his head with that same rushed look of anxiety in his eyes.

Richard could almost read his thoughts as Van surveyed the slaughter that had occurred. He could see when Van began to think of the consequences of leaving. Eolian's army had been few compared to the Dark Knight's men, but the enemy had hoped for the element of surprise. It had not happened. Van had a spy in the ranks of Eolian's army and he had brought him the message of the ambush the night before.

Most of Eolian's men had fallen in the battle, but some had escaped. Eolian Montgomery was among them. A lone rider would be easy pickings.

Van groaned gently, looking toward his horse once again. The men watched as Richard confronted him. Richard did not want to cause a scene in front of them, but he could not let his lord ride into the night alone.

Richard sighed in relief as Van relaxed. "Give him a fresh horse, I want to leave now." With that, the parchment was thrust into Richard's chest. Richard released his friends arm and Van took a shuddering breath before walking away.

Richard watched him check the saddle on his mount. Concern ate at him as he gently opened the crumpled missive.

> Dearest Van,
>
> I need you to come to me. I will not live to see you if you do not hurry. I have waited too long. Doctor Burgess is with me. He is unsure of how much longer I can fight off the lung infection that has ravaged me. Please Hurry to me. I love you. I must see you.
>
> Love, Patricia

Richard did not know what the relationship was between Patricia and Van, but he did know she was not one of the many mistresses that the young man kept. He had wondered many times if she was his mother. Never once had it been said, although there were lots of messages. All were responded to and most would take him away to see her.

"Men, mount up, we are moving." Richard's hearty bellow found all the men and sent them rushing to mount their steeds.

Richard came to a stop before his lord and placed a gloved hand on Van's long leg. The knight sat astride Damien, the big destrier the King had given him three years ago at his knighting ceremony. Richard looked up at the knight's blood-encrusted armor.

With Eolian escaping, another attack could come at any time. It would be an uncomfortable ride, but it was best they all rode in full gear. "The men are ready, my lord. The wounded are few and none that cannot wait for treatment. All are in condition for a hard ride."

Van grasped Richard's hand, desperately clinging to it. In all the battles that he had fought beside the young knight he had never seen him so badly shaken. Fear tingled at the back of Richard's mind. Van was clearly upset about Patricia, but there seemed to be something more. "I need to talk to you, my friend,"

"Of course, my liege." Richard could see the despair, the emptiness in those coal black eyes—things he had never seen before. The hair stood up on the back of his neck. He was scared for his young friend.

"If something were to happen," Van took a deep breath. "If I had to leave you—" His hand trembled slightly as he struggled with his words. "I need to know you understand how I feel about you. I love you like a father. Without you I would not be who I am today." Richard glanced around him at the men who appeared to be out of hearing range. "I want to thank you for all you have done." Van's voice trembled and his eyes shimmered with moisture. "Everything I have and everything I am is to your credit."

Richard was unsure of how to deal with the unexpected emotional outburst. He wanted to say something. He needed to say something. He tightened his grip on the clutching hand and smiled. "You have always been a son to me and you always will be."

Richard's stomach twisted in protest at the thought of losing the young boy he had taken under his wing eight years ago. Van was irrational and unpredictable, but Richard had been honest in his answer. He had always thought of him as the son he had never had. It was hard to see him as the ferocious knight with the unearthly appetites that the story tellers described him to be. No, Richard would always see the Dark Knight as the scared little boy who refused to admit that he was scared.

♛ ♛ ♛

Van looked back to her men. They were weary and withered, but not one of them would complain. Her stomach lurched at the mere thought of leaving them. A deep breath did little to contain the overpowering emotions. Anger, fear, loneliness, and despair crushed at her like a boulder. A few deep stinging breaths and she was able to shove the feelings down to a place where they were at least manageable, even if not completely gone. She concentrated on the rough ride instead of her useless emotions. Fear and worry would do nothing to help. All it would do is make things worse.

The night's ride was rough on all the men and morning had led into afternoon before the small, yet tidy homes of Junket village came into view. Van knew the men were all about to drop from exhaustion.

The people fled before the thundering hooves of the army's horses. The fearful villagers gathered children to their bosoms as they ran from the deafening sounds of chain mail and weapons. Van scowled in irritation. Normally she felt great pleasure and pride at the way people trembled at the mere mention of The Dark Knight's name, but not here in this village. These were people Van knew and had grown up with, but all they knew of Van was that he was an overzealous boy with a quick and violent temper that had grown up to be dangerous.

Van took a shuddering breath that hurt deep inside. She threw up an arm signaling the men to stop. Then she rode the massive destrier back through the men to where Daniel was slouched in his saddle. His head bobbed to the rocking of his borrowed horse as the creature shifted nervously from leg to leg. Van pulled Damien to a stop in front of the messenger and touched the old man's shoulder. Daniel jerked his head up in surprise.

"Easy, old boy. Time to wake up." Van held a small bag of coins out to Daniel.

There was still fear in Daniel's eyes as he took the offered coin, but he smiled weakly and dismounted on wobbly legs. An older woman rushed, without hesitation, into the group of warriors. She threw her arms around Daniel, nearly knocking him off his feet.

Van reined Damien around and headed back to the front of the army. She snorted impatiently and looked back at the couple who kissed and hugged. Tears of joy flowed as they reunited with each other. That same swirling rush of emotions threatened to overcome Van once more and the torrent of feelings had to be shoved back down.

She smiled as Richard handed a small bag of coins to one of the men. Four of her warriors broke off from the group to retrieve supplies. Normally, the army would hunt and gather, but they were all in need of rest and recuperation. Van rode back to the front of the army and they passed quickly through the town.

Van led the army through the dense woods that lay to the east of Junket. She had spent almost every day in these woods, running and cavorting with the boys of the village. The tree line thinned suddenly, showing a small clearing before them. Her heart thudded heavily as a small cottage came into view.

She forced a calm façade as they approached the quiet house. While growing up here as a young boy Van had never felt welcome at the village or in this home. She shook the thin webs of memory from her mind before they could grow and consume her. There was no time for reminiscing.

A short, thin girl stopped in her tracks in the middle of the yard. She was frozen as she watched the army of men and horses descending upon her. She stepped back, one step then two. Suddenly she screamed and raced for the house, her long blonde hair streaming out behind her. Van was not concerned about the girl. She would tell Patricia about the knight and the army and Patricia would calm her.

She flung open the door and slammed it closed behind her. The sturdy door was well kept, but looking it over, Van took in the thatched roof that was once again in need of repairs and a missing shutter over the front window that had been boarded up. Van took a deep breath, signaling the men to stop.

Richard stopped his horse at her side. Van glanced at him and pointed off into the woods. "Take the horses through there…" Van's voice left her. She knew she could not face this death alone. "Bloody hell." She took a deep breath and turned, reluctantly, to the men. "Devon. You are in charge."

"Sir?" the young man nearly squeaked in alarm.

"Take the men and the horses—"

"Sir?" Devon protested again.

Van understood the problem and kept the anger at being questioned contained. Devon was afraid he was taking Richard's place. It was Richard's place as first in command to take charge when The Dark Knight was gone. Devon was probably afraid Richard would kill him. Van did not have time for this, or the time or energy to get upset about it. Devon was young and he would learn.

"Take the horses through those trees. There is a small lake. Feed everyone and tend to the wounded."

Devon looked terrified. Unsure of what to do, he looked from Richard to Van and did nothing. He froze.

"Move!" Van was tired of waiting and lashed out at the hesitant man-at-arms.

Devon moved, kicking his horse into action. The steed lurched forward, running headlong and encouraging the others to move along with him. Soon she and Richard were alone in the courtyard.

"He was afraid he was taking my place." Richard smiled, but Van did not respond. They walked across the yard.

Van pushed against the door. Nothing. The girl apparently had not gone to Patricia. Nay, she had bolted the latch. Van pounded a gloved fist heavily on the door. "Open this door, you insolent little wench, or I will break it down."

The door swung open. The small blue eyed girl stood holding a pitchfork out before her. Van raised one black brow, in a mix of annoyance and amusement, and took a quick step forward. The tines of the implement raked across her thick armored breast plate and she grimaced as the fork screeched along the heavy metal.

The girl winced as the impact shook her.

"I like my women with some spirit." Van grasped the handle of the fork and ripped it from the girl's dainty hands, pulling her into a tight one-armed bear hug.

She stared deeply into Van's eyes before fainting. Van stood there, just holding her limp body.

"Is she all right, my lord?" Richard stepped to the side as Van tossed the pitchfork into the courtyard. He laughed when she snorted in disgust.

"Do you want me to take her?"

Van glanced at the short, fat balding man who stood off to the side of the doorway.

Paul Burgess shifted nervously as he quickly added, "I told her it was all right if you came in. She would not listen."

She flung the girl over an armor-covered shoulder like a sack of grain. "Nay, I got her. Where is my mother?"

Paul led them through the house.

Van paused in the doorway to her mother's room. Her breath caught in her throat to see how frail her mother had become. She had been so full of life just a few months ago.

"Van, what did you do to that poor girl? Lay her on her pallet." Her mother's quiet whisper resounded loudly in the silent room.

Van took a deep shaky breath and crossed the room. The girl's head fell to the side when Van dropped her roughly onto a pallet that was laid out in the corner of the small room. Her long blonde hair spilled over her face hiding her pretty features.

"Why did you not get in touch with me earlier?" Van asked gruffly and turned back to her mother. "I would have come sooner."

"Who is this?" Patricia completely ignored Van's question as she looked at Richard. "You have never brought one of your warriors here before."

"Richard Devenroe, my first in command. Richard, this is my mother, Patricia."

After the introduction Patricia added, "I should have liked you to come visit me while I was well. You have the look of a man who could give a woman great pleasure. It has been a long time. A good rutting could have done me some good." Her breathless words shocked Van.

"Mother!" Van's voice cracked in surprise.

Dr. Burgess looked up. "Forgive her. She has been prone to saying strange things of late. I believe the high fever is…" Paul drew a deep shaky breath. "Well, it is confusing her. I try to just ignore the odd things she says."

Van opened her mouth to respond but Patricia interrupted. "Oh, posh. I may not live through the night. If I cannot be impertinent now, there will never be a time I can." Her skin was sallow, thick black circles stood out under her eyes, and her limbs trembled with every breath.

She looked so frail and helpless. Van's heart felt like a great warrior had it in his fist and was trying to drag it forcibly out through her throat.

Much to her amazement and Patricia's apparent delight Richard walked across the small room to her side. Pulling off his glove, he grasped her hand, pressing it to his lips.

Dr. Burgess smiled weakly, but it faded quickly from his trembling lips. Van knew he loved her mother and that this must be very hard on him. Paul had been with Patricia since Van was born according to the stories they told. Her death would be devastating to the man. He not only loved her, he worshiped her.

Richard remained bent with her frail hand in his massive warrior's paw. "My dear, it would have been my great pleasure to rut with you. I still would not mind if I did not think it would push you over the edge."

With a racking cough that brought Van to her side, she laughed. "Oh, but what a way to go." She took in a deep gurgling breath and coughed again.

Van pulled Richard away from her side with a look of reprimand. "All right, mother. That is too much. I don't think I can handle any more of that. Nay, let us just talk."

Van's shaking hands stopped midway to taking off the black helm when Patricia blurted out. "Your father came to see me."

"What?" Van's eyes jerked to her mother. As a child Van had shuddered at the mere mention of her father. That fear had driven her to practice obsessively with a sword and dagger in order to protect herself and her mother. As her skills increased the fear slowly ebbed and, in its place, anger took seed.

"He wants to see you. I told him we would send him a message when you arrived. I agreed to send you to him." Patricia struggled with another deep gurgling breath.

Van blamed her father for putting her mother in this position. The hairs tingled on the back of her neck and her stomach twisted and cramped as the anger blossomed within her, sending its deadly shoots into her every nerve.

"He has arranged a marriage for you."

"Mother, please. You cannot be serious. You expect me to go back to my father? You expect me to be married?" Van's breath became shallow and nervous tension threatened to tear apart all her well-practiced control. Van's eyes darted nervously from Patricia to Dr. Paul. "Paul, tell me she is…confused now."

"No. I am afraid not."

Van felt out of control. The swirling emotions were getting harder to ignore. She concentrated on the anger because it was the easiest. It was not weak. Fear and pain were useless and weak. She refused to allow herself to feel those emotions.

Van looked down. She was still in full battle garb and the chain mail hauberk glinted in the sun coming through the window of the small room. Most of the blood had been washed away at the small stream where they had rested their mounts in the frantic rush to get to her mother's side, but it was still apparent. Van rubbed at the large blood stain and tried to regain her composure.

Patricia Fordella smiled and whispered so low that Van had to drop down beside her bed to hear her. "This is my last wish. I want you to marry. I want grandchildren." She coughed deeply, a thick wet sound as breath wheezed in and out of her lungs. "I may never get to see them, but I want them."

Van's mother slipped farther away with each labored breath. "Your father has changed. He now has two sons and he wants to make up for the past. Please, love. Let your mother die happy. Promise me." Her voice was a bare wisp. Her eyes closed.

"Yes, Mother," Van answered reluctantly through gritted teeth. Patricia's voice became nothing more than soft breath on Van's cheek. The words were more felt than heard as she leaned in close to her overly-warm face.

"Thank you. I love you..." Van strained to hear her fading words. Patricia sighed. "You will make a good wife, a good mother."

CHAPTER 4

Van watched helplessly as her mother's eyes drifted shut. The hard metal of her protective chest plate did nothing to stop the pain that invaded her heart as she pulled the limp, frail body against her. Tears stinging her eyes, she felt for the breath that no longer filled her mother's sickened lungs. She held the lifeless body tightly to her and took a slow deep breath against her mother's hair.

The sweet smell of roses that had always surrounded her mother had been replaced by the pungent aroma of sickness. Van had always loved the smell of her mother. It had made her feel like she was home the way nothing else ever had. The chest plate suddenly seemed too tight and much too heavy.

Van trembled. She could feel the hot knot of tears swelling, but refused to allow their escape. She took shallow, gulping breaths around the lump that had lodged in her throat and with each labored breath she shoved her tears away.

She pushed away the pain, burying it deep inside, where she had hidden her feelings ever since she was little.

Dr. Burgess gave her a gentle shake. "Van…"

Van couldn't respond. She was not in control and her breathing was still labored. She did not trust herself to speak.

"Van." He gave a more urgent shake. "Van, let me see to her."

Vanessa Fordella, who thought of herself as Sir Burgess, The Dark Knight, Van—but never Vanessa—gently laid her mother down onto the bed. Tears swam in her eyes blurring her vision, but she refused to release them. Her heart still thudded within the tightness of her chest, but her breathing was calm and her armor no longer threatened to crush her to her knees.

Richard grasped her arm. "Van…come. Let the doctor see her." She didn't resist as he pulled her away from the bed. He stood beside Van for only a moment before laying a comforting arm across her shoulders.

Van leaned into him, allowing the heavy arm to give her strength. The deep throbbing pain in her chest ebbed a little at a time until all that was left was a controllable ache.

Van watched as Dr. Burgess felt Patricia's neck for a pulse before gently covering her, head and all. He bowed his head and silent tears fell, staining the white sheet.

Taking a deep breath that shuddered through his wide frame, he turned to Van. Pain swirled in his aging face and she struggled to remember when he had gotten so old. Her mother's illness had taken its toll on him.

"Do you want me to take her?" Dr. Burgess asked pointing to the small girl on the pallet, her long blonde hair still hiding her face. She hadn't made even a sound.

Van's eyes narrowed suspiciously as she watched the motionless girl. It was a long time for someone to stay unconscious from passing out. Too long, she thought.

"Nay, I've got her." Van had to do something, anything to keep her mind off the loss of not only her mother, but also the loss of the man who stood loyally by her side.

Van glanced at Richard's concerned face and sighed. She didn't want to lose him, but she knew there was no choice.

If it had only been her mother's wish that she marry, she would have stood her ground and refused, but it was more than that. Van had known for some time that she would not be able to portray a man much longer.

She should have left long ago, but had not been able to bring herself to do so.

Richard's hand tightened on her shoulder. She looked away from him as a sharp pain stung deep in her chest. She could not picture her life without her men.

The tears she had been fighting surged like a swollen river on the verge of breaking loose from the confining banks of her self-control. Reluctant to feel Richard's heavy arm slip from her shoulders, she nonetheless stepped away. She knew it was time.

Dr. Burgess stepped toward her. He was one, of only two people, to know who Van really was. He had played the biggest role in making sure everyone believed she was a little boy.

"Van," Dr. Burgess said gently. "It is not good to hold everything in, let it out. Keeping things locked inside will just cause a breakdown. Even a man has to let go, to show feelings sometimes."

Giving him a weak smile, she said, "I have too much to do to break down. Perhaps later. For now, I need to get a message to my father. Tell him I am ready. I am assuming you know where to send it?"

"Aye, I know how to get in touch with him. It will take a couple of days to get to his estates, then a couple of days for your father's men to get here. So if all goes well you will have four or five days before they come for you."

"Good, take care of it and take care of Mother's arrangements."

Dr. Burgess walked out of the room with one last tearful look from the doorway. Van watched till he was gone then turned her now dry eyes to Richard.

This would be the hardest thing she had ever had to face and she didn't know if she could manage it. She looked at him and steeled her heart the best she could. It was best to just get it over with, like pulling an arrow from your arm—the quicker the better.

"I need you to take the men. Find a Lord who will take you in. You are now in charge, but you will still need a place to stay." She ignored the worried look on her friend's face, mostly because she could not deal with the guilt of leaving her men. "Winter is coming on and with Eolian out there, joining forces with someone will be a good thing."

"You knew that you would not be coming with me before we left the camp." Richard said slowly. "That was what that speech was about."

Van felt Richard's eyes bore into her. "I have to take care of this with my father." She heard the soft cracking in her voice and prayed that Richard did not.

Richard heard the pain in Van's voice and wanted to offer him comfort, but knew the proud young man would not accept it. He shook his head and tried to smile. It felt wrong so he let it drop away. "You will be careful. Are you certain you do not want us with you?"

Van straightened his shoulders almost defiantly. "Nay, I am not a scared boy anymore, not like I once was. I can take care of myself."

Richard had no doubts that Van could indeed take care of himself, but he still did not want to see him go. He had spent many years with the boy, first at the castle, then when Van had served under him as squire, and finally as men-at-arms when Van had received the honor of knighthood.

They had spent endless nights talking of anything and everything. He had grown to love the stubborn boy and still loved the arrogant man.

He grasped Van's arm. It was not the embrace that his liege needed, but he knew it was all the support that Van would accept.

Van surprised him when he reached up and grasped his wrist with a weak smile. Gratitude shone in the normally emotionless eyes. Richard thought of the last time he had seen that look and was suddenly no longer in the warm and cozy cottage as memories of the past swept him away…

♕ ♕ ♕

Wind howled around Richard and the rain pelted down at him as he sat at his guard post. He pulled the thick cloak up around his head and cursed the awful night. Movement to his right brought him lurching to his feet and drawing his broadsword. The rain and cold was forgotten as he prepared himself for a confrontation.

Van stepped calmly through a curtain of rain, glanced at the sword, and stopped.

"You know pages are not allowed out of the barracks at night." Richard's voice was gruff, but not as mean as he had wanted it to come out. He grunted. "What are you doing here, boy?"

"I could not sleep." Van's gaze followed the sword as Richard slid it back into its scabbard then his gaze came to rest on his face.

Richard nodded his head.

"I needed to talk to you."

Van's voice trembled and his body shook, but Richard was sure it was from more than just the cold.

He and Van had spent many nights talking and had grown close over the two years that Van had been at the castle. He had learned to pick up on the boy's subtle signs of his moods. Right now Van was scared. He could see it in the way his eyes shifted and in the way his body tensed. Yes, he could see the fear, but he knew the boy would never admit to having it.

Richard also knew that he should send him back, but Van had suffered the icy fingers of the frozen night to find him and he could not bring himself to turn the shivering child away. Carefully, Richard lowered himself onto the wet log and pulled his cloak around his head once more.

He looked up at the boy who stood patiently waiting in the pouring rain. His eyes were dark and emotionless, but Richard could almost feel the tension thrumming through him.

He opened the cloak in invitation. "Sit." Van sat obediently on the log beside him and Richard pulled his cloak around the boy's head to keep as much of the rain off of him as he could.

One thing he had learned about Van was that you didn't push him. Van had sought him out for a reason. Richard held his curiosity at bay and waited. He knew that Van would speak when he was ready.

Van looked up at him twice before finally speaking. "I had a nightmare about my father."

Richard looked closely at Van, but the boy just stared down at his sodden feet. "Dr. Burgess?" he asked gently. Dr. Burgess had been the one to drop him off at the castle. If his mother had been with them she had chosen to remain in the carriage. Richard had not pictured the good doctor as someone who caused nightmares.

"He is not my father." Van's dark gaze jerked to Richard's face and he was sure that Van had spoken without thinking. For most subjects that was normal for the rash boy, but for his life outside the castle and his past it was unusual. He was always very guarded about his personal life.

"Who is?" Richard asked trying to keep the shock out of his voice.

Van just shook his head.

Richard saw the stubborn set in the boy's jaw and tried another question. "Tell me about the dream."

Van just shook his head.

Richard wrapped an arm around his quivering shoulders. "You know you can trust me, right?"

"Yes," Van said quietly and then added, "With most things."

Richard felt a stab of pain at that, but understood nonetheless. There were some things that were private no matter how much you trusted someone. He tightened his grip on the shoulders that had finally stopped shaking. "You can tell me anything you need to."

Van reluctantly told him that his father wanted to kill him. When asked why, he hesitated then shook his head, spraying Richard with droplets of frigid water. When Van spoke it was so quietly that Richard had to drop his head down to hear him.

"I do not know," he whispered. "I just know I have to avoid him at all costs."

Richard was pulled back to the present when the warm grasp of Van's hand fell away from his wrist.

Richard drew his own hand away and heaved in a heavy breath. He released it in a deep sigh, ignoring the sharp pain that exploded in his chest as if the breath itself had grabbed onto his heart in an attempt to remain safe inside.

Richard felt the tears of loss swell behind his eyes and did not trust himself to speak. He looked questioningly at Van, saw only a stubborn determination and unending pride. Knowing his liege was too proud to accept sympathy he bowed low and turned away without a backwards glance.

Van watched with a heavy heart as Richard walked out of sight. Careful not to look at the shape under the white sheet, she pulled off her helm. Laying it on the end of the bed, she made her way to the motion-less girl.

Van slapped her face gently as she said, "Come on. Look at me." The girl lay still. "Wake up now."

Van just grinned and shook her head. The girl obviously wanted to play this game until Van gave up and left her. That would not happen. Van chuckled.

"I am too stubborn for that," she said softly. Then she slapped her harder. The girl opened her eyes in shock, screamed, and began to swing her fists into Van's heavy armor.

"Let me go," she shouted. The blonde-haired girl twisted and fought. Her dress began to rise up her milky white thighs. "Get off me."

"Stop. All you are doing is hurting yourself." Van grabbed her arms and, throwing them above the girl's head, she encircled both delicate wrists with one hand. The girl continued to kick and scream. As her legs flailed, Van lost her balance and she fell between the now bared thighs.

Van threw a glove covered hand over the girl's mouth to stop the in-cessant screams. She leaned close, her angry breath caressing the girl's trembling cheek. "Stop. You have two choices. One, you can shut the hell up, sit, and talk to me calmly or—"

The girl's sharp cries rose, cutting Van off in mid thought as the girl began to wildly kick her legs. Her high pitched squall slashed persistently at Van's twisted and frayed nerves. She closed her eyes and took a deep breath. She did not want to scare this girl, but she knew from vast experience that sometimes violence was the best way to get through to an overwrought female. She opened her eyes and smiled with deadly calm.

"Or...Option two," she said, keeping her voice calm. She pushed herself farther between the girl's open legs. The pretty blonde froze, her eyes opening wide, as Van felt herself come to a stop at the junction of the girl's thighs. Van pushed away the guilt at the horror in her gaze.

"I can always stay here, between your soft white thighs." Van's voice took on a seductive whisper. She arched one eyebrow and gave her a grin that said she was through playing.

The girl calmed and Van was impressed by the effort she had put forth to do so. Van removed her hand from the trembling lips and waited.

"I'm calm, just get off."

Van pushed herself halfway off and stopped. Still between her trembling legs, Van ran a hand along her thigh to check the scratches left by the rough mail. The girl tensed beneath her touch. "Nothing is bleeding. I don't think it will turn infectious, but my armor did scratch you. Dr. Burgess will take a look at it later."

Van pulled down the girl's brown woolen dress as she rose. She lowered herself to the pallet, but remained alert in case the girl decided to run. "What is your name?"

"Amy Devant." The girl's voice was just above a squeak—a terrified squeak.

"Devant? Are you a relation of Dorothy Devant?" Dorothy had worked as her mother's day maid ever since she was ten and had gone to live at the castle to train. She had seen Dorothy occasionally over the last three years when she had come home to visit.

Pain shadowed the girl's face and a tear streaked down her cheek. "She was my mother."

Van reached for her thin, trembling hand. "Was? What happened?"

"She passed away last month, from a lung infection." Amy stared at Van with the same shocked look that she always witnessed when someone first saw her.

Van knew the only blemish on her face was the long scar that ran along her right cheek. She also knew that everyone thought the same thing, but no one except the stupid would actually say it. They thought that it was a pretty face, too pretty for a Knight with the wicked reputation she had.

Of course, that prettiness was the main reason she had turned out the way she had. Her too feminine face had always been seen as sign of weakness and an easy target for the boys she had grown up with. It was a difference that had forced her to fight to prove herself and to build a reputation.

Van raised her brow questioningly "I did not know that Dorothy had a daughter."

"My mother wanted it that way. She had me hide when you would visit." Her voice was smoother now, not as scared.

Van let out a short bark of laughter that caused Amy to cringe in fear. "I am sure your mother was only looking out for you when she kept you hidden from me. Did my mother tell you about me?"

"She said that, no matter your reputation, you were a person of honor. That I was to trust you—I am sorry about the pitch fork, I was frightened. My mother always warned me against you. She said you were…a monster." Amy looked apologetic as she spoke. All the fear had gone from her eyes. A great sadness had replaced it.

"Do you have family, someone to take care of you?" Van twisted her neck first one way then the other, emitting loud pops and cracks as she did so. Her eyes were heavy and stung painfully with unshed tears and lack of sleep.

Amy only shook her head.

Van's shredded nerves were on the verge of snapping under the strain of what her life had become. She had been concerned for quite some time of how she would continue her ruse as a man, but now that she no longer needed to portray the knight, her concerns were compounded.

Eolian was a bigger threat to her as a woman than he had ever been to her as a man. To add to her troubles, she still felt responsible for her men and worried how they would fare without her.

"How old are you?" she asked the girl and grimaced at the weary tone in her own voice. She rubbed her temples momentarily as the pain bounced sharply behind her eyes.

Van did not know how to accomplish all that was necessary. A knight or not, she was still responsible for many women and several children. She had no idea how she was going to take care of her responsibilities and carry out her mother's dying wish.

"I am seventeen," Amy said quietly.

Van let her hands drop from her temples and glanced back at her.

Amy wrapped her arms around herself and looked down. She shrugged slightly and when she began to speak again it was in a small timid voice. "Nay, I do not have any other family. After my mother died,

Lady Patricia took care of me. Now I have no one." Tears slipped from her reddened eyes, cutting a streak down the dust on her trembling face.

Van's gaze moved across the room, avoiding her mother's bed.

"Maxwell Enoch said he would marry me."

Van's gaze shot back to Amy, anger clouding her vision momentarily.

"Now I will have to accept," Amy squeaked and the tears came hard then, unbidden, rough sobs that tore from her throat.

Van's fingers tightened into fists until her knuckles were white and her weariness forgotten. Maxwell Enoch was a monster of a man. He had gone through three young wives as it was. There was rumor that he had killed them as he had grown tired of them, just to move on to a newer, sometimes younger bride. She was not about to turn over this innocent girl to him.

Van took a deep breath and tried to ignore the sound of tears beside her so that she could weigh her options. As the Dark Knight she would have made her one of her mistresses, as she had the other girls she had rescued, but things were not that easy now.

She could still take her as a mistress. There was still money set aside for her women and their young ones, but it would not last long and she had to plan for a time when the gold ran out. She took a deep breath, held it, and closed her eyes. One more mistress would only deplete it that much sooner.

She released a deep sigh and opened her eyes to the dimly lit room. A room she was surprised to find that she was not going to miss.

She shook her head slowly. There was a second option available to her now, but it was not without risk.

She could take Amy with her, but she was reluctant to take this option.

She was unsure of her ability to protect Amy. There were men, like Eolian and the ones under him, who would give anything to know who she really was. If they found out she was the Dark Knight, then everyone around her, as well as her women and their children, would be in danger.

A deep breath shuddered through her. There was more than Amy's safety, there was her own as well. If Amy turned out to be untrustworthy...could she trust her secrets to a girl she just met?

Amy sniffled loudly and the cracking sobs cut through Van's head like a sword.

"You need to get yourself together," Van growled in irritation. She had never had tolerance for emotional outbursts. Nevertheless, she reached across and laid a comforting hand the Amy's trembling thigh. Anything to get her to stop, Van thought impatiently as Amy took her hand in a tight grip.

Amy's tears slowly began to ease and then finally stopped. She looked toward the mound on the bed. "I loved her."

Van's gaze turned toward the bed without really seeing it. She took a slow breath and growled softly to herself.

She would need a maid for two reasons. Her soon-to-be husband would expect one and more importantly she had no idea what to do as a woman. Her experience with women was limited to whores and bar-maids, the only women comfortable being around rowdy knights.

She laughed bitterly. She was sure her betrothed would not appreciate her acting like either.

She could hire a maid once she was a woman again, but that would not help her become a proper woman. She needed help and unfortunately that meant confiding in someone.

Van turned her gaze fixedly back to Amy. She stared at her for so long that Amy dropped her head shyly. There were few choices for Van at this time and she decided reluctantly that she would place her trust in Amy and do everything in her power to protect her.

"You will not marry any man you do not want to marry. You were in my mother's care and now you are in mine. If you give me your trust, I will take care of you."

Amy's head came back up and she regarded Van intently. Whatever she had seen in Van's eyes must have convinced her of Van's sincerity, because she smiled. "Thank you, Sir Burgess, I trust you." Amy tightened her grip on her hand and glanced at the bed once more. "Patricia told me that I could. She said you would take care of everything."

Amy's brows furrowed and her concerned gaze lit on Van's face. Van raised a black brow and waited curiously to see what questions had come to her. "What if the woman you are supposed to marry does not want me around?"

Van grinned at her. She pulled her hand out from under Amy's and patted her thigh as one would pat a child who had asked an obvious question. The young woman was innocent, not knowing that the men had all the say, women had none. Well, most women—she intended to have a lot of say.

"First, you will call me Van. I will tell my new betrothed that you will be coming. There will be no argument." She knew that her new husband-to-be would not care if she brought her own day maid, would, in fact, expect it. This removed two problems at once. "Go to your bed chamber, and get some rest. I will let you know of the arrangements to be made."

♔ ♔ ♔

Her mother's funeral began close to sunset. The men had crowded around the small grave site as the preacher said his prayers. He kept looking nervously at the multitude of warriors who stood respectfully at attention.

Van stood next to the grave with Richard on one side and Amy, dressed all in black including a black veil covering her face, on the other.

As the sun sank down behind the tall trees her mother was lowered into the ground in a sweet smelling cedar box. Van's breath threatened to quit on her. Her heart felt heavy and empty. She now had nothing. No mother, no men, no Dark Knight. She did not hear a word the preacher said as he recited the final prayers. She didn't even notice when he walked away, she just knew he was gone.

Richard touched her shoulder gently and she realized it was over. She turned to the men and at once they fell to one knee. Tears trembled on the edge of her eyes and her throat constricted in protest. This was not what she wanted. She wanted to scream at them to stay, that she needed them. Instead she smiled bravely and forced her eyes to dry once more.

Richard stood between her and her men. "We will always be loyal and faithful to the Dark Knight, my liege. If you need us, find us, let us know, and we will be there."

She knew she was doing the right thing, yet letting them go ripped at her heart. Richard dropped to his knee and held his hand up in an offering of allegiance. Van shook violently as sorrow and fear gripped her. She placed her booted foot on his outstretched hand and all their heads bowed in unison.

Van placed her foot back on the ground and Richard stood. He leaned close to her ear, placed a trembling hand on her shoulder, and spoke gently. "I will always be here for you, my child."

Van only nodded not trusting herself to speak. She knew Richard understood. With that the men mounted up and, with one last look, they reined their horses around.

Pride swelled in Van's heart at their loyalty as she watched them ride away. None questioned their leader now, not as they had in the beginning. Van had fought for the last three years for the respect now so freely given. She had indeed fought for respect ever since she was ten years old.

At ten she had been the youngest to ever be accepted at Grayweist Castle for page training and unlike most of the other boys she did not come from a long line of knights or from the line of a rich lord. From the very beginning, Van had struggled to earn a place among the boys.

As the men faded from sight she was swept back to her youth…

Van's eyes squinted against the bright sun and dust stung at her nostrils as the boys circled her. There were five of them. Van smirked at them. Excitement raced through her blood. Her stomach was knotted in fear, but she would never allow the others to see it. She would never allow them to have that power over her.

Angry and hurt because she was celebrating her eleventh birthday alone, Van had left her bunk that morning looking for a fight. Her muscles twinged as she forced her body to remain calm. She had searched out these boys. Prowling the grounds, she had come across several boys, all of them alone. Alone they would no longer fight her no matter how much she provoked them. Alone they were no match for her.

Finally she had found a group of older boys. She had barraged them with insults and taunts until they had circled her. Now she trembled in anticipation. She knew she would lose, but they would not walk away from this unscathed. They would know she was one to be respected and she would get her frustration out at the same time.

They closed in, closer and closer until she could feel their breath on her skin. Taking a shaky breath, she ignored her fear and prepared herself for the upcoming battle. Honor and dignity was all she needed to concentrate on as she fought.

The boys attacked.

The images of the boys blurred as fists connected. Time slowed as bodies collided together. Van growled deeply as she scrambled for purchase in the pile. She felt a bone crush underneath her fist as it drove into a nose. She heard a boy scream in agony as her knee drove into a crotch. Two boys pushed at her, driving her face into the dusty ground. She struggled and fought to get free. Blood flowed freely across her face, but whose and from where she did not know.

Then the crushing weight and grunting bodies were gone from her. Jumping to her feet, Van was stunned to see Peter Lawston lecturing the boys on the duties of a page. You do not attack as a group. You do not attack defenseless boys."

Defenseless boy? Van puffed up her chest and took a shaky breath. Defenseless. Her innards twisted in pain as she fought to remain calm. This was the lord of the manor's son. This was Peter Lawston, the Dragon Knight and the king's champion. This was the man she secretly loved.

The boys walked away with only a glance over their shoulder. They were beaten and bloody, but it was not good enough for Van.

Now they believed that Van had needed help and they believed that, because of this man, this man who thought of her as defenseless. Van's anger grew at what she saw as a transgression against her. How could Peter do this to her?

Peter turned to her with a helpful, look-at-what-I-have-done smile.

"Helpless," Van whispered as she attacked. Peter grabbed for her. The helpful, happy smile turned to shock as Van connected with him.

🝆 🝆 🝆

Amy touched her arm and Van lashed out barely missing her. Van shook her head and focused on the present.

Fear clouded Amy's face. She stood tensely, appearing ready to run if necessary. Guilt stung at Van and she winced. "I am sorry. I was lost in thought."

She waited until Amy smiled and relaxed before taking a step toward her. Amy had quickly become comfortable in her presence which boded well for Van, but she was still nervous about trusting her. It was the best course of action, though, and she would just have to pray that Amy would not betray her, either consciously or accidently.

Van took a deep breath and grinned, hoping that her concerns were hidden from view. "Now, it is time to put your, and my, trust to the test. Can I trust you with my life, with my secrets?" Van reached for the young girl, lifting her veil to see her face. "Do you think I will hurt you? Do you trust me fully?" Van asked.

Van stood steady beneath Amy's penetrating gaze. She relaxed slightly as Amy smiled and nodded. "You have my loyalty and my trust, my lord."

"Good, then I guess I must give you the same. Come, help me get undressed."

Alarm showed in the blue eyes. Alarm, but not fear. "Okay."

No fight. Van took a deep breath and ignored the worry that raced through her veins. She had promised to take care of Amy, and she would. She would protect her with her life if need be.

Back in the cottage she stood still as Amy began stripping off the gambeson that she had worn to the funeral. She struggled to keep the unease under control. Who was this young girl who so willingly put her trust in someone else? Van was not sure she could have done the same thing, not until that trust was earned. Not even if her mother had said to.

Van focused on the wall before her as Amy gripped the bottom of her long, baggy black tunic. Amy grunted as she stretched to lift the thick material over her head and when she wobbled Van knew she must be on tiptoe. She closed her eyes as the material slipped across her face throwing her into darkness.

Cool air caressed her bared arm and she flinched when Amy gasped and stepped away. Van held her breath self-consciously and waited for Amy to speak. When nothing came, she cautiously opened her eyes.

Amy's eyes were wide as she looked up at Van. Van looked from Amy's face to her own body.

She stood in a pair of long leather boots that stopped halfway up her thighs. Above those was a pair of close fitting tights that rode snug against her long legs and fit tightly against her flat pelvic area. Her tight undershirt did little to conceal the shape of her breasts even with the tight wrap below. She had never felt so vulnerable or so exposed.

Dawning thought seemed to light Amy's beautiful face. Her light brows arched. "You are a woman?" There was awe and disbelief in her soft whisper.

Van shook her head, taking a deep breath and holding it until small flashes could be seen in front of her face before releasing it in a whoosh. "We have only—" Van stopped. She cleared her throat. The voice that had come out was that of the Dark Knight. A deep male voice she had spent all her life perfecting—a voice that would give her away faster than the scar on her face.

Amy tilted her head and looked at her expectantly. Van groaned and started over, this time in a softer tone. It cracked gently. "We have only four days. I need you to show me how to be a woman."

Amy's brows rose in question, or concern, over her task, Van was unsure which. Whichever it was Amy did not interrupt. Van took a deep breath. "I need you to stay by my side as much as possible. I have a bad feeling that the Dark Knight will show his head if I am provoked. I do not know how to be anything else because I have never been anything else. I do not think my new husband will like who I am."

Van pulled the dingy white undershirt over her head and allowed Amy to assist her with untwining the tight bindings that pressed down the breasts that Van had cursed since they had begun to sprout. She had always thought them a burden. Van stood patiently as Amy stared at her half-naked form.

"How did I see you as a scary Knight? You are so shapely. You look very feminine." Amy looked up at her, her voice still light with wonder and amazement. To Van she sounded as if she were a child who was finally allowed to stay up late enough to see the wondrously brilliant sunset.

Van tensed and must have scowled because Amy's smile fell away and she took a half step back. Those were words that would have resulted in the speaker's death only days before. Van struggled to relax, but could not.

"Van?" Amy asked anxiously.

Van knew she was a woman now and she was just going to have to get used to it. Feminine was a good thing for a woman, but twenty years of training was hard to ignore. She could hear her mother's voice, echoing in her mind telling her, to think like a boy. She could hear the voices of the boys telling her that she looked like a weak girl, and then she smiled as she remembered the blood that had sprayed from their broken noses.

"It's nothing," Van said with a smile.

Amy didn't look as if she was convinced, but smiled as she stepped behind Van and unwound the thick leather strap from her hair. Van could feel her fingers deftly pulling apart the tangles made by her frantic ride to get to her mother's side.

No one had ever touched her hair and she could not decide if it was a feeling that she liked. The gentle tugs at the locks of hair as Amy untangled the mess sent small shivers down her spine. They were not totally unpleasant, but it was a strange feeling.

Amy's hands slid against Van's shoulders and arms as she worked with her hair. She said in a distracted voice, "You are extremely muscular."

Van looked down at her arms and realized that they were well muscled, but they were not massive. She had never thought of herself as muscular. Her strength came not from size, but just from sheer determination and cunning. She'd only had the other knights and soldiers to compare herself to and she had always come up lacking.

She had always worked harder than everyone else, wishing that she would grow as big as the men around her. Now her thoughts went in another direction. She was not massive as she had hoped to be, but neither was she petite or tiny. In her mind, no matter what Amy had said, she was not feminine.

Breath shuddered through her as she strengthened her resolve. Being a woman and a wife should have come natural to her, but she had spent all her life as something she was not. She was unsure that she could become what she was born to be.

A knock came at the door. Van quickly tugged her tunic over her head as Amy went to answer the door. She looked down at the shirt, now stretched against her unbound breasts.

Amy screamed in what sounded like horror and Van's head jerked up. It took her only a moment to pull her sword from its scabbard and tear through the small cottage. She fought a panic as images of Eolian's men surrounding the cottage swarmed her thoughts. She did not believe that he had found her so quickly, but it was an image that refused to release its hold on her weary mind.

She slid around the doorway of the room and came to a stumbling halt before the front door of the cottage. Verges, a very large and unearthly-looking man, stood holding Amy to his chest.

Tension eased from her body as relief swept over her. He was her spy in Eolian's army and he was her friend.

Verges' massive arms wrapped around Amy and a thick, dirty hand was held tight against her mouth. Amy's eyes were wild and desperate as she kicked and struggled. A low chuckle came from beneath the large hood that covered Verges's entire face. Her struggles went unnoticed by the massive man.

"Verges, put her down."

When he released her without hesitation, Amy fled toward Van. She opened her arms without thought and Amy burrowed deeply into her chest.

Van wrapped one arm distractedly around her and spoke quickly to Verges. "Come in before anyone sees you."

He slipped his wide shoulders through the door, having to turn slightly to accomplish it. "I saw the funeral."

Van knew that was his way of telling her he was sorry for her loss. "I was not going to knock, but I saw you through the window, with your binding off and your hair down."

Van sucked in a breath. She had no concerns of Verges seeing her. He knew all her secrets, from the fact that she was a woman to the identity and location of all her mistresses. No, she had no concerns about him, but she had been careless. If it had not been Verges, if it had been one of her enemies that had seen her undress all would have been lost.

Van's concerns slipped from her mind as Amy's tiny squeak of a voice spat out in outrage. "You saw her almost naked? You were looking through the window?" She spoke with conviction, but would not look directly at him.

"Amy, easy. This is a good friend of mine." Van grinned when he shifted uncomfortably at her statement. He had told her once that she was the only one who would consider him a friend. "Verges, this is Amy Devant."

She turned to Amy with a smile and let her arm drop away. "Amy, will you get us all something to drink?" Turning back to Verges, she smiled. "Are you hungry?" At his nod she instructed Amy to get something to eat as well.

Amy gave Van a look of relieved gratitude and nearly fled from the room. Van's smile fell away. She nodded to the long couch sitting before the fireplace. "Please sit with me."

Van took a seat on the couch and Verges took the chair that sat beside it. He turned the chair to face the couch and Van.

With a quick look toward the kitchen area, she sighed. Verges shifted to get more comfortable. She looked at his shadowed face. He looked at her expectantly as if he knew she wanted to talk.

"You saw the men leaving without me?" She already knew the answer.

He nodded.

She shifted uncomfortably on the soft couch. She wanted to explain to him her situation, but she had come to realize that she did not fully know it. She did not know where she was going or who she was going to be with. What she did know was that her lack of knowledge angered her.

She took a deep breath, turned to face him, and forced the words out. "I am to be married. I do not know who my betrothed is or where I am going." Her eyes narrowed and she scowled. She hated that she was not consulted on this, that she had had no say in who or when or even if she would marry.

She growled thickly and kicked at the small table before the couch. It shivered dangerously and she waited for it to collapse. It did not.

She looked at him and forced herself to relax.

He just smiled calmly.

"You know who my father is. I will be there in a week. I will go there first, that is all I know." She shifted her weight and cracked her neck for what seemed like the hundredth time since she had arrived at her mother's home. "Go there and find out what you can. I am sure people there know of the arrangements."

Even if I don't, she thought bitterly and kicked at the table once more. "I need you to take some money to the girls."

He nodded once again.

She heard Amy coming in from the kitchen and shook her head. "I need a day maid and someone to help me. Amy has agreed to do that for me."

Verges shook his head and allowed the hood to fall across his face as Amy walked into the room with three plates of food balanced on a tray.

She joined Van on the couch, sitting almost on top of her as she drew away from Verges, almost spilling the food as she did so. Van felt a trembling shudder run through Amy's small frame. Van took the tray from her shaking hands and laid it upon the table. "Easy, he will not hurt you."

Amy looked at her as if she was crazy. "How do you know? How do you know him?"

Van could barely hear her small, scared whisper. She grinned even though irritation swam through her veins at being questioned. She was accustomed to telling people what to do and having them do it. "I know." She took one of the food laden plates and handed it to Verges without taking her eyes off Amy. "Because, he takes care of my girls for me when I cannot."

"Your girls?" Amy's attention was finally off of Verges as her head spun toward Van, a look of shock on her face. Van, having no intention of explaining her mistresses to Amy, just shook her head.

As the Dark Knight she had rescued many women all over the country and had taken responsibility for them. It was easiest just to say they were the property of the Dark Knight, that they were his mistresses and their children his. It protected them.

"Aye, my girls." Van grinned at Verges and he chuckled.

Amy cringed and glanced at him before looking back at Van.

"He would never hurt one close to me, even if he might have the urge." She knew that he had had those urges before. Some of the women she had rescued had been a handful. They had done nothing drastic of course, but enough to annoy the big Verges. He had always held his temper, allowing Van to dish out whatever lectures or punishment was required.

She smiled down at Amy and gently handed her a plate of food before taking the last one for herself. "And I met Verges three years ago."

Without looking up, the big man interrupted her. "The Dark Knight saved my life. We were crossing a river that was swollen and flooded with a storm. Trees were uprooted and one hit my horse. I was left for dead by the men I was with. Van came along and pulled me from the river."

"You do not seem surprised that she is a woman." Amy relaxed and pulled slightly away from Van.

Van was proud of her bravery as she questioned Verges and looked at him while she did. She was once again impressed by her ability to trust in the word of someone. Her mother told her that the Dark Knight was trustworthy and she trusted her. Van told her that Verges was trustworthy and, from body language at least, it appeared that Amy was taking Van at her word.

"I am not surprised." He shifted in his seat to face Amy better. The hood fluttered around his face, but revealed nothing. His voice thickened. "While she was bringing me to shore, a large tree hit her. She was knocked unconscious and luckily I was where I could touch, since I cannot swim."

His voice took on an edge of disbelief as he continued. "She had seen me as the enemy and still knowing that, she had saved my life." He chuckled again.

Amy tensed, but did not retreat away from him.

"I could not let her die. I made a fire and had to get her out of her wet clothes." He looked up at Amy, allowing the hood to fall away and his face to show in the flickering glow of the lamps that burned brightly in the room. "I have given her my life, in return for all she has done for me."

Van felt Amy tighten in fear at the distorted face before her, not a pleasant sight at its best, but she did not retreat away from him. She just smiled, a sweet light shading her face. Verges looked surprised and then he flashed a gruesome smile. "I think you have made a good choice, my lord."

"I do as well."

Verges rose to his feet. Gesturing for Amy to remain on the couch, Van followed him to the door.

He turned and looked at her with a soft smile.

"Find me." The two words sounded to her like a desperate plea and she supposed they were. He was her only link to her past and the only one who could help her if things went badly.

She watched him disappear into the darkness and told herself that becoming the woman she was supposed to be would be easy. She smiled and believed it.

The next few days were spent trying to make Van into Vanessa. Van hated everything that women were supposed to be. She despised the cumbersome dresses women were supposed to wear and she was beginning to resent Amy for constantly telling her to be more malleable, more docile.

Van's doubts rose a little more every day. She worried that she would never make a convincing woman. She did not walk like one, she did not sit like one, she did not talk like one, and she definitely could never be docile and malleable.

She didn't have any of the mannerisms of a woman and she hated the name Vanessa. "Milady," she did not seem to have a problem with. She was, after all, a woman and she was not ashamed of that fact. What she hated was the name. It represented everything that she had had to fight to overcome, all the shortcomings she had started out with. Weak, soft Vanessa had been gotten rid of and she had been ever so glad to see her go. Now, she was reluctant to allow her back.

The nights were spent much the same way as they had been for the last three years. Van tossed and turned, lost in dreams of the man she had saved in battle. Night after night he haunted her, again and again rubbing his calloused hand along her cheek, telling her she was beautiful. The man she had loved ever since she was ten when he had welcomed her to the castle.

Five days later, Van waited in the door yard, watching her father ride up with several men. One was leading a horse with a sidesaddle and another led a pack horse ready for a trunk to be loaded onto his back.

Her father did not take his eyes off of her as he rode up.

Van was surprised by how much she looked like him. She was identical to him, even down to the thin, erect nose and the high, sharp cheek bones.

Van trembled as she willed her legs not to turn to jelly. She took a deep calming breath and shuddered as she released it.

She shifted self-consciously beneath the gazes of the men who rode toward them. She wore a long, dark blue dress, one of many that Amy had tailored for her over the last few days. Van felt exposed and uncomfortable as the soft breeze ran its fingers along her bared thighs and legs.

She wore a thick layer of face powder to disguise the telling scar across her cheek. The powder and the huge waves of pitch black hair that swam around her face did well to hide the mark.

Her flowing hair was another thing she didn't think she could get used to. It had never been worn any way but braided and it now rubbed and itched against her face and neck.

The chalkiness of the face powder made her want to sneeze, but Van knew the makeup was necessary. If Eolian found out she was a woman, his revenge would be swift, and he would use anything that he could to get to her. That included the young girl who had put her faith in Van.

Her father, Matthew Fordella, Earl Thereamong, of Thereamong Estates, dismounted. He came confidently toward her. "Vanessa. I have been anticipating meeting you."

"Aye, so I have heard for years." Her hand hovered near the dagger that was strapped to her thigh beneath her dress. She scowled irritably, knowing she could not easily get to it and thought it was fortunate for him that she could not.

Matthew took another step forward. "I am sorry I did not bring a carriage. It takes longer over the rough roads than riding astride. I did bring you a horse with a sidesaddle."

"I need neither your horse nor your saddle." Her angry words brought a pained look to her father's black eyes. She spoke in the arrogant, low pitched voice of the Dark Knight and instantly felt a violent tugging at her arm.

Van tried to pull her arm away, but Amy held firmly, pulling heavily on her sleeve as she pleaded with her. "Stop it, Mi*lady*." She put an extra emphasis on the word lady, stressing it strongly.

The desperate tone in Amy's voice cut through her anger more than the words themselves. Van scowled, sucked in a deep breath and forced herself to relax. When she spoke again it was in a lighter, phony voice.

She had attempted a soft feminine voice many times over the last few days. Much to her dismay and frustration it would crack and groan every time she tried. The only thing she could manage was a high pitched falsetto that hurt even her own ears.

"I have my own horse and saddle, although I can use the mare that you have brought, and the woman's saddle. This is Amy Devant." She gestured to the annoyance behind her without looking back and kept her focus on her father's tense face as she spoke. "She will be going with me." Her voice rattled her teeth and grated at her nerves and she irritably hoped that it did the same for everyone else.

She took a shallow breath and held her arm toward the door in an invitation that she did not want to extend. "You and your men must be tired, please come in. Amy has prepared a mid-meal for us."

Without awaiting a response, Van walked quickly into the cottage. She did not want to be cordial to the man. He had brought her and her mother much pain over the twenty years since her mother had run from him.

Once in the cottage, she said little to him. He talked to her about life in Junket and looked irritated when her answers were short and vague, but there was little she could tell him. She just didn't know very much of what went on in the town, she was seldom ever here and when she was she didn't leave the cottage.

Matthew took a deep breath and dismissed the seven men who had accompanied him. They would bed down in the stable.

Matthew arched one questioning brow that caused Van to think of looking in a mirror as he looked toward Amy Devant. "Should she leave the room?"

"Nay." It was the same monosyllable answer she had given since they had entered the small home.

He gave a tight growl. "I had thought you were going to give me a chance, now I see it is not to be so."

"My Lord, I am giving you a chance." She glanced at him and dropped into the chair closest to her. Amy took a seat next to her. She shifted uncomfortably in the long skirts and tried to remember how Amy had told her to sit. Unable to get situated, she gave up. "That is the only reason you are here."

Van wanted to stay angry with him. She had at one time been frightened of him, but the fear had left her long ago. She had thought she had held onto the anger, but now she found she was only curious. "Why have you come to find me after all these years?"

"I have been looking for you since your mother left me. I am not sure of what you were told all these years, but I would like to tell you what happened." He sat in the chair facing her and waited.

Curious she nodded her head for him to continue.

"You were a little over a year old and the joy of my life when Patricia caught me with my mistress."

Van sucked in a shocked breath and he paused.

Her mother had always said they ran on the night she was born. Not a year later. Not trusting herself to speak, she impatiently twirled her fingers at him to continue.

"I was drunk and when she dumped the chamber pot on us and then hit me on the head with it I lost control of my anger." His voice dropped to a dull whisper. "I hit her."

She clenched her teeth and tightened her fists into hard balls. Honor and understanding warred within her as she listened to his soft voice. Honor bound by pride and held by a deeply rooted set of values meant she could not stand aside and see a woman abused, but understanding caressed her anger and softened it.

She could see the same shame in his face that she felt on the rare occasion that she herself had hit a woman. Her fingers loosened and pain filled her heart.

"When I awoke the next day, she and you were gone. I have searched for you for years. It got back to me about four years after she had left me that she had gotten an annulment and remarried. I remarried a year after I found out." He shook his head and smiled sadly. "I stopped looking for her, but never stopped looking for you."

Pain filled his eyes and Van could not stop the pity that tightened her chest. She clenched her jaw in anger, but knew she was only angry at herself. She felt not only that she was betraying her mother with her pity for him, but if she believed him then her mother had betrayed her.

Her stomach turned painfully and she clenched her throat tightly against a wave of nausea. That lie was responsible for her entire life, a life that had been full of pain and war. She could not even imagine the kind of woman she would have been if she had lived the soft life of a normal female.

Anger at herself, at him, and at her mother boiled together into a dangerous potion within her stomach. It churned and tightened, sending tendrils of hot rage through her senses and she lashed out. "And now after all these years you think you can just come into my life and all will be well, just because you say you are sorry. Nay, you didn't even say that, did you?" The fake voice cracked slightly, but she managed to hold it together.

"Nay, but I am sorry." His face darkened with a deep look of sadness. Taking a deep breath that shuddered through him, he shook his head. "I will let my men stay here tonight, first thing in the morning I will take you to your new husband. He is waiting for you."

"Husband? You make it sound as if he has already been wedded to me and is not just my betrothed?" Van could feel the rage radiating from her and her fingers whitened as she gripped the smooth wooden arms of the chair in which she sat. The rage swirled around her and threatened to overpower her. She was losing control. It worried and excited her all at once. She wanted to let her temper loose and release some of the pent up energy that had been plaguing her for days.

She ground her teeth together painfully. The knowledge of what was at stake was all that held her together. She had given her word to her mother and honor would allow nothing less than fulfilling her promise.

Matthew looked at her, but appeared uncertain of how to answer. A deep sense of foreboding settled across her. She clenched her fists tightly and reminded herself of all that was at stake.

Her honor was all she had left to her. Her word had been given, and not just to her mother. If she broke her word to her mother, it would only affect her, but if she broke her word to the women and children she was responsible for, it would devastate their lives. These women had no one to turn to and were dependent on her care.

She glanced around at Amy and sighed. Amy was one more person who was now depending on her. She looked back at her father and cleared her throat. The anger was pushed down, but for how long she was unsure. "Well?" She was sure of one thing. She did not want to hear his answer.

Matthew looked at her and shook his head. "He has, by proxy. I sanctioned the marriage and it is legal. It will be satisfied as soon as it is consummated."

Her reasons for staying calm faded from her mind like wisps of morning mist under the heat of her anger. She clenched her hands tightly into fists and tried to rise. She felt Amy grasp her shoulder.

Amy tightened her fingers desperately into her flesh. Van dropped back down into the uncomfortable chair, but could not stop the violent shaking that racked her body.

"Milady, calm down. You knew he had picked a husband for you." Amy sounded panicked.

"Aye, I fully understand that, but I was under the mistaken impression I would have an ounce of say in the man I was to marry. What if I don't like him, what if he is mean and cruel? Then what do I do?" She nearly leapt from the chair and began to pace furiously across the small room. She had never felt so out of control in her life. She, the master of all situations, had just been thrust into a situation she had no control over at all.

"I am sure he has good qualities or else Earl Thereamong would not have chosen him." Amy said softly stepping in front of Van to cease her stalking across the floor. Van knew the girl was trying to calm her, but it wasn't working. Anger still swirled dangerously.

Van turned to the man she had been raised to fear and, feigning a calm she didn't feel, demanded, "Fine. Why did you choose this man?"

"His estates are adjacent to mine. I can see you and the grandchildren whenever I please," he said in a calm, rational way that made Van want to scream. "He is a good man."

Van knew there was no use in fighting it, not now. If she didn't like the man that her father had chosen, she would get the marriage annulled. Her father may want her near him, but that did not mean that she had to stay married to the man he had shackled her to. If she didn't consummate the marriage, she would be free. If there was too much of a fight, she would just disappear. Even though she was getting too old to be the Dark Knight she would never be found if she didn't want to be.

Even with that knowledge, she hated the fact that something had been arranged that involved her and she wasn't in charge of it.

The rage she had been feeling for the last week was on the verge of ripping free from its fragile constraints. Van turned and walked off trying, unsuccessfully, to keep the Dark Knight controlled.

CHAPTER 5

Van squinted against the sharp morning light as the sun breached the horizon behind her father. He huffed and puffed and paced before her, dust billowing with each stomp of his feet. Irritation swirled within her as he ranted about the proprieties of sidesaddles.

His eyes bulged in anger and he shook his finger at her. "It is indecent for a properly bred young lady to ride astride."

Images of her upbringing raced through her mind and she snorted lightly. Properly bred, indeed, she thought.

Van put her hands on her hips. She did not want the extra attention that a scene would cause, but she was not going to ride in that silly contraption they called a saddle.

"You did not bring a carriage. I have never used a sidesaddle and I am not going to ride for two days in a saddle that I have never used." She took a deep breath and tried to control the uneasiness that swarmed around her head like a swarm of gnats.

He came to a halt and stared at her with his mouth agape. "Never ridden a side…How could you never…How could your mother…" His words came in a stuttering rush that boiled her blood.

She clinched her fists until her nails dug into her palms. She stepped toward him, but only managed to get her fist half raised when she felt hands grip her arm. Amy yanked. Van ignored her and stared defiantly at her father. "How dare you question my mother?"

Amy pulled hard at her arm. Van arched one eyebrow as she faced the man she had hated for so many years that she could no longer count them.

"Mi*lady*." Amy's voice was nearly a screech.

Van winced. She would have liked to swat at Amy like a wretched gnat. Unable to ignore her maid any longer, she swung her head around to glare at the short, stubborn woman. "Nay, I will not budge on this, not now," Van barked at her. She pushed away the smothering guilt as Amy cringed away from her icy stare.

Van turned back toward Matthew and forced her voice back into the high falsetto, the high-pitched tones breaking across the still morning air. "And definitely, not with you."

Matthew Fordella scowled at her ferociously. Then finally he threw up his arms in apparent surrender and stormed away. He called back to Amy as he stomped off, "Good luck with her, my child. You will need it."

Relief soothed Van's nerves as she watched Matthew bark at his men to saddle her horse. Damien swayed from foot to foot as the men approached. Ears pinned to his head he snorted and pawed at the dusty ground.

Van stood calmly as the men closed in on Damien. She was the only one he trusted. This would not end well, but she did not say a word. A little revenge would do her heart some good. Her unease faded and a grin spread.

The first man cursed loudly as he took a bite to the arm. A second man received a bite to the side. The men fled out of Damien's reach as the huge destrier reared up, slashing the air with his sharp hooves.

Van took a step toward the men and the rearing horse but was stopped by Amy's soft words. "Milady."

She took a deep breath, but didn't look back. "No." She walked past her father and the men without even glancing at them.

Damien held out his muzzle and nickered softly as she approached. As she watched the tension slip from her steed's muscles she could feel some of the stresses drain from her as well.

Matthew grumbled something inaudible about stubborn asses as he turned and stomped away. She wondered in amusement if he was talking of her or Damien. Perhaps both, she thought and smiled smugly as she threw a saddle onto the now calm horse.

Soon Van sat proudly on her stallion and watched Amy receive help onto a docile mare. The poor girl clutched at the reins until her knuckles turned white and her hands shook, but she gave Van a weak smile.

Amy had confessed to her over the short time they had spent together that she was terrified of horses. Now to see Amy braving her fears, for her, made Van's chest tighten. Loyalty from the men assigned to her, men she had proven herself to over the years was expected, but the loyalty this girl showed her was surprising.

The pack horse was loaded with a large trunk that held several newly made dresses, a pile of chain mail, a black helm, a long sword, and a thick chest plate. The men grumbled about the weight and threw glances her way. She was not positive if it was in suspicion or if it was just her guilty conscious that pricked at her.

Van watched her father spur his horse forward and grudgingly followed. She patted Damien's neck, as much to comfort herself as him, and looked back at the cottage one last time.

She would make arrangements with Verges to fix the thatching on the roof and the windows that needed to be replaced. She had never been close to Dr. Paul and even though she would always make sure he was well taken care of, she didn't believe she would ever return to see him.

A sudden feeling of loss assaulted her. She would never see this little house again and that disturbed her. Tears welled behind her eyes so she squinted into the sun to conceal them.

"We need to discuss your saddle." Matthew's irritated voice sounded next to her, pulling her from her reflections.

Van turned to him, grateful for his interruption.

"You need to be appropriate when you meet your husband. Come to think of it," he said staring at Damien. "You just need to be in a carriage, not on that beast."

Van grinned lopsidedly, patted Damien on his heavily-muscled neck and looked up at her father. She opened her mouth to dispute him but Amy's soft voice stopped her.

"Mi*lady*, your father is correct. No matter what your feelings are, you need to make a good first impression if you plan for any of this to work."

Matthew looked closely from Van to Amy. Van turned and glowered at the young girl, but held her tongue. After all, Amy was right. If she was going to pull off this charade—and she had to in order to keep her secret—it had to be convincing.

Van turned to her father and conceded that once they arrived at his estate they would take a carriage, with Damien hitched to the rear of it.

Matthew smiled and nodded his head. "Good." His grin widened. "You can meet my sons and their mother as soon as they return from their visit with her parents."

Van's breath hitched at the thought of his sons, the sons he had always wanted, the son that she was supposed to be. Anger boiled beneath the calm façade that she held before her like a shield. The anger didn't surprise her, but the twinge of jealousy that accompanied it, did.

It was more than jealousy. She admitted, though reluctantly, it was envy. Envy of a life she had secretly dreamed of as a small child. To be the son of a rich lord, to not have to fight for everything she had accomplished.

She pushed away the lost dreams and the envy. She focused instead on the anger, the deep, painful thudding of her heart, and the memory of how good her life had been, despite all the tribulations.

She reminded herself that she could not be angry with his sons. They were innocent and not responsible for the sins of their father, and they were more than his sons. They were her brothers. "Brothers," she whispered.

"Aye, two of them, though neither look like me." He glanced at her and smiled. "Like us, nor do they have my temperament." His flicked the reins and his mount moved smoothly into a trot. Damien matched speed without encouragement.

He turned and studied her closely. His intense scrutiny slid across her skin like a caress. "Though you seem to have it."

Goosebumps tickled right beneath the surface of her skin and she fought to suppress a shudder. She forced her gaze to remain on him. She could feel her shield slipping and a sneer twitching on her tightened lips.

His eyes met hers and his smile widened. "I would like the chance to get to know the girl who seems so much like me."

Van wrenched Damien to a stop, nearly unseating Amy who rode close behind her. She whipped around and glared at her father. "I am nothing like you, Matthew."

He recoiled and pulled his mount to a stop. His eyes widened and his mouth grew slack. She was not sure if his surprise came from the comment or the low deep voice.

She forced herself to straighten and concentrated on her voice instead of the darkness that boiled from within her, clouding her vision and threatening her judgment. "I would never do the things that you have done." Her fists tightened into white trembling balls around the reins and her arms shook with the effort to remain seated. The darkness swirled and caressed her, whispered to her to get revenge on the man who had wanted her dead. For years she had wanted to see him pay, and now she could accomplish that.

Her mother's pale face appeared before her and her last wish, her trembling words, echoed in her mind. Van fought a tear that threatened to spill. She had to get away, had to be alone, if only for a moment.

She spurred Damien into a gallop, leaving Amy and the men behind. She raced across the hard-packed road, trying to dispel the darkness, to leave it behind as she had believed she had done so long ago.

Her jaw tightened until it ached and her teeth grated. She had not felt this anger and need for vengeance in many years and had mistakenly believed she had mastered it. She took a deep breath and reined in her steed.

A quick flare of pain erupted from her clenched jaw. She forced it to relax. Anger flamed within her chest at her father's careless words. She did not want to believe there were any similarities between her and the man she had grown up despising.

"I am not like that man," she said with conviction. She looked at Damien as if he would agree with her and snorted when he only flicked his ears to roust the flies. "Some help you are. I am not like that man. He has done awful things."

She looked back at the approaching party and sighed. Painful flashes of dead men strewn across the battlefield, of running blood, and men who would never return to their families raced across her exhausted mind. A broken and beaten woman lay dead within the recesses of her memory. Tears blurred her vision.

She reminded herself that part of living a life of honor was being honest, even when you did not want to be. "I too have done awful things," she admitted reluctantly. Perhaps there was more resemblance between them than just appearance, after all.

Damien looked over his shoulder at her and drew her gaze back to him.

"Shut up," she said irritably. She took a deep breath and forced herself to calm.

Looking back again at the men, she knew she had no choice but to wait for them to catch up. She patted the quivering horse and she spoke softly to him. "After all, I do not know where we are going." She hung her head limply against his mane until she heard the sound of hoof beats catching up to them.

The entourage rode on in silence with only the soft snorts and nickering of the horses sounding into the still air. The quiet was broken occasionally by the soft questions of her father, but her sharp, one-word answers soon left him silent.

Her mind was focused on her uncertain future. How would she pull off this pretense? What her husband would be like? Those ranked amongst the main worries. She pictured the men that she knew, the angry, the kind, the gentle, and the violent. Which would her husband be?

She wondered tremulously what her new husband would expect of her.

Her concerns rampaged through her mind, balling her into a tense knot of nerves that nipped at her self-control.

The scenery went unnoticed. Van took little conscious stock of where she was. She kept watch for anyone who might be following behind and for possible ambush sites up ahead, but this she did with the subconscious ease of time and experience.

Soon the scenery became more familiar and she sat straighter in her saddle. Her gaze roamed the well-traveled road and took in the large boulders that were strewn beside it.

The trees were tall and old. She grinned. They were heading toward Lynton. Castle Grayweist sat in Lynton—Castle Grayweist and Peter. She was unsure of how she would get to see him, but she would try. It would be nice to have him see her as a woman. A small shudder of excitement raced through her.

Her delighted smile fell away. What good would it do for him to see her? She thought irritably to herself. He would not be seeing her as a woman; no he would be seeing her as a married woman.

Another thought crossed her mind, what if he had married? News of his father's death had reached her several months ago, and with it had been rumors that he had arranged a marriage between Peter and some unknown woman. Others had said the rumors were untrue, so she had chosen to dismiss them. Now her heart sank at the reality that they may indeed be true.

The thought left a jagged line of pain deep between her temples. She raised her hand to massage the sides of her head and tried to make the thought go away, but it refused to release its dark hold on her.

Van's mood was foul when they reached Matthew's manor. She grumbled crossly as she slipped her leg from the saddle, only to have the flowing skirts of her dress hang up against it. She cursed foully, yanked it free, and jumped to the ground.

Amy came to stand beside her. "Are you all right, my lady?"

Van replied with a snort. She watched quietly as her father's dark, black carriage was made ready and her heavy trunk loaded onto it.

Matthew offered to show her his home, but she just scowled at him and shook her head. She had no desire to see the home she should have grown up in.

She climbed into the carriage and sat tensely on the hard seat as they made their way to her new husband. Her breathing grew painful and her mood darkened with every rough step of the horses.

"The castle grows near," Matthew announced, pulling her from her troubling thoughts. Van pulled the curtain from the window and leaned her head out. Castle Grayweist sat proudly before her. The dark cloud of regret that had encircled her was gone as if it had never been there.

If this was her new home, then there was no doubt as to the identity of her new husband. She smiled, her heart racing with excitement. She was the unknown woman to whom Peter was to be wed.

She allowed her mind to drift to Peter and relaxed against the side of the carriage, still staring out the window at the castle she had called home for three years.

Her heart raced faster than the galloping horses pulling the carriage, as if it wanted to get to the castle before them. She had not seen Peter for three years, not since the day she had saved him and become a knight.

Doubt began to cloud her excitement and a tickle of concern brushed against her. Peter had seen her only three years ago and she had changed little in those three years. When she looked in the mirror she still saw herself as Van the knight, no matter the amount of powder she spackled on. She pushed away the doubts the best she could, but they remained low in the back of her mind.

She took a deep breath and closed her eyes. She could only hope that his injuries had made his memory foggy and he would not recognize her for who she really was.

She opened her eyes to the sprawling old castle that sat high upon the rugged cliffs, overlooking the sea. The massive grey castle looked the same as it had when she had been a young child there. She had changed so much since she left and she was surprised to find that the castle had not.

The heavy salts from the sea wafted through the carriage, tickling at her nose and flooding her mind with memories. She sucked in a sharp, painful breath.

This was where she had endured her page training, where she had met Peter and Richard, and where she had always felt at home. She could almost see herself wandering the halls of the castle when she was supposed to be in the barracks. She smiled deviously, recalling that she had never been caught.

The driver pulled the carriage into the courtyard. Van saw a large number of warriors, all in full battle garb. She recognized several of the men that she had served under as a squire and a sad smile crossed her lips.

An empty sense of jealousy washed over her. She was finally in the only place she had ever truly felt at home, but now she felt as if she were an imposter. She missed her time in the castle, she missed her training, but mostly she missed her men. A deep hollow opened up inside her chest and beckoned her toward the cool darkness. She sank into it.

The carriage pulled to a stop in front of the men. She could see maybe a hundred more disappearing over a hill in the distance. She smiled in disheartened recollection. The lists were right over that hill. She had spent many a hot afternoon training in those grassy fields.

Matthew swung the door open and stepped from the carriage. He turned and offered her his hand. She arched one brow and stared at his outstretched hand. She didn't want to accept help from him or anyone else.

Amy nudged her from behind and she realized it was more than pride that made it difficult to take his hand. She was afraid to face this new step in her life. Unease swelled, closing her throat and threating to stop her breath.

Van tightened her shoulders and her resolve. Unwilling to give into her fears, she reluctantly took her father's hand and, on shaking legs, allowed him to lead her into her new life.

She glanced across the courtyard, taking in the men. Her gaze locked on Richard and her heart lurched painfully into her throat. He stood before about twenty of her men. They all were staring at her.

Surprise quickly turned to fear. If by some chance Peter was unable to identify her, the men she had left mere days ago would have no trouble seeing her for who she was.

Loneliness hit her hard in the pit of the belly as if from a physical blow. Her hand flew to her stomach, and it was all she could do to keep her feet beneath her. She had never felt as alone as she did staring at the men she cared for, men she could not go to. A sudden sense of loss overwhelmed her. At least if they were gone she could move on with her new life, but how could she forget them if she had to see them from a distance every day and not be able to be who she truly was with them.

CHAPTER 6

Peter's stomach rolled uneasily as he watched Matthew's carriage come to a dusty stop before him. He took a deep breath and, though his innards twisted and complained, threatening to bring up what little he had managed of his morning meal, forced himself to be outwardly calm.

He had been a nervous ball of tension ever since Vanessa had been located. It had been easier to agree to a marriage with a woman who was lost than it was to face that same marriage once she was found.

The carriage rocked and the door swung open with a slight creak. Peter watched in anticipation as Matthew jumped lightly to the ground before turning back to the carriage and extending his hand to what could only be Peter's new bride.

Peter was anxious to have this first meeting complete so he could get back to the training of his men, but he found he was curious, curious about her manner and her looks. He could picture her mother, small and dainty. He smiled, wondering if there was a resemblance from mother to daughter. He had always had a soft spot for petite women.

As the moments slid by and no one took Matthew's outstretched hand Peter began to worry, tension hammering at his already rolling stomach. The horses hitched to the front of the carriage seemed to echo the anxiety that tormented him as they snorted and pawed at the dusty ground.

He had heard rumors that Vanessa had been a shut-in and that no one in the village had ever seen her. His mind captured the image of a small, shy woman.

Afraid of people and perhaps even her own shadow, he thought, shaking his head sympathetically. The longer no one took the offered hand, the more his mind insisted that his assumption must be true, and the more his anxiety grew.

It didn't matter that society, and his father, had said he was getting old and should have married long before now. He was not ready for a wife. At least, he thought—in hopes to placate himself—a shy and timid woman was more likely to keep out of his way. The last thing he needed was a woman under his feet. He hoped that she would be as obedient as his mistress had been.

His despairing thoughts were interrupted by slow movements beside him. His men were casting quick glances at the carriage and each man was taking his time to gather his weapons. Peter knew they were lingering to catch a glimpse of his new bride, and understanding their curiosity, he did nothing to rush them.

He sighed deeply and wished he could go with his men to train. It was where he belonged. Not here, trying to pacify some petrified little woman that he had no desire to be wed to.

He pushed away his doubts, forced himself to smile, and hoped that it looked more convincing than it felt. He took a step forward to offer his warm welcome to the terrified creature. He paused when she finally outstretched her hand and allowed her father to draw her from the carriage.

Her hand was not small or dainty, nor was it made of the soft pale skin he had expected. His smile faltered. The deep bronzed hand spoke, not of one who had never left her house, but of one who had spent many hours out in the sun and weather. His mind twisted with curiosity as he watched her step almost reluctantly from the carriage.

His breath caught as she slowly stood to her full height. She was almost as tall as her father and he was sure she towered at over six feet. Definitely not, mother like daughter, he thought with a sigh, but she did look familiar.

He tried to catch a full glimpse of her face, tried to place where he might have met her before. He looked from Vanessa's profile to her father and realized why she looked so familiar. Vanessa Fordella looked exactly like her father.

Her gaze skittered nervously across the large group of warriors. She was not the petite creature that he had been expecting, but she did appear to be timid and shy as she looked from man to man. This calmed his mistrust, at least momentarily. Perhaps, he thought, he was inventing worry where none should be.

He focused on her profile and watched avidly as her jaw grew taut. She shook her head. He could see the shock on her face. Her hand flew to her stomach and she looked as if she may faint. He moved quickly to reassure her. Smiling in what he hoped was a warm and welcoming way, he stepped in between her and his men.

She turned her gaze to him and her eyes widened. He found himself looking into the blackest eyes he had ever seen. They peered at him from a face coated in a thick white powder. He had never understood why a woman would go through the trouble of hiding behind a mask of makeup. He had always thought that the women who piled on the makeup were trying to hide something, felt they were dishonest. He took a deep breath, but it did nothing to calm him.

The horses snorted and pawed at the ground. Matthew held out his hand. "Good evening, my boy."

Peter grasped his hands and shook it heartily. "Matthew. Good to see you." Peter tried to focus on him, but his attention was drawn back to his bride as a soft breeze pushed raven black strands of hair across her face.

His fingers itched to reach up and push the shiny black strands from her high cheekbones. The soft waves fell along her sun kissed arms and ended well past the middle of her back. His eyes narrowed as he studied her. The dark tanned arms were bared below the elbows and her black kirtle, to his disappointment, started well above her bosom, giving no hint to what treasures lay beneath.

Peter realized with a start that he had not said a word to her. He bowed slightly. "It is a pleasure to meet you, my lady."

She bowed her head in acknowledgement, but did not respond. Her eyes flicked over his shoulder and then back to his face.

He could hear the men's weapons rattling behind him as they took a slow walk past the carriage on the way to the lists. He looked closely at her and tried to see her as the men might. She stood tall and erect, her shoulders thrown back with a pride that did not adhere to his image of a shy, little maiden, even though her actions did.

She was beautiful. That he was sure the men would see. A soft wisp of concern slithered through him, wrapping around his heart and giving it a quick squeeze. He pushed it away in surprise. He had not felt jealousy in a long time.

Her gaze darted once more over his shoulder and this time remained. He turned back to see Richard staring intently at her. The jealousy he was denying swelled within him so quickly that he had to bite his tongue to keep it from erupting from him like a volcano. He took a shaky breath and motioned jerkily for the men to depart.

Richard opened his mouth as if he might speak, shook his head instead, and led the men off. Peter watched him go and told himself that Richard may just be feeling the same familiar tugging that he himself felt when he looked at her. His eyes narrowed, hoping that was all that Richard was feeling. But the long looks between Richard and Vanessa worried him. He sighed, telling himself that he was being ridiculous.

He took a shaky breath and made sure the smile was still full on his face before he turned to face his bride. Peter was surprised to find her staring at him, her lips slightly parted and her brows arched. Sure that she was scared by the men, he pointed off to the larger group who were about to disappear over a ridgeline.

"Those men will not hurt you," he started in the voice he reserved for small children and women. It was a voice he hoped would calm her fears, but her mouth dropped open more prominently. Fearing that she had not understood, he lowered his voice and smiled sweetly. "You see, over that ridge?" He pointed once again. "That is where I train my men. They are my warriors…"

Vanessa's mouth snapped shut so hard he heard her teeth clank together. "I am not two, and I would appreciate if you would not talk to me as such." Her high pitched squeal was full of indignation and her eyes flashed with anger.

He felt his own jaw drop slightly as shock exploded through him at her blatant disrespect. So much for shy and docile, he thought as she continued her tirade. A pleasant sounding wife would have been a plus he thought irritably.

"I realize fully that those men are warriors and I know what it takes to—"

Behind the angry temptress Peter heard a loud clearing of a throat. He looked around her at a pretty girl, who jerked roughly at the puffy sleeve of his new bride's black dress. The girl, obviously the day maid, who if he had been informed correctly would be Amy Devant, desperately hissed, "Milady. Please, milady, stop."

He was surprised first by the gall of the girl and then by the change it brought to Vanessa. Her jaw tightened and she took a deep breath, held it a moment before releasing it through clenched teeth.

She raised her chin and stared directly at him, at eye level. It was disconcerting to look straight at a woman. He watched her closely as a quiet calm took over her features. He knew it was not a true calm as he could see the anger that sparked deep within those beautiful, mysterious eyes.

He had to look hard to see any emotion and had a feeling that it would take time to learn how to read her fully. He felt a smile tug at the corners of his lips as he realized he was looking forward to learning more about her.

"If you are not too scared, perhaps I may take you to see the men train. We do not have to get too close," he said casually, testing her character and seeing where her limits lie. He expected the same reaction that he always got when he spoke to women, a scared and frightened look.

"Aye, my lord, I would like to see the way you train your men."

Vanessa's voice grated at his nerves, but it held no fear. She had looked terrified and on the verge of tears, looking at the men only moments earlier. Now there was not a trace of reluctance to be close to them. He wondered what had changed her attitude.

The familiar looks that had passed between Vanessa and Richard swamped his mind. His suspicions leapt to a thundering peak and then crashed down upon him like a landslide. Anger exploded and he fought to get a hold of it.

A smug grin twitched on Vanessa's lips, and he realized in irritation that the thick powder hid much of her emotions.

"You wear too much powder. I do not like it. You will wear none from now on." He stepped forward running a finger along her jaw, taking a strip of powder off.

She gasped and jerked her head away from him, recoiling with a look of horror as if he had taken a blade to her instead of his finger. She opened her mouth and just as she stepped toward him with clenched fists a violent ruckus erupted behind him, drawing his attention away from her. A huge black destrier reared up yanking the small carriage off the ground and giving a loud scream of frustration.

Peter smiled widely as he watched the horse's long mane flowing in the slight breeze. He took in the well-defined muscles, marvelous conformation, and shining coat as the aggravated animal pawed at the ground.

"Tell me please, my dear friend, that you have brought that magnificent creature for my stables." He spoke to Matthew without taking his eyes from the horse. "Tell me he is for sale." He looked eagerly at the man who had been his father's friend for many years.

The fifth earl of Thereamong laughed. "Aye, I have brought him for your stables, but nay, he is not for sale."

"He is like a gift?" Confused, he glanced from Matthew to the horse and then back again. "Maybe for the wedding?"

"Nay, not a gift. He is my daughter's steed."

Peter gasped and Matthew's smile disappeared. Peter whipped around to face his new bride who only grinned at him.

He could clearly imagine Vanessa struggling to control the unstable looking stallion. His stomach knotted and his breath hitched. Women had no business riding and definitely not on a horse such as this wide eyed creature.

Fear clenched his muscles, and for a moment all he could do was shake his head. His mind raced with images of her lying sprawled somewhere broken and battered after being thrown.

He took a deep breath and forced the words out through gritted teeth. "Nay, no woman of mine will ride a horse like that."

Vanessa's grin widened, but he could see the anger blazing in her eyes. "Just because you have become my husband does not give you the right to tell me I am not allowed to ride my own horse." She spoke calmly, the smile never leaving her lips. She held herself with a pride that wrapped his stomach with tendrils of fear, fear for her safety and his sanity.

It had been many years since his demands had been challenged. Anger rolled through him. "Does not give me the right?" His voice cracked painfully as he nearly shouted at her. "You are mine and that gives me the right."

She took a jerky step toward him. "I am not yours, I am mine. I can and will ride my horse." Her voice had taken on an edge betraying her anger.

Her day maid rushed to her side, drawing his attention. She pulled heavily on Vanessa's sleeve with a desperate look in her eyes, but Vanessa did not even glance at her. The small maid tugged at her sleeve.

Peter had a clear image of her tearing it completely off. "Milady, please," she pleaded.

Vanessa ignored her.

"I have never seen a capable rider who was a woman." He had known women who had been killed by horses. He knew his anger sprouted from fear and he fought to gain at least a semblance of calm. "It is dangerous."

"I am more capable than you are at riding and being a woman does not limit me in what I can do." Vanessa's eyes widened and she snapped her lips shut. Amy gasped loudly.

Disbelief swarmed him, she could not possibly believe what she said was true. "That is not possible, my dear. There are few *men* better than I." He held her stare without wavering.

Amy tugged at her sleeve, and Peter swore he heard the seam begin to let go. "Not now, Milady. Everyone is watching you." Amy spoke in a bare whisper.

Vanessa straightened her spine and smiled a wicked grin at the young girl who stood nearly a foot shorter than her. Vanessa's voice was low and menacing. "All right, I've got it."

Amy flinched away from the soft, deadly voice.

Vanessa swung her attention back to him. Peter held her glare with a challenge of his own and sighed in relief as she remained silent. He had hoped for a shy and quiet wife and it seemed he had received a hellion instead.

He turned his back on her and hoped she would remain quiet. He glanced at the stables and saw his stable master looking off into the distance, but casting quick furtive glances toward him. He knew he was watching the fight between Peter and his new bride, but he was trying not to be direct about it. Peter groaned under his breath.

"Ponsworth, get that horse to the stables."

Corey Ponsworth came forward, holding a short riding crop.

"I would not do that, if I were you." Vanessa spoke haughtily and wrinkled her nose at Peter when he turned to her.

His barely held temper frayed almost to the breaking point. "How dare you tell me what I would do or would not do? You will remember you are now my wife, and you will learn your place."

Vanessa shrugged and the smirk, that he was quickly coming to dislike, spread across her soft looking lips. He might not like the grin, but he liked the twinkle it brought to her eyes.

No, no, he told himself, as he shook his head to focus his thoughts. He did not like that twinkle. All it meant was trouble. He didn't like it at all, especially the warmth it created low in his stomach. Peter growled and clenched his fists tightly, as he tried unsuccessfully to convince himself that was true.

"The stallion is a handful, Peter," Matthew said and the horse screamed in anger as if in response to his quiet warning.

Peter whipped his head around to gaze at the volatile animal. Ponsworth grasped the lead rope. The horse reared and bucked, pawing at the air. The groomsman, large in stature but still dwarfed by the horse's sheer size, was nearly lifted off his feet.

The massive horse lurched toward them. Matthew leapt out of the way and Amy threw herself into the carriage with a scream.

Peter glanced at his bride. Fear constricted his throat to see her stand calmly as if nothing were amiss. He looked back to Ponsworth, who fought with the lead rope to force the enraged stallion into the stable, but he was only dragged around like an insolent child.

Ponsworth yelled hoarsely at his stable lads to get more ropes. They raced to do his bidding. Once the horse was securely tied, with three ropes looped around his heavily muscled neck, the four men began the tug of war to get him to the stall.

The horse suddenly charged and threw his full weight against the ropes. He tossed his head wildly as he pulled free. Sweat lathered and wild eyed the horse galloped full tilt toward Vanessa who, to Peter's ire, was perfectly calm.

Peter's heart slammed into his throat. He knew she was going to be killed and fear fell over him like a shroud. He threw himself in between her and the charging beast.

Vanessa quickly side stepped him, throwing off his restraining arm and putting herself between him and the panicked horse. He grabbed her arm, but didn't have time to move her aside before the horse skidded to a stop, slamming its muscled chest into her.

He heard Matthew scream out Vanessa's name as the impact threw her backward. She collided with Peter, the breath whooshing out of her in a sudden gasp. He staggered backward and wrapped his arms around her to keep her from falling.

She took several shallow shaky breaths before her breathing finally calmed. Relief washed over him as he realized that she was not seriously injured.

The terrified horse continued to push his head into Vanessa's chest forcing her body tightly against the length of him. He pulled her tighter into his embrace and was unprepared for the feeling of her bottom pressing against his groin. Every woman he had been with had been small and petite. When he had held them closely their hips had caressed against his mid to lower thighs.

He had never held a woman who fit him so fully, so completely. As he began to harden beneath her soft curves, he decided it was a feeling he quite enjoyed.

He watched intently as Vanessa soothed the trembling horse. She spoke quietly under her breath and caressed him. Her long fingers trailed slowly up and down his wide jaw. Peter was entranced by her soft movements. He could almost feel her fingers running across his own jaw line and tracing down his neck to his chest.

Lust exploded into a hot white fire within him. He felt drunk on the soft waves of aroma that caressed his senses. He turned his head, inhaling the deep scent of lavender. Her smooth hair felt like silk as it brushed against his hands, and his fingers involuntarily tightened against her firm stomach as the silky strands tickled across them. A shiver raced down his spine and through his limbs, making them tremble.

His gaze followed the line of her silky black hair to her long straight neck. Its tanned skin showed clearly beneath the sharp line of powder that hid her face. He took a long deep breath and the mix of lavender and face powder overwhelmed his senses. His eyes drifted shut. His mind was encompassed solely by the sweet smell of her body and the way it moved gently against him.

He pressed his lips onto her long bare neck, opening them to lightly bite her warm flesh. Vanessa stiffened even as she pressed herself more fully into him.

Her body trembled and he wondered if it was from fear or excitement. Images of how she would fit beneath him raced through his mind. Would she fit as perfectly beneath him as she did standing here before him? Would he have to bend to take her lips with his?

Those thoughts led rapidly to others as he wondered if she would be as aggressive and strong willed in bed as she was out of bed. He was intrigued by this idea. He had never been with a woman who was anything but compliant, and he wondered what it would be like to have a forceful woman in bed.

He took a deep breath as the muscles of her back shifted against his chest. A sharp flash of heat exploded in his groin and shot hot sparks through limbs that shuddered as if a cold wave had suddenly washed across the land.

A thick groan penetrated his senses and the realization that it was his own threw him back to reality. He shook his head to clear the heady fog that invaded his senses. But the powerful tendrils of lust weaved deeply and refused to let loose their greedy hold on him. He didn't understand what was so different about this woman. He opened his eyes and stared at her.

Her profile was beautiful, her hair gleaming in the sunlight. Her eyes drifted closed and a small smile played at her lips. An insistent heat settled low in his stomach, a pleasant tingling that seemed to warm his whole body. He wondered once again why this woman, who he had known for mere moments, captivated him in ways that the women who had spent years in his life did not.

He had not groaned with a woman since he was a randy boy feeling up one of his father's youngest maids. He didn't make sounds when kissing a woman's neck, hardly made them even when at the peak of his pleasure.

He never lost control and he wasn't about to start now, not with this giant of a woman. Fighting a painful, throbbing lust that argued vehemently with his oath of self-control, he pulled quickly away from her.

Vanessa gasped, stumbled backwards, and threw her arms around the ears of the now calm horse to balance herself. The horse threw his head up and snorted. She instantly began to caress him. He calmed quickly. Peter wished that his own worries could be calmed so easily.

He pulled his wits together long enough to remember that they were not alone and glanced quickly around the courtyard. The servants were doing their best not to watch the goings on with their master and their new mistress. They busied themselves with luggage, but he caught the secretive glances they threw his way.

Matthew stood silently by the carriage, his brow wrinkled in what Peter knew well to be his concerned look. Matthew shook his head and Peter smiled, but the smile felt awkward so he let it drop. Matthew smiled in return. It looked as forced as Peter's had felt. Matthew returned his attention to his daughter. His fingers were laced so tightly together before him that the knuckles were white.

It was expected that no one would interfere with the way Peter handled his wife. She was his property to do with as he wished, but he wondered how hard it was for Matthew to just stand aside and say nothing regarding his daughter.

With a sigh, he followed Matthew's gaze and studied Vanessa closely. He had only seen two women who were almost as tall as him. Both had been about as big around as a sapling willow.

This woman was not. She was decidedly bigger than a mere sapling and decidedly more muscular than any other woman he had known. She looked as if she could take on half of his army without breaking a sweat.

Peter's gaze slid down her body and stopped on the round bottom that was pushing against the soft material of her dress. Lust threatened to bubble forth and he jerked his gaze away quickly, focusing instead on the way she handled the horse. She handled him well, but he had been unpredictable from the moment Peter had noticed him. He seemed to have a wide range of emotions. Peter didn't trust him in the least.

Vanessa looked over her shoulder at him and smirked. She looked very smug about being able to handle the horse. His stomach wrenched in concern. She moved to the horse's shoulder, patting his heavily muscled chest as she went.

She had an air of invulnerability that worried him and it was more than just the horse. She was not afraid of going to see his men train and she had no qualms about telling him what to do. She had not even batted a pretty eyelash in the face of his anger. That stunned him. He had never had anyone stand toe to toe with him and not back down.

She did not seem to hold an ounce of fear and that alone terrified him. He could see her being hurt by her over-confidence. He would have to make sure she was safe. He watched Vanessa turn calmly back to the horse like nothing was amiss.

He had to exert control in order to protect her. He was the husband. He was the master. He was the stallion of his herd.

Peter appraised the scene before him. The large stallion stood calmly before his wife, his head hung low, allowing her to stroke him as she wished. He was meek and controllable beneath her ministrations, and Peter realized that the stallion was not always the master.

He barked out a laugh, causing the horse to jerk his head up.

Vanessa spun her head around at him. "What is so funny?"

Her voice cracked. Peter realized it had several times before. "I was thinking of a stallion and a herd," he said with a soft smile, his suspicion growing as he thought of her voice. Something wasn't right but he couldn't decide what.

He ran his gaze over her, his brow furrowed in concentration. Her eyes widened and she glanced away, either unable or unwilling to meet his eyes.

He took a quick breath, holding it as he forced himself to concentrate on her, going over each of her actions since she had arrived.

He released his captured breath in a sharp exhale as the answer flashed before him.

It was her voice. It was all wrong. He thought of a lie told by a small child. Sometimes you couldn't tell how you knew they were lying, but you knew they were. A look? A gesture?

She shifted uncomfortably as he appraised her closely.

A small crack in their voice, he thought, a sly smile sliding across their lips.

What she was hiding? And why? He didn't know but he was going to find out. He glanced over at the young day maid, who still cringed in the seat of the carriage, and wondered why she was trying so hard to keep her mistress controlled.

He looked back at Vanessa. He needed to be sure of the voice, not just a suspicion. He needed to hear it again and the best way to do that would be to keep her off balance.

He grinned inwardly but forced himself to keep a calm face, to betray nothing of his plans to antagonize her. "I think it incredulous that a creature as large as he ran to a small wisp of a woman for protection."

Her shoulders pressed back, her chin rose in arrogance, and a gleam sparkled in her dark eyes as anger blossomed across her every feature. Peter smiled, pleased that his plan had worked so well.

Vanessa stepped unsteadily toward him, her fist clenched and her mouth parting.

"Milady." Amy slowly climbed from the carriage interrupting Vanessa before she could speak. "Milady, you need to calm."

Peter scowled at the young woman. He was sure Vanessa would have spoken outrageously and was disappointed that she had been censored once again.

Van visibly relaxed and turned her back on him. "My lord, I am not exactly a wisp of a woman. You have seen me, have you not?" Without looking back at him she began removing the ropes from the horse.

"Aye, my dear, I have seen you and have indeed just felt you against me." He glared at Amy as he finished speaking, in hopes to censor her, but her eyes were only on her mistress.

Vanessa gasped, clenching her fists. Amy grabbed her arm and Matthew pushed himself away from the carriage with a defined growl. Peter had forgotten the Earl of Thereamong, but apparently he had heard enough. By the time he reached them, he had on a wide smile that twitched tightly at the edges, proclaiming it to be an effort for him to hold it.

"Peter, my boy, take me to the stables and let me see those prize mares you recently picked up."

Peter turned his attention fully to him with a sigh of resignation.

He would have to get her alone before he would be able to discover any of her secrets so he did his best to push it from his mind. "Yes, I have gotten three new breeders for my stables, with…" He turned back to Vanessa who stood motionless beside him. He could almost see the fumes shimmering around her as she struggled with her anger. "What is his name?"

She opened her mouth and snapped it shut again. She closed her eyes momentarily and took a deep breath. Peter raised his brow at her. "Well?"

"Beast," she said, but he had a feeling that was not what she had planned to say. He didn't know why she would lie about the horse's name, but he would find that out as well. All in good time, he thought with an internal grin.

"Appropriate at least." He focused once again on her father. The resemblance between the two was stunning. "With the addition of *Beast*," he emphasized deeply as he glanced at her. "I will soon have the best breeding stock in all of Yorkshire." Peter took several deep breaths and the tightness eased from his chest as he forced himself to relax.

Matthew grasped Beast's reins and gave them a soft tug. Vanessa's fist was clenched around them so tightly that her knuckles were white. Peter was sure the leather must be biting into her skin.

Matthew arched one dark eyebrow and waited. Her small maid tugged gently on her sleeve. Vanessa scowled, but allowed her father to pull the reins from her grasp.

Peter was surprised she had given in without a fight, but was grateful for the assistance when Matthew ran his hand through Vanessa's arm and positioned her in between himself and Matthew.

"Come, my dear, you can look at the pretty mares he purchased. You would like that wouldn't you?" He handed the reins to Peter and not waiting for an answer turned and began walking to the stables.

Peter looked from Matthew to the large horse and realized what he had done. Matthew had given Peter the reins, but had placed Vanessa in front of the horse. Peter might hold the reins, but he was sure, as Beast nudged her gently on the back, that the horse was unaware of anything but his mistress before him.

If the horse bolted or reared up now, Vanessa would be right in his path. Peter's stomach lurched, but he knew it was pointless to continue the same fight. Once the horse was safely in the stables, the situation would be easier for him to control.

He adjusted the reins so that he could offer his arm to his new bride. Vanessa glanced at it and with a soft push from her day maid accepted it. Pleased that Vanessa had not declared war over this little act, he allowed himself some hope for a calmer future.

Peter looked back at the day maid. She was throwing quick glances between Vanessa and Beast. Peter wondered which of the two she was more nervous about.

Irritation sprouted once more within him as he thought about how the mere child seemed to control his new bride with a few simple words while he struggled to even keep her civil. It gnawed at him and he could not seem to let it go.

It had become a challenge to see who she really was beneath the voice that cracked at odd times and the flaring temper that her maid was able to tame with a few words. He had no doubts that what she was showing him was not who she truly was.

He saw glimpses of her in her anger, the sparkle of calculation in her eyes, the deep pitch of her voice when she was uncontrolled, and he wanted to see more. It excited him, stirring feelings of life that he had thought dead long ago.

When he was a young boy he used to throw pebbles at the wild boars that roamed the forests until they would chase him. He had many close calls, several leading to jagged scars, and he had never felt anything like the exhilaration of the chase.

That rush was what he felt now. He looked closely at his bride and wanted nothing more than to throw another stone at her. He only hoped that in this chase he would escape scar free.

Recalling the quick flare of anger that had glittered in her eyes at the mention of incompetent horsewomen, he knew the best stone to use to antagonize her. "Aye, darling, you should like to look at the mares."

He carefully felt the weight of the stone in his hand, decided it was a good one, and threw. "I am sure we shall find a nice tame one, one to look good under a sidesaddle. One more fitted to your riding abilities...as a woman." Her head whipped around and she pierced him with an angry gaze. He smiled his sweetest, most innocent smile.

She had not even opened her mouth when the young girl loudly cleared her throat. Vanessa groaned and Peter cursed under his breath at her interruption.

Matthew turned to her, a look of mischief crossing his face. "My dear, you should see the doctor about that." His lips twitched with amusement as he spoke. "Winter is coming, and lung problems are much more prevalent in the cold."

Peter knew, without a doubt, that Matthew had not missed the byplay between the two women. A blind man would not have missed it, Peter thought with a grin of his own.

Vanessa's anger faded from her face and she laughed at his words. It was a sweet tinkling laugh, but she stopped it quickly, biting her lip and looking away.

Peter was disappointed that she had gotten such quick control of it. It had sounded real and welcoming. Warmth spread through him and his heart longed to hear it again.

A fleeting image sparked within his mind at the sound of that laugh. It slipped quickly through the fogs of memory like a ghost through the night, disappeared through his fingers before he could see it clearly, and was gone. He looked at her closely and considered what it would take to get her to lose control of that laugh once again. If he could hear it once more, he might be able to catch the memory that his mind had alluded to.

He wondered briefly if it would be harder to get her to lose control of her temper or of that laugh. The laugh, of that he was sure. He would work on the temper first. Once he had discovered her secrets, he would work on the laughter and the memory.

They quickly reached the stables. Beast became irritated again as he was lead into a stall. "Easy, Beast." Peter spoke softly to him, as the monster pranced erratically. He rubbed him down personally, instead of leaving it to a groom, wanting to establish a bond with the magnificent creature.

"He is a beautiful horse." Matthew's voice was tinged with admiration.

Peter and Vanessa both agreed in unison.

Speaking quietly to Beast, he did a quick rub down on the unstable horse. Peter smirked cockily when the new arrival to his stable grew calm. That satisfaction lasted until he looked up to see the new arrival to his life leaning against the wooden gate, gently rubbing the horse's damp face.

Peter shook his head and his smile fell away. He decided to let it go for the time being. When the horse was rubbed down, fed, and comfortable, the four people roamed through the stable and looked at all the horses, including the mares Peter had just purchased.

Peter led Vanessa to an older, sway backed mare, long past her prime. "Rain will be perfect for you." He glanced at her.

She was staring at the mare incredulously. He patted the sloped neck of the old mare. Rain once was a spirited horse, but now she was happy to plod along. Raising a ruckus would be much too much effort. She was a mare that he felt comfortable allowing Vanessa to ride on her own.

Van looked at him and was sure he was baiting her once again. Anger spread through her like a wildfire. Her breath was so expanded in her puffed out chest that her breasts strained against the buttons of her riding habit.

She took a deep breath. Why was she letting this man get to her? She knew why. She was out of her element. She was standing before the world, vulnerable and unprotected by her armor and sword. She could feel every breeze beneath a kirtle that she had never before worn and feel the pain of every rock beneath her small slippers.

She wanted her tights, she wanted her boots, and what she wanted most was her sword so she could run it through the infuriating man in front of her.

Matthew stepped forward taking hold of Amy's arm. "Come, my dear, let us go to the manor. The newlyweds need a chance to be alone, to get to know each other before the celebration tonight."

Amy's gaze darted from Van to Peter in a panic. Nervous energy tingled through Van at the knowledge she would be alone with her husband. Her first thought was of how she would enjoy being unrestrained by her maid, but that joyful thought was quickly squelched as she reminded herself she still had to keep up the pretense of a woman.

Amy tried to argue, but Matthew pulled her away. Van felt a twinge of pity for the girl and wondered if Amy would have still agreed to do this job if she had known how stubborn Van was. She stood contemplating Amy's plight for only a moment before she was pulled from her thoughts by Peter's deep voice. It slid across her like a cool length of silk and a small shiver of pleasure ran up her spine.

She turned and met his gaze, the soft blue of his eyes twinkled in amusement and his lips were turned up in an amused grin. Her breath quickened and her heart pounded somewhere in the vicinity of her throat.

"What?" She could hear the weakness tinged in her voice and it frightened her. Weakness was not something she could allow. She silently cursed herself.

"In all the commotion I was never introduced to your maid." He closed the gap between them, his wide chest now so close that the warmth of his body enveloped her.

"Amy Devant." Her voice was a mere whisper. She fought an urge to step away from him. His breath caressed her face and she shivered. A hot flush swam through her blood, boiling it until she feared she would melt right there at his feet. She barely managed to surpass a shudder and prayed he could not see the heat that tinged her face beneath the powder.

Struggling to take command of the chaos that had invaded her traitorous body, she took a deep, calming breath. But it only heightened her arousal as his light male musk invaded her already reeling senses.

Her mind raced back to her childhood. She remembered standing in the shadows watching him from a distance and wondering what it would have been like to be as close to him as she was now. Anticipation shivered across her spine. She longed to reach out and touch his cheek, but trepidation stopped her.

"Aye, I know her name. I just was not introduced. You do know that if you want to bring someone into my home, you should at least ask me first," he said softly, his voice remonstrative, as if scolding a bad child.

His words were like a wave of cold water, dosing the flames of desire that had threatened to consume her. She wanted to be angry at his words, but she was only grateful that her thoughts were now once again under her command.

She had not even considered asking his permission to bring her maid. She was unaccustomed to having her actions questioned, but she knew he was correct. As her husband, it was his right to govern who and what came into his home. Her mind spun painfully. She worried that she would not be able to become a woman of any worth after being a knight for so long.

The corner of his lip twitched and he stepped a little closer. "I am after all the master of this house."

Irritation churned, no man was her master. She clenched her fists, her nails digging into the palms of her hand.

He looked at her expectantly.

She wanted to tell him who he was dealing with, that she was her own master, the master of others, and that no one was *her* master. Anger cut her deep. She bit the inside of her lip against the rebuke that jumped dangerously at the back of her throat.

When she made no remark, he shrugged almost imperceptibly. "We have plenty of time before our wedding celebration, would you like a tour of the grounds?" His tone was soothing and sweet, but the wicked twinkle in his blue eyes spoke differently.

Suspicious of the sudden change, she wanted to refuse. Knowing she could not, she nodded. "Yes."

"Good." His lips spread into a lopsided grin, giving her the impression of a hungry wolf patiently on the prowl. Gooseflesh tickled her skin.

He pushed past her. Her heart skipped a beat as his shoulder grazed against hers. She turned and watched him grab a sidesaddle and walk toward the swaybacked mare.

The mare swung her head lazily toward them as they approached. She was well past her prime and Van had a sharp vision of breaking the poor creature in half. "You cannot be serious?" Her breath hitched. "I cannot ride that horse. Do you see the size of me? I will hurt her."

"I have ridden her. You will be fine." He opened the stall, and Rain did not hesitate. She came walking slowly out of the stall without encouragement. He turned to gaze at Van, his smile falling away from his lips, but not his eyes. "You are not afraid of her, are you?"

"*For* her, not *of* her," she said impatiently. "I would be more comfortable riding my own horse." She tried to keep her tone civil, tried to keep at least a modicum of subservience to her voice. Her pride pricked at her, but she ignored it.

He smiled at her patiently and turned away. He saddled the poor mare and bridled her as if Van had said nothing.

She was beginning to realize that the only way she was going to get out of riding in that damnable saddle was to put up more of a fight than she was willing to do. Out of viable options, she resigned herself to giving in to his wishes. She straightened her shoulders and sighed. Nervous energy surged like waves, crashing into her until she felt as if she would drown.

She stared malevolently at the wide expanse of his back. His muscles rolled beneath the light woolen tunic as he pulled the girth up tight across the patient mare's belly.

"I know," he said, his voice chipper. "You are afraid of making a fool of yourself in front of me, but do not worry, I am your husband." He looked over his shoulder at her, a smug smile on his lips and a superior, haughty twinkle in his eyes. "I will not think any less of you."

Anger pushed at her, but she refused to give in to it. "There is no way you can think less of me." The bitterness she felt at his treatment of her tinged her words.

His smile faltered. His eyes scrutinized her for a long moment before he turned back to his task.

Van was shocked when she realized that indeed she was scared to make a fool of herself in front of him. She cared for him and respected him. As a knight and as one of his men at arms, she was confident and sure of herself, but as his bride she was in unknown territory. She felt as if she had lost her bearings under a cloud covered sky and had no idea where she was or how to get back to familiar surroundings.

CHAPTER 7

P eter watched as the anger slid from Vanessa's features leaving behind a nervous reluctance. He smiled. He was once more in control of himself and ready to gain control of Vanessa as well.

"Come. Let us get you onto your magnificent creature." He gestured to Rain and to his surprise Vanessa came forward without argument. Her teeth worried her lower lip. She looked nervous, unsure, yet determined.

"Are you certain I will not hurt her?"

"You will not hurt her." He reached for Vanessa, drawing her close. "You are a magnificent creature yourself, but not so big that you will hurt any you are astride." A vivid image of the two of them lying naked in the fresh hay assailed his mind, her hips spread wide as she rode him. He could almost feel himself pulling her down, crushing her breasts against his sweat dampened chest, and pressing his lips onto hers.

He felt himself harden at the fleeting images. Damn, he was losing his control and all he had done was touch her arm. He had been doing so well. Perhaps it was not such a good idea to be alone with her. He took a quick step backwards.

"Are you well? You look to be in pain." She was at his side in an instant, her hand rubbing along his chest and down his abdomen. "Are you hurt?" The concern in her beautiful eyes hit him like a stone.

A soft groan escaped him at the heat he could feel through his soft wool tunic everywhere she touched him. Irritated by his sudden and unexplainable loss of control, he grasped her hand and shoved her away. "I am fine." It came out gruffer than he had intended.

Her eyes widened and he silently cursed himself as she stepped away.

"Let us just get you on that damned horse."

Peter gestured jerkily toward her mount. Her eyes narrowed stubbornly. Peter was prepared once again for a battle, but to his surprise she went willingly. He enfolded her waist in his hands and lifted her onto the horse. Rain shifted nervously under the weight of a rider and Vanessa grasped his shoulders.

She let out a soft laugh as she fought for balance. "You must be jesting. I cannot ride this." He barely heard her words and could not respond. Her long fingers were digging into him as she held herself up. Heat seared him. He wanted nothing more than to bury himself deeply inside her until the flames burst around him and freed him from this incessant desire that she provoked in him.

Just as he was about to haul her down on top of him, Vanessa removed her hands. He felt a sudden loss. His shoulders were cold, empty where her hands had been.

Vanessa found her balance. One leg hanging down and the other thrown over the saddle horn, she slipped her left foot into the stirrup, showing a goodly amount of white calf when she did. He sucked in a hot breath at the sight of soft skin and turned away to saddle his own destrier.

Jackal was a light tan with thick black mane and tail. Vanessa smiled as she watched him lead the horse out of its stall. "Such a grand specimen." Her high pitched squeal echoed through the barn.

"Thank you." Peter grinned as he readied his horse. "But do not say that too loudly around Jackal. He is jealous. It is good although to hear you think so about me, since you will soon be seeing all I have to offer you, later tonight, in bed." He stared at her intently. The shocked look in her eyes told him she had reacted to his teasing, while to his annoyance the powder hid any blush she may have had.

Van felt her face heat in embarrassment, but said nothing. She had seen many marital beddings during her three years as a knight, but was not prepared for one of her own. Excitement and fear battled deep inside her, churning her stomach until it rolled and boiled.

For the first time she wondered what it would be like to lay with a man. Would he be gentle with her or would he be rough? She looked at the large size of his body and wondered how she would accommodate him. A tingle of worry tickled at the back of her mind and she tried to push it away.

Peter smiled at her. Without another word, he pulled himself onto the prancing horse and guided him out of the stable.

She took a deep breath and patted the old mare's neck. "This is it," she whispered and gently kicked the horse's side. Van wobbled slightly as they followed Peter out the door, but she steadied herself easily.

She followed along without too much trouble, but she felt on edge and struggled to keep her balance. Feelings of inadequacy that she had not felt in many years overwhelmed her.

She had not been very good on horseback when she had first arrived at the castle for training. She had struggled to get good, practicing until exhaustion left her spent, every time she could manage to sneak away. She had crawled into her cot bruised and battered many a night, but she had managed to become the best.

"That is Joseph Pittman. Both his parents and his two older sisters were killed in a fire." Peter's voice, tinged with kindness, drew her attention and she followed his gaze.

A small boy, appearing to be of less than ten years raced between the fences. His tattered yellow tunic and long brown hair fluttered behind him as he disappeared into the stables.

The horse shifted unevenly beneath her. Van tightened the grip on her reins and returned her attention to Peter.

"They were tenants of my father's. When I came home three years ago, Joseph was here. My father had taken him in." Peter's profile was relaxed and a sad smile played on his lips as he looked in the direction the boy had disappeared.

She smiled at the softness in his voice, but said nothing. It was a relief to know he had a kindness toward children, even if not toward women. Having his child would not be awful.

Van started as the idea crossed her mind. She had not considered children before. She wrinkled her brow and stared at his wide back. Her hand drifted to her stomach as she tried to picture herself swollen with child. She had seen many women heavy into pregnancy, but had never given them a second thought. Never once had she imagined being in their position of life.

Peter's hearty hale to the men at the front gate pulled her from her reverie. He gave them a friendly wave as they rushed to push the gate open. She nodded to the men. A jolt of surprise hit her when they smiled in return and gave a small bow.

It was much different than when she visited castles as the Dark Knight. She had rarely received a smile, other than from the women who hung around the men late at night. The bows she had always received had seemed to be given grudgingly, given more out of fear than from the respect she saw on these men's faces.

Anticipation filled her as the big oak gate swung shut behind her. She had been many places on these grounds, but never with permission and rarely while the sun was still up. As a page she was restricted to inside the castle walls. Not, she thought with a grin, that that had ever stopped her from going where she wanted.

Peter stopped, looking back at her until she was beside him. "Now stay close by me. I want to be able to help you if you fall." His words were kind and seemed sincere, but she bristled at the condescending tone that accompanied them.

"I will not fall," she began, but her words failed as the mare rocked to a stop. She shifted on the unfamiliar saddle.

He stared at her, his brow raised as if he didn't quite believe her words as she shifted in the saddle, trying to find her balance. "I see." He kicked Jackal in the side softly and started off without looking back. "I like to keep the tenants close to the castle."

As they rode, he explained the dangers of enemies and the need to be able to get the tenants inside the castle walls quickly in the event of attack. "I can replace crops and animals, but the people I cannot."

His soft words and the care he showed toward the lives of his people warmed her heart. She smiled finding it impossible to be irritated with him and admire him at the same time. She settled into the uncomfortable saddle the best she could and was determined to enjoy the tour of the grounds.

Tenants came out of their homes to greet them as they rode. Van was unsure of how to react. She had never been through a village where she had been received with anything besides fear and suspicion. She considered which she liked better, the fear or the friendliness.

She found the decision easy as she returned waves and smiles, stopping to talk to people as they held children up to meet her. This was to be her home and here she would much prefer the open welcome.

Were she to go somewhere else, she might just prefer the fear, she thought. Her soft smile turned to a wicked grin.

They soon left the homes behind and skirted fields of healthy crops. Peter was silent as he led her into a dense grove of trees.

Fragrant smells delighted her senses. Multicolored blooms intertwined through the underbrush, creating a cascade of brilliance that took her breath away. She inhaled deeply and wondered when the last time was that she had been able to relax enough to just enjoy the smell of flowers. Sadly, she could not remember.

"These trees were my father's favorite place on the grounds." His voice was wistful. His hand reached out and his fingers ran across the rough bark of a moss covered tree.

"They are beautiful." She leaned gently in the saddle, hand still gripping the pummel tightly, and ran her free hand along a massive tree trunk. As the trees thinned, a small meadow could be seen just ahead of them. Peter led her into it.

In the center of the quiet meadow was a pristine lake. Sunlight shimmered and sparkled across the minute ripples that moved along the surface of the deep blue water. Birds flew noisily around calling to each other. Her thoughts touched on her childhood as she drank in the splendid beauty of the lake. She had come here often as a page. Peace had always caressed her when she looked upon the still waters. It did the same now.

"I would take you to the other side of the lake, to a small set of caves over there...if I could trust you on a horse." His voice, once again patronizing, shattered her illusions of peace.

Anger rolled through her, quickly dispelling the charms of the lake. She had fought hard all her life for respect. She had fought hard to prove herself and when someone had insulted her she had quickly and painfully made them aware of their mistake. Disrespect was always dealt with the same way. Quickly and violently. It was how she wanted to deal with it now, but she forced herself to stay silent.

She tightened her fists through the reins and clenched her jaw until her teeth ached. She did not trust herself to speak. She knew it was imperative that she keep her temper under a tight rein. She must remain in control if she was to protect her identity.

"I should have brought a carriage with us. At least that way, I would not have to worry so much about you falling," he said with a heavy sigh.

Without turning to look at him, she snapped, "I am just as capable of riding as you or anyone else. I have been riding for a long time, and I do not need to be on this broken down mare that should have received the respect due her and been left alone." Van was afraid she would lose her balance as she was still not used to the angle at which she was sitting with one leg strung over the saddle horn.

Self-conscious of the way she held tightly onto the saddle, she forced her hands to relax. She shifted uncomfortably. The mare snorted and pawed at the ground. Van felt herself slipping from the saddle and gripped it once more.

"I am enjoying showing you my grounds, but would feel more secure if you were not on the back of a horse beyond your abilities to control," he said in a soft calm voice. "You seem to be having difficulties with that mare. I am glad I did not allow you to bring that creature you believe is your horse."

The flames of her anger greedily consumed every twig and branch of insults he threw at her, building in strength and power until she could feel the heat of it erupting around her. "He is my horse and you cannot stop me from riding him." She heard her voice crack and cringed.

He arched his brows and he scowled. "I can make you do anything I want." He edged his stallion up next to her.

"The hell you can." Her voice slipped farther into its arrogant growl as she challenged him. She spun toward him, slipping and off balance. Peter pushed his horse into hers. The mare panicked over the sudden movement on her back and bucked. Van was unprepared for the sudden liveliness of the broken down old mare.

She hit hard into the ground and the beauty of the small lake was forgotten. Her rage, controlled on such a shaky level for days now, boiled over. She was on her feet before he could dismount.

Van had gotten control of herself as she struggled to her feet and started toward him—gotten control of her mind, but not her anger. No, her rage still flowed through her like deadly lava, but the Dark Knight had come. He broke through all her insecurities and brought with him the calm of battle, of knowing what to do and how to do it.

Van grasped Peter's leg and yanked hard. He planted his foot into the stirrup and grasped the horse's thick mane. He laughed. "You cannot best me, I am a man. I am your master."

"So pompous...so full of yourself...men are barely the masters of themselves." She spoke with a well manufactured voice, one that spoke of uncontrolled rage, uncontrolled thought, all the while pulling up dramatically on his leg.

She faked labored breathing and deep painful gasps as she struggled. Peter laughed, but did not try to stop her. He looked down at her patiently as one would a child, with an air of superiority and amusement as she pretended to unseat him from his horse.

She smiled inwardly as she forced deeper, harsher breaths as she positioned him, pulling his leg higher till his balance teetered. Gripping the girth it took her less than a heartbeat to release it. He didn't have a chance.

Saddle and all slid off as Jackal lunged away from her. She barely registered Peter's loud grunt as he hit the ground. She rushed toward him. Intent on doing bodily harm, she forgot her dress. It tangled around her legs and feet like a serpent springing up from the tall grass.

The dress twisted and constricted around her as she kicked wildly to get free. Her balance slipped and she sprawled along the whole length of him.

Peter had barely untangled himself from the saddle in time to catch her, keeping her full weight from slamming the breath out of both of them. She tried to sit up, tried to untangle her legs, and was unable. She cursed loudly as she yanked at the stubborn material.

Peter clutched her dress. His other hand wrapped around her waist, steadying her. He gave several hard tugs. The material gave out a soft ripping sound, but still refused to release her legs. She fought and kicked and soon they were both wrapped in the length of her gown.

Peter added his curses to hers, his voice tight and pained. She knew she was large and was sure she was heavy against him. His breathing was harsh and his arms trembled. Not wanting to hurt him further, she renewed her struggles to release them both from her dress.

She let out a string of oaths that would have made some of her men blush and finally managed to free one leg. Cool air brushed against her sweat laden skin and relief washed over her.

Peter grabbed her raised thigh, shoved the dress from her other thigh and pulled her into a sitting position, astride him.

She froze. His lust was apparent as she felt the rough material of his tights straining against her woman's mound. She felt a strange pulling sensation deep in her belly and alarm replaced the sweet sensation of relief.

Unsure of what to do, wanting to run and wanting to stay, she did nothing, only sat stiffly upon him not daring to move. Her breathing came in short gasps. Warmth spread from her chest to her stomach and settled deeply between her legs.

Peter ran his hands up her arms, causing them to tremble uncontrollably. She tensed her muscles to stop the vibrations that were overwhelming her, but the shudders continued.

He stared up at her. His hands slipped beneath the bunched material of her dress and came to rest on her hips. Heat raced across her skin.

Images of him beside this very lake, water dripping down his topless frame impaled her and she gasped.

Peter looked up at her questioningly, his grip tightening. Sucking in a deep breath and biting her lower lip, she averted her gaze and focused on the shimmering water and the wild call of the loons at its banks. She closed her eyes, but could still see him clearly as he had been so long ago.

She had been at page training for almost a year when she had come upon him waist deep in the lake one night. Hidden beneath the thickets, she had spied on him, staring raptly at the water droplets, glistening in the moonlight and running in small rivulets down the defined muscles of his chest as he bathed in the cool water. That had been the first night that she had fancied herself in love with him.

His fingertips ran along her arm, drawing her from her sweet memories. She opened her eyes and reluctantly met his gaze.

Her heart thudded erratically until she thought it would burst forth and reveal itself to him. Feeling as if she was an awkward child once again, she pressed her hands against her chest in an attempt to still the hammering within.

His hands traced a scorching path up her arms. He stared at her intently as he had the night she had saved his life, as if he were unsure of what he was seeing. Alarm tickled in the back of her mind, but it was faint and hard to distinguish beneath the passion that blazed within her.

His fingertips grazed her hands and tickled across her heaving breasts. Small shivers of anticipation buzzed through her head, completely overwhelming the alarm that struggled unsuccessfully to be heard.

He smiled softly and, pushing her hair out of the way, grasped the back of her neck. Lost in the passion she saw in his eyes, she did not fight him as he pulled her down to him.

Her nose brushed his. She held her breath anticipating his kiss, but to her disappointment he did not kiss her. He held her closely, staring deeply into her eyes as if trying to see into her soul.

She tried to draw her eyes away, to protect her secrets, but was unable to escape the hold he had on her. Not that of his hand on her neck, but that of his captivating gaze.

Staring into her eyes made Peter feel as if he were floating upon the surface of the lake, dark into the night, with only the shimmering glints of moonlight to hint at the secrets hidden within the water's black depths.

Fear, desire, and uncertainty blazed in the darkness of Vanessa's eyes, and he was lost in the swirling emotions.

Vanessa trembled as his hands pulled up the gown. He was convinced she was untouched by man. She had to be innocent, given the hesitant way she responded to his touches, the way she leaned toward him in eagerness, only to stiffen in fear a moment later.

He wondered if her shudders were from fear or excitement. Perhaps both, he thought and the realization shot sparks of desire through his loins.

He slid the gown slowly across her legs, and delighted in the way her muscular thighs trembled against him. Her skin was smooth and warm beneath his calloused hands. His cock jumped eagerly, pleading for entry. He clutched at her bared bottom and pushed away the insistent desire that tore at his restraint.

She stiffened. Her eyes shifted nervously toward the horses and then back to him as if she were hoping for escape. He was prepared for her to run, to struggle, and to fight once more, but she surprised him, remaining as she was, sitting stiffly upon him.

A moist, teasing heat soaked through his braies, caressing his throbbing shaft, and divulging her passions to him in a warm invitation. His heart raced painfully at the knowledge that she wanted him.

He took a deep breath and forced himself to remain still and calm. She was innocent and he knew that, though her body might know what it wanted, she might not understand the emotions rampaging through her. He wanted to take his time, to give her pleasure.

He smiled up at her in what he hoped was encouragement, but he could not quell the trembling in his lips. She did not relax, but neither did she pull away or try to move his hand. His heart swelled and thudded loudly in his ears, drowning out the sounds of the various birds that surrounded the lake.

He wrapped the long silken strands of cascading hair around his unsteady fingers and pulled her mouth to his, pressing his lips onto hers.

She dropped her hands to his chest. Heat seared through his thick tunic, branding him. A chill raced across his spine, and he clenched his jaw to keep a groan from escaping.

He ran his tongue gently across her lips and reveled in the small gasp it elicited from her. His heart danced somewhere in the vicinity of his throat. He swallowed hard to get breath around it. Pressing his hardened cock against her, he rocked slowly, gently.

Her eyes closed and her hands clenched the front of his tunic, pulling erotically at the thick hair of his chest beneath it. He moved slowly wanting to take his time with her, to enjoy her fully as he brought her to pleasure. Her lips trembled against his and she shivered enticingly in his arms.

Desire flared brightly within him, battling with his control and slowly taking over. "Open your mouth." He tried to make his words gentle and seductive, but they came out in a harsh, almost painful, command.

Her lips tightened and trembled, and then to his surprise they opened slowly, cautious and unsure. He smiled against her parted lips, amazed that she had obeyed so willingly.

He inhaled deeply as she surrendered to him, her hot breath mixing with his as his tongue invaded her parted lips. He shuddered.

She held herself stiffly through his ministrations, her tongue retreating whenever his grazed its tip.

Vanessa groaned deeply. It was a hauntingly familiar sound. He closed his eyes, tried to place it, and was lost in a dream as he kissed her soft lips. Wisps of memories caressed him. He tried to concentrate on them. A voice, a touch, they teased him gently and raced away. The sounds of a pounding and violent rain whispered to him seductively. The memory was within his grasp. Then Vanessa tentatively touched her tongue to his and it was gone.

Swirling desire fled in the way of a pulsing painful lust, and Peter lost all control at this sudden response from her. Her willingness, her eagerness sent him over the edge. He tumbled her onto her back, staying between her thighs as he rolled with her. He pulled up his tunic and fought with his braies and hose to free his engorged member.

He felt the heat of her sex scorch him as he ran his cock between her trembling thighs. Her tightness swallowed him as he plunged deep into her and with one sudden thrust he tore through her maidenhead.

Vanessa gasped, sucking in a deep whistling breath. He felt her hands on him, her strong fingers digging into his shoulders, clutching at his clothing.

Wrapping his arms tightly around her shoulders, he buried his face into her fragrant hair and crushed her to him. He increased his pace, harder and faster as the tight pain of his lust built inside him like a hurricane.

He felt her begin to struggle beneath him, her hands shoving at his shoulders. Her legs tightened around him, hips rocking as she fought. Her deep shuddering moans vibrated through his body and she dug her nails painfully into his back.

He looked down into her face and caught a glimpse of fear in her eyes as she stared straight up at the sky above her. He tried to stop and slowed his thrusts. Her muscles tightened and released around his cock as she struggled, creating a pulsing, pulling sensation.

The violent storm within him was peaking. He was too close to the swirling winds of desire to pull free. The tempest called to him and he could do nothing but obey. He closed his eyes and everything was lost to him as he plunged into her faster and deeper, screaming his release, a release like nothing he had ever experienced before.

He collapsed on top of her, guilt quickly filling the void that was left as the storm dissipated.

Van lay shaking and confused beneath Peter, unsure of how to interpret the rush of emotions that had overtaken her during his rough lovemaking. She drew in long slow breaths and tried to swallow the thick lump in her throat. Her eyes closed, she went over the past few moments in an attempt to understand why she had panicked.

She had enjoyed the kisses he had given, but the moment he had rolled her onto her back she had begun to feel trapped, overpowered, and helpless. The loss of her virginity had not hurt as she had heard other women complain that it did, but the feeling of complete domination had suffocated her.

Her body had ached for him to continue even as fear had overwhelmed her. She did not understand how her body could want something that her mind rebelled against.

As he had slammed into her, a tight ball had started in the pit of her stomach and a building heat had swelled from between her legs. The flames had threatened to engulf her. That was when she had begun to fight.

Peter's body trembled, drawing her from her thoughts. She listened to his raspy breathing and waited for him to move. He continued to lie still, even though she could feel him softening inside her.

She dropped her arms to her sides, the cool grass relieving some of the stress that wrapped her in a tight grip. The tension slowly eased from her muscles.

Her legs trembled as if she had run a mighty race. She shifted beneath him, adjusting her hips to find a semblance of comfort.

To her horror, she felt him begin to harden once again and her eyes flew open. "Nay, move not," Peter said without lifting his head. "I did not do that well."

She could feel his hot breath against her neck as he spoke, his voice a weak whisper.

Her breathing stopped, her heart raced, and she held herself perfectly still, hoping he would not want to take her again so soon.

She silently cursed herself for her weakness. She was not a weak woman and had indeed proved that fact over and over throughout many battles and injuries. So why was she afraid now? The fear of losing herself to him? The fear of liking it? She had no answers and shifted uncomfortably.

Peter shuddered as she shifted beneath him, pushing her hips into his. He groaned. "Do not move. Hold still and get used to me." His words were muffled in her hair.

He inhaled its soft lavender scent and wrinkled his nose when the fine strands tickled at his face. He did not want to face her. He had acted like a lust starved child instead of a grown experienced man and could not understand it.

He wanted to stay buried in the safety of her hair, but knew he could not. He had to make sure she was not hurt or frightened. He hoped he could make her understand what he himself did not.

With a tight moan, he pulled himself up onto his elbows to look down at her. The thick powder on her face was laced with small rivulets of sweat. The fear was gone from her eyes and her face seemed calm behind the thick mask of powder. The overly sweet smelling powder hid her expressions, hid her feelings and irritated him.

"How much powder do you have on your face?"

Vanessa began to struggle, her eyes widening in concern or fear. He was not sure which. What he was sure of, was that she needed to stay still. "Do not struggle."

Her sudden movements stroked and throbbed around his already painful erection. He had not wanted to take a woman more than once since he couldn't remember when, but as she continued to struggle he could feel a hot desire build within him.

"Nay, do not, whatever it is that you want to cover is still covered. I can see nothing, but powder." He pulled out of her before he did something else he would regret and lay still, holding his weight off of her with shaky arms.

She fell motionless and stared up at him. He pushed the uncontrolled strands of hair from her face careful not to disturb the powder. He smiled gently and gave a shaky chuckle. "Well, that decides the public bedding."

CHAPTER 8

P ublic bedding." Van sucked in a sharp breath. "Nay, I will not allow it." Her voice was a tight squeal that pricked at her ears and strained her throat. She had attended many a public bedding and could not stand to think of herself up cn display as those women had been. She shuddered at the thought of being utterly exposed after so many years of hiding within the safety of the Dark Knight's embrace.

Peter's eyes danced with a hint of worry, and she felt some of her own anxiety fall away. Her hungry gaze roamed across his rugged face and she shuddered. She took in the square of his jaw and the slight bump in a nose that had been broken more than once. She had fantasized about him a lot over the years since she had last seen him. She found that she still desired him, and that desire concerned her.

"Do not panic. There will be no need for a public bedding." Peter smiled in what he hoped was reassurance. "I have no way to reproduce your virgin's blood for all to see. Not now."

Peter pulled away and cringed at the large amount of blood smeared on her pale white thighs. Guilt swarmed him and he felt lower than he ever had in his life.

The soft silk of her skirts was cool against his hands as he slid the dress down her shapely legs. "It is all right, sweet one. Do not be afraid. You are not hurt." He kept his voice soft and low, a bare whisper.

Vanessa groaned, shook her head. Her eyes slid closed and she took several deep breaths before opening them again. She struggled to her feet, but faltered.

Peter was at her side in a moment, an arm wrapped around her in support. Vanessa leaned into him as if she wanted comfort, but to his frustration it lasted only a moment. Then a look of confusion swept across her face and she pulled away.

He sighed as disappointment swelled within him, but reluctantly pressed on with business that had to be taken care of. "If you are not scared, I will need to check to see if I hurt you." He paused long enough to steady the tremble in his voice. "To see what damage was done."

He took a deep breath and forced himself to make the offer he did not want to make. "But, if you would prefer, you may wait here while I retrieve the doctor to do it." He needed to make sure she was comfortable. He had already made a mess of things and did not want to make them any worse, if it was possible to get worse from here.

"Nay, that is not necessary, I am not afraid of you." Her voice trembled and she looked at the ground. "Not like that." She looked embarrassed or ashamed, Peter could not decide which. Maybe it was both.

He fought an unimaginable urge to pull her against him, to fix the problems she had, especially the ones he caused. He took a step toward her, but did not take her in his arms. "Not like what?" He gently touched her arm. It was chilled and he could feel the gooseflesh that had erupted upon it. She jumped, looking up at him.

She shook her head sadly. Peter shoved away the guilt at pushing her so hard and extended his hand.

She stared at it, but did not move. He groaned exasperated. He grasped her hand and pulled her gently to the water's edge. As he guided her onto the grassy bank, he prayed that he had not injured her too badly. Her nose wrinkled and she let out a slight grunt as she sat on the cool grass. He could not help but smile. She was a beauty.

Vanessa looked up at him with a mixture of distrust and fear. His smile fell away. The anger he could take. He even liked to provoke it, to see it flash in her eyes. The fear was something different. It made him feel like a monster that terrorized women. That was not him. Well, he thought sarcastically, thinking of the past few hours, it usually wasn't him.

He pulled her skirts out of the way and slid her to the edge of the gently lapping water. She tried to pull the dress back down, but he caught her wrist in his hand. He felt a trembling, but was unsure if it was coming from her or from him. "Sit still and we will be done all the faster. I thought you said you weren't scared of me?"

"I am not scared." She sat still while he pulled the dress back up. The blood was drying on her smooth white thighs. There was a lot of it and worry rippled through Peter's stomach.

"Don't be." He tore a strip from the bottom of her chemise and wet it in the cold water of the lake.

Vanessa closed her eyes as Peter gently washed away the blood and seed that covered her sex and thighs. He sighed deeply. "There is slight tearing. I am sorry. It was not well done of me at all." He trembled with embarrassment, with guilt.

Vanessa's head leaned back, her body relaxing. Peter smiled and continued to gently rub the wet strip of cloth along her skin even though she was clean.

Sunlight glittered across the pale blue surface of the lake. Peter glanced up as several white kingfishers swooped over the lake, squawking loudly at the intruders. Small purple flowers grew from vines throughout the small meadow, sending soft scents of light perfume wafting over Peter's senses.

Vanessa rocked her hips forward. The soft warmth of her sex grazing his hand pulled his attention back to her. He took in the look of pleasure that swept across her face and shivers ran across his skin, leaving hot tingles in their wake. He could almost feel her pleasure as if it was his own. He wanted her, wanted her bad, but would not allow himself to hurt her once again.

Irritated with his own lack of control, he yanked down her skirts and silently cursed himself.

Confusion swept through Van as Peter roughly pulled her to her feet and stomped away. She had begun to relax and she didn't understand why he was angry again. He had taken her, violently, submitted her to embarrassments, and now he had the gall to be mad at her.

She glowered fiercely as she watched him retrieve his saddle. She could hear him cursing as he threw it back onto his stallion. Jackal swung his head to look at his master and laid his ears back. Peter told him to shut the hell up and continued to saddle him.

Van grinned as she thought of how she had outsmarted him as he had acted so superior sitting upon his horse. A sudden image of his saddle slipping from beneath him filled her mind. Giggles bubbled up inside of her and erupted uncontrollably.

He looked up at her in surprise only reinforcing the image of his shocked look as he had gone off his mount. She could clearly see his blond brows raised in shock and his arms flailing for purchase, but finding none. She could almost hear his grunt as he hit the ground. Her giggles quickly became a full bellied laughter that she couldn't stop, even though she tried desperately to do so.

Peter stalked toward her, a grin of his own starting. Van grinned in return. She could not remember when the last time was that she had laughed. She had always needed to be so in control of herself. She took a deep breath, trying to contain her laughter, but the vivid memory of her own fall over her dress flashed through her mind.

It was the dress that had gotten her. Of all the enemies that she had faced, she was done in by a dress. Her sides ached and her stomach hurt, but the laughter gripped her once again.

Peter stopped before her and shook his head. Grasping her arms tightly, he gave her a playful shake. The wide smile sparkled all the way up to his blue eyes. They shimmered with laughter as he spoke. "What is so funny?"

She jerked from his grasp still laughing and began to run. "I was thinking of you falling with your saddle," she yelled breathlessly over her shoulder.

Peter took chase, catching her in an instant. He threw her to the ground and rolled on top of her. "You think that was funny, do you? Well, I think it funny that you couldn't even run in your dress without falling over on top of me."

The mention of the dreaded dress brought on another round of laughter. Van struggled nominally beneath him, but no longer wished to get away. Her fear was completely gone, leaving only the admiration that she had harbored for him since she was a page at the castle.

He smiled down at her and her laughter died as her breath caught painfully in her throat. Van could feel her face getting hot beneath the thick powder as she lost herself in his warm embrace.

The brush around them rustled as Grant stepped through the foliage. "Sorry, my liege, to interrupt, but you told me to inform you when all was ready at the castle."

Peter didn't answer, only grunted. He grasped her arm and pulled Van to her feet as he stood. She gained control of her racing heart for only a moment before he pulled her against him. She trembled deep within his tight embrace. Her heart thudded against the walls of her chest and she fought to gain control.

"We are not finished with this," he growled deeply, drawing her back to reality. "You keep thinking it funny that you made me fall, I will get even with you."

Van grinned widely in anticipation. She and Richard Devenroe had played pranks on one another. It had started out as a training method to teach the young squire how to be prepared for all situations. It had ended as a competition to out-best each other. Van had loved it and missed it.

Now it seemed that she had the same opportunity and from the look on her new husband's face, it was a challenge she was going to love once again. It was something she could see him following out fully, and she was prepared.

She pulled away from him and whispered, "Think hard on how you will get me, I do not surprise easily. I do not know if I see the skills in you that it will take to get even with me. I am quite good at this."

Peter was left standing in dismay as she walked toward his horse, his horse of all things. Did she expect him to ride the sidesaddle? Ha, it wouldn't surprise him one bit. Relief swept through him as she turned with a smile and waited.

His own smile had found its way back to his face by the time he had crossed the meadow and reached her side. He arched a brow as a sweet squeaky voice came from his wife.

"I would like to ride with you back to our home. I am uncomfortable upon such a large horse by myself. I would feel much safer if I were to be with you." She uttered such nice words that did not match her smile. Well-manufactured and looking nothing like the sweet sound coming from her, it was a look of mischief that had him worried.

She was planning something and he knew it, but he would not give her the opportunity to win. "If that is your wish, my bride." Peter mounted Jackal who pranced and swayed beneath him. He waited for his steed, and himself to calm, and then pulled Vanessa onto his lap. With her legs draped across one of his thighs, she wrapped her arms around his neck for support. His breath caught and he tried unsuccessfully to ignore the shapely hip that pressed between his legs.

Peter motioned to his second in command and watched only long enough to make sure that Grant had hold of Vanessa's mare before heading off. The rocking of the horse slid her hip against his sensitive manhood. His breath thickened and he closed his eyes.

Van smiled at his quiet groan. She was getting to him. She knew the ways that women used men, teasing and promising things they would do. She had been the object of desire for several women during raids. They would rub up against the Dark Knight to throw him off guard, not that it had distracted her.

It had a lot of the others, though. Pain stung at her eyes and clouded her mind as she remembered the men that had been killed in battle because they were distracted by those women. She had always thought it ridiculous that the men had been so blinded.

More than once though, she had wondered if it was possible for her to distract a man with teases and promises. Now as she watched Peter's eyes flutter open she realized she had the chance to find out.

Peter looked startled to find her staring at him. He smiled nervously. She grinned. Did she have what it took to distract him with her body? She knew she was playing a dangerous game, and she trembled with excitement.

He pulled her tighter into his embrace as the horse gained some speed. Comfort flowed from his arms and beckoned her. She wanted to snuggle deeper into his chest, but she resisted. She intended to take control. To show him that it would not be so easy to take advantage of her again. She was determined to take control of her traitorous body. She was the Dark Knight after all and no one could get the best of her.

Van took a deep breath and focused on the task at hand—unmanning her husband and gaining control. Confident that she could master this situation as she had all others, she gently pressed herself into his tight embrace and ignored the warmth that softly caressed her. She tried desperately to concentrate only on the soft groans that escaped him, but an insistent heat was spreading through her veins and warming her. It swirled around her mind and crashed through her body, gathering heat as it went.

Hestlay had passed them quite some time ago and was now out of sight. Knowing they were alone gave her strength and confidence to forge ahead. She took a steadying breath and pressed her hip into the hardening shaft that strained against her. Turning, she pressed her breasts more fully into his hard chest.

The heat that had been pulsing through her settled suddenly between her thighs and she knew she was lost. When he leaned his head down to her, she parted her lips in eager anticipation. He clung to her, kissing her passionately, driving his tongue deep into her mouth. There was no struggle this time, no coherent thought of stopping him.

Van wanted this kiss, wanted the warmth that this man provided her. But fear slithered through that warmth, making it dangerous and forbidden. She tightened her arms around him and tentatively pressed her tongue forward, following his lead.

A groan escaped her and Peter jerked away. Van struggled to catch her breath. She didn't understand what had happened or how things had gotten out of control so quickly.

"I know you are planning something and you will not get away with it."

Van jerked her head up at Peter's angry voice. "You are not the only one who will be ready, who will be good at this. I am a great knight, a man prepared for battle and you are but a lowly woman. How can you hope to best me?"

Peter didn't understand how things had slipped from his control so fast, but he did not intend to let it happen again. Vanessa glanced at him, a look of confusion clouding her dark eyes. She shook her head and jumped from the horse.

She smiled up at him, this time a sad smile, and before he could dismount she said. "I wanted—" She stopped, shook her head, and walked away.

Peter stared after her. She had looked lost, confused. He didn't understand her. What had she wanted? Was she really not trying anything? Was she interested in him? Nay, that couldn't be possible, not after what had happened. Could it? he wondered as he watched her disappear into the large, oak entrance doors.

He stared at the doors before following his new bride into what had been his family home for many generations. A young maid stopped him just inside the door to inform him that his bride had been escorted to her room and was preparing for dinner. He smiled at her distractedly and nodded his thanks, but his mind was filled with the afternoon's activities.

He was looking forward to the little game they had begun, but felt no concern at losing. No, he would win. It was an unseemly notion that a woman would be of any competition to a man.

He made his way through the great halls toward the master's bed chambers without giving thought to anything but the woman that had been bestowed upon him.

She was nothing like the women that he had believed to be acceptable bride material. All were small and quiet without real opinions of their own, at least none that he had ever heard. They were well trained in the ways of a woman. They knew what a man wanted to hear and said it. They knew their place and stayed in it.

This woman, although she seemed to know what a man wanted to hear, did not want to say it. She was stubborn and mouthy. Neither of which he was interested in. So for the life of him, he could not determine what it was about her that he found so fascinating.

He paused outside his chamber door and looked down the hall toward the mistress's chambers. He wanted to go to her, to see her again. He shook his head. "Why does that woman drive me out of my head so easily?"

He pushed the door open to his chambers and realized he knew the answer to his question. He hated to admit it, but he knew it was correct. Vanessa was just like his mother and that terrified him.

👑👑👑

"Milady, what are you doing?"

Van cringed at Amy's chiding protest as she shredded the soft material of the thin chemise Amy had coerced her into. She had begun pulling it off the moment Amy's back had been turned.

"I can handle wearing the dresses, I can even tolerate it. I would prefer not, but that is not to be." She tossed another piece of clothing to the floor. "I cannot and will not wear all these layers. It is hot and sweaty under all of this unnecessary clothing. I will have to make a compromise with you on this. I will wear the dress, but not anything else." Naked once again Van stood stubbornly. "I need to be able to breathe and to move." She was not going to budge on this. She remembered all too well what those dreaded layers of ruffles and lace had cost her. They had been more than a mere nuisance, they had been disastrous.

"Milady. Please, there are going to be a lot of guests. It is unseemly for the lady of the castle to be going around in only a dress, and where are your slippers." Van could hear the stress and irritation in Amy's voice. Amy rolled her eyes and rubbed her temples. "You cannot go bare-footed."

"It can be no worse than that cloth you try to tell me is a proper foot covering. You fix a sole of some kind onto the bottom or I will wear my boots." She made a move toward the large blue trunk in the corner.

"Nay," Amy threw up her arms. "I will fix them, please just get dressed. If I can get you to wear a dress, then I will settle for that, but you are not making my job any easier. When you told me I had to help, I didn't realize you were so stubborn."

It took less time than Van had expected for Amy to modify a pair of kid slippers with a thick fold of leather stitched discreetly onto the bottom. They were slightly stiff, but felt solid on her feet. She walked around the room to accustom herself with the feel.

Catching a glance of herself in the full length mirror she stopped. The soft blue gown hung delicately along her hips and thighs, while the puffed style of the sleeves did well to conceal the size of her arms. All in all she looked presentable. She could live with it.

"That dress shows way to much of your assets. I strongly suggest the chemise." Amy said.

"Shut up and let's go."

☙ ☙ ☙

Peter quickly changed his clothes and headed for the feast. He was lost in thoughts of his mother and Vanessa.

His mother, Analise Lawston, was a self-assured woman. She was outspoken and disobedient. James, Peter's father, had loved her more than anything. Peter loved his father a great deal, but their relationship had been strained in the years after Analise had left them. Peter had only been eight and had not realized the extent of all that had happened, but learned later that his father had blamed him for her leaving.

Peter started down the long stairway as his mind drifted back to when he was twelve...

☙ ☙ ☙

Peter lay sprawled in the front courtyard, looking up at the sky. Small white clouds drifted across the bright blue. He had fought with his father again and was now sure his father hated him. Pain swirled through him and anger kicked at him insistently, although he tried to ignore it.

He tossed a small clod of dirt into the air and watched it explode beside him as it hit the hard earth. Peter closed his eyes and tried to recall what the fight was about this time. He couldn't remember.

A cool shadow fell upon his face and he opened his eyes. His father stood above him, tears glistening in his eyes. "May I watch the clouds with you?"

Peter, unsure of what was happening and filled with anger, only shook his head. His father lowered himself onto the ground and laid back, his shoulder brushing Peter's. Warmth caressed Peter, driving away the pain and padding him against the prods of anger.

His father lay silent for a long time before his shaky words began. "I need to tell you what happened, and I should have done so a long time ago." Peter heard a deep breath rattle through his father and shuddered. "Your mother never wanted me. She never wanted anything from me, including a child."

Peter turned his head to watch him speak, but when a tear slid down his father's weathered cheek, he looked back uneasily at the sky. The breeze picked up and the clouds hurried along as if they didn't want to bear witness to this private confession.

"Analise had been unhappy about the marriage before we wed. She had wanted an annulment. I had paid a large dowry for her. She had two older sisters who were not wed and custom said they should have married first, but with enough money customs can be overlooked."

Peter did not understand exactly what his father was talking about, but did not ask. He could not bring himself to interrupt. He watched from the corner of his eye as his father's chest rose and fell unevenly.

"I had loved her for years before I could finally convince her father to allow us to wed, but by then she was in love with someone else. I never found out whom, although he was a man from a lower class."

Peter never understood why that mattered. People were people to him, but he knew that not everyone felt that way.

"I had been alone for a very long time. I was thirty-five, she had barely turned sixteen. She did not want a child with me and fought me every time, but I was insistent on getting an heir."

Peter slowly turned his head and looked at his father.

"She despised me for it and I came to blame you." Another tear slid down his now dusty cheek. "She had wanted nothing to do with you or with me."

His father smiled sadly. "I still loved her and began to think that if it were not for you we could work it out."

He turned onto his side, propped his head with one hand and looked down on Peter. "I know it was not your fault. It was her fault and it was mine. I knew she was against the union, but had hoped that she would come to love me."

His father's tears stung his heart and Peter felt helpless to do anything. He had never seen his father cry, never seen him so vulnerable. He vowed silently to himself that he would never allow a woman to make him weak. Peter laid his hand across his father's.

"Promise me something, Peter."

Peter tightened his hand around his father's and said that he promised.

"Promise me that you will marry a woman who was bred to marry. One who is as honest as a woman ever gets, obedient, without an opinion to bother you with, and not very smart. A smart woman thinks too much of herself, she is too proud."

His father sat up and looked down at him. The seriousness in his features held Peter's attention. "A proud woman will not allow herself to be dominated, and a woman not dominated will not know what to do with herself. Women cannot handle things on their own. They have to have a man to keep them safe, even from themselves."

"I promise." Peter reiterated. I promise, he told himself again.

♛♛♛

Peter was jerked back to the present when his foot slipped across a step and he almost tumbled down the stairs. He shook his head and berated his stupidity.

He took a deep breath, thinking again of his father's description of the perfect bride. That had been his daily lecture from his father ever since that day in the courtyard.

It had been challenged by Grant Hestlay, who Peter had been a squire under. Grant had been in love with one of the upstairs maids, Dorothy Tyrece. Peter smiled, remembering the fiery woman that had stolen Grant's heart. Another proud and self-assured woman who had disappeared one night.

Even though she had run off, Grant had said he had no regrets. He was constantly telling Peter that he shouldn't live his life in fear of being hurt. It made for a lonely life. He said Peter should love fully and completely.

Peter shook his head to expel the contradictory voices that rattled in his aching head. Neither man's advice was helping him with his present problem, his bride.

Not only was she not the obedient and not very bright wife that he had always planned for, she was hiding something. He could feel it deep within him, and if he could keep his wits about him long enough he would find out what it was. That was the problem though, Peter thought in irritation. She had a way of distracting him from his task.

He rounded the corner and a hand pressed into his chest bringing him to a dead stop. His head jerked up, surprised to see his mistress standing before him.

"Rebeka, what are you still doing here?" He was shocked to see her still in the castle. "I told you to leave. I will make sure you are taken care of until you can find a new protector. I told you that, you have nothing to worry about." He was not used to being questioned, especially by his mistress. She had always been so pliable to his demands and wishes. Never once had she questioned him or disobeyed.

"Aye, but I know you," she said sweetly. "You are only trying to do what is proper. You have been forced into a marriage with a dreadful woman you had never met." She ran her hand seductively across his chest. He ignored it. "I have heard she is like a giant, a loud giant who tells you what to do. I understand you are under a great deal of stress, not meaning what you say." She smiled sweetly as she continued to rub her hand across his body. "Besides, you did not give me enough time to pack, and I do not yet know where to go."

Van peered around the corner as a small framed, yet very well-endowed blonde slithered against her husband. She felt an unaccustomed emotion wrench at her chest as she fought the urge to rip the long blonde locks from the obvious doxy. This was a woman he had spent intimate time with, had held in his arms, and the thing that bothered Van the most was that she cared.

Peter body was rigid. He pushed at the clinging arms that tried again and again to enfold his neck. "Look Rebeka, I will not parade my leman around in front of my wife."

Still she clung to him. Her seductive look turned to panic as Van stepped around the corner.

"I am glad to hear that, my lord. Although, holding her so close to you might constitute parading, do you not think?" Her face remained calm, even though she wanted to scream and injure them both.

"I–It is not what—" he growled deeply, shoving Rebeka away. "I do not have to explain myself to you. I will do as I want, when I want, and you will not question me again."

Ignoring his ranting, Van kept her attention on the much smaller woman who was trying desperately to regain her composure. "Did I hear you say, my dear, that Peter did not give you plenty of time to leave? When did he tell you?"

Van forced herself to remain calm, but that was not what she wanted. What she wanted was to slip her dagger from beneath her dress, where it lay snuggled comfortably in the sheath strapped to her thigh. She wanted to stab this whore until the twisting ache in her stomach and throat went away and she could breathe once again without pain.

"Not that it is any of your business, but he told me this morning," Rebeka snarled.

"Today? He allowed you to stay until the very day I was to arrive?" She clucked her tongue in mock sympathy and shook her head sadly. "That is shameful. Do you need help getting your things packed, a place to stay? I can help you in any way you need."

She forced a smile as anger blossomed across Rebeka's reddening face.

"I don't need anything from you. I will be well taken care of, in all ways, by Peter. I may not be allowed to stay here, but Peter will not turn his back on me. Look at you, you are a giant."

"Rebeka, that is enough." Peter's stern voice rang across the hallway, but Rebeka's words continued to pour from her.

Rebeka was near tears, but her tirade continued unbidden. "How do you hope to satisfy a man like Peter?"

Peter grasped her arm. "Stop now, Rebeka."

Rebeka jerked her arm away, but did not step away from Peter's side.

Van twisted her hands into fists but stood calmly as she listened to Rebeka's shaky voice. She could hear the fear beneath the words and that pleased her

"He is not interested in a woman like you. He will be lucky if he is capable of rising to take care of you, and he will come running back to me."

Rage swarmed through Van at the thought of losing Peter, to this woman, or any other. The anger scared her, because she had not expected the fear that came with it.

"He likes his women small, large bosomed, and fair skinned. How do you—"

Peter reached once more for his wayward leman, but Van's temper snapped before he could reach her. She grasped Rebeka's arm in a vice-like grip, stopping her words as she ripped her from Peter's side. She held her tightly with one arm around her narrow shoulders. Van ran her fingers down Rebeka's trembling cheek, wrapped them tightly around her long slender neck. She tightened her grip on Rebeka's throat until her eyes bulged in fear and she began to struggle.

Van glanced at Peter who stood with his mouth slightly agape, staring at her as she let go of his mistress's throat and slid her fingertip into the low cut dress to gently caress the rounded swell of Rebeka's breast. She looked back down at the small trembling blonde. "You are beautiful. I will give you that. If I were in the market for a leman, I would choose one that was as small and as well endowed. I can see nearly to your feet from up here, as low-cut as your dress is. It is quite fetching."

Peter shook his head. Van watched as the shock seemed to disappear and the anger spread across his features. He stepped forward quickly. "Vanessa, let her go. Now."

Amy rushed around the corner and grasped Van's arm. "Milady— Milady—My—Vanessa! Vanessa, let her go. What are you thinking?" She pulled helplessly at her. "Remember who you are now! Van!"

"Get your damned hands off me!" Van barked through clenched teeth as she violently ripped her arm free of the nuisance that pulled at it.

Released suddenly, Rebeka fell into Peter, who was forced to catch her. Amy took a step away with a look of fear on her face that caused guilt to slap at Van, refusing to be ignored.

Anger quickly made way for black rage as Van fought to keep herself from losing total control. She had never felt so helpless in her life. Emotions collided upon her like waves of a violent ocean storm. She felt trapped and alone. The ground beneath her seemed to suck at her feet, trapping her as the waves crashed into her again and again.

She saw one of her men in the halls not far away. "Devon, here," she yelled in a voice that was far too deep. She prayed that no one noticed. She took a deep breath and turned her attention back to the terrified leman. The woman shuddered and stepped closer into Peter.

Peter stepped half around Rebeka to protect her from another attack. "Vanessa. Stop."

Van ignored him and spoke around him, once more in control of her voice. "I may not be what Peter wants, but no matter how many times he takes you instead of me, I can give him the one thing you will never be able to: an heir."

She noted the sharp intake of breath and the devastated look on Rebeka's face and knew she had struck a sour nerve with the woman. She turned her attention to Devon as he walked up to them confused.

"Aye, my lady?" Devon looked closely at her.

"Miss Rebeka is going to be joining us for supper tonight to help celebrate our marriage, then in the morning I want you to find a couple of men to help her pack and to make sure she has decent housing arrangements made for her. We will be taking care of her for two months." She put two fingers up. They trembled slightly so she dropped her hand quickly. With that she turned to leave, only to be stopped by fingers painfully digging into her arm.

"How did you know his name?" Peter snarled.

Her eyes widened as she realized that in her anger she had made a huge mistake. She had not been introduced to any of the men except for Grant.

"I told her, milord." Amy smiled shyly at Devon, as he slightly blushed. "Devon and I met earlier in the day while you were out on your lands. I pointed him out when she returned."

"Everyone will leave us now." Peter ordered. He waited until the three were out of earshot before turning his enraged face toward her. "What in the Devil's name did you think you were doing?"

She had stood calmly, waiting until they were alone. Now she ripped her arm free from his grasp. "I was taking care of things the way you should have. How dare you wait until the very day that I was to be here before asking your whore to leave? You should have more consideration than that, since I have been told we have been married for several weeks now." Her breathing was shallow and painful. The world spun around her and faded out of focus. His face doubled and then snapped back together as her heart raced.

"It is bad enough that I have been married to a man that doesn't like me, but I will not suffer through having mistresses thrown at me like I am some second woman. I do not need to be reminded that I am not what a man desires."

With that she was gone and he had been so dumbfounded by her response that he did not even try to stop her.

Not desire her? My God, he had taken her and had wanted to again. Did that not stand for proof of his desire? How could she not know? Guilt stabbed deeply at his heart and twisted the blade over and over. She had been untouched by a man. How could she know what desire was or how to see it? He had done what he hadn't wanted to do and that was to hurt her.

He had seen the pain in her eyes when Rebeka was holding him. He didn't want to hurt her, although, he didn't know how to break her, and turn her into the wife he had always promised himself he would have, *without* hurting her.

CHAPTER 9

Peter stood staring at the emptiness left by his rebellious wife. It was more than an empty space in the hallway and it seemed to be spreading. Thin fingers of cold slithered over him and left a void that he could not understand.

A deep breath shuddered through his frame, but it did nothing to release the tension that cramped his muscles. Regret over the way he had treated his wife cloaked him like a shroud, but he didn't know how to fix it.

Images of his mother plagued his tired mind. His father doted on her, allowing her to come and go as she pleased, allowing her to do as she pleased. He knew his father was hoping to win her love, but he had been wrong. Peter knew in his heart that if his father had enforced more control over her, she never would have left. Peter had no intention of making the same mistake.

He trudged to the dining hall in no mood to face the crowded room. It would be packed to celebrate his joyous day. What he wanted most was to retire to his room and hide.

By the time he stepped through the archway into the loud and overly crowded room, he had resigned himself to the celebration. He wanted to eat quickly and get it over with. These big gatherings did not engage his interest for long. They never had.

His gaze scanned the room, taking in his men, both those that had been with him for years and those who had recently joined his ranks. Among those who had just joined were the men of the Dark Knight. Peter scowled and wondered where the high-spirited knight had disappeared to.

His scrutinizing gaze sought out the Dark Knight's first in command. Richard Devenroe sat at the head table where he had sat three years ago before joining with Van Burgess.

Richard had sent scouts out to look for Van, but they had all returned empty handed. Peter's eyes continued across the head table as he pondered on the disappearance of the knight.

He glanced at his chair at the head of the main table. His gaze drifted to the right of his seat and came to a stop where his wife should be sitting. To his shock and dismay Rebeka sat there instead. A trencher of food was already sitting before her, waiting for him to come and share it with her as he had since she had become his leman two years before. His breath lodged in his throat as his airway constricted.

He forced in a deep inhale and looked to the left of his seat. There sat Vanessa. Her head was held high and her spine was rigid. She was a beautiful sight in the soft blue gown with its puffy sleeves that stopped before her elbows.

Peter released the breath with a shudder. Tension cramped his shoulders and neck once more. Unsure of his next actions, he motioned for Grant, who appeared about to share a trencher with Vanessa.

Grant nodded and rose. He bowed to Vanessa with a nervous smile and walked toward Peter. Peter shook as he fought against the rumbling emotions that boiled uncontrolled within him.

Grant looked to be very uncomfortable. "Aye, my Lord."

"What are you thinking? How dare you allow the seating arrangement that is taking place? Do you intend to share food with my bride?" Peter shot off the questions rapidly without giving Grant time to answer any of them.

Grant shook his head as Peter spoke.

Peter took a deep breath and forced himself to wait. Grant sighed and shook his head once again. He looked at the two women as he spoke. "My Liege, it was not my doing. Miss Constance sat herself down and before I could tell her to move, Lady Vanessa arrived and placed herself on the bench beside me."

Peter glanced over at his wife. Vanessa had not moved a muscle from what he could tell. She stared straight ahead with a blank expression on her face. He could hear Grant speaking in the background, but he was having trouble focusing on anything but his beautiful bride.

"Your new bride announced that you would be arriving within the moment and ordered the food to be brought."

Peter glanced back at Grant who stood staring at Vanessa with an intense look that Peter could not discern. He felt a rush of jealously that surprised him. He was not a jealous man.

Grant looked back to him and continued, "I was not sure at first that she understood what was happening, but then she tells me she will be sharing my food if I do not mind, and if I do, she will go and sit with the other men. She said she was sure that she would be welcomed there. I did not doubt her. What would you have had me do?"

"I would have had you move her to where she belongs," Peter grunted in exasperation. He could think of no way out of this situation, short of making a dreadful scene in front of everyone and he was not quite willing to do that.

Grant held a look of worry that left Peter feeling unsettled. He looked closely at Peter and said quietly, "I think they will both create an uproar if you try to move either one of them. I tried to talk Lady Vanessa into moving. She growled at me. Growled at me, my liege. She knows where she is supposed to be and there are already murmurs going through the guests about the seating. They are not sure what to think, but it has been noticed."

Peter closed his eyes, hoping it would all be gone when he opened them. He opened his eyes slightly and peeked out. Everything was still as it had been. "Well, hell."

"Excuse me, my liege?" Grant asked.

Peter opened his eyes fully and shook his head as frustration pounded at the sides of his temples, creating a resounding headache. "I know they will make a scene. I just need to get through this one night and then Rebeka will be gone in the morning."

"I don't think that one will go easily, my lord."

Peter looked over at the small blonde who glared at the new lady of the castle as he considered his friend's words.

He shook his head as he watched the two women at his head table. Rebeka turned back to Vanessa and scowled furiously, but was completely ignored. He chuckled, turning back to his lifelong friend. "Oh, nay, Grant. Rebeka will leave. Lady Vanessa made that perfectly clear to her. Even assigned some of my men to help her along the way. Get with Devon. He is in charge of seeing to her comfort." Peter waved away the shocked expression on Grant's face and made his way toward what he hoped would not be a complete disaster.

"My lady," He bowed politely to his wife and ignored his leman altogether. He would eat with his wife. It did not matter which side of him she sat on. He would not make a big stir, but he would make sure all knew who his choice was. It was not a wonderful plan. Hell, it was not even a good one, but it was one that would have to suffice, and one that would dissuade all doubts and rumors without disrupting the entire celebration.

Peter glanced around the head table. It was filled with his higher ranked men-at-arms. They fidgeted uncomfortably as their gaze darted between Peter and the two women.

Peter nodded to the table in general and turned to Vanessa. Every man at the table seemed to relax. They turned without question to share with the person on their left instead of their right, as was custom.

"Looks like I get to share with you, my dear." Richard said quietly to Rebeka and slid his trencher of stew toward her.

"I will not share with you. You are only up here, because Peter knows your men will not listen to him yet. When they do, you will lose all your power," Rebeka snarled and pushed his trencher away from her.

It slammed into Richard's goblet spilling it across the table. Peter spun his head around to her. He opened his mouth to tell her to leave, but Richard spoke first. His soft voice sounded deadly in the silent room.

"No matter what his reasoning, I am here because it was requested that I be here. Unlike you, who have no business being here at all." Richard sat his goblet back up and pulled his food close in front of him.

He stabbed a slice of beef with his dagger and started ignoring her. Peter smiled and relaxed when the other men followed suit.

It was not much of a celebration at the beginning. All the guests were silent as they glanced at Rebeka. Anger flourished within Peter as he glared at his mistress. She sat stiffly, without eating or drinking.

The guests partook of wine and ale and quickly seemed to forget the extra woman at the head table. The laughter and talk spread throughout the large dining hall. Peter smiled sweetly and turned his full attention to Vanessa. He placed his hand on her trembling arm. She looked up at him in surprise.

He laughed gently and caressed her arm. He did not dislike her and he wanted no misunderstandings. He would accept nothing less than obedience, but he did like her. He opened his mouth, but was unsure of what to say to reassure her.

Several drunken people stood at once, interrupting Peter. He closed his mouth and grinned. He turned to them as they began to give their congratulations to the new couple.

It did not take long, with the wine flowing abundantly, for the good wishes to turn to lewd advice. Within moments the celebration had gotten loud and the ruckus was starting to disrupt the tables.

Rebeka stood and slipped away from the table. She quietly joined the ranks of the drunken soldiers. Most of the men at the head table were well into their cups and did not seem to take notice when she left.

Peter noticed, for he had drunk little. He wanted to show Vanessa pleasure, and he had enough trouble controlling himself when it came to her without being encumbered by drink.

Van took notice as Rebeka slinked off into the crowd. Van had drunk nothing. She had never drunk more than a few mouthfuls of anything other than watered down ale. She had never been in a position where she could relax her guard. When she was the Dark Knight, she could not risk compromising herself and she had the same fears now. She had no idea how alcohol would affect her, but knowing it made most men loose of lips, she had never pushed fate.

"Relax, my dear." Peter's voice pulled her thoughts away from the Dark Knight. She turned to him with a forced smile. "All will be well," he continued. "I will show you. This union has not started off at the best pace, but we can make something work out of it." He slid his hand down her arm and took her hand. Shocked at the jolt of heat that raced through her fingers and arm she stared down at it.

"Get on with the bedding. We have had our fill of food and drink, get on with the entertainment," the drunken man shouted above the noisy room.

Van jerked her head up as cheers erupted through the crowd. Rank comments and lewd suggestions followed.

She smiled. This was part of why she missed the life of a knight. It was rare that a woman of any ranking got to see this side of men. She glanced across the room at the maids and whores who lounged across the laps of the men. She smiled at her men, but it concerned her to see them separated from Peter's men.

Van looked toward Peter. He sat staring intently at her.

He was surprised, and a little irritated, by his bride. She did not seem in the least ruffled by the graphic language. She should blush and act the part of the innocent young girl that he knew her to be.

He looked at the young boy who had loudly insisted on the bedding. Christopher Dalton had been a foot soldier in Peter's army for less than a year. Rebeka stood next to him with a satisfied grin. Peter knew she had planted the seed in his head and left the shouting to him. Peter was shocked to see this vindictive side of her.

He pushed her from his mind and stood holding out his hands. "That is not a possibility," he shouted over the commotion. "I am sorry for the lack of entertainment, but the marriage has already been consummated." He held his hands higher as an uproar echoed through the hall.

"You cannot have. She cannot excite you." Rebeka raced toward him, stumbling over the crowding men as her voice rose to a fevered pitch. "Not the way that I do."

She stopped breathlessly in front of them and glowered down at Vanessa, who looked up at her with a deadly grin.

Tension dug its claws into Peter's nerves and refused to release its painful grasp.

"There is no way you could entice him to take you. You are lying. You have no honor—"

Peter had no time to react as Vanessa lurched up from her seat and threw Rebeka off balance. She grasped Rebeka's arms and yanked her slender frame up against her own. Vanessa spoke unsteadily through tightly clenched teeth. "You will listen to me, and you will listen real close."

All the men were instantly on their feet, ready to come to their lady's aid. Peter grasped Vanessa's arm and tried to pull Rebeka from her steel grasp. She tightened her hold, refusing to let go.

Vanessa's voice was a mere whisper. "There are a lot of things you can do to me. A lot you may call me. I will forgive you a great deal, for you are after all, just a woman, but even at that, you will never question my honor."

The soft gravel in her voice was unlike any of the voices she had used throughout the day, yet Peter found it familiar.

Small white dents appeared in Rebeka's arms as Vanessa dug her fingers deeply into the soft white flesh, lifting her completely from the ground. As Rebeka's tears began to fall, Peter yanked at Vanessa's arm.

"Vanessa, let her go, you are making a scene. We can deal with this when we are not in front of everyone." He pulled at her arm until Rebeka squealed in pain. "Vanessa!"

Vanessa yanked her arms away. Rebeka fell to the floor with a scream. Vanessa turned her dark gaze on Peter once again. She sighed deeply and shook her head. He saw the pain that swirled in her black eyes, and it ached within him as if her pain had caressed him.

"This was a bad idea. I am never going to be able to do this. I cannot." She turned and fled the room.

Peter glanced down as a small figure brushed past him. He shook his head and grasped Amy's arm. "Nay, I will take care of this."

"Pray, let me go to her."

"Nay, I will speak to her." Peter started to walk past her, but her small hand stayed him.

"You do not understand." Amy pulled weakly against his arm. She looked up at him pleadingly with tear moistened eyes.

"Do not cry. You are right. I do not understand a lot about that woman, but I will be the one to see to her." His gaze caught all the staring faces of the men and servants as he turned to follow Vanessa up the stairs.

Guilt pricked at him. He had wanted to avoid a scene, but things had ended up worse than he had imagined. "I should have just moved her," he said quietly as he trudged up the stairs. "It would have been less of a scene in the long run."

He reached his chambers only to find them empty, though he wasn't surprised. He knew she wouldn't run to his room. He made his way across the floor and tried the door between the rooms only to find it locked. He knocked. "Vanessa." Nothing came from beyond the door.

Anger began to swell within him at being locked out. Pounding loudly on the heavy oak door he shouted. "Open this blasted door."

No answer, but he could think of nowhere else she would have run. "Open it now. This is your last chance to let me in." No answer. Pain splintered through his arm as it collided with the wood once more. He growled at the offending object and caressed his throbbing hand.

He stomped to his bed side and ripped open the top drawer of his bed stand. He had a moment of concern when the key to her door was not lying on the top of the parchments where he thought he had left it.

Cursing vividly, he dug through the drawer. Relief washed away some of the frustration when his hand closed around the small cold key. Peter rushed back, turned the key and threw the door open.

Vanessa stood defiantly in the center of the room, hands on her narrow hips. Peter could feel the anger radiating from her like the heat of a blazing fire. Its dangerous flames threatened to engulf him as he encroached upon her. "How dare you just walk into my chambers? This is my chambers, is it not? I cannot believe you would allow your whore to humiliate me like she did, and you said nothing."

Peter shook his clouded head in an unsuccessful attempt to clear it. Guilt pricked its hooks into him once again. She was right, he had said nothing. The pain dug in deeper. From the way it looked, Vanessa probably thought he had defended Rebeka. He had not. He just had not wanted Vanessa to hurt her. "Damn it, woman, I did not want to cause a big scene, but I guess you took care of that anyway." He closed the gap between them. "Do not ever lock your door against me and nay, these are not your chambers. They are mine. This entire castle and everything in it is mine. That includes you." He had to gain control of her now, or he was afraid she would never be the wife he needed her to be.

Vanessa stiffened and her chin rose up a notch. Her eyes flashed with anger and pride. Peter scowled. How could one woman drive him so mad? He took a deep breath.

"As such, you will act accordingly." He had trouble focusing on anything except the way her dress pulled into her curves, unencumbered by even the thin chemise that decent women wore. He could see the candle light through the bottom of the dress and although he could see nothing specific, irritation began to turn to anger as he thought of the way the men looked at her throughout the night. He could not allow her to dress so in front of his men. He did not want her near the men and would allow nothing to encourage the men to take unwanted notice of her.

"It reflects badly on me that you dress so and wear so much face powder. From now on you will wear the clothing you were meant to wear."

"I do not believe you would like the clothes I was meant to wear." She grinned lopsidedly at him before she continued. "And nay, I am not yours. I belong to no one. You cannot tell me what to do. You cannot say this is how it will be and expect me not to have any say over my own life." Her face was reddened beneath the powder, and he could hear the passionate anger in her raised voice.

Fury swarmed his thoughts and invaded him with images of his defiant mother screaming relentlessly at his father. The way she had humiliated him with his men, the way she had spent time alone with them in the barracks. He could see the devastation on his father's face when she admitted to her affairs with his men, and the tears, that he was afraid would never end, the night that she had left with one of them.

All he could see through his rage was his mother standing before him. "You damned bitch, you will not speak to me in such a way." He raised his hand to hit her and Vanessa's face swirled back into his view.

He gasped, dropped his hand and took a step back. All he wanted was his calm life back, wanted things the way they were before she had invaded his peaceful existence.

Vanessa stared at him, but remained silent. He wanted more than anything to know what she was thinking, if she hated him. He could not bring himself to ask the questions he did not know if he could face the answers to. Peter looked around the room at the dingy tapestries on the walls and the layers of dust that covered everything. He shivered. The large room had been vacant for a long time, since his mother had left them. It felt alive with the ghosts of the past. "I will have them send up a bath for you."

"Nay." Vanessa's voice was icy and calm.

Peter knew he had made a mess of the whole day and could only hope that tomorrow would bring better. "Come then, if you are too tired than we can just go to sleep."

Peter took a slow step toward her and held out his hand. He wanted to take her in his arms and tell her how sorry he was, but he would not, could not. She held his gaze and then slowly looked down at his extended hand.

Van looked at his hand, but could not take it. She was angry that he had yelled at her. More, she was angry that she had to force herself not to react. But mostly, she was scared of what it meant to willingly take his offered hand.

She glanced up at his face and was surprised to see the sadness fill his eyes. He dropped his hand. "Change and come to bed." He walked into his chambers. Stopping just inside the door, he turned and waited.

If Van was going to make this work, it would mean sharing a bed with him and postponing it would not make it any easier. She took a deep breath and nodded.

Peter smiled and disappeared from sight but left the door standing open in a quiet invitation.

Van changed slowly and made her way to Peter.

He turned as she walked into the room. "Clean off the powder and come to bed."

Van stopped, her breath catching in her throat. She could not take off the face powder. Fear coursed through her as she considered the ramifications of Eolian discovering her true identity. He would stop at nothing to get his revenge on her.

Van had not only defeated his army in battles many times, but she had also taken from him a young girl who was pregnant with his child. The young girl had been held against her will until Van had rescued her. Although Eolian did not know the child was his, he swore his revenge on her for taking the woman he professed to love.

Peter took a step toward her drawing her attention back to him. "You cannot sleep in that mess."

She folded her arms across her chest and looked at him in challenge. "I cannot take off my face powder. I cannot."

Peter looked at her closely and his soft, concerned voice surprised her. "Tell me why. Tell me and I may allow you to wear it." Peter stripped off his shirt.

She watched his every move and smiled when she saw the jagged scar on his upper chest and shoulder. It seemed so long ago that she had saved him. She had been a lowly soldier and had known then that she cared more about this man than she could admit to.

"I cannot tell you why. Not now. It is important to me that I am allowed to keep it on."

Peter sat heavily on the bed. His intent stare never left her face.

Her eyes stung and her breath came in hard little gasps. "I am not what you think I am. I am not the kind of woman you should have married. You can tell them you made a mistake." Tears built behind her eyes and threatened to drown her. "Tell them you want an annulment. If you tell them it was a lie, that we did not consummate the union, it can be dissolved." She sucked in a shuddering breath and continued in a bare whisper. "I am not what you want."

She felt a deep sadness pierce her heart at offering him his freedom. She was afraid he would take her up on it, and she didn't understand that. It was what she wanted, wasn't it?

"I have no intention of doing any such thing. You are my wife and you will have to get used to it." He slipped off his brown leather boots and then his hose. He rose slowly and walked toward her in nothing at all. His voice was gentle and caressing. "If it is that important to wear the ridiculous stuff, I will allow it, for now. Soon though, it will come off."

Her eyes never left his manhood as it steadily hardened beneath her gaze. Her breath thickened as she took in the rippling muscles in his thighs. Panic rushed through her system and she had to fight the urge to run. Away from him or into his arms she wasn't sure.

"Are you even listening to me?"

His amused voice tore her from her thoughts. She took a deep breath and forced herself to relax.

"If you don't want that reaction to you, then you really must not stare at me the way you do." He laughed and held his hand out to her. His eyes held a hopeful look. "Come to bed. I can control myself." At least he prayed that he could.

Vanessa shook her head, but did not take his hand.

Peter dropped his empty hand once again, pain and guilt pricking at him. He turned toward the bed, held back the covers for her, and waited. He was determined to make things right, though he was not sure how.

Vanessa climbed beneath the bed coverings of his massive bed and lay stiffly as he joined her.

He pulled her close to him, her back to his chest. He could feel the roundness of her bottom pressing into him. "Okay, this will not work," he mumbled grumpily.

He turned onto his back, pulling her head onto his chest. Closing his eyes, he tried to ignore her gentle breath and her long fingers as they explored the soft curls of blonde hair that covered his chest.

Her hand stopped on the rough scar that still dominated his shoulder. She gently placed a kiss on it, before laying her head comfortably upon it and finding sleep.

Sleep eluded Peter for quite some time. He lay watching her in the guttering light of the candles. He didn't remember falling asleep. He thought he had stared at her face all night, but when he opened his eyes the sun was rising, the candles had burned themselves out, and she was gone.

CHAPTER 10

A my ignored the wavering nervousness that coursed through her rolling stomach. She rushed up the stairs in the early morning light and let herself into her lady's chambers. The bed, though rumpled, did not appear to have been slept in and a quick glance around the room proved that it was empty.

She took in the large dust filled room and her gaze stopped on the closed interior door between the suites. Sure that Van had spent the night in the master's chambers with her husband, Amy slouched on the bed to await her mistress. Her thoughts were riddled with concern as she pondered all that had happened since they had arrived at the castle.

She closed her eyes and let her mind wander back to the day before. She had been a nervous wreck, terrified of what would happen as Peter got to know Van without her there to censor Van's run-away mouth. Unable to just sit and wait for them to return from their ride, she had wandered the grounds of her new home.

That was how she had met the handsome Devon Horacio. She had remembered him from Patricia's funeral and was relieved when he had not recognized her. Her heart fluttered as she pictured the tall green-eyed man and she was looking forward to getting to know him better.

She opened her eyes and a smile spread across her lips. She looked again at the middle door. Her smile slipping away, she shook her head and sighed sadly. The entire castle had heard the fight that had went on between Peter and Van.

She had spoken with several of the house maids as the couple had fought. All were shocked by Lord Grayweist's behavior. They had gone on and on about how dignified he was, how stoic, the perfect gentleman. Amy giggled when she remembered their wide-eyed whispers. "He is acting just like one of his men."

The door swung open and Amy jumped from the bed. It was not Lady Vanessa as she had expected, but a very naked Lord Grayweist. A scream escaped her before could get control of it.

"Nay, don't scream." Peter hastily picked up the shimmery night robe that lay across the end of the bed and slipped it around him. "I did not mean to frighten you. I was looking for Lady Vanessa. Have you by chance seen her?"

"Nay, milord, I was looking for her as well." Amy's fought to control her rapid breathing. Her brow furrowed as fear swept through her. She didn't want to believe that Van would have run, but she knew it was a possibility.

He looked around the room and shook his head. "I need some things seen to." He turned a sober face toward her.

She smiled nervously and nodded.

"As I am sure you have been informed, this was my mother's room. Everything is how she left it. No one has been allowed in this room since the day she left. The servants have not even been allowed in this room to clean." He sniffed indignantly and looked around. "Obviously." He smiled softly and turned his attention back to her. "My Vanessa may not spend much time in it, but it should at least be hers, and clean. You will see to that, won't you?"

Amy felt a grin spread across her lips. My Vanessa, he calls her, she thought, and her grin widened. When Peter looked at her, eyebrows arched in a silent question, all she said was, "Aye, my lord."

"My lord," a shaky voice said from beside them.

Amy and Peter both turned toward the adjoining door. Peter's second-in-command stood with a smirk growing on his face. He bit his lip, struggling to keep a straight face. He lost and cleared his throat before continuing. "You look very nice in that pink and lacy robe, but shall I call for Miceal to help you dress?" Grant turned to Amy and gave her a big wink. "See what happens when he is left to dress himself."

She looked back to Peter with a grin, but he only scowled.

Grant turned back to his lord and added. "You have promised to take Lady Vanessa to see the training of your men. She is waiting."

"I promised her no such thing." Peter shot of the bed and left it rocking beneath Amy.

She took a deep breath and groaned.

"Where would you get an idea like that? Nay, do not answer that. I take it you have seen my meek little bride this morning." Peter slapped his hand on his forehead, slid the hand down his face, and shook his head with a groan.

"Aye, my lord, I saw her this morning at the stables. Now I am not sure where she has disappeared to," Grant said a bit hesitantly.

With that, both men rushed into Peter's chambers. Amy headed directly to the stables. She needed to make sure Van's horse was still safely in his stall. She was almost to the stables when a deep voice resonated from behind her. Her heart jumped to her throat at the familiar voice.

"Miss Devant?" he repeated.

A shiver ran through her and she could not contain her smile as Devon's voice rumbled behind her.

"Mr. Horacio." She turned toward him slowly, trying unsuccessfully to feign nonchalance. Her heart thrummed erratically in her chest as she looked into his sparkling green eyes.

"Pray, call me Devon." He smiled as he took her hand. He turned it softly, brought it to his full lips, and kissed her palm. "How are you today? Things as good as they were yesterday?"

Her breath caught. She had to force her numb lips to respond. "I am fine," she said, pulling her hand away from his. She took a deep breath to control the butterflies that beat relentlessly at her stomach, demanding to be released into the brightness of the morning.

"Things are no different today than they were, and it is highly improper for me to refer to you by your first name. It is awfully forward, seeing as we have only just met." She protested, but she wanted nothing more than to say his name over and over as he pressed his lips to her hand. It was hard to concentrate on anything beyond his brilliant green eyes and the thick brace of red hair that flew wild and free.

They turned and walked to the stables together. Despite her protests, she was comfortable with the warrior. She glanced up at him several times before opening her mouth to speak. "I spoke with several of the housemaids yesterday. They all seem to think that the lord of the castle is not acting like himself since my lady arrived." She looked up at him questioningly. Heat flushed her cheeks as he smiled down at her.

His deep baritone voice caressed her as he spoke. "I had only just joined with the Dark Knight a couple of years ago. Until we arrived here four days ago, I had never met Lord Grayweist." He stepped closer to her as they walked.

Her heart raced around her chest bounding off the walls like an excited puppy whose master had just returned from a long voyage.

His voice only increased the pounding as he continued. "I do know that the men think highly of him. I am sure he is a man of honor and will do nothing to harm her."

She laughed before she could stop it. Smiling she shook her head. "That is not exactly what I am worried about."

"So what, you think she will hurt him?" He asked in a voice that sounded like he was jesting, but his smile faltered when she smiled grimly and nodded.

"That, or she will try to disappear." Her voice hitched painfully as she considered the possibility of that happening. She had only known Van for a short time, but she cared for her. Van was all she had left now.

Devon looked at her closely, a concerned look crossing his face. "You do not think she would take her horse and go, do you?"

"I am afraid to think so, but it is a high possibility. That is why I am heading there now." Amy felt sorry for Van. She was unsure of how to help her. She wanted to help her, not because she had agreed to take on the job, but because she liked the big woman.

They continued on to the stables in a comfortable silence for several moments. Devon's hand brushed against hers several times as they walked and she forgot, momentarily, how to breathe as his warm hand connected with hers. After the first few times she was certain it was not accidental. She said nothing to discourage him.

They passed several soldiers who smiled and said their good mornings to her. She smiled back. As the warriors went on their way she leaned toward Devon to whisper conspiratorially, "I have always been afraid of soldiers."

Devon looked from the small, feisty, and very beautiful young girl to the huge, dirty, scar-riddled warriors that roamed the courtyard. He looked back at her and worry tightened his chest. "These men are on good behavior here, but that does not mean you should trust the majority of soldiers that you meet. Do not trust them too far. All men have it in them to be brutes at one time or another." His voice sounded much too gruff even to his own ears, but he did not want to see anything happen to Amy. "You need to be wary of them."

Amy stopped and looked up at him. He had expected to see fear, but what he saw swelled his chest with warmth. What he saw was trust and a little more, or perhaps that was just his wishful thinking.

"Even you? Am I not to trust you, Mr. Horacio?" She looked up at him with almost devotion in her shining eyes and he did not believe that he was imagining it.

"You are so beautiful." His voice was husky. "It is me especially that you should not trust. Please do not think me a nice man, a man whose motives are pure. I am still not sure myself if friendship is what I have in mind for us." He pulled her against him, smiling at the shocked look that crossed her face. "I may be after much more from you."

"Let me go. Look at all these people," she whispered breathlessly. "They will see." She blushed to an almost purple color as she tried to push him away with a laugh. "Let me go. I may scream."

He pulled her closer and kissed the top of her nose. "Scream. See how many people are watching us then." He laughed as he unwillingly set her away from him and looked down at her. "You are such a small little thing. I would not want to fight me off if I were you. I could overpower you easily," he said and made a halfhearted reach for her.

Amy squealed as she stepped out of his reach, but she laughed and smacked playfully at him. "You may be a foot taller than me and your thigh may be as big as my waist, but I know how to hit a man where it will hurt. So do not try me."

He gasped mockingly. "You would not do that to me. That is fighting dirty." Devon knew he could block her kick if she tried and he lunged at her.

Her leg moved, an obvious attempt to decimate his manhood. He pulled his thigh to catch the blow that never came. Sudden pain flashed through his face as her small fist smashed into his eye, throwing him off guard.

"You hit me." He was dumbfounded. "You lied to me. That is not what you said you would do." He could feel the eye beginning to puff even as they spoke.

"Did it hurt?" she asked pompously.

"Yes it hurt. That, my dear, is a stupid question." He was not angry at her and fought the urge to laugh at the smirk on her face.

"Then yes, I did exactly what I said I would." She turned to walk away from him, a scream tearing from her as he threw her over his shoulder.

"Put me down," she screeched. "Devon."

His name came from her lips like a cool breeze on a hot and humid day. It raced over him, sending chills across his skin. He placed her on the ground and smiled. "Now, see, that was not so hard, was it?"

She giggled as she turned to him. "What?"

"Calling me Devon. You will get used to it." She did not answer him, just swung her fist into his chest. He laughed. "Come, my dear. Let us see if we can find that lady of yours."

Angry voices echoed across the courtyard as they approached the stables. Just outside the stable doors Lord and Lady Grayweist stood toe to toe.

Amy moved to rush past him and toward the couple. Peter caught Devon's gaze and he grabbed Amy, pulling her back against him. Devon wrapped an arm around her waist keeping her still as Peter turned his attention back to the furious woman before him.

"I will not allow you to just leave my chambers without an escort. It is unseemly for a woman to just wander the grounds without someone to protect her." He looked at the thin black dress that shrouded her. The breeze pulled the thin material across her muscular thighs and narrow hips. Lust rushed through him and he could only imagine what it did in the minds of the other men.

Anger gave way to rage as Vanessa nearly screamed in his face. It boiled in his veins like lava just begging to be set free.

"I do not need an escort of any type. I think I can take care of myself on my own land without some arrogant man trying to make himself feel important by telling me what to do."

Peter could feel his face heating up as the anger pushed at him incessantly. "Do not interrupt me when I am speaking to you. Where were you raised that your mother did not teach you better manners than this? Did she not—"

Van's unstable emotions had had enough and the mention of her mother propelled her over the edge. Her throat burned as she screeched at him, and her voice wavered, but she held it together. "Do not ever speak of my mother. You know nothing of what she had to go through for me. Do not think that just because I am standing here before you dressed like a meek woman means—"

Peter reached forward, grabbing her arms, giving her a rough shake. "When I speak to you, you will shut that hole under your nose and listen to me. You will show me the respect that I deserve."

Van began to struggle in his tight grip, her anger building and clouding her thoughts. A dirt clod hit her painfully in the shoulder and she fell silent. She stared down at the dirt spot that showed brightly on her newly made gown. She looked up and saw Devon. He would not meet her eyes, just looked guiltily at his dirty hands.

Amy stood beside Devon, giving her a pleading look. Van was devastated. She was not one to lose her calm control. If she had been on the battlefield, that dirt clod could easily have been an arrow, and she would not be embarrassed in front of all the people in the courtyard. Nay, now she would be dead.

Shame flooded her. She turned her full attention back to Peter. "I am fine, my lord. You may release me." She could hear the deep remorse in her shaky voice, and hoped that Peter could not.

Van was on the verge of a complete breakdown. Tears that had built since her mother had died threatened to drown her as she thought of mounting Damian and charging away.

Peter watched her closely and she could feel her skin tighten beneath his probing gaze. He didn't release her, instead pulled her tightly into his warm embrace. "Everything is going to be all right, my love. I know things have not worked well for us, but it will get better."

His soft whisper tickled across the side of her face. She turned it away from him. She held herself perfectly still in his arms. She could feel his warmth trying to seep into her and fought against it. She barely held the tears at bay and could not allow them to fall in front of all these people, in front of him. She fought against the desire to lose herself in his caress.

He finally released her, smiling a confident smile. It lasted only a moment as she began to speak. "Nothing will be all right, not now, not ever. I can never be…" She did not add, the woman you want me to be. She couldn't. "Never mind." She had regained a semblance of her iron control and now smiled. "I would like to accompany you to see the men now."

"See my men?" His face tightened and she smiled. At least he would not be holding her and threatening to tumble the walls that she held precariously around herself. "Nay, I will not allow you to accompany me to see my men train. You have no business going onto the training field. Do you understand me?"

Van snorted. "I understand you are going back on your word, my lord. You are the one who offered for me to see them. It was practically the first thing out of your mouth."

Peter crossed his arms stubbornly in front of him. "Vanessa, I am not going back on my word. I remember well the first time I met you and I also remember saying, perhaps I would take you. I have decided it is not a good idea that you see the men train with me now."

"Then when will I see the men train with you?" Van tilted her head to the side and gazed at him. Irritation swirled, but she held it at bay. The dirt clod had done well to remind her of her delicate position. She just hoped it would last.

"Never. You will not be allowed to go with me. I will not allow it. Now, tell me you understand." Peter glanced around them and shook his head. He looked back at her and scowled.

Van conceded that she could not win this argument, but smiled knowing that at least part of the battle would be her victory. "I understand that I will not be allowed to accompany you to see the men train." Careful wording and she could agree to almost anything. She smiled sweetly.

Suspicion rose within Peter as he watched the docile smile spread across her soft lips. He felt an urge to kiss her, but fought it. "Good, now go back inside and finish getting dressed. You spend so much time plastering yourself with that powder you do not remember to dress all the way." Peter felt excitement try to harden him every time the wind pushed the silky material against her. He was quite enjoying the view and thought perhaps he might like to see her like that in private later, but was angry to think that his men were thinking of her intimate curves.

"I will do no such thing. I am dressed. I will wear what I have on. If you think it is easy wearing such layers of fluff around your legs and walking then you do it." Her voice faltered as a laugh was heard from somewhere around them. It was quickly smothered and she continued, unabashed. "The time that you make it through a day with them on is the day that I will wear them."

Did she have no sense at all? He thought one moment that he was getting through to her and then the next she acted like she was the one who was in charge. "I will not even dignify that with a response, but you will do as I say. Now go to your chambers and get dressed."

Amy stepped into his line of sight and approached with a nervous smile. "Milady let me assist you, please. I can take her to her chambers, milord."

Vanessa turned with a look on her face that said she was miles from the courtyard and no longer participating in their conversation. She scowled and walked away without a word.

Peter was dumbfounded as he watched her disappeared into the stables. Anger blurred his vision as he went after her. Amy, Devon, and Grant followed.

Before they had reached her they heard a livid shout, "What the Hell do you think you are doing? This is none of your concern." Recognizing his horse trainer's voice Peter rushed into the large building, his three followers close on his heels.

Peter's mind froze as he stepped through the stable doors and gazed in horror at the scene before him.

Corey Ponsworth stood with his legs apart and his arm pulled back, his bull whip arched behind him. Lady Vanessa walked confidently toward him, pulling her hand into the end of her sleeve, wrapping the material tightly around it.

Peter's heart flew to his throat and he could not breathe, could not demand a stop to this nightmare. Fear and anger overrode his senses. It took only a moment for him to catch his breath, but before he had his mouth open, Corey thrust the whip violently forward. The whip flew close to his wife's face and Peter thought his knees would give out.

Her covered hand flew up catching the whip and twisting it around her wrist. There was a gasp and a grunt issued forth as Corey's arm jerked forward, the whip ripping from his fingers.

Vanessa pulled the whip through her hand and grasped the tightly wound leather grip. She stalked toward him with murder in her every feature. Peter could clearly see her flailing his head horse master with his own whip.

Peter gained control of his traitorous limbs enough to rush forward, blocking her path. "Stop, what do you think you are doing?" He looked behind her at the magnificent horse that stood before him. He understood her anger. He felt that same anger at what must have been Corey using his whip on his prize stallion.

Lingering fear for his stubborn bride added to his anger, building it as he quickly scanned Jackal's hide for signs of whip damage. Satisfied the horse was not injured Peter turned on Corey. "You will leave my lands at once. I cannot tolerate a whip taken to my prize horse, but it would only cause your dismissal. Taking the same whip to my wife, or any other woman, will get your head separated from your shoulders."

The color in Corey's face drained till he looked whiter than Vanessa and all her powder. "Milord?" His voice was a bare whisper.

Peter ignored the shock and fear in the man's voice and continued. "You will take this opportunity to leave, because it is a short one. You are only getting it because you did not manage to hit her."

Corey began to stutter his defense. "But, m–milord, s–she interfered with—"

"I do not care what it is that she did. No one deserves to be treated like that, with the exception of you." Peter turned back toward Vanessa, expecting her to be gloating over her victory. He had seen women do it all his life. Every mistress he had had and most of his female acquaintances had all been the same. Well, he would let her know it was not her victory, he would...

Vanessa was not gloating. She was not even there. Peter ran his gaze along the dim interior and found her running her hand along Jackal's flank. She gently pushed him out of the way and stepped behind him.

Peter realized she was not checking him for wounds and, curious, he walked toward her. He listened to her annoying voice and was thoroughly convinced now that it was a fake. "It's all right. Nothing else is going to happen to you. There is nothing for you to fear anymore. I am here."

Jackal snorted and pawed at the ground as Peter approached. "Easy boy," he said gently.

Van crouched behind the quivering animal's dangerous hind legs. Lady Vanessa, for a woman of large stature, still looked small behind the thick swishing tail of the massive destrier. Peter tried to pull Jackal from the stall, only causing him to rear.

Terrified his steed would hurt the woman who seemed ignorant of the danger she was in, he let the horse go. To his relief, Jackal calmed. With the horse quieted he could hear the woman speaking once again.

He took a step forward and glanced around Jackal's wide backside. His bride held a steady hand out to a bleeding Joseph Pittman who crouched terrified in the corner of the stable. Peter bellowed out a command to detain Corey Ponsworth. Jackal lunged forward, the boy screamed, and Lady Vanessa remained crouched calmly.

"Easy, boy. Did not mean to be so loud. Come, calm down now."

The stallion's breathing slowed and, in the hands of the man he loved and trusted, Jackal calmed once more.

"Vanessa, when I get you out of there I am going to thrash you until you cannot sit straight." Peter tried to sound angry, but worry shook his voice.

"Do not listen to him. He is full of talk, but that is all. Your name is Joseph, correct?"

His forehead furrowed but he didn't answer. Joseph gave a wide-eyed look to the lord of the castle and shrank farther back into the corner. Peter felt like an ogre and sighed.

"Come now. Look at me, not at him, all right. He is actually a very nice man. He would do nothing to hurt me...or you. I will make sure no one bothers you. Come now. You can trust me." Van pushed her hand closer to the trembling child. She extended her other hand and opened her arms invitingly.

"Are you sure? You will help me? The dark lady will take care of me and protect me?" Joseph's small voice trembled, but hope seemed to light his eyes.

Peter stepped around Jackal, laying a supporting hand on Vanessa's shoulder, and placed himself in between her and the horse's lethal hooves.

Joseph lay curled, nearly in the fetal position, blood pooling from two long whip marks across his arm and side. Vanessa had not gone to save a horse, although he was sure she would. Somehow she had heard Joseph cry out. "Joseph, come now. The dark lady will take care of you. You can trust her. We are not safe here behind an aggravated horse."

Vanessa looked up surprised. It seemed as if she hadn't even considered the danger.

Joseph rose and slowly came forward until he stood within the comfort of Vanessa's outstretched arms. She remained as she was until he carefully wrapped his thin arms around her neck, then she closed her arms around him and stood.

She smiled sweetly at Peter, all the grief and squabbling forgotten. She allowed him to lead her out of the stable without argument. Joseph cried softly against her shoulder as they made their way to the castle. Peter's heart swelled with pride and warmth as he listened to her coo nonsensical sounds to the boy to calm him. Peter wrapped his arm around her shoulders and pulled her close as he walked beside her.

In the massive kitchen, he took charge. Vanessa allowed it without question, which surprised him, and pleased him.

Vanessa sat on one of the kitchen benches, resting Joseph on her legs. Peter offered a dagger to Vanessa who took it with a thankful smile. As Peter commanded the servants to get hot water and clean linens she carefully began to cut away the dirty shirt. Joseph began to cry and fight and Peter turned quickly back to them.

"Am I hurting you?" Vanessa's gaze darted between Peter and the boy. Concern wrapped like a mist around Peter.

Joseph shook his head. "No." His voice hiccupped with tears. "You are cutting my only shirt."

Vanessa and Peter's eyes met. The shock and sadness that he saw in the dark depths of her eyes tore at his soul. Peter walked forward, kneeling before them, enveloping the boy's small knee with his massive hand.

"You have only one shirt?" He looked up at Vanessa and shook his head. "My father passed on, not long ago and I have not had a chance to see to everything that needs taken care of around here. My men needed me on the field."

She smiled, running her hand up his cheek. It rasped across a day's worth of beard that he had not yet shaven off. He liked to keep it off in the heat of the summer, while in winter he would allow it to grow for the warmth of it.

Vanessa's eyes sparkled gently. "Then it is good that I am here now."

Peter took a deep breath and turned back to the boy. "Where have you been staying since the fire?"

"In the stables. Your papa allowed me to stay in the castle. Then he got sick. Magdala said I had to go. Servants let me eat, but then have to hurry and go. Most nice to me, but some just say I in way." His tears had stopped, but the red rimmed eyes still looked concerned.

Peter turned to Vanessa who was looking at him curiously. "Magdala was my father's mistress after my mother...left." He took a deep breath. She opened her mouth and he was afraid she was going to ask about his mother. He quickly turned back to Joseph and smiled. "Magdala is no longer here. You will have new clothes and you will no longer stay in the stables." He tried to think of what to do with the boy when it was settled by his new bride.

"Amy will take care of you. She made the clothes that I wear. She can make some for you as well. You will stay in the nursery for now, until you feel comfortable enough for your own room. Would you like that?"

"To stay in the castle? Oh aye, very much." He turned pleading eyes to Peter. "Is that all right if I stay, milord?"

"Of course it is. You are more than welcome to stay in the castle. I am sure if my father had known what his mistress had done he would have put a stop to it." He knew he would have. His father may not have had a great opinion of women but he was always good to children.

Van continued to cut away at the shirt then allowed Peter to wash the wounds and place a soothing salve on them. Once the boy was doctored, Peter gently placed him on his feet. Peter arose, pulling Van with him, immediately wrapping his arm around her narrow waist, drawing her close. Resting a comforting hand on the lad's shoulder, he smiled at the small woman that approached. Amy was really quite a contrast to the man following protectively behind her.

Devon was at least a foot taller than the small blue-eyed, blonde girl. She looked almost like a child standing in front of the massive red headed warrior. Well, she would, if not for the well-endowed bosom that pushed at her plain servant's shirt.

Joseph looked up questioningly at Vanessa. "It's all right," she said gently and caressed his head. "You can go with her. I trust Amy with my life. I am entrusting her to take care of you as well, but if you need me or just want to see me you can find me. I will see you in a couple of hours to make sure you like the nursery and the clothes Amy will make for you."

Joseph leaned in close, standing on his toes to get even closer. Van leaned over, placing her face aside his. "What about the big man?" He whispered.

"That is Devon. I trust him as well. He is important to Amy, just don't tell anyone yet, all right. It has to be our little secret." Her voice was a conspiratorial whisper that carried well throughout the kitchen.

Peter grinned as Joseph smiled widely with the knowledge that he knew something special, something no one else knew. He was too young to realize that all who looked at the two young people could see the beginnings of something sparking between them.

Vanessa rose and stood beside her husband, his arm never leaving the comfort of her back. They watched Amy take Joseph by the hand. Devon followed them to the staircase where he shook hands with the boy and made his way to the training field.

"I am going to see to Ponsworth. I need to find out exactly what happened before I make a final decision on what is to be done." Peter was taken aback by his own comments. He had surprised himself, never thinking he would explain himself to a woman. His actions were his and no one else counseled what he did.

Vanessa shook her head and grunted. "What difference does it make? He has to be punished for what he did. It is unacceptable to strike a helpless child with such force and malice."

"I have to question him. I have to know all the circumstances. What would you have me do, flog him with his own whip without an inquiry?" Peter shook his head with a laugh. "Aye, that you would, wouldn't you? I have never met anyone so impetuous. Do it now and damn it all, is that it?" Peter thought he had known someone like that, but who he could not say. Someone he had known a long time ago.

"Fine. If you are to question him, then at the very least you can allow me to accompany you, to make sure it is done correctly." She started walking, as if he had already agreed.

"Nay, you will stay here. Go into the castle and wait for me to get back. I will tell you what happens. Do not worry. I will take care of things, I promise." He pulled her close, kissed her deeply and reveled in the response that was drawn from her, before walking away.

Van had not taken more than one step to follow him when a restraining hand pulled her to a stop. "Now is not the time, Amy." Van said as she spun around. Her eyes widened in surprise, and joy.

Richard shook his head. "I am not Amy, but aye, now is not the time. Husbands do not like to be challenged by their wives." She opened her mouth to object, but Richard just waved her words away. "Nay, listen to me. It is not wise for a woman to push her husband too far. You would be wiser to sit back and allow him to think you meek and controllable."

"Meek and controlled. That ought to throw him off." She smiled dev-ilishly. It might be just worth the effort to see the look on his face.

"I think it would be best if we go watch the men train now. It would be best if we awaited your husband there." He gestured in the direction that Devon had disappeared.

"Watch the men?" Van looked questioningly at the wide chested man she had grown to love over the years. She decided he had obviously missed the beginning of the argument.

"Yes, James Rothman, the stable boy?" Van just looked at him, nod-ding her head; she knew who he was referring to. He was a very quiet young man of perhaps thirteen. She had told him James that morning that she was to accompany Peter to see the men.

"He came to me this morning to inform me of your intentions. It would be better if we just met Lord Grayweist at the field."

Van knew it was not safe to spend time with Richard or any of the men, but she needed the comfort. She desperately wanted her old life back, but knowing that would never happen, she wanted the next best thing: to be close to those she cared about, even though they would not know who she truly was.

Richard smiled, but stared at her intently. "He will not be happy if you barge in on his questioning of that man."

Happy? Happy indeed. Richard had no idea how unhappy he would be to see her on the field. He may prefer to have her burst in on him now. "Aye, right you be. It would be best to meet him there." Her anger evaporated in the warming sun and she grinned deviously.

Richard's green eyes narrowed suspiciously. She just grinned wider.

CHAPTER 11

Peter relentlessly pushed his domestic problems to the back of his mind as he stepped into the guard house at the front gate. He registered the dull click of the latch behind him, but did not turn as Grant pulled the door closed.

Corey lurched to his feet. "I demand to be let loose. I have been with your father for years and I have taken enough—"

"Sit down." Peter rammed a hand into Corey's chest, shoving him back onto the bench. "I will tell you when you have taken enough."

Corey grunted loudly in protest but kept himself planted firmly in his seat.

Peter ignored the disgust he felt for his horseman and forced himself to begin his questioning. "Tell me what happened." He was in no mood to deal with this situation. Vanessa had him doubting his methods and it irritated him, mostly because he thought she might be right.

Corey shifted uncomfortably and looked up at the two big soldiers who stood stiffly to each side of him. "I was trying to get that damned horse of your wife's to calm down." He turned his focus back to Peter. "I was moving him to the bigger stall, as you instructed. He is a worthless beast and if you ask me—"

Peter raised his brows at the squirming man. "I did not ask."

"Aye, well. That devil of a creature is perfectly content to stand in the stall as if he is waiting for someone, yet if you go near him, he screams. I tried to open his gate. He bit me. I went for my whip and that insolent little child ran between me and that horse." Corey went to stand, looked into Peter's face, and sat quickly back down. He looked at the floor as he continued speaking. "I told him to get out of my way, milord, but that child is undisciplined. When I lightly touched him with my whip, he began to scream and upset all the horses."

It took everything Peter had in him not to knock that barbarian of a man from his seat and pound him until he was senseless. He clenched his fists so tight they began to tremble.

"He ran for Jackal's stall. I knew you would not want the boy to upset him, so I touched him again with my whip." Corey remained sitting, not looking at Peter. "I have done nothing wrong."

Peter shook with the effort of staying in control. "Touched?" His voice was soft like the calm eye of the storm while the hurricane raged, unchecked, throughout his body and emotions.

Corey looked up and his gaze darted between Peter and Grant.

Peter could see the fear on his face and that satisfied him. "Touched him with the whip?" Peter glanced back at Grant and held his hand out calmly. Grant gently slapped Corey's whip into his open palm.

"Touched," Peter repeated quietly. Without looking back at Corey he swung the whip. In the small room he was unable to get a snap out of it. Nonetheless, it took skin from the man's arm.

"Milord, please, no," Corey cried out as the whip once more connected with the flesh, blood began to well from the resulting welts.

"I am just touching you." Peter's anger mounted. "I should have you flailed for your insolent behavior. I do not have the time or the effort at this moment. You will leave these grounds. Now."

Peter swung the long leather whip back and forth, the tip of it ran across the floor and the tops of his boots. "Do not set your foot on my land. If you do, I will tell you, my sweet little bride may lose some of that iron control she has over her temper. I will not stop her or anyone from flaying you with a whip again. Do I make myself perfectly clear?"

Corey jumped to his feet in protest. "Where am I to go, milord? I have no one to turn to. I have a home here. I have been here all my life." The words began to blur together as they tumbled quickly from his pleading lips. "If it gets around that you let me go for this, I will be an outcast. No one will go against you." The tremble in his words increased until Peter could hardly understand him.

Peter looked at him without pity, shook his head, and walked out. He heard Grant giving orders to remove Corey from the grounds before following Peter out. Outside the small building two stable hands waited with their saddled mounts. The horses pawed impatiently at the ground and nickered lightly at the men as they approached. Peter did not believe he had ever been as eager to get away as he was today. He looked forward to a hard day of training to help clear his mind, or at least distract him from his eccentric wife.

"What are you thinking, my lord," Grant asked, once they were away from the castle.

"That I should have allowed her to whip him," Peter scowled at the reins and sighed. "What am I going to do with her? She acts more like one of the men than she does a docile wife. How is it possible that she could have been raised like that?" Peter considered asking about Vanessa's voice or if Grant thought she was hiding something, but decided against it. He wasn't sure he could deal with the answers.

"I know very little about her, my lord, but I can find out." Grant was a talent at uncovering secrets and Peter seriously considered it, before deciding it was too early.

He took a deep breath and shook his head. "Nay, I will talk to her. The trouble is, every time I get around her I want to strangle her. She is as undisciplined as a woman can get. I would like to take her over my knee and give her a good thrashing."

This brought on gales of laughter from his riding companion. "Aye, my lord, I can see you now, trying to take that giant of a creature over your knee. You may get her there, but I bet she is not there long enough for a thrashing."

Peter glared at his friend, but couldn't help the grin that tugged at his lips. "Very amusing, I do not recall asking for your opinion. I can tell you one thing. I will have her tamed before you can laugh at me aga—"

Peter stopped, dumbfounded, on the rise. He stared down at his wife, surrounded by a circle of his men. Terror raced through his veins chilling his blood as weapons flew around her and anger warmed his face. Angry that she stood so calmly as swords fell around her. Angry that he could still see the soft silhouette of her body beneath a dress without the proper under garments. Did she have to disregard everything he said?

She reached for the daggers that Gary had just been juggling. Peter sucked in an infuriated gasp and his patience snapped.

He kicked Jackal into a gallop and raced toward them. Gary saw him, his eyes widening and the color draining from his face. One of the daggers slipped from his now limp fingers and fell to the ground at Vanessa's feet. Vanessa looked at him, turned to the men, spoke, and looked back, patiently waiting.

As Peter had entered the guard house and Vanessa had started toward the lists, Richard had a sinking feeling deep in his gut. He had overstepped his bounds when he had approached her and now he worried of the consequences.

The silence between them was uncomfortable as they walked side by side. Lady Vanessa looked at him several times before she finally opened her mouth to speak. "Are you doing all right back here with Lord Grayweist?"

He ran his gaze across her face and tried to place her. He knew her. He recognized the resemblance to her father, but he didn't believe that was all there was to it. "You know I was with him before?" It had been three years since he was under Lord Grayweist and few people outside the armies knew he had been.

"Aye." She didn't look at him when she spoke.

"Aye, I suppose that sort of thing gets around?" He fished for a better answer, but had a feeling he would not get it.

"Aye, I suppose it does."

Richard looked at her out of the corner of his eye as they walked. She walked stiffly, and kept her eyes straight ahead. The answer she gave told him she knew more than she was saying.

"I am doing fine here...my lady," he added as an afterthought, realizing he was being very informal with the lady of the castle. "My lady, I apologize for speaking to you the way I have. I hope you will accept my apo—"

She waved her hand, turning to look at him. "Nay. You may speak to me the way you wish. Consider me a good friend." She smiled and returned her gaze forward. "I have heard that Peter is no longer in the war with Eolian."

Richard stopped and stared at her. "You know of Eolian?" His suspicions peaked. Not many people knew of him, at least not by name. "Where did you hear his name? It is strange you should know of him, except perhaps by the Knight of Fear. I have known no woman who does." She stopped, but refused to meet his eyes. "If Peter is no longer involved in the King's armies, then why all the training?"

He smiled. "If you are not going to answer my questions, then I am not going to answer any more of yours, my friend. Unless you want to change your mind on how I can speak to you, my lady?"

"Nay, my friend." She took a deep breath and began to walk again, looking around nervously. He followed along beside her. "I have heard the name. I am sure many women have. Just because they do not tell you, does not mean they do not know."

He eyed her carefully. "Aye, I suppose. I am not sure of your answer, but I'll let it pass for now."

"Thank you, Devenroe. Now, as to the training?" she asked.

"This has always been a training facility for pages and squires, now we are going to become a full time institution. Lord Grayweist has spoken to folk from all over who will send their sons to us to train. The king will also be sending us several new men."

"What of the men? Some will surely want to leave, return to the wars?" Their gait drew them close, walking as old friends, the awkward silence now gone.

"Aye, some have already requested to go. We have only a few weeks with the king's new men before he sends for their return. They are young, without any training and he has given Lord Grayweist only a small amount of time to turn them into warriors."

Vanessa shook her head. She listened closely and seemed genuinely interested, darting glances at him while he spoke. "That is terrible. He must know it takes more time than that." Her voice broke as she spoke.

He glanced at her quickly. She smiled nervously and looked away. Suspicion grew like a vine, winding through his thoughts.

"That is why it is so important to begin this institution. It is the first of its kind around. Training needs to begin as soon as possible." Richard walked along comfortably beside her, forgetting himself for a moment, forgetting who it was that walked with him.

Vanessa grumbled and shook her head. "Warriors with page training are more dedicated, more meticulous about their work and their loyalties. Young boys pulled from behind the plows are a danger to them-selves as much as they are to the others in the group."

Richard looked closely at her as she spoke. Most women would not even consider such a thing, but he was sure it was not unheard of.

"Aye, that they are. When the King comes for his men, some of the younger men, have received permission to go. The ones who have been with Lawston for years, and the men with me, have decided to stay. We will be here to teach and to protect the tenants." He thought it just as well. Only a certain amount of men were necessary here and more men were needed in the wars.

Cresting a small knoll the men came into view. He watched Lady Vanessa, looking for signs of fear, but expecting none. None came.

Vanessa looked across the sea of bodies that began to gather. "I can fully imagine the tenants are relieved to have the warriors here all the time."

Richard noted her eyes come to rest on several of the men as she scanned the individual groups. He would almost swear it was his men she looked upon. Just a coincidence, he was sure—Maybe.

He had almost convinced himself of that when her gaze stopped on a massive group, all his men. She looked over each one, seeming to count each man before moving on. He was mostly sure her eyes landed on only his men, but he was also half sure he was mistaken. All doubt was re-moved when a look of concern crossed her face and she began to scan the crowd once again.

He shifted his feet as he watched her. He had noticed four of his men were missing and was sure she had as well. Although how that was pos-sible he did not know.

Van glanced at him, worry tickling at her mind, but could think of no way to ask about the missing men. She had been so occupied at the meal the night before she had not kept a good count on her men.

Now she wanted to know if they had come here, if something had happened to them. Had some been more injured than she had previously believed? Anxiety wormed its way to the base of her thoughts and began to eat at her.

One of her missing men topped a rise on the far side of the lists. Her heart fluttered as the other three followed a moment behind him. Relief hit her hard before she could think to hide it. She glanced quickly at Richard, but he didn't say anything, just raised an eyebrow.

Van resumed walking toward the men when Richard stepped in front of her. "You cannot go down there until Lord Grayweist arrives," Rich-ard said, his voice rose in the familiar way that told her he was anxious.

She knew very well the power she had over the castle and all the in-habitants. She grinned crookedly at him. "Are you going to be the one to stop me?"

"Nay, I would like to tell you though. Lady Vanessa, Lord Grayweist is not going to be pleased if I allow you to get close to the men. Even someone of your status can be in danger from warriors." His eyes darted behind him and then he scowled at her.

"I will take my chances with the men, and as to Peter, well." She took a deep breath and smiled apologetically. "I will apologize now, for he is not going to be pleased that you have allowed me this far."

His jaw dropped. She turned and walked directly into the center of the men, smiling at the shocked expressions that stared back at her. "Good morrow, men. I thought I would formally introduce myself."

"My lady, we know who you are. You are the Lady Grayweist, Lady Vanessa Lawston," Devon said from the ranks of the men. He pushed his way to the front of the group.

It was her turn to feel shock. She had not considered who she now was. It was like she was an entirely different person. Lady Lawston, her breath came heavy as if by a physical blow. She had lost another part of who she no longer was.

Devon was not detoured by the sudden change in her. His smile grew and his voice rose. "Mostly we know you are the protector of the small, friend to the animals, mainly us, and above all you are the Dark Lady." Behind him cheers went up.

Before she could speak one young man that she didn't recognize shyly asked, "Did you really grab that whip? That would have been impressive to see."

She grinned at the youth. "And you are?"

"Sorry, my lady. I am Francis Devlin. The story has spread all over as to how you saved that little boy, without thinking of the danger to yourself." He stood proudly before her as he spoke and Van shook her head. Her smile widened, though she did not believe she had done anything special.

"Well, Francis Devlin. What can you show me that's impressive?" She enjoyed the glow brought onto his face. His smooth features would soon be ravaged with the grief of war, but for now he still had a child-like quality that touched her ragged heart.

"I can do this and I am the best at it." No sooner were the words out of his mouth than he had pulled his broadsword from the scabbard, balancing the worn hilt on his open palm, the sun glinting off the upraised blade.

He tossed the sword into the air and then the plan went awry as Robert Dauphin, one of the younger of Van's men, hit his shoulder and laughed. "You are not the best. I am—" Robert's laughter died as the sword hilt bounced from Francis's awaiting hand, and the blade stuck into the ground between Van's feet.

"Oh, my lady." Robert and Francis both stuttered, stepping back. The color drained from their faces. The men standing around waited with wide eyes to see her reaction.

Van looked down at the quivering blade and just smiled. "That was impressive. Imagine, throwing a sword like that, even with someone hitting you, and still landing it safely between my delicate feet. Amazing. Can you do it again?"

"Nay!" Francis took a deep breath, mortified. "I mean, nay, my lady."

"Too bad. Can you do something better then? Like catching it perhaps?" she asked with a laugh. All the men seemed to relax.

"Aye, my lady."

He leapt forward and grabbed up the sword, ripping it from the ground. Dirt and grass flew onto her black skirt. Van waved him off when he started to make more apologies. She smiled widely, enjoying herself for the first time in weeks. He beamed as his sword was once more balanced precariously on his open palm.

"If you are going to hit him, Dauphin, do it now where he can stab his own feet, or yours, not mine." This brought teasing, yells and laughter from the men.

Not shaken by the sudden noise, or the harrying by Van, he tossed the sword. It came down hilt first, wobbled, and almost fell. Manipulating his arms and legs in an awkward dance, he got it under control, tossing it once more. The second catch was smoother. The sword wavered only slightly on his calloused palm.

"That was impressive." Van was fascinated. Never had she seen such a trick before. She considered asking for his sword. She was sure she could get the mastery of it. "Why do you do that?"

"Lord Grayweist says that if you are one with your weapons you have the advantage. It is one of his training tools and Francis here is not the best, I am."

This came from another of Van's men. He was a tall blond-haired man, his skin fair, reddened by the sun. She had always felt sympathy for Jonathan. He was not a man who tanned, only burned and peeled.

"How can you be the best? You have only been practicing for a couple of days," Francis cried.

Jonathan had been new to Van's men only the year before. Her heart reached out to them. She hated lying to them, but she was thankful to still be in their lives.

"So, you are the best as well. Let us see what you have learned in just four days, Jonathan." She gasped gently at her mistake and sucked in a breath, but in the excitement no one wondered how she knew his name.

His attempt was comical, but he did manage to get it balanced and even got one catch out of his five attempts. This brought on gales of laughter, screams, and jests from the others. It also brought on a competition, first one claiming to be the best and beginning to show off for Lady Vanessa, and then another would join.

Loud laughter sounded from behind several men, followed by a snide voice. "All these new men are weak and useless." A short barrel-chested man with shaggy black hair stepped between the men. "They could not manage to be one with their weapon if it was run through them."

Anger flooded Van's senses and shook her entire being. "And you are?" She fought to keep her voice calm and level.

He dropped a jerky, insincere bow and smiled. "Ryan Deumount."

A tight shiver raced up her spine at the smile. It stopped well before it reached his eyes. It twitched lightly at the corners, but he showed no amusement.

"Do you always speak so rudely, Deumount?" Her voice was low and she could barely maintain the falsetto she had been portraying.

"Only honestly. I speak what I see—"

"Your vision is bad then, because these men are some of the best at what they do." Van forced herself to stop speaking before she went any farther and said something she would regret.

Ryan only laughed. He walked away with two men following him. She recognized Christopher Dalton who had yelled for the bedding, but the other man she did not.

Richard stepped close to her side and whispered gently "I do not trust that man nor do I trust his little puppies. That is Christopher Dalton and Gregory Penchiot and he leads them around by the nose."

She nodded and turned her attention back to the men. The laughter had died from them and they shifted uncertainly.

Van turned her head as one of the boys she had attended page training with stepped forward. Gary Puelo was his name, she believed. He had been older than she by a couple of years and had not been one of the boys that tormented her. He had kept mostly to himself, and if she remembered correctly, they had never had occasion to speak.

He spoke to her in a slow gentle voice. "My lady, I cannot safely show you the sword toss, but I can show you something." Taking up three daggers, borrowed from the men around him, he began to smoothly juggle. The men began to laugh and talk once more, Ryan and his snide remarks forgotten.

"Oh, now that I know I can manage. Let me try..." Her voice trailed off as Gary stared into the distance behind her, dropping a dagger he was handing her.

Van turned to see Peter thundering toward her with rage coloring his every nuance and feature. Taking a deep breath, she smiled at the men and was surprised to see the concern in their eyes. "Everything is all right." She turned to Richard. "Meek and controlled? We shall see."

♛ ♛ ♛

Jackal slid to a stop in front of her. Peter remained seated, feeling more in control looking down at her. "What in the name of God's eyes are you doing here?"

Looking down at the toes of her slippers, she said quietly, "I cry your pardon, my lord, I was just watching the men."

He was thrown off by the sudden change in her. She was not attacking him or telling him what and how she was going to do things. Suspicion exploded within him. She was up to something. "What did I tell you, my lady?" He fought to keep his voice calm.

"My lord, you have told me so much since I have arrived. If you were to be more specific, I could give you a more accurate answer."

Her voice was still grating on his nerves, but now it was a sing song tone that at least portrayed her as docile.

He growled darkly. "I told you something of seeing the men train, did I not?"

"Aye, when I first arrived, you said I could come with you to see the men train."

He glanced at Richard, who rolled his eyes and shook his head.

"Later than that." Anger seeped from his pores. He scowled at the ring of men and they all fell back a step.

"You told me, I would not be allowed to accompany you to see the men, my lord." Her eyes stayed downcast, her voice tilting and malleable.

"So you deliberately disobeyed me?" He wanted more than anything to throttle her right here in front of his men. Strangle her until she was unconscious and could no longer make him feel this confusing swirl of anger, desire and jealousy.

"Nay, my lord. I did as you commanded." He raised his brow and opened his mouth to speak. She shook her head, never looking up from her submissive position as she continued. "You said I was not allowed to accompany you and I did not. I accompanied Richard."

Peter's gaze jumped from the top of her head to Richard's shocked face. He caught his gaze and expected him to dispute the claim, but Richard held his tongue.

"So, it is Richard to you, now?" His stomach cramped and knotted at the thought of them spending time together. They seemed to be standing too close when he had arrived. He pushed the petty jealousy from his mind the best he could and turned his attention back to his conniving wife. "So, not only do you disobey me you try to involve my men."

Vanessa's eyes flew to his face, a challenge burning deep within them. Her control had been lost and Peter wondered what had caused it. "You cannot blame *my* men. They are to do as *I* command them."

Peter leapt from his horse and stopped so close to her the sweet aroma of face powder caressed him, he ignored it. "Your men? Just how in the bloody blazes do you figure they are *your* men?" He gestured widely, encompassing all that watched. He yelled directly in her face and to his dismay she didn't back down. She stood toe to toe with him once again. "Do you think all these men yours?"

"Nay, but at least half of them are my men." Vanessa's face registered shock. She pulled away from him and glanced at Richard before dropping her head.

"Half, which half, pray tell would that be?" He thought of her quick glance at Richard and added, "I understand you consider Richard one of them, I want to know the rest." He glared at Richard. Richard dropped his eyes and Peter turned his attention back to his wife.

He watched her chest rise and fall with several deep breaths. The smooth silk of her dress pulled tight across her breasts, distracting him. When she finally spoke her voice waivered slightly, pulling his attention from her luscious diversions.

"That is not exactly what I meant my lord. I simply meant to say—" A nervous deep breath. "—that as the lady of this castle, it is my right to claim half of what is in it." As the words came out, she picked up speed. "A marriage is like a partnership. If you went into a partnership with my father for horses, to share the land and the responsibility you would have half. That is the way it should be."

"Half, my dear, you are right." He grabbed her by the arms dragging her close. Her flesh was warm beneath his tight grasp. "As a partner with your father, I would be responsible for half. As a husband, I am responsible for not only all of *my* men, but for you as well." His voice rose to a bark that tore through his throat like a fire. He had let his anger get the better of him once again.

Damn it, he thought, and released her so quickly she almost fell. "I do not have time for this. You will return to the castle and you are not allowed to come with Richard again to this field. Do you understand me?"

"Aye, my lord." She glared at him defiantly and spat out the words. Then she turned and began to walk away.

"Stop." His voice sounded tired and weary and he desperately hoped that the others could not sense it. Peter cringed at the intent looks of the men watching as she turned back to him. "Just so I do not have to do this every day, I will make myself clear now. You are not allowed to come to this field with anyone. That includes me, Richard and any of...the men or the servants. Now, do I make myself clear?"

She did not answer him, just stared, an arrogant black brow raised in challenge.

"Do you understand me?" No answer. "Tell me you understand."

"I understand." With that she began once again to walk away.

Peter watched her smooth form sway beneath the dress and realized it was not see-through. He could see nothing of her body and it was made of thick enough material that she was decent. The only difference was the dress alone did not hide the roundness of her curves.

He groaned in frustration and desire. Letting out a soft oath, he yelled for her to stop. She did, but did not look back. "Grant, take the men and get them started, I am going to take my *wife* back." Remounting Jackal, he walked the horse toward her.

He held out an outstretched hand. Vanessa turned, but only glowered at it. He let out a dramatic groan that left several of the men chuckling. He cocked his head slightly at Richard and then at Grant. Understanding his silent command, both men walked around behind Vanessa.

She eyed them suspiciously.

Peter shot his hand down and grasped her arm. He began hauling her up onto his lap. She kicked and fought and Peter nearly lost his grip. Richard and Grant each grasped a leg and boosted her onto the horse. Vanessa renewed her struggle, but they had her in a sitting position before she could slide back to the ground. Peter wrapped his arms tightly around her waist. "Vanessa, stop. You will throw us both off if you continue."

"You change spots with me then. I will sit back there and you can sit on my lap." Laughter erupted behind them, but Peter didn't even bother to turn around. "If you would just allow me to ride like a person, it would not be so bad. I would not wiggle."

Vanessa once more began to fight him. They both almost went off the side as she kicked her legs. Jackal snorted and sidestepped beneath them. He swung his head around and whinnied at them.

Peter told him to shut up, grasped his aggravating wife's thigh, and pulled it over the horse so that she sat straddling the prancing animal. "You want to ride like a man, here." He wrapped his arm tightly around her waist and yanked her back against him. The hard evidence of his lust pressed into her back. "Although I quite enjoyed you rubbing against me as you fought," he whispered into her ear.

She stiffened. He smiled.

He spoke calming words of support to Jackal until the big horse was once more relaxed. He kicked him gently in the sides and guided him away from the snickering men. They would pay when he returned. He would work them extra hard this afternoon, he thought with a grin as they fell out of sight.

He pulled her deeper into his embrace and rocked his hips. Pressing his hard shaft against her bottom, he reveled in the sensations as she rocked against him. He groaned, but ignored it. Her heady scent swarmed his nose and invaded his brain like the swooping troops of an army. This time he didn't fight it.

Vanessa groaned in response and pressed harder against him. With one arm still holding tightly onto her waist, he ran his other hand up the bodice of her dress. He gently cupped her breast, running his thumb across her nipple until it budded enticingly beneath the silk. He had an urge to feel it between his teeth. He smiled as her head fell back against his shoulder.

He turned Jackal toward a thick line of trees as he ran his tongue across her neck. She moaned softly and pushed her throat into his lips. He ran kisses along her neck from her shoulder to her ear, closing his teeth around her earlobe and sucking gently before returning to her shoulder. He made his way back to her ear, stopping every so often to bite gently. Every time his teeth pressed into her flesh she shivered and his body jumped in response as if the shudder had run through him.

Once they were hidden in the shadowed confines of the forest, his hand left her waist. He curled his fingers around the soft material of her skirts and slid them up baring her left thigh.

Vanessa gasped and turned toward him, trying to re-cover herself. She opened her mouth to protest, but he quickly dipped his tongue between her warm, waiting lips. Need exploded through his loins, pushing his control and his sanity to the edge. His mouth caressed hers and he gently sucked her full bottom lip.

She was rigid in his arms at first, but soon began to relax. He pressed the kiss deeper running his tongue along hers, encouraging her to respond. She released her skirts in surrender and turned deeper into his embrace.

Peter knew he was standing on the rim of a dark chasm. Passion and desire called to him from the black swirling depths. He closed his eyes, took a step, and allowed himself to fall.

He ran his tongue along her trembling lips and placed kisses across her cheek, her ears, and her neck. She tasted of warm moist heaven. Her scent, her movement, the soft way her skin slid beneath his fingers and lips, all tore at him, urging him to pull her from the horse and take her.

Her body began to quiver, and her hot breath kissed his cheek as she moaned against him. Her head fell back. He kissed the tender hollow at the base of her neck.

He ran his left hand along her bared thigh as his lips found hers. He cupped her bouncing breast with his right as he guided Jackal along with his legs. Following the rhythmic stride of the horse, he trailed his fingers beneath the bunched up skirt until it came to the soft damp folds of her womanhood. He groaned in ecstasy. She felt like satin.

Her hand flew to his wrist, her tongue stilled, and she began to pull away. He hit the small nodule within her folds. She froze. He pushed harder against it. Her grip tightened on his arm and she leaned back into his kiss.

Peter needed to last just a bit longer, and on the horse was the best place to do it. To keep him from throwing her to the ground, he had kept the horse moving, plus he enjoyed the rocking of the horse as it pressed her tightly against him.

Vanessa kissed him hard and rocked her hips gently forward into his roving fingers. He massaged her breast gently, carefully, but when she pressed herself into his hand he asserted more pressure.

He pinched her hardened nipple and pulled firmly on it. She cried out and bit gently on his lips. Pain flowed through his hardened shaft and pressure screamed to be released.

Her hand tightened almost painfully on his wrist, pulling his thoughts from his own need. He slid his fingers across her folds, caressed the entrance that he most wanted to explore, and forced himself back to the magic nodule. Her breath stopped momentarily as he began to gently manipulate her, moving his fingers slowly at first, increasing speed with her breathing.

"I cannot allow this—" Her breathing came in hot, hard pants and her words were soft and frightened, but she made no move to stop him. His fingers slowed.

"Do you like to kiss me?" He hadn't realized his breath was as ragged as hers until he heard the words tearing from his raw throat.

"Aye."

His heart jumped at her breathy answer. "Then kiss me. Kiss me and think of nothing else. You have no idea how badly I need you now. How much I want you, desire you. You are so beautiful. Kiss me." He waited for her to lean forward, to open her mouth to him. His fingers resumed their frantic pace as she came closer and closer. He pressed his fingers into her breast and she arched toward his hand. He tightened his grip.

Her body tightened suddenly and she cried out, digging her fingers into his wrist as she came to pleasure. Her warmth coated his fingers as he plunged two fingers into her. He pressed deep, rocking his fingers within her, urging her onto more pleasure. It did not take much to bring her forth once more. Clinging desperately to him, she smiled weakly.

He urgently brought Jackal to a stop on a grassy hill, beneath a large oak tree.

"If that is how you feel when you are above me, I understand why it is you lose control so easily," she said breathlessly.

Without a word, he swung himself to the ground and pulled her from the horse. Feeling good about finally holding his control long enough to bring her to pleasure, he pushed her into the tall grass. "I am not through yet. I am hoping my control will last just a little longer. Then we will see who loses control."

Van ignored the challenge, managed to pull the sheath free from her thigh, and hide the dagger within the folds of her dress as Peter kissed her deeply. Her breath came in hard painful gasps but her body purred with the afterglow of pleasure.

He pulled off her suddenly. To her surprise she reached for him without conscious thought to do so. He smiled, yanked her up against him, and began to remove the laces of her dress.

She held her unease at bay and allowed him to pull the dress over her head. Keeping hold of the dagger, she hoped it appeared as if she were just assisting him.

He smiled and she relaxed the best she could. She placed the dress beside her as he laid her back and resumed his caresses. He took time to lather each breast with kisses, sucking the nipples into his mouth and biting them gently before working down her tight, muscular stomach. Her body quivered and shook each time his lips scorched across her skin. She didn't understand what had happened within her on the horse but she wanted it to happen again.

When he didn't stop at her stomach and placed a kiss between her open thighs she gasped. She sat up and put her hands down to cover herself. "Are you sure you should do that?"

"Trust me."

She had a moment's doubt, before allowing him to push her back down. Her breath caught and she held herself very still as his tongue gently opened her folds.

Her breath came in short gasps and she began to see the same swirling stars behind her closed eyes that she had on the horse. She rocked her hips into his face and wrapped her hands through his wind tangled hair.

He drove his tongue into her again and again, faster and harder causing her to cry out. He nibbled and sucked until her breaths were tight and she thought she could not stand anymore. He licked and nibbled until the trembling in the legs could not be controlled. Then he stopped. She moaned as he pulled away.

Peter smiled and removed his shirt, then started again. Once again he took her to the trembling edge of bliss and stopped. This time she growled and tried to hold his head as he sat back. He looked at her for a moment, as she wiggled impatiently, then removed his boots and hose. Then he dropped his head to her again.

His tongue and teeth teased her until her muscles ached and she wanted to cry. The pleasure started to build, throbbing within her and keeping time with the pounding of her racing heart. Her muscles tightened and then he was gone. Her eyes flew open.

He left her as the pressure became painful, wonderful, and she had thought she would soon have a release to this sweet torture. As he pulled away she grabbed his hair. "Wait." Her voice was barely heard.

He removed her shaking hand and smiled. "Trust me." He gently tweaked her hardened nipples, covered her with his body and kissed her deeply. He pulled his face from hers, looked down at her and asked, "Do you want me? Tell me to take you and I will bring you great pleasure."

Van just shook her head. She didn't know what she wanted, but she did know that his voice sounded just as tortured as she felt.

"Tell me, please. I cannot last much longer. I will not take you until you tell me I can, until you tell me you want me. I have already hurt you too much. Please." His voice sounded pained and his deep blue eyes were clouded and dark. "I promised myself I would not hurt you again. I will spill my seed on the ground between your sweet thighs, but I will not take you until you are ready." His voice cracked with strain and his body shook with effort. She looked up at his sweat glistened face and shook her head in confusion.

She didn't know how to ask for what she wanted because she didn't understand what she wanted. Her eyes stung with tears and her body ached with need. She shook violently and her hips rocked it seemed of their own accord.

Peter smiled ruefully and shook his head. Small patters of sweat dripped upon her upturned face. He put his hand between their bodies and gently rubbed the swollen button.

She cried out. She needed release. She needed…her head rocked back and forth and she pressed her hips hard into his hand. She trembled and panted, her hot breath tearing from her in painful gasps. Grasping his thick blond hair in fingers that didn't seem to be her own, she yanked him down to her face and kissed him, hard. Again and again she kissed him. She pulled her head back long enough to utter tortured words. "Take me. Now. I need you."

Grasping her hips, tilting them upwards, he plunged deep into her wet well, driving in hard and kissing her as he did. He pounded into her again and again, until they reached the peak together, both plunging into the abyss of ecstasy and pleasure as one. Matching screams echoed against the trees. Two sweating bodies clung to each other as the world around them, all too soon, came back into focus.

"You need to let go, love. I can't breathe."

Laughing she relaxed the grip around his neck, but didn't let go.

"Are you all right?" His eyes scanned her face.

She self-consciously thought of the powder. He smiled and she relaxed.

"I think so," she said. "I think I am better than all right. Although I am angry with you," she said, managing to keep a straight face.

Peter pulled off of her enough to see her face. "Angry?"

Pushing him off, she grabbed her dress careful not to let the dagger slip out. She smiled. "Yes, angry. If you knew how to do that, you should have done it yesterday."

"Very funny. You are lucky I do not have the strength right now to take you over my knee and give you the thrashing you deserve."

CHAPTER 12

B ack at the castle Van went to check on Joseph. She was sure that Amy had taken good care of him, but she needed to make certain. She laughed gently as Richard's long ago words came to memory. "You, my son, have control issues. Everything does not have to be your way."

Van walked through the halls with a smile that just didn't want to go away. Amy turned a corner not far from her and the young girl's face lit with obvious relief.

"Where have you been? I have been looking all over for you," Amy said frantically. "I was beginning to think you had ran away"

Van grinned. She had definitely considered it, but she wouldn't tell that to the nervous girl. "I was with my men. Watching them train." Van had to fight a laugh thinking that probably was worse than telling her she had thought of leaving.

"You were *what*, Lady Vanessa?" Amy's voice echoed through the empty hall.

Van's grin fell away and she scowled at her young caretaker. She hated that name. Amy either didn't notice the evil look or chose to ignore it. Van thought it was probably the latter.

Amy lowered her voice conspiratorially. "I cannot really help you if you insist on putting yourself in a position like that. You are the one who insisted on this act, with the makeup and the help from me." Amy shook her head and grabbed Van by the sleeve.

Van was impressed with the fortitude Amy showed. Guilt flowed through her as she thought of what she was putting the girl through.

Amy gave her arm a gentle shake. "If you really want this to work, it can only happen if you try. If you don't want it to work, then you are wasting your time with all the face powder and irritating everyone with that horrid voice for nothing."

Van knew Amy was right even though she didn't want to admit it. Self-doubt tried to assert itself within her mind, but Van shoved it away. "Amy—" She began, but Amy tugged on her sleeve harder and shook her head.

"You need to realize they are not your men anymore. They are your husband's."

Pain filled Van's heart for she knew this was true. Her life felt empty once again. Her good feelings from earlier were quickly dying.

Amy threw her hands in the air as if in surrender. "It is not going to get any easier if you continue fighting it."

Van's gaze took in the hall and she listened carefully for anyone who might be listening on the other side of the wall. She looked back at Amy sadly. "I know. I did not think it would be this hard. It was easy for me to pretend to be a man, to pretend to be the Dark Knight. That came easy to me. If I could pretend to be something I am not, how can it be so hard to just be who I am?"

Amy smiled. She touched Van gently on the heavily powdered face. "And do you know who you are?"

Van just looked at her. She didn't know. Her brow furrowed. She didn't have an answer and felt momentarily lost and confused.

A noise penetrated Van's concentration. She looked up. A young girl with long brown waves, that spilled unbound around her pretty face, walked around the corner already talking. "That is a silly question, if I have ever heard one. Everyone knows who they are." The girl was all of about fifteen and her beautiful brown eyes were set deep in a delicate face.

"May I ask who you are then?" Van smiled at her and thought that she was about as innocent a child as she had ever seen. Her eyes were that of a child, but that was well surpassed by the body of a grown woman. It made for a dangerous combination.

"I am Anna Puelo. I stay here in the castle, milady. I hoped to meet you yesterday, but I imagine you were tired." Anna talked with the open abandon of a child—a sheltered child.

"Aye, that I was. How is it that you came to be here in the castle? I assume you came with your brother. Gary Puelo is quite good with the daggers. He showed me his juggling trick."

The young girl's eyes grew wide and her words came rapidly. "He must really like you. He does not show many people that. I did come with him. He's been here a long time. I was seven and Momma and Papa..." Her eyes welled up, but she sniffled back the tears before they could completely form.

Van's brow furrowed and Amy laid a comforting hand on the girl's shoulder. "It is all right."

The young girl smiled sadly at Amy's soft voice. "They died," she said quietly as a tear slid down her cheek.

Van fought a jolt of worry. She felt drawn to this child. Caring for people was a weakness, and she knew if anyone found out she had a weakness they would use it against her. She shuddered as a chill swept across her now sweat-dampened skin.

Anna's voice continued louder and surer now, the grief pushed away at least for the time being. "Gary came here to be a warrior and I came to be with him." Anna's face brightened and the sadness faded to nothing as she was off onto another subject. "I heard you saved Joseph. Me and Joseph are friends."

Van couldn't help but smile in spite of herself as the girl's chipmunk chatter continued uninterrupted.

"I had come in to see him. Is that all right?" She looked unsure for only a moment, before Joseph came bounding around the corner in a freshly made shirt and pair of trousers.

"Anna."

His bright smile brought warmth to Van's heart. She had hoped he would not retain any ill effects from the treatment he had been given. And from the look on his freshly washed face, it didn't appear that he had. "Anna, you met the Dark Lady? She saved me."

He threw his arms around Van's legs and her heart stopped. All she could do was look down at Joseph in wonder. Her heart seemed to skip a beat and a pleased smile touched her lips.

Joseph pulled away after a moment and she looked down at him. He was a small boy, even for only being eight. He walked with a slight limp, but with his thick black hair and dark brown eyes, he made a handsome child.

"I have been asked to stay by the castle and away from the men training for today—"

Amy shook her head with a smile. "For today, milady?"

"—and as that is the case—" Van didn't even look at her insolent little maid, but could feel the corners of her lips twitch as she fought a smile. "I am in need of a couple of guides to show me around. I want to see some interesting places. Lord Grayweist showed me all the ordinary places. I would like to see something special."

Anna was the first one to speak. "I can show you. I have secret place." She bit her bottom lip and looked pleadingly up at Van.

Van smiled and nodded her head in encouragement.

Anna took a deep breath and nodded in return. "You cannot tell anyone. I go there to be alone. Gary does not like me to spend much time around people, but I hate to just stay in my chambers all day." She stared shyly at her feet. "You will not tell anyone will you?"

"Certainly not. I would never betray a friend." Van's heart lurched. The concern was stronger now. She was risking a lot by allowing herself to care for these children, but looking down at their anxious and excited faces she could not bring herself to push them away. She took a deep breath and smiled. "If you trust me, you can take me to your special place." Van grinned as Anna bounced up and down in excitement.

A half an hour later Van, Amy, Joseph, and Anna stood in a small, hidden glen. Wild flowers wove a carpet of vivid colors that was surrounded by a tall wall of hedges and bush. From the inside you could see nothing of the world and from the outside you could not see the small sanctuary unless you knew where to look. It was just large enough for the four of them.

They sat in comfortable silence for several minutes. Van turned to Anna. "Anna?" She kept her voice light.

Anna looked over to her with a smile. "Yes, my lady?"

"Would you mind telling me about what happened to your parents?" Van cringed as the beaming smile disappeared from Anna's face and her eyes clouded over. Curiosity about Anna and her brother Gary had pushed at the back of Van's mind since she had met the young girl, but she forced a smile and patted her on the arm. "If you don't want to tell me, you do not have to."

Anne shook her head, looked at the hands on her lap, and was silent. Van thought that meant that she did not want to talk about it, but the girl began to speak in a soft, trembling voice. "Our village was raided eight years ago. I was seven. Gary was fourteen."

Van turned her attention to the loudly chirping birds that flitted from branch to branch above them as she listened to Anna's sad voice. "He saved me from the Knight of Fear."

Van's head spun back to her fast enough to pop her neck with a loud crack. "Eolian," she hissed almost silently.

Anger slithered into her like worms through the dead and rotting corpses of all the men, women, and children Eolian, the Knight of Fear, had slaughtered. Her hands tightened into fists and Anna sucked in a deep breath. Joseph moved away and Van struggled to get control of her hatred.

"My lady?" Amy's trembling voice inquired.

"Nothing," Van tried to smile but could not manage anything more than a sneer. "Tell me the rest."

This time there was no hesitation, but Anna continued with a look of fear on her face that stabbed deeply into Van's heart and conscience. She enjoyed the look of fear, but not from someone she was beginning to care about.

"Gary pulled me out of bed and dragged me into the woods." Anna's voice cracked. "We did not stop running until Peter found us and brought us here."

Amy put her arm around the girl. "I understand. I have lost both of my parents as well." She then told of her father dying the same way her mother had, of a lung infection. "I loved them both very much."

Van turned to Joseph and asked if he wanted to talk about his parents, but all he said was the fire was too much to talk about."

His eyes welled up and Van quickly changed the subject. They spoke of the woods, flowers and the animals around the castle.

Soon they fell into a companionable silence, listening to the chirping birds squabbling. The birds soon faded from Van's conscious thought as she allowed her hatred and rage against Eolian to boil silently within her.

☙☙☙

When Peter returned to the lists, Devon approached him. Stopping nervously before Peter, he stuttered that he needed to go back to the castle. "I have to see to Rebeka. I should have stayed, but with all the excitement…"

"By all means, I would hope you get to her before Lady Vanessa does." Peter watched him and three of the men, all men Richard had brought, leave to take charge of his former mistress. Unease itched at his thoughts. "Richard, I need to speak to you." He gestured for Grant to join them. Peter steered them to a private spot out of earshot of the men. "Richard, I have noticed the men are still separated into groups. Yours and mine. I think it would be best to come up with some way of drawing them together."

"I do not think the two groups quite know what to do. My men are not my men, my lord. They are the Dark Knight's men." Richard shrugged and looked apologetically at him, but Peter just waved it off. He understood.

Damn nuisance boy had always been a problem. Now he had just up and disappeared, leaving his men and heading off to God only knows where, Peter thought irritably, still in shock over his disappearance.

Richard nodded and continued. "Almost all of them have ridden with him for three years. He left us so quickly. It is a hard adjustment for us. They are loyal to him, but are still trying to find a way to be loyal to you without breaking that trust." Richard's gaze darted across the men and Peter thought he saw guilt on the man's face.

"I understand," Peter said, and he did understand. He understood that Richard himself was still loyal to The Dark Knight. "I understand what they are going through, because you are having difficulties with it and you were once one of my men. I am expecting much from those who were never my men, but we need to come up with something to pull us all together." He turned and walked back to the men.

Van followed behind her three companions on their way back from the woods. She grinned and picked up her pace as she saw Devon leading three men to Rebeka's door. She smiled widely and told Amy to take Anna and Joseph into the castle.

"Milady, what are you going to do? Let them take care of it."

"I will. I just want to watch her go." Van could not understand the completely joyous feeling that warmed her at the mere thought of that woman being gone.

"Promise me…promise me you will not hurt her."

Van promised and grinned when she was alone. She could not hold in a small, enthusiastic laugh as Devon banged on the mistress's door, but she did keep out of sight. She wanted to kick the door down herself, but figured it easier to keep her promise if she didn't get any closer than necessary.

"Go away."

Van could hear her muffled voice from behind the heavy door.

Devon gave it another thunderous hit. "I cannot do that, Miss Constance. You must come out now."

"Go away." Her voice was shrill now, scared.

Van's grin widened.

"I have orders to remove you in any way I see fit," Devon growled.

Van beamed in pride. Her smile faltered momentarily as a wave of desolate emptiness crashed over her. She missed Devon and all her men.

She pushed away the self-pity as Devon spoke again. "I have an axe to remove the door, or it has been approved for me to burn this place to the ground, with you in it."

That did it, the door opened. "I am not ready yet. You can just go now. Peter would never have agreed to this."

Van leaned from her hiding place, but was unable to catch sight of the angry sounding woman.

"I am here until I get my things together," Rebeka continued. "I will let you know when I am ready for a carriage."

The door began to slam shut, but Devon put out a large hand stopping it and pushing it fully open giving Van a view of Rebeka's livid features.

"Nay, Miss Constance. We have our orders. We are to assist you in getting what items belong to you. I would like to be done before the midday meal."

Her face darkened to a deep red as she strained futilely to shut the door against him. "You cannot do this. Peter would not have told you to do this to me. I will speak to him." She shrieked the words, but they seemed to lack conviction. "I will show you he did not order this," she yelled directly in his face before slamming her full weight against the door. It shivered, but did not close.

"You are right about one thing. Lord Grayweist did not order our assistance, but speak to him all you wish. You will just have to do it from Hillsford."

Devon sounded exasperated and his neck was reddening. Van grinned. She knew he was losing patience.

"Hillsford, that is so far away. I will not go there." Rebeka was nearly screeching as she lost the battle for the door.

"Look, my orders are coming from the Dark Lady."

Van groaned and shook her head. She needed to put a stop to this Dark Lady name. It was too close to the Dark Knight to be comfortable.

Devon motioned with his free hand, never taking his eyes off the sputtering leman. His three companions stepped closer to the small house. "She has made your housing arrangements. If you do not want to stay there, don't, but it is the only one that will be taken care of—" Rebeka stuttered and squealed. Devon kept speaking as if she were silent and acquiescent. "—it is paid up for two months and you will get an allowance for the same amount of time. That is all."

Standing in the center of the doorway, Rebeka blocked their entry. "I have been here for two years. I should have your loyalty."

Van was quite enjoying the show, staying to the shadows where she was hidden.

"Aye, you have been here a long time and, though it could cost me my life, if you were the lady and she the whore, between the two of you, she would still get my loyalty."

Van's heart swelled with pride.

Devon shoved Rebeka from the entryway. It took them less than half an hour to get her into a carriage and on her way. Van watched with elation as the carriage disappeared.

She glanced up as Devon approached her. The entire way, he looked at her in that scrutinizing way that all her men and Peter seemed to inspect her with. It made nervous gooseflesh break out on her skin. She held her breath as he stopped before her, absolutely sure he was going to say, "I know who you really are."

"Is everything all right, my lady?" Devon asked.

She relaxed and the breath whooshed quietly out of her. "Yes, Devon, thank you for all that you have done. Are you heading back out to the men?" She hoped her voice sounded calm through the boiling emotions coursing through her.

"Yes, my lady. Is there anything else I can do for you?" At the shake of her head he opened his mouth, just to close it again.

Van waited nervously. When he didn't continue, only stared closely into her eyes, she said, "Can I ask you something?"

He stared at her closely. But even knowing that he was being disrespectful, he could not bring himself to look away. He tried to convince himself that the familiarity was only because she looked like her father. "Of course, you can ask me whatever you wish, my lady." He knew he recognized her and it was beginning to gnaw at him. He could feel the aggravation to his insides like he could feel the sun on his shoulders at mid-day.

"When are the king's men arriving tomorrow? First thing, I assume?"

Surprise overcame his contemplation of where he had met her before. "Aye, my lady, they should be here at day break. You will not be there, will you?" He hoped not for her sake, but he had a feeling that she would be there bright and early.

Her thickly powdered brow raised. Her black eyes widened in an expression that did nothing to appear innocent, but it seemed to be the look she was going for. "No one can rightly predict what will occur with the rising of the morning sun."

"I think it wise if you were not to arrive, my lady. I can only imagine how angry he would be." He knew that no matter what anyone may say, he would see her in the morning where she was not supposed to be.

"Head back." With that she walked away.

Devon watched her go, wondering what was in her mind. Shaking his head, he turned to leave, and then thought better of it. He had sent the other three men with Rebeka. They would escort her and return. He could afford to be absent for at least a few more minutes, he thought with a widening grin.

Devon nearly ran to the servants' entrance of the castle and made his way to the Amy's quarters. He pushed open the door.

Amy turned and let out a squeal. "What do you think you are doing in here?"

He raised a thick brow and stopped right before her. With a smile, he ran a calloused finger down her smooth cheek.

She jerked her head away.

He grasped her arm and pulled her close. "What *am* I doing here?" he asked rhetorically and then grinned wickedly. "Well, I am trying to decide if I want to be more than just friends with you."

"You need to get out," she said in a low hiss.

But she did not move away and her eyes shone with desire. He took a chance and leaned forward. She did not fight him when he pressed his lips to hers. Excitement swirled within him.

"Open your mouth, for me."

His voice was thick, his body tight with lust and need. She resisted only slightly before allowing his tongue the entrance it demanded. Devon grasped her tightly, crushing her to him. He kissed her passionately, marveling in her sweet attempts to follow his lead. Her tongue moved slightly forward and then retreated once again as if embarrassed and unsure.

He frantically pulled open the laces of her blouse and marveled at her beauty. Amy shuddered in his arms, a small groan escaping, and pushed herself deeper into his embrace as he massaged her bared breasts.

"Stop that now!"

Devon jerked away as if he was physically torn from Amy's body when Lady Vanessa's angry voice cracked across the small room.

"What do you think you are doing in here?"

Devon stepped protectively in front of Amy.

Amy covered herself, shrinking away from her mistress. "Milady, I am sorry—"

"Nay," Vanessa interrupted her. "You are not to apologize to me, ever."

It took everything Devon had not to back down when Lady Vanessa turned her icy gaze upon him. "You, on the other hand will apologize and explain yourself. What do you intend to do?" she growled angrily at him.

"My lady?"

Lady Vanessa voice tickled at the back of his mind, but he could not place it and she was not giving him time to think.

"You know very well what I am asking, and if you think to stand in between me and her, you are sorely mistaken."

His mind whirled as her voice changed and lightened to a higher pitch. She took a tight step toward them, drawing his thoughts away from her voice.

"Lady Vanessa, please," Amy pleaded from behind him. Her delicate hand lay on his lower back as she peeked around his shoulders. Even in the volatile situation, the warm weight of her small hand sent shivers through his loins.

Lady Vanessa didn't seem to take notice of Amy at all. She took another tight step toward Devon. "What are your intentions? Are you looking to marry her?"

"My Lady, Lady Vanessa, we just met. H–how am I to know if m–marriage is what I want?" Devon stuttered, still unsure of what he really wanted. He knew he wanted Amy, but for what, he did not know.

Vanessa glared at him and her gaze never wavered. "Until you know, I expect you to act with some decorum around her."

Devon dropped his eyes self-consciously and had to force them back to Lady Vanessa's face.

"Until you know if you want it to be something more than a toss, you will both keep your hands on the outside of the clothing." She stepped quickly toward him, closing the gap. Chest to chest and eye to eye, he fought the urge to retreat and lost. She smiled a satisfied grin as he took an involuntary step back. "If she ends up pregnant and you do not marry her…How far can you go to hide?"

"Vanessa!" Amy squealed.

"You—" Vanessa glanced over his shoulder at Amy and he felt her hand tighten on his tunic. "I will deal with you later." Turning her attention back to him, Vanessa smiled an arctic smile that chilled him to the very core. "Do I make myself very clear?" she said softly.

The soft, calm question scared him more than her angry growls. "Aye, Dark Lady."

There would be no argument from him. He would do his best to keep his promise to her. It was more than fear of her. It was an involuntary loyalty that seemed to overtake him, the feeling that he needed to show her respect as well as fealty.

"Good, then I would suggest you get back to the men, like I already instructed." Van was relieved that she had arrived in time to stop them. She shook her head as she watched him leave. She trusted Devon and had no objections to his marrying Amy, but she would not allow him to take advantage of her if marriage was not in his heart.

He had almost reached the door when she spoke his name. He turned back to her with his hand resting on the latch.

"Do not make me give you an order twice, ever again."

He bowed low. "Never again, my lady."

Van grinned as he walked out. At least he had stuck with my lady instead of Dark Lady as he had called her when he was so distracted. She turned her attention back to Amy who stood red faced in embarrassment and shame.

Amy struggled to re-lace her blouse, but her fingers were trembling to the point of uselessness. Her eyes shone with unshed tears and her voice trembled nearly as bad as her fingers. "I do not understand how it got to…well to where we were."

Van smiled. "I know that you like him. I understand. You do need to be careful, although I think he likes you as well." She pushed away Amy's trembling hands as the girl's face lit in a bright smile and her gaze jumped to Van's eyes.

Van just shook her head and finished the laces. "I came to ask you if you would like to help me in the gardens. I already have some of the servants starting on it." The gardens had been the pride of Grayweist Castle when she was a page, but had fallen into a mess of weeds and grasses. The garden had been her favorite retreat during her training, and she wanted to bring it back to that glorious state once again.

"Aye, milady, if that will take your mind off what you have just seen, then I will gladly dig in the dirt," Amy said in a weak voice.

CHAPTER 13

Rebeka sat slumped in the jolting carriage as it made its way to Hillsford and thought of the hovel she was sure Vanessa had deemed to put her in. She was certain that in her spite, Vanessa would place her in the worst ramshackle of a hut she could find.

She cursed Vanessa Lawston violently, every so often kicking the seat before her to punctuate those curses. "The new lady of Grayweist," she snorted snidely into the empty carriage.

The carriage came to a sudden jolting stop. Her two laughing escorts jumped to the ground. She straightened her back and lifted her head proudly, determined not to give them the satisfaction of seeing her fall apart.

She sucked in a deep breath and steadied herself the best she could, but she still jumped when one of the soldiers tore the door open. When he looked in with his round white face and grinning mouth, she barely suppressed the urge to kick him in his crooked teeth. She had no idea who either of them were, but they were new to the castle. Perhaps if they had been Peter's men she would have gotten more sympathy.

She shook her head. No, she thought foully. Even Peter's men seemed enamored of the giant woman.

Rebeka raised an eyebrow at the man who had opened the carriage door, but he just stepped away. She scowled deeply. He smiled in return.

"You are an ass, boy," she spat at him. "Do you not know you are to help a lady depart a carriage?"

"Oh I know and I do help *ladies* down," he said with a gentlemanly tone that did not match the condescending smile that lit his eye as he smirked at her.

"Get away from me then," she snapped with as much loathing as she could pack into her words.

He stepped back with a mock bow and gestured for her to step down. She kept her gaze on her footing as she slid unassisted from the coach.

"Welcome to your new home."

Rebeka glanced up as the second man unceremoniously dropped her luggage onto the stoop. She made no reply but ran her gaze across the house. To her amazement, it was not a hovel or a hut. It was a nice, clean, and cozy house. She snorted at it loudly and turned to the two men who were climbing back onto their perch. "It is smaller than the house I am accustomed to," she brayed in a loud voice that echoed across the still air.

They made no reply and, with a flick of the whip, the horse's hooves clattered against the hard packed street. She stood there trembling until they were out of site, and then she turned her frown toward the house.

The door was silent as she pushed it open and the interior, much to her grudging approval, was warm and inviting. A hard heavy lump settled deep in her stomach and she didn't even step inside. She closed the door with a slam, picked up her luggage, and walked away.

By the end of the day she was less than two miles from Lynton, sitting at a small table in the dining room at the Doveslane Inn. She had walked for only a short distance back toward Lynton and the Castle Grayweist when an elderly lord had stopped to offer her a ride.

He was heavyset and graying at the temples. Once in the carriage, he had smiled at her lecherously and ran his hand against her thigh. She had smiled sweetly, hiding her fear and disgust. He had told her he wanted more than her gratitude for the ride, and she had thanked him thoroughly more than once.

Rebeka shuddered in revulsion as the memory flooded her mind. She bowed her head on the table. Luckily, he was old and quick, she thought. She took a deep breath and steadied herself, pushing thoughts of the sweat laden man away.

Her plan was to stay out of sight for a few days and then return to the castle. She was fairly sure that it would not take longer than that for Peter to tire of his new bride. She still could not fathom how he managed to consummate the marriage.

She could hear the other guests of the Inn bustling around as they checked in and out, but she did not raise her head nor pay them much heed.

The scraping of a chair drew her attention. Her gaze shot up as a large man wrapped in a filthy cloak sat down without a word.

"Pardon me, can I help you?" she said with more bravado than she felt.

She eyed the big man cautiously and concern started to worm through her. He was dressed in black and bulky clothing and looked out of place in the somewhat respectable inn.

Without lifting his hooded head, he gave a small laugh. The sound splintered through her like an axe through rotted wood. The chair groaned and protested as he shifted his massive bulk. "You talk awfully arrogant for nothing more than a whore." His raspy voice sent violent chills of fear through her.

Rebeka sucked in a deep breath. She looked around her and saw to her dismay that every person in the Inn was casting long sideways glances at the big man. She shook her head and prayed no one noticed who she was. Peter could not know she was here until the time was right.

She could not afford to draw any more attention to herself than necessary and decided her best course of action would be to leave the man sitting where he was. She started to rise. Long rough fingers wrapped around her slender wrist. She could feel the blood drain from her face as her bones scraped together.

Sharp pain tugged at her wrist and arm, dragging a sharp cry from her dry lips. "Let me go or I will scream." She stood in a crouch and struggled against his iron grip. Concern over being caught by Peter was being overrun by a steady pulsing fear for her safety.

"Scream. From what I have been told it will come as a surprise that you are not in Hillsford." His words were soft and calm as if this were tea time in the parlor.

He tugged her forward and she sat so quickly she issued a grunt. His grip loosened and she pulled her hand away, absently rubbing her wrist.

"I have a message." He shifted his bulk closer to her and whispered conspiringly. "The Knight of Fear wants to see you."

Fear turned to icy terror at the sound of his name. "Why?"

"I do not ask things that are not my concern." A rancid smell of decay and old food wafted over her as he leaned even closer. "I am to bring you to him. He thought you might be a little reluctant, so he sent me. I have a way of…bringing around hesitant folks." He stood suddenly and she heard several people gasp behind her. He held out his hand in invitation.

Rebeka sat there like a stone, staring at him. He tilted his head and the hood slid back, revealing the sharp, jagged angles of his almost sunken nose. His dark brown eyes were dull and pained, but showed intelligence and a deep seated anger. The man smiled widely. Grimy blackened teeth showed between cracked and bloody lips.

"You can take it or scream. I don't care one whit either way. It has been awhile since I have killed a lot of nice-dressed folk." The chilling words were said in that same even tone.

She rose without taking his hand and followed him out to an awaiting carriage. The man on the driver's perch sat rigidly, staring forward, and did not even acknowledge their approach.

The big man pulled open the door to the windowless carriage and placed a large sweaty hand on her arm. A violent tremor overtook her muscles and raced throughout her body. She tried to pull away, but he propelled her into the carriage as if she were a child's ragdoll.

The door closed and she let out shaky breath when she realized she would not have to ride with the odoriferous and terrifying man.

The interior was lit by two candles that adorned the candelabras attached to each side of the carriage. The air inside was slightly smoky, but not overpowering. She watched as the smoke swirled along the ceiling and then disappeared out a small slit in the covering. A sliver of fading daylight beckoned her through the vent and she started to cry.

She could hear the horses whinny and snort in restless anticipation. The leather harnesses creaked and strained as if the horses were fighting against their restraints. She closed eyes and laid her head back against the seat. The jolt of the carriage bounced her head painfully.

All her life she had been the one in control. She knew very well where her power had come from, but she had never been above using whatever was necessary to obtain what she wanted.

First, it had been due to her father. He was a man of no land and little worth, but made up for it with malice and fear. Rebeka had learned at an early age to use that to her benefit, throwing her weight around, knowing her father would back her up.

She shifted in the uncomfortable carriage seat and smiled weakly as she thought of how good her life had been before her father had died. No one questioned her, no one contradicted her.

Never had she been afraid of anyone. Well, besides her father, she thought, brushing impatiently at her wet cheeks.

She was not a woman above tears, but they were always used to get what she wanted. Very seldom in her life had she had need to actually cry.

Rebeka scrubbed at her weeping eyes and shifted along with the rocking of the quickly moving carriage. She took a deep breath, retaining an unsteady hold on her racing emotions.

Dragging in a sharp, painful breath that wheezed past her heavy heart, she forced herself to focus on the memories of her life. It was easier than to think of what her future now held.

Rebeka remembered being uneasy when her father had died, avoiding the people who might not have been so accommodating to her now that he was gone. It was then she decided to find a protector.

She opened her eyes and smiled as she thought of Peter. She had met him two years ago. He had been in mourning over his father and unnerved by an arranged marriage to some girl he had known when she was only one. He had been distracted and consumed with only his men. It had been easy to coerce him. She had soon taken over the run of the castle.

Rebeka's smile fell away. Vanessa, she thought with a snarl. Her tears were completely forgotten as anger assailed her.

She had heard rumors of a shy and secluded girl, young and sheltered, and never seen even by those of the village where she lived. Rebeka had thought to intimidate her. She had been expecting a weak child and had been taken off guard by the giant of a woman who had arrived.

Rebeka had little experience with fear, and yet she could not imagine a greater fear than she had felt on the day of Peter's marriage celebration, that first night in the corridor. She shivered uncontrollably as she felt the chills that had run rampant over her spine that night. She could almost feel the tight grip on her throat and gagged slightly with the vivid memory. She had seriously thought the new Lady of the Castle was going to kill her.

The carriage came to a jerky stop thankfully throwing off the painful memory. Her heart thrummed in anticipation and dread.

The door opened and someone held out an almost delicate hand to her. She looked beyond him at black trees and shadows. She took note of the dark, star-sprinkled sky through the tops of the trees and realized they had traveled into the night.

She looked back at the man who patiently held his hand out to her, surprised to see a wide, friendly smile and bright blue eyes. Knowing she had no choice at this point other than to acquiesce, she placed her hand in his and allowed him to assist her onto the moist, leaf-strewn ground. Her foot sank slightly.

"Where is my abductor?" she asked quietly, looking around.

"Verges? Oh, he had other things to take care of. Come, let me take you inside." His voice was gentle, but it did nothing to calm her.

"Inside where?" she said timidly.

He smiled sweetly, placed his hand on her arm, and pulled her gently along.

A small cabin seemed to appear within the darkness of the trees as they approached it. She relaxed slightly.

He opened the door to the cottage. Warm air wafted out at her. She shivered and her feet stopped once again. The man just chuckled lightly and pushed her through the open door. Her muscles twitched as a torrent of fear threatened to drown her.

"Close the door," a deep voice said from a tall backed chair facing the fireplace.

Rebeka turned toward the door, but her escort was gone. She took a deep breath and thought to run. Her body slumped. There was nowhere to go. She did not know where she was and she had an idea that if she ran, she would not get far before they caught her.

She pushed the door closed soundly and gathered all her courage. It wasn't much, but when she spoke her voice did not betray the scared little girl she felt like. She turned back toward the chair and forced herself to take a step forward. "Are you the Knight of Fear? I have heard much about you."

"Have you now?" The eerie voice floated up from the far side of the chair.

"There is always idle talk after the meals." This time her voice was weaker. The scared little girl peered out from beneath her façade of bravery.

He stood gracefully and turned to face her. Her breath caught. He was a handsome man with thick black hair, light brown eyes, and a wide nose. It was not a delicate face, but it was a rugged one.

"My name is Eolian Montgomery. I have asked you here, knowing that you were turned out of your home, a home you have known for the past two years." He spoke with a passion and a deeply embedded anger that frightened her. "I know you are without a protector and that you have refused both the money and the housing that the new lady has provided you."

She quivered as he stepped closer. "What does that have to do with you?"

"I am offering my protection. More importantly, I am offering you a way to get back at the self-righteous Sir Peter and perhaps a way to get your rightful place from the woman who took it."

"How can you give me back what was taken?" she asked, her interest peaking. Her fear faded beneath a lustful desire for power and prestige.

Eolian did not answer, only smiled, sending chills down her spine. He beckoned her forward and unable to refuse, as she looked deep into his eyes, she took several steps forward.

"Take your clothes off." His smile fell away and his dark features became passive, his voice calm in the same careful tone he had used to tell her to close the door.

She took a step back, fear trying to insinuate itself into her mind again. She pushed it away the best she could, but still it remained to taunt her seductively. A knot formed deep in her throat threatening to cut off her breathing. "What?"

He took another step toward her and she retreated again keeping the same distance between them. "If I am to be your protector, I will see my new property." He shrugged indifferently and shook his head. "Take them off now or I will send you back to Hillsford and you will stay there."

She took another step back to widen the gap. "You cannot make me stay there."

"You are right. I will just take you to Lady Grayweist. I am sure she will have plenty of time to deal with you before she becomes occupied with giving her husband an heir," he said calmly and turned away.

"Wait," she said weakly and began to hastily remove her clothing. She fumbled with the fasteners as her fingers trembled uncontrollably. A tear slid down her face. Once she was standing naked she stared at the floor.

The warmth of the fire caressed her lovingly. It reminded her of the heat that had flowed through her in response to his smile. She wondered irrationally what it would take to get him to smile at her once more.

She stole a glance at him then focused again on her slipper-clad feet. "How can you promise to return me to Grayweist?"

"When I take over Grayweist, I will be in need of a woman to stand at my side and bring heirs to my home."

Her gaze shot to his face. He did not appear to be jesting and her heart skipped erratically. She took a careful step forward, never taking her gaze from his arresting brown eyes. "I can be the Lady of Grayweist castle and not just your mistress?"

He smiled. That small act of approval thrilled her more than anything she could ever remember. The warmth of the fire was suddenly over-powering and she pressed her thighs together to stem the quivering antic-ipation that was building.

This time when he approached her, she stepped forward to meet him.

CHAPTER 14

Peter had thought of nothing besides his aggravating wife since he had left the lists. With his mind not on the training, he had made mistakes and took several good hits.

An hour before the sun set, and training would end, he took his leave and headed for the castle. He told himself he was tired, dirty, and wanted nothing more than to bathe and rest, but he knew what he wanted was to see his wife.

Looking forward to a bath, he had sent Grant ahead of him to see to it. Now, Grant met him at the foot of the stairs. "Your bride is not in here."

Peter tried to scowl at him, but a smile touched his lips. "Did I ask about my wife, Hestlay?"

Grant snapped off a mock bow. "No, my lord and liege, you did not." His artificial military demeanor made Peter's grin widen.

"I told you I was coming early for a bath." Peter had known the men were not fooled when he had left. He very seldom left the training field before his men and then it was for something more important than a bath. He grunted.

Grant's face lit with a knowing smile that made Peter want to smack him upside the head, perhaps with his sword. "I know what you said, my lord. I also know you want to check on your new bride."

He shook his head in objection. "Of course, I want to check on her. I need to make sure she is not whipping the help or training the men."

Grant burst into laughter. "Nothing as drastic as that. Amy told me she is out in the garden. They have spent the day out there, cleaning and planting new flowers."

"The garden, you say?" Peter nodded as if this information meant nothing to him and then finally gave up the charade. With a grin he turned toward the door. "Tell Miceal to keep my bath ready," he said, pushing the door closed to shut out Grant's good natured laughter.

Peter walked silently through the darkening night. The smells of freshly-dug earth tugged at his senses. The crew had made a remarkable difference in the mess of weeds the garden had been. Flowers, transplanted from the surrounding woods, were freshly planted and watered. They already dominated a large part of the area.

He stopped when he spotted Van leaning on the back wall of the garden, her head leaned back, eyes closed. Hiding behind a large tree, he watched her. Just watching her breathe in the cool night air seemed to charge him. The feelings of exhaustion lifted, the bath forgotten. Her chest rose and fell gently. Her face and neck were bathed in the orange glow of the setting sun.

Vanessa smiled, but her eyes remained closed. It excited him just to watch her relax. He was proud of what she had done in the gardens and happy that she had gone to such pains to restore his home…their home, he amended with a smile.

"Vanessa."

Peter jumped as Amy's voice sounded close behind him.

Vanessa's eyes remained closed. "Do not call me that, Amy."

Peter wondered what she did want to be called.

"It is time for you to come. Your bath is ready. The men will return soon for the evening meal." There was no response and Amy disappeared. Peter listened to her soft footfalls until they were gone. Then Vanessa pushed herself away from the tall wall.

Peter ducked back behind the tree, trying not to even breathe. Silently he watched her. She walked slowly through the garden, stopping here and there to smell a newly planted flower.

He began to grin in anticipation as she drew closer and closer to his hiding place. A grunt was torn from her as he grabbed her, throwing her to the wet ground. He did not wait for her to regain her composure. He rolled on top of her and began to kiss her, firmly and passionately. Without encouragement, her lips parted.

His lust was a painful throb that screamed its need at him when she wrapped her arms around him and returned his kiss. Peter fumbled at her dress until the nuisance was out of his way and forced his way between her legs, opening them to him.

He pulled his painfully hard shaft free and drove it into her. He kissed her, tasting the sweat tang of sweat and dust. He drove himself into her harder and deeper as she clung to him. A fire grew within his stomach and settled in his loins. He panted and groaned, marveling at how good she felt beneath him. An explosion of fiery ecstasy filled him. He called her name into her mouth as he spilled his seed inside her.

Peter pulled off of her, kissing the tip of her nose. He adjusted his clothing and walked away. He turned at the edge of the garden. She had adjusted her clothing and was starting to rise. "I think, my dear, that ought to teach you that I am the master. You do not stand a chance against me." He grinned as her eyes narrowed and her brows furrowed in irritation. "I will always be able to outsmart you. You may be able to uncinch a saddle, but I am the master of the ambush."

Seeing the anger that spread across her features, he ran for the doors, with her hard on his heels. He saw servants stop and stare, mouths agape, as he tore through the hall, but he ignored them. He knew they were shocked by his unaccustomed behavior. He was always so proper and restrained and now he ran, laughing, as the dark figure of the new lady of the castle chased after him.

Making it to his chambers first, he threw the key into the lock, laughing as he heard her banging on his door. He slipped into the bath as her footsteps faded.

Van was angry with him for taking advantage of her. She was also exhilarated from the passionate love making and the chase through the halls. With a wide and satisfied smile, she made her way down the servants' stairs and out into the cool evening air.

The mortar of the castle walls was cool to her back as she leaned against it. The cool breeze wafted against her heated skin and she closed her eyes. When she opened them again, she saw light from the men's barracks.

She watched the wavering light and a lonely feeling washed over her. "No," she said gently to the night air. It was dangerous. She had seen their looks. She knew they were curious about her. She could not mess this up. There were too many people who now could be used against her.

She made up her mind and turned toward the servants' door. Her hand froze on the latch. Emptiness enveloped her, weakening her resolve. There was an empty hole in her that her men had once filled. It was deep and dark, aching with a hunger that jabbed painfully at her, insistent on being fed.

Cursing herself, she carefully looked to make sure no one watched and raced across the courtyard to the barracks of her men. She had learned that once the king came for his men, hers would move into the castle and the barracks would be used for the new pages that would be arriving.

When she slipped silently through the door to the barracks, the men stopped and stared. Those undressed quickly covered themselves.

Richard rushed to her side. "My lady, is everything all right? Is something wrong?" There was concern in his voice. His eyes darted to the swords that lay beside each man's bed.

"Everything is fine, Richard. I have come to see if there is anything that you need. I am sure that Lord Grayweist keeps you well stocked with weapons and armor, but I know the men get overlooked. So if you need something. Shirts, blankets..."

The tension in his frame seemed to disappear. He smiled and shook his head in blatant exasperation. "This is too much, my lady, but we could use some more blankets."

"Stockings, my Lady." Robert Dauphin shyly looked down at the three toes that stood out from his worn through stocking.

"Blankets and stockings it shall be. If there is anything else, you will let me know. Now, hurry, we are getting ready to serve supper." With that she walked out, the aching hole in her soul appeased, at least momentarily.

Peter watched her leave the men's barracks from his chamber window. His stomach lurched in fear for her. Anything could happen to her out there. He did not know these men and her status would only go so far in protecting her. Fear gave way to anger.

Anger turned his thoughts to another possibility. She had gone to meet with one of the men. It was apparent that she was not totally happy with him. Perhaps, she was seeking comfort elsewhere.

He remembered his mother's delicate frame, wrapped in the arms of one of his father's warriors. He had been too young to understand. When she said she was only comforting him from a wound, he had believed her. He had promised not to tell his father. The night she left, she left with that man, and he had finally understood.

With a deep growl, he shoved his mother once more from his mind. She had been a constant visitor since his new wife had arrived and he was desperate to be rid of her. No matter how he tried to shut out the past, he could see the pain on his father's tear-streaked face the night his mother had left. He could feel the anger that thrummed through his father when he realized that his man at arms was gone as well.

Peter's anger and jealousy consumed him and, when Vanessa opened her chamber door, he was standing before it. She jumped guiltily. "What do you think you were doing out there?" he demanded. "It is not proper for a woman to be out with men, not at all." He was angry even as he pulled her against him, but he had been frightened for her as well. He was relieved that she was safe, and now that she was in his arms, the idea of her taking a lover seemed farfetched.

"You are right, my lord. I did not think."

Peter had expected her usually self-righteous sermon, and her response shocked him. He pulled away and looked down into her contrite eyes, wondering what the change was.

"I only wanted to see to the men's needs. They are in need of blankets and stockings. It is new to me to have to worry about what my appearance in things will be." She shrugged. "I am used to doing as I wish. I understand I have an image to uphold. I will try harder."

Peter shook his head, once more amazed at her. He wanted to be angry, but could not. He wanted to chastise her, but found he could not do that either. Instead, he kissed her gently and left the room. He made his way to the dining hall, leaving her to bathe and change.

♔ ♔ ♔

Ryan Deumount stalked along the halls of the castle in search of some feminine entertainment. He walked with confidence and bowed low as Peter walked past him, on his way, more than likely, to the dining hall for the evening meal.

If all went well Ryan would be done with his wench and at his table before the meal was served. He looked with loathing around the well-lit castle. He would be glad when his work here was finished and he could return to the man he had pledged his loyalty to long ago.

Eolian had sent him here six months ago when word had spread that Peter Lawston was going to start a training facility for squires. The great and awe inspiring Dragon Knight, the former king's champion, Ryan thought sarcastically as he glanced at Peter's retreating frame.

Ryan's task was to watch and learn. Eolian thought it was a trick, that Peter would never leave the wars behind.

Ryan had recruited Gregory and Christopher, not long after he had arrived, to help him if the need should arise, but it had not. He had seen little that was of interest to Eolian and was convinced there would be nothing to learn.

He was looking forward to disappearing within a few days and informing Eolian that Peter had indeed gone soft and was giving up the battles, that there was nothing of interest here at Grayweist Castle.

He ran his hand along the rough stone of the walls as he made his way toward the servants' quarters. He had hoped with the arrival of The Dark Knight's men he would have something interesting to do. But unfortunately, the only thing that had followed was a mammoth woman who irritated her husband and squealed when she spoke.

He was sure Eolian would not be interested in her.

Footfalls came rushing around the corner. Ryan smiled as Amy Devant hurried into view. He felt his lust rise and his breathing increase.

He wanted the feisty little day maid more than he had wanted a woman in a long time. She hung on Devon like he was a god, but looked at Ryan himself as if he were scum on the pond.

He had approached her the day she arrived, but she had turned him down. He had grabbed her arm and she struggled, but fear thrummed through her so strongly he could feel it. He had hardened painfully. Then Devon had come along to her rescue.

He began to harden as he watched her approach confidently. She nodded to him politely and he returned it with a grin. She would fear him and that excited him. She would fight him despite the fear, and that excited him even more. As she walked by him, he gave a low bow and decided he didn't want some malleable maid, he wanted the fight as well as the fear.

He shot his hand out and grasped her arm. She did not scream as he had worried she would, but she did begin to struggle. He yanked her back and shoved her against the rough wall. He kissed her clenched lips and pulled his dagger from its place on his hip.

He pushed himself against her, her breasts heaving against his chest. Pulling his lips from hers, he pressed the dagger to her long pale neck.

He could see the fear in her wide eyes, could smell it on her as she trembled in his arms.

Ryan felt iron hands upon him as he was violently shoved into the wall beside her. He let out a loud grunt. His eyes widened in shock as he looked up into the enraged face of Lady Vanessa. He felt the cold steel of his own weapon pressed into his throat.

"What the bloody hell do you think you are doing?" she asked him in a deep growl. "I should kill you where you stand."

Fear invaded Ryan like an attacking army, but before he could even open his mouth to speak Amy was tugging on her arms.

"Please, my lady, let him go. He is not worth it." She tugged again, harder, but the steel grip on his tunic did not loosen. "Please, my lady. Let him go."

Vanessa let him go and stared at him. "You are lucky, but if you ever come near her again, you will not be."

With that, Vanessa grasped Amy's arm and they walked away. Ryan slumped against the wall and took several deep breaths. "You have no idea who you are messing with, my lady," he whispered to himself. "You will regret this."

Peter watched Vanessa and Amy walk into the dining hall. He rose to his feet at the look of panic on Amy's face and the rage on Vanessa's. Amy rushed to Devon's side but only shook her head when he leaned close to ask her a question that, Peter could only guess, would be the same as the one he would ask Vanessa when she sat beside him.

He waited until she was seated and took his place at her side. "What is wrong?"

Vanessa shook her head. "Nothing, my lord." She smiled and took a deep breath. The next smile looked slightly more real, but not quite. He asked her several more times, but the answer was always the same.

He gave up and said little more through the entire meal.

He was unable to come to terms with his feelings and concerns. Unable to determine if she was playing the meek woman once again to trick him or if she was being sincere, he drank more than usual.

That night he took her twice, making sure she came to pleasure each time. At the end of the second bout, he was unsure if he had fallen asleep or fallen unconscious. It was late into the night, and he had drunk deeply into his cups at supper. The last thing he remembered was hoping his head would not pound in the morning.

Reaching across the bed sometime in the dark of night, Peter found nothing but cold empty space. He slowly opened his eyes. It was still dark and his pounding head felt fogged. "Vanessa?" He got no answer from the darkness.

He assumed she had gone to her chambers. He was sure she was just unaccustomed to sleeping with him and had gone to her own bed. Well, he thought with irritation, if she did not want to be in here with him then he was too tired to argue.

He closed his eyes and rolled over. Her side of the bed was cold. He groaned and shifted to find a comfortable position. When that didn't work, he moved back to his side. It was now cold. He tossed and turned for a several long minutes before cursing loudly and getting up.

If she didn't want to sleep in his chambers, then he would go to her. He walked naked to her room. He moved toward her bed slowly, but it was empty. He scowled and went back to his room. Looking longingly at his bed, he considered going back to sleep.

He cursed again knowing it was useless, but not understanding why. He had slept alone for many years. Even with Rebeka he had slept alone most nights.

He stood there for a moment then realized what had to be wrong with him. He was worried because she was wandering out in the dark and when he knew where she was he could sleep.

Peter pulled on his dressing robe, lit a candle, and he walked out into the hall. He opened his mouth to yell for her before reminding himself impatiently that everyone was asleep. He looked up and down the long hall. Where would he look? "Knowing her, she could have gone anywhere."

"Excuse me, milord?"

Peter jumped, spinning to the sound of the voice. It was one of his oldest maids. She had been around since his father was young.

"Margaret, my dear, what are you doing up at this hour?"

She was an old woman, who had no responsibilities in the home anymore. She also had no family, no one to take care of her, and he was loath to let her go. So he had asked her to stay.

"Oh, my boy. I did not mean to wake you. It is just hard for an old woman to walk silently."

"You did not wake me, I reached for—"

She smiled knowingly at him. "It has only been a few days and you already feel her absence." Her laugh quickly turned to a cough.

"I did not say that. Do you happen to know where she is?" His head was beginning to pound, his stomach rolling.

"In the nursery." With that she walked back toward the servants' hall, and to her bed.

In the nursery, a single candle lit a beautiful face. She lay with her arms wrapped around a sleeping Joseph. Her head lay gently against his, his face against the silk of her robe. Her eyes were shut and her breathing gentle.

Joseph opened his eyes, letting out a soft cry.

"It's all right, it is just me," Peter said in a low voice. "Are you all right?"

"Aye milord, I had a bad dream."

Weaving gently in the doorway, Peter watched a tear slide down Joseph's cheek. "Can you sleep now?"

"I should…" He pulled at Vanessa who had awakened and was now holding him tightly. "I am all alone and it is so strange to be here. I dreamed of the fire."

Peter's eyes drifted shut. He leaned his head against the door frame. His mind had fogged further and his thoughts were slow. He could not see straight. Between the drink and the lack of sleep, he was about to fall where he stood. "I am sorry, my boy. As tired as I am, I could not return to sleep with an empty side on my bed." He took a deep breath and swayed. "Insolent old woman was right," he added to himself.

"What woman, my lord?"

Peter's eyes opened. Vanessa's brow was crinkled with wonder and surprise.

"Never mind. I am too tired for this. Come. Let's go. Bring him. He can sleep in your chambers, so he can be close to us, at least until he gets more comfortable in the nursery." With that Peter took her hands, pulling her and Joseph up.

With the small child tucked into her large bed, and Vanessa back in his, Peter pulled her tightly into his embrace. Sleep found him quickly.

♛ ♛ ♛

Walking silently through the servants' chambers, a dark figure made his way into the castle without the aid of a candle. Accustomed to seeing through the darkness, no candle was needed to accomplish what he needed to do.

He crept silently past many closed doors, but did not pause. He knew exactly where he was going. He shifted the rag that he carried in one large hand and slinked close to the walls.

He stopped before Lady Vanessa's day maid's chamber. He lifted the latch and pushed the door. It swung open silently on well-oiled hinges. Slight moonlight fell through the openings in the walls, illuminating Amy's sleeping face.

She lay comfortably and undisturbed by his presence. He walked silently toward her. Towering over her sleeping figure, he smiled. Excitement thrummed through his veins and he began to harden.

He shook his head and forced himself to focus. He must get her out of the castle first. Once safely out of the castle, he could take her. Then, when he was sated, he would complete his task.

He adjusted the rag once more and clamped it over her mouth. She struggled violently, but was unable to scream as he tied the rag tightly behind her head.

She kicked hard and swung her arms as he threw her over his shoulder. He rushed out into the darkness. He noticed with elation that clouds had concealed the moon. His movements were lost in the darkness as he rushed to the stables. He wrapped an arm around her tight round bottom in order to keep her from falling.

Once inside the stable, he gently tossed Amy to the hay littered ground inside one of the stalls.

He pulled the rag from her mouth and pressed his lips to hers, cutting of her screams just as they had begun. The horses snorted from the stalls beside them. Amy pressed her lips tightly together and punched and kicked.

Kissing her harder, he ran his hand down her leg pulling her sleeping gown up and out of his way. He forced his knee between her legs and pulled off of her to speak.

Her knee connected. His words were lost and his swelling manhood retreated in agony as he groaned loudly and rolled off her. Amy tried to run, but he shot a trembling hand out and caught her ankle. She fell.

She began kicking at him, but his words finally stopped her. "Wait. Amy, please."

"Devon?" The moon peeked from behind the clouds, and she stared at him dumbfounded. "What were you thinking?" She pulled herself toward him and laid a hand on his heaving chest. "I am sorry if I hurt you, but you are lucky it wasn't worse."

"How could it be worse?" He laughed breathlessly, the movement causing pain to shoot up his stomach. Horses grumbled and pawed at the ground in their stables while Amy helped him to a sitting position.

"I could have been wearing the dagger Lady Vanessa gave to me," she said with a small, insolent grin.

"Aye, well." He pulled her quickly into his lap and was pleased when a small grimace of pain was all that was detected. "I started to tell you who I was, but then your knee found me."

He didn't wait for a response. He began kissing her roughly and hoped that she had not hurt him too seriously, for that would spoil all the plans he had for the night.

Her response was warm and inviting. When her hand slid into his shirt, twinning into the tight blond curls, his response showed him that she had done no permanent damage.

Amy did nothing to stop him as he flipped her onto her back and followed her over. He pushing her night rail around her waist and pressed her thighs apart with his knees and freed himself. He would love to feel her skin on his, but that would have to wait. He had to be prepared in case someone came in.

She hesitated only a moment when he lay upon her. Then she relaxed and returned his kisses. He placed his throbbing member up against the warm folds of her sex, allowing her to feel the way it moved and jumped in response to her. He rocked the head of it across the small knob where her folds met. She groaned lightly and clung to him.

He would take his time with her. They had all night. He had only been with one virgin, but the older women he had been with had taught him how to go slow, how to ready her. So that he would not hurt the next one as he had the first.

He slid his hand between them, feeling her, caressing her, until she rocked her hips in time with his searching fingers. Her head fell back and he ran his tongue along her exposed neck. He kissed it gently and then more aggressively careful not to leave marks. Her body shuddered below him and her hands threaded through his hair as she began to writhe and moan.

He listened to her harsh breathing and soft moans and moved his lips back to hers. He kissed her deeply. Sliding his fingers down between her swollen folds, he slipped one of them into her now moist hole. It was tight, but he would not hurt her more than necessary.

She gasped and tried to struggle beneath him. He pulled his lips away, but left his finger inside her warmth. "All you have to do is tell me to stop."

She said nothing. She looked up at him with trust and he had to struggle to keep control. He began to kiss and nibble at her neck and ears as he pushed his finger deep inside her. He could feel the thin membrane that spoke of her purity.

He increased his rhythm to match her rocking hips as he pressed on the walls to loosen them. He gently added a second finger and, pushing them into her gently, readied her to accept him. He allowed her to set the pace, although it was hard. The feeling of her body beneath him had his blood boiling and his heavy shaft jumped with anticipation.

Her face glowed with pleasure and her moans washed over him. Her eyes widened in shock when he hit a spot that must have sent jolts of ecstasy through her. He was almost undone and had to fight to keep himself from plunging into her before he felt she was ready.

Just as he was sure he was going to lose the battle of wills with himself, her rhythm suddenly became frantic and her cries so loud that he quickly covered her mouth with his. As she lost herself in the feelings he had drawn from her, he positioned himself. He pulled his fingers from her and quickly pressed the tip of himself into her. It was all he could do to keep from plunging it in deep.

He pushed in until he felt the restraining barrier and then withdrew. She stiffened below him and he slid his hand between them once again. He began to manipulate the pulsing knob at the apex of her folds. "Relax," he said against her lips.

Kissing her, biting on her lips, her chin, and her neck, he fought to hold on. Amy began to squirm beneath him and he increased his speed.

Suddenly her muscles tightened around him and her fingers dug painfully into his shoulders. He deepened his kiss and caught the sound of her cries as the waves of pleasure grew. She rocked her hips forward and he plunged deep and hard inside her. She stiffened in pleasure as the waves crashed over her. He moaned her name against her lips as her warm juices pushed him over the edge.

With one hard thrust he plunged forward and spilled his seed. Lying still, he began to kiss her gently and lovingly as she began to cry.

"Did I hurt you badly? It will not hurt the next time." He rose up on his elbows, easing some of the weight from her, while still remaining inside her. She would soon get accustomed to him, and if he were a lucky man, he would get to take her again this night.

"Nay, it did not hurt too awful, but we promised Lady Vanessa that we would be respectful. That we would wait," she said in a small tearful voice.

Relieved that that was her only problem with it, he smiled, kissing her again. "Nay, I promised her I would not get you pregnant and not marry you. That I would leave you be until I made a decision. I would like you to marry me."

Her eyes widened in shock and she just stared at him. Letting her have time to think it over, he began to kiss her. Gently at first until he felt the stirrings of life in him once again. He made love to her gently once more, smiling when he brought her to pleasure.

He pulled himself out of her and cringed at the blood on his manhood. He moved to her side and pulled her against him. "I decided, I think, when I first saw you, that I loved you. I know I still need to get permission from Lord Grayweist, but I would like for you to be my bride."

"Lord Grayweist?" she asked in apparent confusion.

"It is the way things are done. He is my Lord—"

She waved his words away. "He should not be." She jerked her head up, glancing in his eyes, then away. "I cannot marry you, unless you ask the permission to marry from Lady Vanessa."

"That is not the way things are done. Why would I ask a woman?" Devon was drawn to the lady as well as the other men were, but to treat her like the lord of the manor would be unheard of. What would Peter say?

Amy looked to be almost into a panic. He tried to draw her close to him once again, but she pulled away. "Would you not ask my father if he were alive?"

"Of course," he said humorously.

"And if my father were dead, would you not ask my mother if she were alive?" Her voice was still low, but had taken on a desperate tone.

"Yes." He knew where she was leading, and if it were that important to her, he would do it. He would probably do anything she asked of him, reasons or not.

"They are both gone," Amy said. "Please, you have to ask her. Van is all I have."

Devon wondered for a moment about the name, but let it go as a stutter in her fear and excitement.

"Please, Devon. She is all there is for me, and she is responsible for me, not Lord Peter. She is the one who promised to take care of me."

"All right."

"All right what?"

He pulled her close. "The sun shall rise soon, and if I am to talk to Lady Vanessa in the morning, I should get some sleep."

Amy jumped to her feet and all the horses whinnied in response to her cries of joy.

Flying up, he threw his hand over her mouth. "If you scream, everyone will know we are out here, and if Lady Vanessa kills me, it will be difficult to marry you."

CHAPTER 15

Verges stood in the early morning shadows off the side of the road and watched a large group of boys marching toward Grayweist Castle. The boys trudging along the dusty road were still too far away for him to see individual faces. The sun had not deemed to show her head over the horizon and only sent teasing lights up to color the clouds and to whisper promises of the warmth it would bring.

He could tell by the way they walked that they were all mere children, fresh from plowing the small plots of land allotted them. He hoped there was a boy among them that he could use.

For his purposes, or more for the purposes of The Knight of Fear, a weak, pliable man was useless. A man who was too strong would be just as worthless. He would recognize the type he needed, of that he was sure. He had used many a boy and they all were the same.

Eolian's first instinct when he had learned that the King was sending these men to Grayweist for training had been to send his men to kill them before they arrived. Then he had thought about it for moment and grinned. He had told Verges he had a better plan. To find a man or a couple of men who would be willing to spy for him.

This worked well for Verges. It gave him reason to be close to the castle and to keep an eye on Van.

Verges leaned against one of the stout trees. Van had always been an enigma to him and now it was much more so. He tried to picture her in a gown and proper settings, but his mind could not form the image, even though he had seen it over the last few days. He laughed lightly and shook his head.

He had not yet sent her a missive, letting her have time to come to terms with her new surroundings and to make some decisions. Today, he would send her a message to let her know that he had found her.

He would do whatever was necessary to help her. He had told her little maid Amy that he had pledged his life to her and he had. It was not something he took lightly. Van had been the first thing in his life that had been good and decent and he intended to keep her safe.

Pain and persecution were all he had known as he grew up. An outcast, abandoned by his parents, he was beaten and abused for his grotesque appearance. He had become full of rage and had used all his intelligence to take revenge on those who had scorned him. Murder and rape had come as second nature to him and he felt no remorse for his actions, believing all people were the same and deserved whatever punishment he doled out.

He closed his eyes and took several deep breaths. His life had been full of strife. He had thought that over the years all the decency within him had been lost. That had changed when Van had saved him.

For reasons that he still could not comprehend, she had risked her life for him, throwing herself in a raging, flood-engorged river.

He opened his eyes, but he could still see her face shimmering before him. He chuckled deeply and thought that her risking her life was not the oddest part to him. The oddest thing was that this beautiful woman had shown him trust and caring, even after she had seen him up close. At that time he had pledged his life and his loyalty to her, and only to her.

Loud arguments drew his attention back to the soon to be warriors. Two boys were being obnoxious, speaking of rank and crude things, pushing and shoving. They were bigger than the others. These were boys who had seen the end of a whip many a time. Not weak, but maybe a little on the stupid side. The kind he could use.

As the others began to walk faster, the two boys, brothers from the looks of them, began to fall behind. They watched the group walk away from them. Verges watched the group as well, pleased that not one of them looked back.

He pulled his hood tighter around his head and stepped into their path. He didn't say a word as they stopped and regarded him warily.

"Why, we have no coin if that is what you are after." The older of the two boys was the first to speak up. His large eyes betraying the fear he was trying hard to hide.

Verges smiled beneath the dark hood that shadowed his face as he regarded them closely for a moment. He took in the way they shifted uncomfortably and eyed the direction where the group had disappeared. They were probably wondering if it had been wise to fall behind, after all.

The younger boy slipped behind his brother. Verges smiled wider. The older boy was the one to use. The other would just go along with whatever his older brother said to do. It is always the same, Verges thought.

He chuckled and the boys both jumped and took a step back. Deciding they had stewed in their fear long enough, he asked in an amused voice, "Would you like some?"

"Some what?" the older boy spat out, raising his fists.

Verges shook his head in aggravation and deadly humor. "Coin, you said you had none."

They looked confused for a moment and the older of the two dropped his hands. Verges patiently waited for them to figure it out on their own and nodded when they seemed to grasp what he was saying.

"If I like what you have to say you will have plenty of coin, enough never to return to the rear of a plow." He waited patiently for them to talk. If he had judged them correctly, and he thought he had, then they would agree.

"What do you want from us?" The fear was still evident, but now greed had overcome it as he knew it would. He really liked predictable people. He almost laughed as he realized that was why Van confused him so often. She was anything but predictable.

He pushed her from his mind and focused on the task at hand. "Nothing but a moment of your time. I will tell you what is expected of you and you will agree. If not, you will go on your way." That they would die right here in the road if they declined was information he thought best kept to himself, at least for now.

The boy's eyes darted around him, but neither made a move. "We will be late. We are supposed to be with that group."

"Go then." Verges turned away and made it to the trees before the two boys caught up with him.

"Wait." There was a desperate note in the boy's trembling voice.

"Wait for what?" He turned back to them quickly and his hood slipped back. The night air felt cool against his heated skin.

The boys almost fell over themselves as they stepped back quickly. "Are you going to kill us?"

"Nay, at least I am not planning to. What tomorrow brings, no one knows." He shrugged. "Does this mean you are willing to talk to me?"

The older one nodded. The younger just stood staring.

"You are going to the Grayweist manor to train for the King." It was not a question and Verges did not wait for an answer. "What I want from you is to watch, that is all. Watch and tell me anything you see, that you think I want to know."

"How are we supposed to know that?" the young one said from behind his brother's shoulder.

"What are your names?" Verges wanted to be done with these two. He was tired and still needed to send a message to Van.

"I am Edward Hurtado and this is my younger brother Harry."

"Edward and Harry, you will use your judgment. If you think I want to know then I probably will. If you need to get in touch with me you can find me at the Doveslane Inn." He pointed to the east where the inn sat not more than a mile down the road.

"If I am not there leave a message with Annette." Verges was sure they were going to say yes, but a little incentive always helped, so he added for good measure. "She is the small red head that takes the boys upstairs for half a bit." Edward's eyes lit up at that little piece of encouragement and Verges held out a small pouch that jingled of coin. "Are you interested?"

Without a word, Edward reached out and snatched the coins. Verges's smile widened and he walked away, disappearing into the darkness of the woods.

"Now do we go to the castle?" Harry looked at his older brother. He was unsure if this was a good idea or not, but he would not argue with Edward. He had looked up to Edward all his life. He may not be the best at the things he did, and he certainly wasn't a nice boy, but Edward was his brother and he loved him.

"Not just yet. Just to be safe I think we should acquaint ourselves with the location of the inn. And get to know Annette a little more on the personal side." He laughed as he shook the hefty sack.

CHAPTER 16

P eter felt his head pounding before he was even fully awake. He rolled on his side without opening his eyes. The smell of Vanessa's face powder wafted up from the pillow beside him. He slid his hand across the wrinkled sheet, but found nothing.

"Damn," he muttered and the soft sound echoed through his head. He opened his eyes to bright sunlight streaming into the room and sharp pain stabbed his pounding head.

He clenched his eyes shut for a moment then opened them a little at a time, until he could peer around the room. It looked to be well into the morning. He could not remember the last time he had not risen before the sun.

He swung his legs over the side of the bed and sat up. A wave of nausea crashed over him and he closed his eyes, breathing slowly and deeply. Several shallow breaths seemed to calm his irritated stomach and he opened his eyes cautiously. He had not drunk so much in a very long time. He was not accustomed to it as he had been when he was seventeen. Age was catching up to him, at thirty two he felt like an old man.

He dressed as quickly as he could manage and made his way through Vanessa's empty chambers. His first stop would be the kitchen. Coffee and a bit to eat should settle both his head and his stomach.

The cook, who had been with his father since Peter was a child, brought him food to break his fast with a sweet and almost toothless grin. "Good morrow, milord."

"Good morrow, Cook. Have you, by any chance, seen my bride? She is probably with Joseph." He was already beginning to feel better. Being up and about limbered up his stiff muscles and joints. The smells of sweet rolls and meats eased his stomach and the thought of seeing his new bride relaxed his heart.

"Aye, milord. Lady Vanessa broke her fast early, the sweet boy with her, Miss Amy and Miss Anna, too. The four of them are rapidly becoming friends. They were together almost all of yesterday." Cook rushed through her words and darted quick nervous looks around the kitchen.

Peter's stomach twisted in concern. He shook his head to clear the doubt and decided the cook was just anxious to return to work.

"Where have they run off to today?" He thought he might find her before he went to see what kind of men the King had sent him to work with. Just to make sure she was behaving.

When Cook looked quickly down to her feet, Peter felt his stomach knot. So, he thought, she wasn't just anxious to complete her work. Once again his head began to pound and his stomach rolled.

"Where are they?" He pushed back his chair and the screech of the legs jolted through the bottom of his feet and seemed to explode out his head.

"Amy and Anna took little Joseph to the stream to fish before his studies. He is becoming quite the charming young man, my lord." Without meeting his gaze she busied herself straightening the large overly bright kitchen.

Two long strides were all it took to reach her. He grasped her chubby arm and spun her to face him. She kept her eyes straight forward and seemed intent on the rise and fall of his chest.

His face became hot with the anger that wormed its way through his aching head. "Where is my wife?"

She just continued to stare at his rapidly rising and falling chest.

His head thudded as if the devil himself were kicking the walls trying to get out. "If I have to hunt for her…" He let his voice trail off and glared down at her, but she remained silent. "If you are trying to protect her, it would be best just to tell me. The longer I have to search, the angrier I will become." He gave her a gentle shake.

"I don't think it's gonna make one wit of difference, milord." Her voice was almost silent.

"What will not make a difference?" He released her and she quickly retreated a few steps.

"If you have to look or not." She was now looking at his feet instead of his chest and he sighed wearily.

"What is that supposed to mean? I would urge you to tell me what you know, Cook."

She said nothing, just shook her head sadly.

He threw his hands up in exasperation. "How is it that I have lived here all my life and she is here only one day and already she has your loyalty?" He glared at her menacingly, but he felt no anger at her loyalty to Vanessa. In fact it pleased him to no end and he knew that Cook was only trying to protect his rampant bride.

Her eyes shot to his and she shook her head. "Milord, you have my loyalty, it's just that—"

"My lord, there you are." Grant's strained voice sounded from the doorway behind him. "I heard Amy telling Anna something I thought you might need to hear."

Peter turned toward Grant cautiously and caught Cook slipping away out of the corner of his eye. He let her go.

"What is it, Hestlay?"

"Anna said—" Grant took a deep breath and seemed to prepare himself for what he was about to say.

Peter was exasperated and well beyond the last frayed strands of his patience. "Just open your damned mouth and tell me."

His angry voice seemed to make Grant more concerned instead of less, but nonetheless opened his mouth as ordered. "She said—that she is not acting very smart. Seeing the men again was stupid and she should not…"

Peter could hear his old friend still talking, but the words no longer mattered. His aches and pains forgotten, he turned and stormed out the servants' door. He heard the door bang behind him and knew that Grant followed, but didn't slow his pace to the stables. "And for the sake of the groom, my horse had best be saddled and waiting for me," he growled foully as he stomped across the dusty courtyard.

♕ ♕ ♕

Van walked toward the men in the lists, knowing that she did not have much time before Peter arrived. She had debated all through breakfast on whether or not to come. She wanted to see the men, but more she wanted Peter to know that she was capable of protecting herself. If he trusted her and had faith in her, then perhaps he would allow her to help him with the men.

She laughed gently at the notion, knowing that was never going to happen, and looked over the king's newly sent men. One quick look showed her that they were not men. In fact they were not much more than little boys.

They were younger than she had expected and wondered if Peter knew how young they were. On that she was sure she was going to have to ask Richard, for Peter would never tell her.

"Richard, Good morrow. How are the men looking?" Every man turned and stared, but she did not see much surprise in their faces.

Van had debated on riding Damien down to the lists. He was unused to being stabled and needed exercise, but had decided against it. One rebellion at a time should be sufficient.

"My lady, may I speak to you alone?" Richard's voice was urgent as he took her by the arm and tried with nonchalance drag her away.

"Nay, Lord Grayweist is eating his breakfast and will be along shortly. I would like to see the men." With that she calmly removed his grip and walked toward the new boys.

"You make that sound as if he has given permission for you to be here. I know better," Richard grunted and shook his head. He had prayed she would not show up, but had known she was going to. He glared at the back of her head, but had to fight a grin.

"I need the king's new men to line up. Single file, facing me." Her voice was loud and commanding. Richard looked at her suspiciously. The voice was not the same high pitched squeal that had been hurting his head since she arrived. No it was different, but he was not sure how.

The boys milled around, looking at one another, obviously unsure of whom this woman was and if they were supposed to obey.

Richard shook his head and waited. If he was a lucky man, they would fail to obey her and she would stay at the castle. Her voice, pitched with a slight gravelly sound that made Richard's mind perk up, boomed across the meadow. "*Now!*" The boys fell over themselves to get into line. The horses screamed and jerked at their leads.

Vanessa paced slowly along the line, her voice once more annoying. "I want to welcome you to Grayweist. It is my understanding we are only to have you for a few short weeks. We will just have to make the best of it."

Richard cocked his head and stared at her intently. She smiled confidently at the scared looking boys and he decided it had been her anger that had changed her voice. The familiar sounding voice still tickled at the back of his mind, but he pushed it away for later thought.

Vanessa stopped in the center of the line facing the boys. She gestured for the horses to be brought forward without turning her head to look at the men.

Richard took a deep breath and hoped the men would not obey. As the men brought the horses forward without hesitation, he groaned. Fear for this stubborn girl cascaded over him. She was going to be in dire trouble and anyone who helped her would be as well.

He took a deep breath and stepped forward, taking his place at her side.

She glanced at him, but did not speak. A small smile tugged at her lips as she turned to watch the horses being lined up facing the boys.

Richard swallowed his concern and stood firmly beside her, even though he knew he should not be here. He should not be before the men and he reminded himself that he should have insisted that she go back.

He had not sent her back for the same reason that he stood here at her side. She seemed to look to him as her personal second-in-command and he felt compelled to play that part. So here he was. Once again about to do something Peter would surely behead him for.

Van raised one black brow at her second-in-command and gazed at him questioningly. "We have too many horses?" Pride that he stood at her side battled with the knowledge that she was doing something stupid once again.

Richard pursed his lips stubbornly and she had to fight a smile. She knew that look well and had seen it many times, right before he gave her what she wanted.

He sighed dramatically. "Two boys are late. Edward and Harry Hurtado. They started out with the group but got separated. Trouble makers from what I have gathered."

Her nerves trembled awake. It was possible that they had just wandered off, but she didn't believe so. Years of training and experience had made her cautious, had made her trust her instinct. "Keep a close watch on them if they arrive."

He nodded and she turned her attention back to the task at hand. She pointed at the far end of the horse line. "Start at that end. The tall chestnut is one, the dark bay is two, and so on." She pointed to each one in turn.

Her gaze took in all the men and her spirits sank. They were separated into two groups, her men and Peter's men. She shook her head slightly and thought, *This is unacceptable*. This would not do, not if they were to become one powerful army.

She quickly considered the options of merging the two groups. She grinned. The answer was simple. Assign them to tasks in combined groups, in essence, not giving them an option.

She didn't need help matching horses to boys for she had been doing it for years, but she knew she would not have many opportunities to encourage the combining of groups. She looked out across her men. "Richard and Devon, please stand behind the new men."

She waited until both her men were in position and looked over Peter's men. She did not know them well and would have to change that if she was going to assign them into tasks together. Men who were well matched and compatible would make the blending of the two groups smoother.

"Douglas and Gary, join them." They joined Richard and Devon without question. "You will walk behind the men and assist me in assigning horses."

She smiled as they huddled close and conferred momentarily. Every so often they would look up or point at either the back of a boy or at one of the horses. She gave them the time they thought they needed. Not so much because she needed their help but because it would bring them closer.

She paced before the boys and watched them closely. Some clearly stared at the horses they wanted. Some were smaller and suited to smaller horses, some were larger and needed a stout horse beneath them.

She'd handed out several horses, using these criteria, when Richard stopped behind a small framed red head and held six fingers up above the boys head. Van looked at the boy and at the sixth horse in line, a small golden horse. She considered it closely and nodded. The horse was given out.

Van handed out a couple more horses on her own and several that her appointed men suggested to her and thought things were going well. She was pleased with their suggestions and waited when they grouped together once again.

There was heated disagreement for a moment and then they seemed to come to a decision. Curiosity itched at her brain and demanded to be scratched. She pushed it back the best she could and waited impatiently—waiting was never one of her strong suits. Nor was patience, she thought with a grin.

Douglas stepped forward and stopped behind a small blond-haired boy who shifted from foot to foot and looked at the horses, clearly terrified. She had passed him several times and each time he had avoided her gaze. It was obvious the boy was afraid of horses and she didn't want to encourage it by putting him with a docile pony. Unsure of what exactly to do with him, she had gone on to the next boy.

Douglas held up nine fingers. Her brow furrowed and she turned to the horses. The ninth horse in the line was a massive black destrier, who snorted and pawed at the ground.

Van stared at the creature with appreciation. This was not a horse she was sure she wanted to put with any of the boys and wondered why Douglas had suggested it for this boy.

If she had not been so impressed with the way they had handed out the horses before, she would have thought he didn't know what he was doing. She turned a questioning look back to Douglas arching one eyebrow, and waited.

He nodded confidently. She glanced behind him to Richard. He did not look as sure of the decision, but he nodded.

She nodded toward the men handing out the horses and the restless stallion was brought forward. The young man took a step back, his hand going to his chest. He swayed and she was concerned momentarily that he would faint dead away, but thankfully he kept his feet beneath him. She knew how hard it was to go through training while being harassed and she did not wish it on any of the boys.

He refused to take the reins that were thrust at him and stepped completely out of line.

Douglas opened his mouth, but Van shook her head at him. She walked calmly up to the boy. "Afraid of horses, my boy?"

His chest puffed out and his head rose in pride. "I am afraid of nothing."

"Nothing? Everyone is afraid of something," she said. "Do you think yourself less a man if you admit to fear?" She did not wait for an answer as she stepped back. She raised her voice to be heard by all.

"I want to ask all of you a question, and I expect you to answer me. Forget what I stand before you wearing and just give me the answer you would if I were not dressed so." She ignored the prickle of discomfort as she decided, too late, that it was not wise to ask them to picture her as anything except a woman.

👑👑👑

Peter and Grant topped the hill overlooking the lists, but no one seemed to take notice. He snorted in irritation. His new bride stood proudly before the men seemingly doing his job, handing out horses to them. His eyes narrowed as he looked at what the king had sent.

They were not men. They were too young and too soft to be men. His line of thought was cut off as Douglas Sheire held his hands above a small blond-boy. He watched, interest rising as a massive black stallion was led to the young boy.

He seemed to panic and stepped out of line.

"He is afraid of horses," Grant said calmly beside him. Peter agreed, but didn't comment.

He watched Vanessa approach the blond-haired boy. She spoke to him for a moment and Peter wished he could hear what was being said.

He got his wish as Vanessa stepped away from the men. Her questioning voice echoed across the lists and Peter listened avidly. "I want to ask all of you a question, and I expect you to answer me. Forget what I stand before you wearing and just give me the answer you would if I were not dressed so. Who among you is afraid? Show me your hands."

At first there was nothing and Peter grinned, thinking that she was going to be disappointed. His men were not going to admit…Surprise overtook Peter as one-by-one, hands began to rise.

Peter turned to Grant who looked surprised as well. "Did all my men just admit to being afraid in front of a woman?"

Grant looked at him, his surprise turning to an ornery grin. "Nay, my Lord. They admitted it in front of the Dark Lady."

Peter rolled his eyes and nudged his horse forward. Van glanced up at him but then turned her attention back to the men. The men were all distracted by the lady of the castle and none took notice of his approach. That could get them all killed in battle and he would make sure to discipline the men when training began today.

Van looked across the sea of raised arms and by the time she spoke again, Peter was within hearing range.

"Fear is something good. Fear, listened to, makes you cautious, makes you pay attention to the situation. It is not fear that makes you less of a warrior. It is how you deal with that fear. If you let that fear run your life than you are a coward." She took the reins from Francis's hands and held them out to the scared boy. "If you take that fear and you overcome it, then you are its master, not its slave."

Peter approached quietly from behind the line of boys. The men who stood with the horses stopped and stared at him.

Peter pulled his horse to a stop and waited. This was an important decision for the boy and he was unwilling to interfere. He folded his arms across his wide chest and merely waited as the boy seemed to struggle with the decision.

His men all seemed to notice him at once and looked nervously from him to the others. He just sat patiently.

Richard, Devon, Douglas, and Puelo must have noticed the gaze of the other men. They looked over their shoulders at him guiltily. He kept his focus on Vanessa.

She did not take her eyes off the boy, but he was sure she was accessing him out of the corner of her eye.

With a trembling hand the boy took the offered reins. Peter smiled, knowing it was more than likely because she had basically called him a coward if he did not.

"I see you have all met my wife," Peter said proudly.

All the boys spun around to face him.

"My dear, I shall like to have a private talk with you." Pride in her had overridden the anger he had felt and he could not bring himself to yell at her. He would, although, make sure she understood that she had disobeyed him once again and that it would not be tolerated.

"I think we can talk here, can we not?" Van looked at him untrustingly and attempted an innocent smile that failed miserably.

"Fine." He would rather do it in private, but perhaps here was better. It would be a reminder as well to all the men who have seemed to forget that she was not allowed here. "You have disobeyed me once more and I would like to see you get out of it this time. I told you, you were not allowed to come here and yet here you stand."

"I did not disobey you, my lord." She said calmly. "You said I could not come here with anyone and I did not. I came on my own. As a matter of fact—"

Peter lost control and yelled, "I do not care about your matters or your facts. You know damned well what it is I had wanted from you. You went behind my back and did as you bloody well pleased once again." He took a deep breath to calm the anger roiling around in his stomach. "You will go back to the castle, you will stay there, and so I have no more misunderstandings I will say this to you."

Peter looked down at her trying to pin her with his most ferocious glare. He felt it slip when she arched one brow at him and smiled. Damn, he didn't understand how she got under his skin so bad.

He took a deep breath and spoke, his voice quiet and deliberate. "You are not allowed to come to this training ground in any way, with anyone or by yourself. You are not allowed to be here. However it is you think to come here, it is not allowed. Now, do you understand that?" Peter knew he had all the possibilities covered leaving her no way of getting around it.

"Aye, my lord, I understand." Van looked at the remainder of the horses and sighed.

"Good, now that we have an understanding." He turned toward Grant who was dismounting his steed. "Grant, help the men finishing handing out the horses, while I take my wife back." He looked at her irritably and added, "Again."

He reached down and pulled her onto the saddle. He kept her sideways until they were into the surrounding trees and then allowed her to throw her leg over the saddle. He felt a rush of lust as a length of pale white calf glittered in the bright morning light.

"My lord, do you have to hurry back?" She pressed against him and he fought a groan.

"That will not get you out of trouble." His voice was gruff, but he wrapped his arm around her waist. "Aye, I need to hurry back. I was late getting there to begin with." His arousal pressing into her buttocks insisted that he didn't need to hurry.

He pushed Jackal to a faster pace before he gave in to his need. As they were coming to the edge of the trees, he reached up and grasped a breast. She gasped. He placed a kiss on her neck and released her.

"Swing your leg back over."

She did so without argument as they cleared the trees.

He pulled Jackal to a stop before the castle steps and reluctantly slid her to the ground. "Stay out of trouble, stay near the castle and away from the men. You will not go back to the men if I leave you now, will you?"

"Nay, my lord, I have no intention of returning to the men now. I have other things on my agenda today." She grinned and he shook his head in exasperation.

"I will see you tonight." With one last suspicious look, he wheeled Jackal around and she stood watching him as he disappeared back into the trees.

"My lady, are you all right?"

Van heard the foot falls of three people behind her. "Aye, Amy I am fine." She turned with an excited smile to greet her friends. She reached down and gathered Joseph up into her arms. "How did the fishing go?"

The excitement in his eyes lit up his whole face. "I caught a big one."

"Good, now how would you like to help me—well, to help the men?"

He nodded and Van led them to the well-stocked wardrobe. She was pleased with the variety of linens and wools they had to choose from. The four friends rummaged through the dusty room until they had large stacks of heavy woolen material. Each took a heaping armload and they made their way to Van's chambers. The room had been thoroughly cleaned and Peter's mother's things had been packed away. It was a little empty, but it was a more comfortable area than she had ever had before. She laughed gently, thinking she had never had much more than a lean-to, so anything above that was an improvement.

Several maids joined them and the day passed as they made stockings and blankets for the men in the barracks. Van sat comfortably as they worked, listening to them talk and laugh. She interjected here and there but for the most part she silently enjoyed their lively chat.

Not long after they finished, Margaret came to the door. "Milady, there is a man here to see the lord, shall I send for him."

"Nay, I will see to him." She walked down the long winding staircase. At the bottom of the stairs stood a man she had met only once. Marcus Teredo, father of Nancy, a friend of Joseph's. Peter had introduced her when he had taken her on the tour of his land, and Joseph had told her later that he was friends with the man's daughter.

She extended a hand of welcome to him. "Mr. Teredo, how may I help you?"

He looked at it unsure for a moment then grasped her outstretched hand and gave it a hardy shake. "I came to see Lord Grayweist."

"He is unavailable right now. You can come back later or you can speak to me." She asked Margaret to send for drinks and ushered him to a chair. She didn't wait for his consent to talk to her. She had learned over the years that if you didn't give someone the luxury of time to think, they were more agreeable.

He sat with that same unsure look on his face. "It's my sheep," he started uneasily. "They are coming up missing. I was not sure what it was until last night. It is men, my lady."

He paused as a young redheaded maid shyly brought two goblets in. He took the one offered to him and smiled in thanks. He drank heartily and when he spoke again he sounded more relaxed. "I was quite sure it was wild animals. I stayed out last night with my arrows, since it was a full moon and there was plenty of light, but it was men. They took some and left."

"Did you see what they looked like?" she asked in an even tone, trying to hide the nervous energy that pulsed through her. She had to know if it was Eolian's men. If it was, why was he here? Did he follow her men or did he know somehow who she was? Her breath tightened in her chest as worry constricted around her.

"I saw them all, but only one stood out. He was a monster of a man, wore a dark cloak with a hood. The hood fell back when he was taking a sheep." He shuddered and stared at the trembling goblet in his hand. "His face…it was not deformed really, but…" He stopped, looked at her, and shrugged.

"Misshapen?"

He nodded.

"A very large man?" she asked, but she already knew.

He nodded.

Verges. She was glad that he was near, but not happy that he was not alone.

"Aye."

"When did they arrive?"

"Four nights ago was the first time sheep came up missing. I didn't say anything when you stopped by because I had still thought it to be animals, milady." He looked at her hopefully.

Relief fluttered through her. Four days. That meant that Eolian had arrived around the same time as her men and before she did. She could only pray that meant they were unaware of her.

"They came last night. That should mean they will not return for a couple of days. I do not want you to tell anyone of this." She stopped momentarily and grinned. She had a devious idea. "No actually, I want you to tell anyone you see, especially ones that will spread the word. I want you to tell them that you think your sheep are sick, that they are dying. That should worry whoever it is that is taking them."

He looked distraught. "Milady, that will mean no one will buy them."

She just smiled. "It will all work out if you trust me."

At the reluctant nod of his head she showed him out. She hoped Eolian had eaten a lot of the sheep by the time the rumor of the sick sheep got to him.

She began to laugh gently as she approached her chamber door.

"What is so funny?" Amy's voice broke into her thoughts as Van pushed the door open.

"Nothing, Amy. We had better get those things out to the barracks. The men will be here any moment."

Peter was weary as he rode back to the castle. The training of the young, inexperienced boys had gone just as badly as he had anticipated.

He rode in between Grant and Richard as they approached the stables. He turned toward Richard but his words were lost as he watched four unmistakable figures run from the barracks to the castle. "What do you figure they are up to now, Devenroe?"

Richard looked from him to the running figures. "My lord, I am not one to guess what your wife—"

Peter shook his head. "Pretend she is not my wife. What would your answer be?"

Richard looked at him seriously. "I would no more try to judge what that woman would do than I would try to judge where I might stand not to get hit by lightning." This sent all the men into hysterics.

Peter ignored them. "Hestlay, go on to the castle with the men. I am going to ride over to the barracks with the boys and Richard's men." He made a mental note to stop calling them Richard's men. They would never become one if even he kept segregating them.

Walking into the dim building, he looked around. Nothing looked different that he could make out. What had she been up to?

"My lord, I found it."

Devon held up a big bundle of cloth that had been laid on his bed. On all the beds they discovered. Peter opened Richard's, smiling as stockings and blankets came rolling out.

Peter looked his friend. "You know something, Richard, that woman will be the death of me. Just when I think she cannot surprise me, she does."

"One thing for sure, my lord. You will not be one stuck in a boring marriage."

Everyone hooted and hollered at that. Peter shook his head leaving them to their fun.

He was having difficulties remaining angry with her, a grin making its appearance on his normally stoic face.

He did not see her before the evening meal, though he found himself looking for her. When he had cleaned up and made it to the dining hall, she was already there, sitting silhouetted in the candle light. The flickering of the flames reflected off the silk of her gown.

He walked directly to her and pulled her to her feet. He smiled when she gasped. "I cannot wait to get you alone tonight."

"Sit, my lord. We shall dine with the men, before we retire." Her face glowed with excitement and pride. It made even the powder glow. His heart swelled with pride even as his mind tumbled with irritation.

When the meal was served and the maids clear of the table, Vanessa leaned toward him. She gestured for Richard and Grant to come forward and Peter gazed at her in distrust.

"My lord, Marcus Teredo came to see me this afternoon," she said quietly.

He gave a massive and injured sigh. "Not only are you training my men, but now my tenants are coming to see you." He raised a brow at her in mock irritation.

She looked at him, opened her mouth to answer, and then thought better of it. She shut her mouth and smiled.

Vanessa looked at all of them in turn and then told the story of his sheep. "I think it should be looked into, my lord."

Peter listened carefully and nodded his head.

"There is one more thing, my lord."

She ducked her head. He saw a grin spreading and he was afraid to ask.

"Yes?"

All the men sitting close to them at the head table burst into laughter as she told them what she had told Marcus to tell people.

"That is more than I can take. I am no longer hungry." He jumped to his feet and swung her over his shoulder like a sack of grain.

As she pretended to fight him, he watched the faces of the men, both his and Richard's. He wondered if he would make it to the stairs, lord or not, if she was actually asking for help.

From the intent looks on their faces he didn't think so. Instead of making him angry, it made him feel more secure. No one would bother her. She would be safe.

It was more than just the way they had looked at him now. He had heard them talking between themselves as well. He knew they would give their lives for her. He grinned as he began to walk toward the stairs.

Vanessa struggled the entire way to the chambers, exciting him all the more as breasts rubbed against him and thighs caressed his arms.

On the stairs he faltered and swayed. He grinned when she slowed her fighting until he was on flat ground once again. He was pleased with the change in her.

Peter pushed it from his mind as he kicked the door to his chamber closed. He laughed as she began to struggle more violently now. She kicked and swung her arms. Then he heard her laughter, low and breathy.

He threw her onto the bed and nearly ripped his clothes off. She followed his example. He stood slack jawed in surprise as she slipped the gown from beneath her hips.

Vanessa lay back and opened her arms, and her smooth white thighs, in invitation. He wasted no time falling atop her. She wrapped her arms around his neck and pulled him closer. He kissed her gently.

He had planned to take his time with her, to make her ready, but it seemed apparent, as she forced the kiss deeper, that she already was.

Van kissed him greedily. Excitement raced through her muscles and settled between her open thighs. The hard tip of his arousal searched her folds for entry and she gasped into his mouth as he rammed his cock into her, hard.

His motions were frantic, needy, and she matched his movements with her own greedy lust, shoving her hips hard into his. They ground together in ecstasy, riding the waves of pleasure until raspy breath echoed throughout the chamber.

Muscles taunt to the point of pain, she clung to him as he took her to new heights of pleasure. Wonderful agony echoed through her with every hard thrust, and she tilted her hips to take him deeper.

He stiffened with a growl. The hot pulsations of his own pleasure pushed her over the edge. Head back, she bit her lip to hold in her cries, but they were ripped from her.

They lay together, wrapped tightly in trembling arms and legs, as they awaited the return of their senses. She expected him to roll off, but was pleasantly surprised when he laid his head in the crook of her neck. She wrapped her arms around him and sighed contentedly, not wanting him to move just yet.

She liked the feel of him. The pressure made them seem like one person, connected in some special way. She marveled at the change in herself. She had fought that connection fiercely in the beginning, not wanting him to have that power over her.

Now she reveled in the power she felt over him as well. It was a oneness she craved, but even that surprised her. Where had her craving for total command gone? She considered this as she closed her eyes.

Peter shifted his weight, worried that he was hurting her. He groaned pleasurably and grinned as her arms tightened around his neck when he tried to lift off of her. He kissed the top of her nose gently and lay beside her.

Covering the both of them, he pulled her tightly into his embrace. He could smell the powder that she caked on and hoped she would not be wearing it much longer. He fell asleep wishing he could see her true face.

That night he dreamed once again of the boy who had saved him three years ago, the same dream that had plagued him since that night. The young dark face leaning over him. The dagger wound dripping blood onto his shoulder, their blood mingling in his wound. Over and over, he caressed the smooth skin of his cheek, telling him he was beautiful.

CHAPTER 17

Van awoke as Peter slipped from the bed. The early morning light was just beginning to peek through the window of the master bed chamber. She reached up checking for the light powdery feel of the camouflage on her face. She could feel the powder thick across the scar. She stretched sleepily and watched Peter's naked backside as he walked toward the fireplace.

"You are the lightest sleeper I have ever seen," he said laughingly, looking over his shoulder at her.

She blushed beneath the powder but did not take her eyes off his flexing muscles.

"Good morrow, my lord." She smiled and thought the only reason she had stayed alive as long as she had was because she was light sleeper. There had been more than one ambush where the sentry had fallen asleep. She had been the first to awaken to someone walking through the camp.

She had always been on guard to protect herself and her secret and had never slept soundly. It had been that way since she had gone to Castle Grayweist for training and she had quickly gotten used to restless sleep.

He took the charred end of the fire poker from its place beside the fireplace and stoked the dying fire. "I do believe it is about time you began to call me Peter. It is quite proper, I assure you."

Once the coals were stoked he added a log to the fire. She was sure the day would warm up as it had the day before, but the morning air still carried a chill.

Her heart raced with excitement as her gaze took in the way the fire light flickered across the crests and valleys of his muscular body. She shook her head gently. She had seen naked men before the fire before and none had ensnared her attention the way Peter did.

She gasped silently as he turned suddenly and walked back to her. His manhood rose as he walked. It jumped and pulsed and her heart seemed to jump with it.

He smiled lustily at her. "I was hoping to wake you in more romantic ways." He stopped beside the bed and cocked his head at her. "Are you listening to me?"

She blushed and ducked her head. "Sorry, my lord."

"No, not listening. I told you to call me Peter. I am your husband.

Van just stared up into his rapturous blue eyes and barked a short laugh before she got hold of herself. Call him Peter? Van did not think she could get used to that. Peter was someone she looked up to, someone she respected, but he was also someone in power above her. Even when she became a knight, he was above her.

"I do not see what is so funny. I do think it is more than proper. I think it is a rule of sorts, to show your respect and your loyalty." He lay down atop her and she relaxed, wrapping her arms around his neck and pulling him close.

He kissed her gently and then rose back up on his elbows and gazed into her eyes. "You will show your respect to me by calling me Peter and to show my respect of you I will call you Vanessa and—"

She stiffened beneath him before she could stop herself.

He grinned. "Sorry, Vanessa," he said, emphasizing her name teasingly.

Van scowled at him.

His grin widened. "Do you have something else you would prefer I call you, Vanessa?"

She sighed. This line of conversation would get her in trouble and she had more pressing ideas for the morning.

She pressed her breasts into his warm chest. His crinkly hairs dug gently into her skin. "I have something else I would prefer you do, rather than talk." She ran her tongue along his ear and rejoiced in the way he shivered at her touch.

Chills ran through Peter's spine as Vanessa's tongue slid across his ear. A welcome warmth spread through him and settled in his groin.

The crackling fire threw shaky light across the large room. Peter looked down at her face. It was tanned and beautiful. He could see only perfection except for the smearing of powder that sleep had not erased.

He caressed the side of her face that was powder free and wondered again why she wore it. He did not ask. He knew there would be no answer.

Gently lowering his lips to hers, he savored the warm taste of her trembling lips. He flicked his tongue across them and grinned as she gasped.

She tried to pull him closer, but he propped himself up on his elbows and continued his gentle assault. He ran his tongue across her cheek, the residue of powder gritty and sweet.

Peter sucked gently on her ear and ran his hand across her quivering arms. His touch was feather light and he could feel the goose flesh spring forth on her arm. He kissed and licked her neck, barely containing his lust as she moaned and arched her back.

He wrapped his hand around a creamy breast and dropped his head to it, grasping a hardened nipple in his teeth, biting gently. He nuzzled each breast and lathered them with kisses.

"Please," she whispered breathlessly. Her voice sounded pained.

He looked up at her for a moment, her eyes tightly closed, her mouth slightly agape. Then he slid down her toned body, trailing kisses along her stomach and kissed the soft hair at the apex of her thighs.

"Peter," she gasped, wrapping her fingers through his hair encouragingly.

He grinned smugly at the use of his Christian name. He pushed her folds apart with his tongue. Her warm juices were sweet as he slid it in and out of her. Her muscles tightened and she rocked her hips. Her breathing increased, her hands tightening painfully in his hair.

Vanessa's moaning increased. His lust was becoming painful and he knew he could not last much longer.

He pulled away from her and she gasped, "Wait."

He smiled up at her gently and covered her with his body. Shaking with need, he slipped his hardened shaft into her warm wetness.

She wrapped her legs around his hips as he rocked against her gently. Pressing his lips onto hers and encouraging her lips open with his tongue, he kissed her sweetly and controlled the lust as much as he could.

Vanessa ran her fingers through his hair, and around his ear, and kissed him back as they rocked together on the bed.

Her muscles tensed and pulsed around him as he slid tenderly in and out. His breathing increased, tightness formed low in his stomach.

A lump grew in his throat as she kissed him lovingly and without hesitation.

She began to move her hips faster against him. She moaned against his lips. He nibbled and bit on her lips and chin and down her neck until her she tightened around him and cried out.

Her face seemed to glow with pleasure. He could wait no longer. He spilled his seed deeply against her womb and collapsed atop her.

Peter reined Jackal to a stop on the rise overlooking the lists. The men stood in small groups, each group with several boys. The boys each held the reins of a horse. Some struggled with their mounts and some looked confident.

Peter watched the boys appraisingly as they worked. The horses whinnied in greeting. Jackal tossed his head, snorting in return. Peter ran his gaze across the groups of men and boys. It took him only moments to pick out two new bodies that were not there the day before. His grin fell away and he rode directly to Grant. He was sure the boys were Edward and Harry Hurtado. The other boys had all said they were disobedient and rowdy on the way to the castle. Now they appeared to be in fine spirits and working well with the others. He narrowed his eyes and stared at them in suspicion.

Dismounting, he handed off his reins without looking in the direction of the man who took them. He nodded toward the two boys. "Edward and Harry Hurtado?" he asked, already sure of the answer.

"Aye, my liege, they arrived just a short while ago." Grant nodded his head gently. He glanced over at the boys. "They claim to have fallen behind and become lost." He snorted and added, "Like they were not on a well-worn and traveled road."

"Keep a close watch. No one has gotten lost on that road before." He watched the boys for a few moments before adding, "How are they doing?"

"I have concerns," Grant said sternly. "The majority of the boys are fine. My concern lies with the brothers. On the trip here it was said they were rude and evil tempered, but since their late arrival, they have been nothing if not polite and well mannered. It does not make sense to me."

Peter nodded his head in agreement. "I noticed that as well. I want to know if they leave the grounds for anything. If they do need to leave, get them an escort."

Peter glanced from Grant to Richard and smiled. He had not wanted to let him go three years ago and was glad to have him back within his army. "How are the rest doing?"

"Some are doing better than others, but all seem to be willing to learn." Richard shifted nervously from foot to foot. "We have some problems with Marshall VanDyke and Ebro, the brute of a horse he was assigned to."

"Aye, he is afraid of horses. Douglas Sheire said he had spoken to the boy and he saw something in him. He just needs to get over his fear." Peter watched Richard closely as he kept looking past him expectantly. A disappointed look crossed his face once more and he looked back to Peter.

"Richard?" Peter asked curiously. "Are you still listening to me?"

Richard glanced at him and grinned sheepishly. "Yes, my liege. It is nothing."

"It is something." Peter let his voice drop to a commanding tone. "Tell me."

"It is just that I was expecting to see Lady Vanessa. I really had not expected her to give up so easily." Richard shook his head and gave a small laugh. He looked over Peter's shoulder again and shrugged. "I know..." His voice trailed off.

Grant shook his head, a look of disbelief crossing his face.

Peter did not need to turn, did not want to see what he knew he would see. Vanessa must have dressed and left right after him. He had been positive that she was bowing to his control, had seen it this morning in the way she looked at him.

He had to be mistaken. Had to be.

Peter watched all the men, and the boys, stop and look and he was not in the least surprised to turn and see his wife.

A wave of anger crashed into him as he watched the woman, who was forbidden from coming to the field, stride confidently toward him.

He was not as annoyed to see her as he was to see the thick powder back on her face. He had seen all of one side of it and had seen nothing wrong. Whatever blemish she had, she had to get over her fear of what people would say or think. That, although, would have to wait.

Now he would make it clear that she was going to obey him. He would make sure she understood him if it was the last thing he did. "What in the bloody hell, are you doing here?"

"I came to watch the young boy that I put with—"

He shot his hand forward, grasping her arm and jerking her to him. "Nay, you will not watch anything and when it comes to my men there is no 'I' involved when you are the one speaking."

She jerked her arm, but he tightened his grip and shook her gently.

"I told you, without any questions, you are not allowed to be here and you promised me." Peter dug his fingers into her rigid arm and glared at her. "You said you would not come out here and you are disobeying me again as well as lying to me. I could have you whipped for what you have done. I—"

His words cut off abruptly as she jerked her arm violently away from him. "I said no such thing. I may be disobeying you, but I did not lie. You told me what was expected of me and asked me if I understood. I did not lie when I said I did." She straightened her shoulders and held her head high. "As much as you rant and rave about it, I am fully aware of and understand what you expect of me."

He slapped an aggravated hand to his forehead as he realized what she had done. Trying hard to fight a laugh, he pulled his weathered hand down his face and forced himself to glare at her. "Fine, you understand. Now you will tell me that you will do as I say."

The corner of Vanessa's mouth twitched smugly. "Nay," she said softly. There was no explanation, no hesitation...no nothing. Just, "Nay."

"What do you mean, nay?" Peter asked incredulously. He could not believe that she had just defied him so openly and she had done so with a grin on her lips.

She just looked at him, the grin widened.

"You will do as I say or..." He shook his finger at her as he considered his options. They were few and none seemed to be effective. The ones that were effective he did not believe he would be capable of doing.

"Or I will have you locked in your chambers until you do," he said finally.

She gasped and took a step back. "Locked in…like I am some sort of prisoner. I am a person and I am your wife." She took another small step back. "What I am not is your slave, nor your prisoner. I will not be locked in anywhere like I am."

Anger screamed through Peter at her public defiance. He lurched forward and threw her over his wide shoulder. "You will no longer defy me."

He watched Richard as well as several other men start forward to help her, but to their credit none moved more than a step or two. Well, some took three before they stopped to watch.

He yelled for his horse. He looked across the men. His gaze settled on two men who had been with him for several years. James Choral, a tall blond-haired man and Brevon Dumont, a short, round, redheaded boy with a face full of freckles.

He pointed to them. "You two saddle up and come with me."

Vanessa kicked and hollered dramatically and almost overturned them both. He watched them lead Jackal forward and was unsure of how he was going to mount with her fighting him so hard.

He grasped the saddle and reins. Grant stepped beside him and steadied him as he swung his leg over, with her still struggling. He felt them sway as he teetered. He cringed as he prepared for both of them to hit the ground. Grant pushed on his thigh and relief flooded him as his rear settled into the well-worn saddle.

She pushed her feet against the horse and they almost went over backwards. Grant grabbed her legs, taking several good kicks in the process. He cursed loudly and Peter watched the pale beginnings of a bruise begin on his arm. "Tie her legs." Peter barely got the growl out. His breathing came in exhausted gasps. He had not worked this hard in a long time.

Within moments, and with the help of several others, Grant had pulled a rope from the saddle bag and had Vanessa trussed up at the ankles and knees and wrists.

Neither struggles, nor her unladylike curses, ceased as they made their way to the castle. Guilt began to worm its way through his thoughts as he swung his leg over the saddle, but he had come too far now to back down. If he let her win now, he would never gain control of her.

Peter almost lost his balance as she renewed her violent struggles when he took the castle steps. He slapped her hard across the bottom, and tried to ignore her gasp. Her curses renewed with new vigor and she hit him across the lower back.

Pain exploded through him, but he ignored her, the best he could. He knew he would have bruises across his back and backside.

He slapped her across the rump again and told her to shut up and stop struggling before they both fell. She ignored him and continued fighting.

He mounted the stairs with the two men right on his heels. He kicked his chamber door open, stalked across the floor and threw her onto his bed.

He turned and left without a word to her. Slamming the door hard, he gave notice to the two men who had ridden with him. "Keep a close eye on her and do not allow her to leave this room." He took a deep breath. "I will send a maid up to undo her bindings."

The men turned and stared as he crested the hill overlooking the lists. They shuffled nervously and Peter shoved down a bout of irritation at them.

Grant took the reins as he dismounted.

"I will see how the boys are coming." Peter kept his voice calm and controlled.

He could allow no hint of the anger that boiled inside him. He could feel it burning at him and pushing to escape its confines. He took a deep breath and stilled his shaking hands.

The anger he felt was not at his disobedient wife, but at himself, at his inability to control a mere woman. It was no wonder Eolian eluded him so many times, he thought impatiently. How was he going to train these boys to be of any use to anyone?

He supposed he could teach them to take orders from their wives, perhaps that he could do, he thought crossly. Shaking off the tendrils of self-doubt, worming through his foggy brain, he made his way to the boys.

They were practicing grooming and hoof care, but he could see from anxious and excited looks that most wanted to be riding already.

Peter stopped and watched them. These boys were not from well to do families or even those of the middle classmen. It was apparent that they had seen days of hunger and sickness. They probably had never been treated as well as they were here.

This was not good.

Conditions here were meant to be bad, to accustom the pages to life as a warrior. These boys were happy here, happy to be fed and to have the opportunity to ride the magnificent creatures put under their care.

All but one. Marshall VanDyke, the short blond boy who had been afraid to even touch his horse. He was having difficulties controlling his mount. While he could hold him steady or pick up his feet for cleaning, he did not seem to be able to manage both. Every time the huge destrier would spook or rear, Marshall would lose grasp of the lead and let him have his head.

Grant and Richard stopped to each side of him. He glanced at them and then back at Marshall.

Grant shook his head. "It has been like that all day, my lord. He does not have the courage to take control. If that horse continues to have his way, there will be no fixing the problem."

Peter knew exactly what he meant. He was having the same dilemma of his own. He forced Vanessa from his mind and tried to concentrate on the situation at hand.

"It will be fine. Sheire is a fine judge of people and of horse flesh." Peter strode toward Marshall and loudly proclaimed, "Boy, I have to see to one of my tenants." Ebro skittered away.

Marshall grasped the reins and pulled the big creature back toward him. He showed no fear when he did it, just frustration.

Peter grinned. He was sure that Douglas had seen the natural way the boy had with horses. He just needed a chance to get over his fear. "Both Devenroe and Hestlay are needed here, so you will accompany me."

"Milord?" Marshall's voice squeaked as he shifted his gaze frantically around the group.

"Saddle your mount." With that he turned away, away from the pleading look and the fear in the boy's trembling face.

Richard quietly asked as he handed Jackal over, "Do you know he has never saddled or ridden before?"

"Aye, Devenroe, I am quite aware." Peter looked into Richard's troubled green eyes and smiled. "He will never get over his fears unless he is forced to, and as bad as it will be for him to make mistakes in front of me, it will be so much worse for those same mistakes to be made here."

Richard nodded in understanding.

"Are you ready, boy?"

Ebro was saddled and it looked to be correct. Peter just hoped Marshall didn't fall off in front of everyone.

Peter mounted Jackal and watched Marshall take a deep breath. He swung unsteadily into the saddle. The horse swayed beneath him. He sat stiffly and Peter waited until the animal settled.

Peter urged his mount next to the young boy. He sat with his head forward and did not look around. "Ready?" Peter asked again.

"Aye, my lord. I am ready." He added under his breath, "As ready as I will ever get."

Peter grinned. He nodded to the men and led the unstable boy away from watching eyes. He did not want an audience for what he had planned. He was not sure if his plan would even work, but he was going to do it anyway. He could use this time away from his own problems and distractions.

When they were a safe distance away, Peter dropped back beside him. "When you come to the fork in the road you will take a right. After that you will take a left and there will be a large oak, struck many years ago by lightening. Behind it is the small holding where you will stop."

"Milord, are you not going with me? Where will you be?" Marshall's voice was a soft weak plea.

Peter ignored Marshall's fear and his own doubts. "I will be right behind you." He hit the skittish horse soundly on the rump and it bolted away. He added loudly, "Right behind you, in case you fall off." He kicked his steed and Jackal bounded after the racing stallion. Peter watched the smooth lines of Ebro with pride.

Marshall clung desperately to the whipping mane and clenched his eyes shut in fear. He was sure he was going to fall and die. He could feel the wind flowing through his whipping hair. Opening his eyes a little at a time, he fought the trembling that wracked his arms and legs.

He thought of all the things in his life he still wanted to do and thought of his loving mother, as he waited for the fall that would end his life. He could feel Peter racing behind him. He could sense Jackal urging Ebro to go faster, competing with the challenging destrier.

The first fork in the road was not far ahead of them. He could see it barreling toward him. It split to the left and to the right and ahead of it were several trees and scraggly brush. If the horse didn't turn the correct way he would be shamed, but if the horse didn't turn at all it would kill them both.

Marshall took a deep breath and forced himself to straighten. If he was going to make that turn, he was going to have to do something. He released his death grip on the coarse mane and pulled tightly on the reins.

He leaned right and pulled the reins, gently at first, in the direction of the turn. Ebro turned neatly into the turn and Marshall nearly shouted from joy. Never had he dreamed he could do this. He had believed the horse to be out of control, that he had no power to control it, and he had been wrong. He had done it.

He relaxed, feeling the stallion's smooth neck muscles ripple against the reins. Ebro tugged against them, wanting his head. He had been constrained in the stables and wanted to run.

Marshall allowed a slight slacking and gave Ebro some freedom while still keeping control. He moved with the rhythm of the horse's long, ground-eating strides. He leaned forward out of the wind and took a deep breath.

Fear swamped him once again as the second fork came into view. He pulled on the reins, slowing.

Suddenly Peter was beside him, slapping Ebro on the rump once again. Jackal pushed forward into the bend and Ebro pushed ahead of him. Fear knotted in Marshall's stomach but he held firmly onto the reins and leaned into the turn.

Peter grinned proudly at the boy. Marshall was doing well with the racing stallion. He held an unsteady control over Ebro, but it was control nonetheless.

Jackal laid his ears laid back and pulled the bit into his teeth. Peter pulled gently on the reins and felt no give. He tugged on them roughly, but Jackal only snorted and nudged his way past Ebro and into the lead.

Marcus Teredo and his son, Kyle, stood in the door yard of their cottage and watched as the racers flew past them. Peter turned Jackal toward Ebro, forcing him to turn as well and they came thundering back toward Teredo's land.

The sheep in the front pasture stood lazily watching the racers go by.

The horses, heaving heavy breaths and lathered to a thick white, skidded to a stop, side-by-side.

Marshall, unprepared for the sudden stop, flew over his mount, landing heavily on the ground. He jumped to his feet before Peter could even ask if he was all right. He happily hugged the big animal tightly around the neck before dancing around the two animals, shouting his exhilaration.

"Careful, boy, look how you are scaring my sheep." Marcus laughed as the sheep lazily moved from grass clump to grass clump, bleating contentedly.

"Sorry, sir. I apologize." The gesture was well meant and honest, even given the mile-wide grin, a new feature to his young, dirt-covered face.

"Marcus, I am sorry if we disturbed you or your sheep. May I come in?" Peter asked. He glanced at Marcus's son and watched the slow smile that crossed his face as he stared at the horses. There was a shiny glint to his eyes and a slight slackness to his jaws.

"Kyle, take the horses and give them a good rub down. Give them little water but no food just yet," Marcus said gently as he looked over the horses. "Don't let them gulp the water now."

"Aw, I know all that, Papa." Kyle took the reins and led the horses toward the small stable yard.

Peter's shoulders knotted in concern as the obviously, slow-witted boy took his prize stallions. "Is he going to be all right with them?"

"Aye, milord. He had the fever when he was little and the doctor said there was nothing that could be done. We thought we had lost him, only lost a part of him though. He is here and that is what matters to us."

Marcus motioned them toward the house. He led the way, opening the wood slat door so they could enter. "He had been damaged due to the high fever. Aye, he is slow, but he is as strong as an ox, willing, and capable of doing anything I ask of him. He is skilled at caring for horses, milord."

Peter turned before he entered the house. "Go with him, Marshall. You need to know how to care for horses that have been run hard. Caring for them properly makes sure they do not become ill."

He did not wait for an answer but followed Marcus into the small warm house and took the offered seat at the small table.

Marcus's wife was beside herself, mumbling irritably about guests giving notice before coming to visit, even if they were the lord of the manor.

Marcus shook his head indulgently and ignored her. He looked expectantly at Peter but Peter waited until the ale was placed on the table and Mrs. Teredo was out of the room.

Peter took a long drink of ale and looked around the small kitchen. It was clean and warm, but looked well used. "I have been told you are having difficulties with sheep coming up missing here of late."

"Aye, milord, as I told Lady Graywest, I believed it to be wolves or some such animal. I stayed up one night to find out. It was men. I did not recognize them, but Lady Vanessa asked me what they looked like and she knew who it was."

Peter looked up at him in shock, but Marcus was taking a long drink of ale. Peter took a deep breath and relaxed. "What did they look like?" he asked calmly, but what he wanted to know was why he thought Vanessa knew who it was.

Marcus repeated his story of the large gruesome looking creature and Peter felt his stomach draw tight. He knew exactly who it was. Eolian was here, of that he was certain, but he was unsure of why Eolian had not made his presence known before now. Why was he keeping hidden?

"I have told people what she told me to, but no one has come to look at my sheep. I did what she asked." He glanced nervously in the direction his wife had disappeared to. "I hope it was the right thing, milord. My sheep is all I have to take care of my family milord. Without them…" He shrugged his shoulders and concern furrowed his brow.

"Everything will be fine. It will all work out in the end. Your sheep will sell, even if I have to buy them all." He gave Marcus's arm a gentle squeeze. "My wife just wanted to worry the men who stole your sheep. Tell people it was a mistake, not today, but tomorrow. Tell them it was coyotes that were dragging away your sheep and not a sickness." Peter took a small drink of ale and leaned back in his chair.

"Yes, my lord."

Peter grinned at Marcus. "That should worry the men long enough, but we want them to come back for some more. Tomorrow night I will post a man on your holding as well as several others' with livestock. We will get the men doing this."

They spoke of the weather and the coming winter before Peter made his farewells. Peter and Marshall made their way back to the castle, more sedately than on the way to the holding.

Peter said very little on the way back. His mind worried over what Marcus had said. "She knew who it was". He had said it so calmly, but Peter had not been calm since he had said it.

Eolian, at last report, had been far away from here. He had been seen around a small town of Junket not long ago. What had brought him this far over?

More importantly, how did Vanessa know it was him? She knew his name, not many did, but it was not unheard of. Knowing Eolian's name, and knowing one of his men by a description, was not the same.

At first he tried to pass it off as a woman's fear. Vanessa knew about the man and was afraid of him and assumed that any man was him. Hysterics would explain it.

He shook his head and snorted. Vanessa was not the hysterical type.

He chewed the inside of his bottom lip as the questions swirled through his mind. How would she know one of his men?

"Well, perhaps I should just ask her," he mumbled.

Marshall looked over at him, but Peter just shook his head.

Peter frowned. He was glad to have a reason to go see Vanessa. He had wanted to see her for most of the day, but could not bring himself to go to her just because of his nagging guilt.

He watched Marshall return to the men. The boy sat tall and proud in his seat. He was now a confident rider. Peter grinned.

He reined Jackal around and made his way to his prisoner. Smiling, he thought of many delightful ways to interrogate her. They may not make her talk, but maybe he could make her scream. He smile turned to a lustful grin.

CHAPTER 18

V an had easily removed the bindings before there was a knock on the door. A maid proclaimed she was sent to remove her ropes. The shy voice was barely heard through the solid oak. Van told her to go away.

Now Van sat on the edge of her bed and wondered what she was doing. "I am going to give myself away," she chastised herself quietly. She forced herself to remember that the Dark Knight was gone, never to return. The problem was she did not know who to be with him gone.

She seemed unable to be the woman she was expected to be and it was impossible for her to be the man she had pretended to be. She sighed heavily, feeling lost.

She closed her eyes against a wave of nausea. Her head felt light and her breathing became harsh. She began to feel a panic she had never experienced before.

Her eyes flew open and her gaze darted around the room. The walls began to close in on her. Her vision blurred as her breath came harder and heavier. As the room began to spin, she ran for the door. Skidding to the stop, she stared at the wide back of a guard.

James Choral turned, opened his mouth, and she slammed the door shut. She walked through the empty master's chamber, but when she opened the door to the hall she saw the back of Brevon Dumont.

Her eyes narrowed angrily. She had somehow managed to go from a great and feared knight, to a lowly woman, and then to a prisoner. Anger exploded in her troubled mind.

The knight that lingered just below the surface fought for release. She balled her fists into tight balls and glared into Brevon's bright green eyes as he turned to her.

"Lady Vanessa, I am sorry, but it is requested that you remain..." A hard-swung fist stopped him in mid-sentence and dropped him to the cold stone floor. She glared down at him, barely containing an urge to kick him violently in the ribs.

Footfalls running toward her drew her attention. Panic filled James's face as he ran to his fallen partner's aid.

He stepped toward her quickly. She slammed the heavy oak door shut and heard a satisfying crack on the other side with a sharp yell of pain.

Storming through Peter's chambers and back into her own, she stomped to the window.

Out in the distance she could see the lists, and the men. Her heart sank and seemed to settle deep in her stomach. They were her men no longer.

She could not stay here, not as a Lady and definitely not as a prisoner. She had to escape. She would just disappear.

Leaning out the window, she looked down at the stables. It was a straight drop to the hard ground far below. Her spirits slipped and she sighed deeply.

Van let her gaze roam to the gardens. It was still her favorite place in the castle and just the sight of them made her calm. Vines grew from the gardens below the Lord's chamber to almost his small window. Her eyes widened and a smile crossed her face as her gaze followed the path of the dark green leafy vines. She returned to his chambers.

"Aye, indeed that is a splendid idea." She spoke out his window to the quiet garden. She threw her leg into the opening and pressed herself through the small window. It was a tight squeeze, but she was out.

She teetered unstably on the small ledge and clung to the rough stones and mortar that made up the walls of her prison. She silently cursed her wicked dress as it caught and snagged on the thick vines. She scraped her fingers repeatedly trying to pull it free. How women managed to accomplish anything in the ruffled contraptions they insisted on wearing, she could not fathom.

The dress clung to the sturdy vines, fighting her the entire way down. Frustration and anger built within her. She looked down and breathed a sigh of relief to see the ground close enough to risk a jump. The dress was worse than getting used to the overly baggy and long tunic she had worn as a warrior. That had been hard to get used to as well, not like the well-fitting clothing she had worn as a small page, before the emergence of her womanly curves.

A hard jolt to the ground was favorable compared to hanging with one arm trying to untangle the thin black material with the other. She laughed, thinking what it would have been like to try her feat of escape if she had been wearing the layers of lace silky undergarments Amy kept trying to force upon her.

She took a deep breath and jumped. The hard landing knocked the breath from her and turned her legs to jelly, but she quickly shook off the pain and made her way to the stables and freedom.

The stables were bustling with activity as the stable hands got acquainted with Mortamor St. Johns, the very small man who came from the village to take charge of the horses. Mortamor was a nice man, small in frame, but not in heart. He owned no whip, tending to his horses and those around him with kindness and gentleness.

St. Johns looked up as she approached. His eyes widened in surprise and she could only imagine what he was seeing.

She could feel the sweat trickling down her body. Her black dress clung to her damp body and dust and dirt powdered her face and hands. She was a good foot taller than him and wider by far.

Fear clouded his widened eyes momentarily. He must have realized who she was as recognition brightened his face. He visibly relaxed though his eyes still held wariness.

She grinned, wondering what kind of stories he had heard about the new lady of the castle.

He smiled charmingly. "Milady, can I assist you?"

She raised her brow questioningly. "You are, who?"

"My apologies, milady. I am Mortamor St. Johns. I came to take over from the last stable master." He smiled nervously and swept a low bow.

"Are you a cruel man, a man who enjoys using the whip?" She sneered at him. She had heard the stories of his kindness, but felt it was always best that you make judgments for yourself in matters such as this.

"Nay, milady." His hands trembled slightly but he stood proudly before her.

She saw no hint of a lie and relaxed slightly. "Good, I am in no need of your service. I have come for my horse and saddle." She nodded dismissively and moved to walk around him.

When he stepped into her path she raised a threatening brow at him. She could see the fear in his eyes, but felt a jolt of respect for the man who stood his ground.

His voice trembled almost as much as his frame. "I have orders. You are not to take out any of the horses or tack. I am sorry, milady."

"Orders? That is fine." She grinned at him and stepped closer. She softened her voice. "I have an order of my own for you." Her quiet demeanor changed and she straightened to her full height. "*Move!*"

He nearly tripped over his feet as he quickly stepped away from her, allowing her to pass.

She walked toward the stalls and almost cried when she heard the familiar whinny of Damien. The tension seemed to flow from her muscles and she increased her step. The large stallion had his head over the gate of the stall when she arrived.

He whinnied once more and she wrapped her arms around the heavily muscled neck. She buried her face into his warm mane and breathed in deeply. She gave her old friend comfort and took some from him as well.

"I cannot leave. I have nothing." She spoke into the tickling fibers of his mane. He stood patiently through her hug and leaned his large jaw against the top of her head. "I need my things, and I have something I need to take care of first, my friend. It will be just a while longer yet, and we will be free." She kissed him gently and reluctantly pulled away. She left the stable, her heart and her mind heavy with her uncertain future.

Where was she to go now? She had no intention of returning, just yet, to her chambers. Though she would have to return to them at some point, she thought despairingly.

She stood outside the stables for only a moment looking around the massive courtyard. Her gaze fell on the barracks where her men stayed, what would soon be the housing of pages from all over. She made her way to it.

In the darkness of the barracks Van breathed deeply the smells of the men. She missed the nights huddled around the fires with her men. Was she wrong to still want it? It was the only life she had ever known.

She could feel the tears clogging her throat, yet she refused to give way to them.

Van plopped heavily on one of the rumpled bunks and leaned back closing her eyes. She thought back to all the troubles she had encountered since the arrival of that dreaded messenger.

All of them, her mind had decided, revolved around the hated gowns. There was her first encounter with her father, where she had felt naked and exposed. Then there was the disastrous first meeting with Peter where she could not even walk in them. She did not believe she could ride in the infernal thing and it had almost killed her coming down the wall.

What would she do if someone found out who she was? What would she do to protect herself and others if she could not even manage a dress. She had already eliminated the thin slippers and the chemise, but it was not enough.

When she had first became a squire it had seemed impossible to maneuver in the bulky hauberk and chest plate. Practice was all it had taken. Was it possible that with practice her gowns would become as secondary skin as had her armor?

Her eyes opened and she smiled. "Only one way to find out," she said with determination.

Her voice echoed in the long, dirt-floored building. Always one to begin training as soon as possible she set about to accomplish the task she had laid out for herself.

Starting at one end of the barrack she first began to run the distance of the men's sleeping quarters. Falling several times only angered her to run faster. Lap after lap she raced down the center of the isle. Lap after lap the dress began to be forgotten.

Sweat began to slide down her face. The quick breeze as she ran was cool and inviting. She ran her arm across her forehead as the salt stung her eyes.

Her confidence began to build as she fell less and less. Soon she changed course. She slid under the bunks or went over the tops of them.

Her breath began to wheeze tightly through her raw throat and heaving chest. Still she ran on; adding jumps, kicks, and rolls to her practice.

Hours later, covered in dirt, sweat, and bruises Van stood assessing the area. On one of the bunks lay a short sword, heavy and well worn. It had been left behind, due to a broken tip.

Practice began immediately. As she feared, the sword caught in the material of the skirt as she swung the massive weapon. It snagged and tore at the silky dress. She did not give up. She practiced throughout the day until she felt one with her weapon.

Van fell to the ground in exhaustion. She was tired and sore, but exhilarated. The high pitched whinny of approaching horses brought her to her feet. She glanced out one of the small windows and noticed that darkness was falling.

She knew the warriors would stop at the barracks to drop off armor and weapons before entering the castle for the evening meal. She opened the door a slight crack and peered out. The men were coming up into the court yard.

Closing the door she ran for the back of the barracks, slipped out one of the rear windows, and laughed as her dress went with her instead of holding her up.

She ran toward the castle, sliding to a stop in the deep shadows of the garden. She realized that practice with the sword was fine, but the main weapon she would probably use was her dagger.

The thigh strap was inaccessible without lifting her skirts completely. The dagger would be useless to her. She looked at the folds in her dress and shook her head. She must be able to get at her weapon.

Looking around the darkening shadows of the garden to ensure she was alone, she gathered the silky material and pulled it up exposing her thighs and the scabbard. She removed the jewel encrusted dagger and dropped the material, allowing it to fall naturally.

Using the sharpened dagger she made a slit in the fabric. The knife slid into the newly made hole perfectly. She pulled it in and out several times to insure it would work properly, and then she began the long climb back to her husband's chambers.

Peter pushed away the guilt for locking up his bride and focused on what pleasures he could inflict on her. He would make her forget his mistreatment in wondrous ways. A grin spread as he mounted the stairs two at a time.

He glanced up at the guards he had assigned. His grin fell away. Dried blood was smeared across both of the men's faces. Peter's heart began to race and fear prodded at him. His first thought was that she had escaped.

He quickened his step, but then forced himself to relax and walk calmly toward them. He reminded himself firmly that if she had escaped, the men would not still be standing guard. They would have sent for him.

"What happened?" Peter impatiently motioned for James to join them in front of the master chambers.

James looked at Brevon almost sympathetically and then focused on Peter's shoulder as he spoke. "She was coming out of the chambers. We told her to stay, milord. She slammed the door into my face."

Peter looked at the slightly bulged nose, the thin smearing of dried blood, and the darkening eyes of both men, and knew without a doubt that both had suffered broken noses.

He turned his attention to Brevon, who stood quietly with his shoulders stiff. He would not meet Peter's gaze. "What did she hit you with, Dumont?"

Brevon quickly looked at the floor and mumbled an answer too low for Peter to hear. Peter glanced at James, but the tall blond looked away nervously. Peter was not positive but it looked as though James was trying not to laugh.

Peter's brow furrowed and he turned back to Brevon. "I apologize. I did not hear you. Can you look at me and repeat your answer?"

Brevon's jaw tensed. He shook his head and looked at Peter. His eyes gaze darted to the ceiling and back to Peter's face. He sighed heavily and reluctantly answered through clenched teeth, "I said her fist. She hit me with her fist, milord."

"Fist?" Peter's mouth dropped open before he could stop it. "How many times?"

He had seen Vanessa's temper, but she had always kept it under tight control. At least usually. She had lost it with Rebeka, but even then she had only grabbed her. Peter had not believed her to be a violent person. He had pushed her hard and she had never struck him. He was surprised she had actually hit the guard.

Brevon's facial color deepened until he looked as though his skin were burnt. "Just once, my lord."

"Once?" He looked at the damage to the two men.

A tingling doubt wormed through him. *Maybe I better rethink pushing her so far. I knew she was strong. I just had no idea how much so*, he thought grimly.

"It is all right. She is a fiery woman to say the least. Have you heard anything from her?" Peter looked toward the door. The room behind it was silent.

"A lot of cursing at first, milord, but she has been quiet for a long time now," Brevon said quietly.

Peter opened the door to an empty room. A thorough search of both rooms sent his angry bellow to the men outside the thick doors. He heard their rapid footsteps rush toward him. They stopped behind him, their breathing heavy and raspy through their broken noses.

"I thought you said she was in here. Where is she?" He spun toward them. "Which one of you let her out?" He pointed his finger accusingly at each of them in turn and then clenched his fists. He took a jerky step toward them struggling to get control of his anger and concern. "Did she persuade you in some way? What did she promise you, did she give you something?" Peter shot his questions rapidly at them, gesturing angrily at the rumpled and messed blankets on his wife's bed.

They stepped back a half step. "N–nay, milord. W–we—" they stuttered together.

Peter jerked his arms up for silence. "I do not want to hear it. The three of us will search the castle and the surrounding lands and when I find her she had better have a good explanation as to how she disappeared into thin air." He glared from one to the other. "For you sakes, she had better."

With the men trailing behind, the entire manor was turned upside down.

Peter was halfway through questioning one of the downstairs maids when he sucked in a deep breath. A sudden worry stopped his words in mid question.

If Vanessa had gotten out, she might run and if she had run she would head for the stables.

Peter turned away from the confused looking maid and rushed from the castle, knowing in his heart that her stallion would be gone, but praying that he was wrong. Guilt slammed into him, knowing he had pushed her too far this time, and she had escaped him. A heavy hand clenched his heart and threatened to rip it out.

The sky was darkening as Peter and the two guards stepped into the courtyard. The men were entering the barracks, but Peter barely registered their movements as he raced for the stables.

Mortamor looked up, startled from the work he was bent over, as Peter slid to a stop just within the stable doors. Mortamor bowed low and asked if there was anything he could do for him. His gaze darted from Peter to the men behind him.

"Aye, you can tell me if you have seen my wife." Peter forced himself to assume a calm demeanor and held his breath as he awaited the man's response.

Mortamor looked back to Peter. "Aye, milord."

Peter could feel the sweat running from his brow and stinging his eyes, but he did not bother to wipe it away.

Mortamor eyed him carefully before cautiously continuing. "I tried to stop her, milord but as the lady here, when she told me to move I had to…"

Peter did not wait to hear more. He rushed for her stallion's stall with Mortamor and both guards right behind him. He stopped suddenly, surprised to see Beast still in it. He looked back at Mortamor questioningly.

"She came to him, but told him she could not leave. She said she did not have any of her things and that there was something she had to take care of first. Then she left. I did not see where she went." He wrung his hands nervously. "I did not think to inform you, milord. She did not take the horse, so I thought—"

"You did just fine." Peter's voice was calm, but his innards rolled in turmoil. He turned back to the two men. "We will go back to her chambers and wait. If she does not return shortly, we will gather the men and start the search."

Once again in her chambers, Peter and the guards stood silently. Peter tilted his head listening closely. He thought he heard a deep breathing coming from his chambers.

He walked carefully toward the door and then was sure he heard several graphic curse words. It was definitely Vanessa's voice. His brow furrowed in concentration. Her voice was sometimes sweet, sometimes low and angry, but now there was a different tone to it. It lacked the high pitched squeal, which he had begun to believe was false. Now he was sure of it.

Peter entered the chamber, but it was empty. He strode to the window and looked down, watching her fight to pull herself up. He grinned down at her, impressed at the skill with which she scaled the twisting and thorn covered vines.

The vine she was holding gave way suddenly. Vanessa cursed and Peter's heart lurched, balling into his throat and cutting off his breath. He was sure she was going to land broken and battered in the garden below. He gripped painfully at the window ledge, the hard rock digging into his flesh.

He stood helpless as she slid down the wall. She cursed loudly as the vines caught at her face and hair. She managed to catch herself and Peter took a deep shuddering breath as relief surged through him.

She began to climb once more. She pulled only slightly with her gown and he was amazed that it did not catch and tear on the vines. But it seemed to move fluidly with her.

"Greetings, my lady."

Vanessa jumped and almost lost her grip on the wall once more. His breath caught in his throat.

She looked up. The vines had left a green and black smudge down one side of her face. A trickle of blood ran across her cheek. Dirt, sweat, and grime covered her face, but the powder was gone.

More than likely, he thought, sweat had washed it away. He wondered if she was aware that her mask was missing. He grinned, thinking that she was not.

Her brilliant smile, full of pure joy, took his breath away. He smiled. "Do you need some help?" He was no longer angry, just relieved she had not run and that she had not fallen. "I am surprised that gown has not tangled on you, though I shudder to think of anyone in the garden, what a sight they would enjoy."

"Very humorous. Nay, I need no help." Vanessa laughed. "I have my dress well in hand, I will be right up." The dress caught on several thorns, but she dispatched it easily enough, and made her way quickly up the wall.

Peter held his breath until she was within an arm's reach. He leaned through the window and grasped both of her wrists drawing her roughly through the small opening.

He pulled harder than necessary. Her weight suddenly came through the window and pushed him off balance. She fell painfully on top of him, knocking out his breath.

James and Devon rushed forward to assist him. Peter just waved them away, gathering the large, laughing woman tighter in his arms.

"Close the door on your way out," Peter ordered without looking at them.

He opened his mouth to lecture her on putting herself in danger, and for disobeying him, and was stunned into silence when she placed her warm soft lips against his. With a deep and insistent kiss, she pressed herself forcibly against him.

She pulled away only long enough to pull her gown over her head and to remove his shirt. She leaned down against him. A moan of pleasure escaped him at the feel of her hardened, erect nipples brushing through the tight curls on his chest.

She caressed his chest, kissing his cheeks, his chin, and his neck as her hand roamed lower. A shaky groan escaped him as her hand first released him from his braies and hose and then caressed the entire length of him.

He did not think he would survive this sweet torture. He thought to roll her over. He pulled her hips up and gasped in pleasure and surprise when she pressed them back down. His hardened shaft slid into her hot sweet moistness.

He shuddered, grasping her, driving deeply. She arched her back, taking him fully. As her breasts swayed over him he found he liked a woman of the same height. She was a perfect match. He wrapped his arms around her, pulling her down to him, taking first one breast and then the other into his hungry mouth.

It took only a few moments before his hands were back on her hips, guiding her, up and down. Sitting up straight she allowed him to control the speed.

Her eyes were closed, her long fingers digging into the flesh of his chest. Sweet joy lit her face. Her breathing came in deep gasps, her lips parting to allow the sounds of the building pleasure to escape.

The look of need on her face excited him beyond the limits of his control. His fingers dug into her hips. He lifted her off him and pulled her back down as he thrust his hips forcefully up to meet her. Up and down she slid against the length of him. He pounded deeply into her. Her breathing increased and her moans became louder.

Pain lingered in his chest as her nails clawed at him in her pleasure. He increased his tempo. His breathing became a painful, searing burn deep in his throat. His eyes closed, his head fell back. He arched his spine and called her name as he spilled his seed deep inside her.

His throat ached and his heart was racing. He opened his eyes and looked up at Vanessa. Shivers ran through her as she rocked her hips gently.

Knowing that she had not come to pleasure, he rolled her over and, without pulling out, slid on top her. He ran his hand across her breast and caressed an erect nipple. He continued his exploration down her flat stomach and through the patch of hair between her toned thighs.

He propped himself up on his elbow and watched her dark, tanned face as he manipulated her wet, warm flesh. Her lips quivered and her head rocked back.

Her fingers gripped his shoulders tightly. She closed her eyes, her breath coming in short quick gasps as his fingers moved faster.

He looked carefully at her familiar face and wondered again why she insisted on wearing so much powder. From what he could see she had nothing to be ashamed of.

Sweat glistened on the dark tanned skin. He enjoyed watching her without the presence of the powder he had come to loath. Even with the dirt and grime on the one side of her face she was beautiful.

His fingers moved faster across her swollen flesh and darted within her warm passage. Vanessa moaned deep within her throat and rocked her hips to match his movements.

He smiled down at her as she cried out, lost in passion. It echoed across the tapestries in the room as the warmth of her pleasure spilled around his fingers.

Peter slowly got to his feet. His words were breathy as he spoke. "I will send up a bath. You can wash up before supper." He smiled, thinking it wouldn't be too bad to be with Vanessa for a lifetime. She lay sprawled across the rug. Her firm body sparkled with sweat. His groin tightened in response and he smiled contentedly.

Peter began to turn away and Vanessa reached up and stayed him with a touch to his arm. He looked backed down at her in surprise. She lowered her eyes for a moment and then taking a deep breath stared up at him.

Nervousness teased Van like a bully from her past. She felt once again like a lowly page. She hadn't felt like that since she was eight. Peter affected her in ways no one else ever had.

He looked down at her expectantly, but did not say a word.

She took a deep breath and forced herself to speak. "My lord, may I speak to you a moment. I have a request."

"Aye, come and sit by the fire " He pulled her to her feet and led her to the matching chairs that sat before the cold fireplace. He wrapped a blanket around her shoulders and pushed her gently into one of the chairs.

Apprehension tensed her muscles. She twisted her neck from side to side hearing the customary and satisfying pop.

Peter wrapped a blanket around his shoulders and pulled his chair closer to her. Their knees touched when he sat down.

A hot jolt of pleasure shot through her legs and settled in her stomach, leaving in its wake a warmness that calmed her taut nerves.

Peter placed his hand against her arm. "What is it?"

She trembled slightly and looked into his deep blue eyes. "I am not sure how to ask this."

He smiled warmly. "Just ask."

She nodded. "What do you know of me?"

Peter's head tilted slightly and his brow furrowed. "I know a little. Is there something in particular that you are asking?"

She smiled weakly. "I know my father and yours were friends. Did you see anything of me as a child?" She prayed his answer was no.

Her mother's story was that she had left the night Van was born. Her father's was different. He had told her that she was with him until she was one. She did not want to learn that her mother had lied to her, but she needed to know the truth.

"Aye, I saw you. You were as much a handful then as you are now. Screamed and kicked. You were indeed a hellion." He grinned at her playfully. "I remember well that I was the only one who could calm you when your mood was particularly foul."

Her eyes darted to his and she could feel the heat of embarrassment color her face. She cleared her throat and tried not to think of how much she had loved him when she was a page in training.

"What do you remember or what has my father told you?" She didn't want to know. She wanted nothing more than to stop this line of questioning and not betray her mother's memory, but honor insisted that she ask. If her father was not the man she thought he was, then she had to know.

"Well," Peter relaxed back against the chair and considered her for a moment. Then he smiled and her heart fluttered within her.

"I was twelve when you were born. My father and I sat with Matthew the entire night as he paced the floor, while you were being birthed." Peter leaned forward and caught her gaze.

She stared into his blue eyes and was unable to look away.

He was unsure of what to tell her and did not like the pained look in her eyes. He did not like the uncertainty that he saw or the uncertainty that he felt. "He was very proud. I even helped look for you after your mo—after you were gone." Grasping her hands he kissed them. "I think it would be best if your father was the one who told you of your first year." He watched Van get to her feet, smiling as he noticed she had not removed her slippers.

"Yes, I shall go to him for a few days. My mother told me she ran because my father wanted to kill me, just for the fact that I was a girl." She looked down at the empty fireplace and shuddered.

Peter wanted to go to her, but held off. He felt that she needed a moment to gather her thoughts.

Her voice was low when she finally spoke again. "I can live with that, being a girl is not an honor or something to be respected, I understand this. I do not know if I can understand my mother lying to me, making me become a—" She jerked her head up and stared back at him.

He waited patiently and then finally asked. "Become a what? Where have you been for the last nineteen years?" Peter had wondered that since he had agreed to marry her, where she had been, how she had been raised. Now that he had mentioned going to her father he wondered something more.

Were the problems concerning her father the something she had spoken to her stallion about, the something that she had to take care of before she could leave? Once they were settled would she then just disappear?

A sudden heavy pressure gripped his chest. He stood and walked toward her barely resisting the urge to grab her and hold her safely to him.

Her eyes were clouded with questions and doubt. "My mother was a good woman. At least I always thought so. She always did what she had to in order to protect me." She shrugged. "But if I did not need protecting, than what was it all for? Just so she did not have to go back to him?"

"From what I remember, she was not a happy woman. She had difficulties with Matthew and his mistress. It is the way of life with men. Your mother was just not able to accept it."

She looked at him firmly. "I will not be able to accept it either. I will give my loyalty to only one man. I will expect the same from him. I will not compromise on this."

He smiled. He had no desire to be with another woman, but was unwilling to tell her that outright. Instead, he moved the conversation to something else he had been curious about. She had mentioned several things that made him wonder if she was ashamed of what she was born.

"You speak badly of being a woman. Is it so bad to be one?" He knew there were some women who were unhappy being female, though they were few and far between. Those women wanted the respect and rights given to a man.

She looked at him for several long seconds as if contemplating exactly what to tell him, or how much. "I have never thought about it. Being a woman does not bother me, but being thought of as a weak woman, a woman with no rights and no honor does. Just because one is born a woman does not mean she cannot do anything that a man can do if given the proper chances."

"It does not work that way. A woman is not a strong as a man." He laughed as she tilted her head at him, looked down at herself, and then back at him. She raised an arrogant black brow and plopped angrily into her chair.

"Put your beautiful brow down. You are not the typical woman. You are strong, but most women are not." Peter shook his head. He was surprised that he had admitted that she was strong. She was, but he didn't like to admit it.

"That is because most women have not had the opportunity to become the best of what they can be."

Peter watched intently as she slipped her slippers from her feet and Peter thought he caught a glimpse of a leather sole on them. He smiled. It did not surprise him in the least.

"Most women would not even want to be anything except what they are." He felt the stirrings of arousal as she massaged the white soles of her feet, running her fingers in between her toes. He turned quickly toward the door, shaking the feelings of arousal off the best her could. "I will send up that bath, and we will arrange for you to spend some time with your father."

With that he was gone, leaving her to wonder if her father did indeed have any of the answers she needed. Something to tell her who she should be. She had not lied to Peter. She liked being a woman. It was a new experience for her, but she liked it nevertheless. She had never before been one, but she had always known she was one. It had always given her extra pride to think she had prevailed over men, given her extra incentive to try harder. There had been no room in her charade for failure.

Now her life was spinning out of control and she felt helpless to change anything in it.

All her thoughts brought her to one conclusion: it was best to be a woman when no one knew you were one.

CHAPTER 19

V an lay staring into the darkness, long into the night. The gentle snores beside her did nothing to soothe her troubled mind.

She wanted back the decisions of battle and knighthood. Those had been much easier problems for her to solve. They were things she was used to. Now she was unsure of what the correct tactics were to insure victory. She was not even sure what constituted victory as a woman, a wife, and a daughter.

Thoughts of her father swirled through her weary mind, tormenting and teasing her. Questions about him danced mischievously right beyond her grasp, not giving her the answers that she desperately sought. She closed her eyes and forced her body to lie still even though she could feel her nerves tickling right below the surface of her skin. She itched to toss and turn.

She took long deep breaths and forced her tightened muscles to relax. Her mind began to relax with her body and she was able to push her father from her mind.

As sleep dragged at her, images of Eolian began to swirl and pull at her mind. She grunted lightly and opened her eyes.

Looking at the slightly darker square of wall that indicated the window, she sighed. There would be no escape for her this night. Not through the window and not into peaceful dreams.

She leaned her head back into the softness of the feather pillow and resigned herself to a sleepless night.

Eolian worried her, but not for herself. She was concerned for the safety of those around her, those she had come to care for.

She thought she had considered the results of her coming here carefully, but now she knew that she had not taken in all the facts. It hurt her pride to think she had so blatantly missed such important information.

She had decided before coming how simple it would be just to disappear. If things were not as she wanted or if someone suspected she was more than she portrayed then she could easily mount Damien and fade into the night. She had blindly assumed that her coming had not been a problem for anyone, not counting herself.

Knowing this, had given her confidence. Now she was not so sure. Eolian had undoubtedly followed her men, thinking they would bring him to the Dark Knight eventually. Now they were here and even if she left, her men would not. The ones here would still be in danger.

How long had he been here watching? Did he follow the men directly here or had he just shown up when the sheep started disappearing? She hoped he had not followed the men directly. That would mean that Eolian had followed her to Junket and that would not do.

Questions swam, unanswered, through her sleep-deprived mind.

Closing her eyes, she struggled to get some rest. Still the questions came. How long would Eolian wait to find the man he had sworn to kill? Did he have someone on the inside doing the watching for him? Her breath seemed to catch in her throat.

Her eyes sprung open and she slid silently from the bed careful not to wake Peter. What was she to do? She grabbed a night robe on her way out of the room, walking down the servants stairs and out into the night. Soon she found herself walking in the garden once again. Sitting on the large marble bench, she leaned her head back. The dark, cloudy sky did nothing to relax her tensions.

She was unsure what to do. She had tried talking to Peter before bed about the men. He refused to tell her anything, saying it was no concern of a woman. Sometimes he was more bull headed than he had the right to be. He had wanted to know how she had known Verges and was even more angered when she had known his name.

Van had tried to convince him that a lot of people in Junket knew who they were. That had only brought silence out of him. He had looked at her with suspicion and worry.

There would be no more discussion of it. He had made that clear. He would not take any advice from a woman. At least not directly, she thought with a sly smile. If it was her advice but told by someone else…like about the boys. She had told them to watch the brothers and when Richard told him he had listened to it.

That brought her to her feet. On the way out of the garden, she sensed movement. She slid into the dense branches of the overgrown brambles, her heart racing. Had they found her so soon? Relief washed over her as Richard stepped into view.

"Richard." Her voice was nothing more than a bare whisper.

Startled, Richard whirled to face the soft voice, his hand slipping automatically to his sword hilt. He took a deep breath and relaxed as Lady Vanessa stepped into view. "My lady, you should not be out here this late."

"Why are you? Just out for a stroll in the garden at this late hour?" She motioned for him to follow her.

He hesitated for a moment as she turned and walked toward the barracks. His gaze followed the path of the vines until they reached the window to Peter's chambers. He hoped his liege was still asleep as he turned away to follow the frustrating woman.

"I saw someone wandering. I heard of your daring escape down the vine." They stopped beneath a large oak about halfway between the castle and the barracks. Richard looked nervously around the empty yard. He turned his focus back to Vanessa. "Those vines might make it easy for anyone who wants into the keep."

She turned toward him. The moon peeked from behind the clouds, glowing lightly against the powder on her face, making it sparkle. "Aye, I have thought of that as well. The grounds-men are to remove them first thing in the morning. I want to talk to you. I was on my way to the barracks to find you."

Richard shook his head, but felt no real surprise. "That would not be wise. If someone were to see us…well I shudder to think what Peter will think." Why him? he thought for the thousandth time since the lady had appeared at his side. Why is it that when she needed someone it was him she went to? If she could not go to her husband, why not Grant as he was second here? Why had she chosen him so quickly?

"Aye, that may be." Her soft whisper pulled him from his musings. "I still need to talk to you. With Eolian here—"

He raised his hand at her. "Did Lord Grayweist tell you that was who it was?" It had not been mentioned that she knew.

"Nay, where I know it from does not matter. Are you listening to me?" At his nod she continued. "He got here, according to Marcus Teredo, not long after you and m—the men arrived. I think they followed you here."

"Why would they have done that?" He knew full well why. Eolian still wanted revenge for his losses to the Dark Knight and for the loss of the poor girl that Van had rescued from his clutches.

He was curious what Vanessa thought the reasons were, but was sure he would not learn them this night. She always seemed to keep her knowledge well hidden.

She smiled, her white teeth flashing quickly in the moonlight. "I am sure he has his reasons, just as I know you are aware of what they are. Men do not follow others across the countryside without both knowing why it is they do it."

Richard grunted as much in irritation as consent. She had an aggravating way of talking without answering questions and without agreeing to anything.

"If Eolian is looking for someone," she continued, stepping closer to him. "He is not going to just stand around and wait for him to show up. When he does not find him, he will do something to help his search along."

Richard's eyes widened. He understood where she was going with her thoughts. He agreed with her. It was not like Eolian to wait for something to happen. He would force his hand if necessary.

Van looked around the dark night carefully before turning back to him. "The two brothers were gone more than long enough to have had a talk with him or one of his men, someone like Verges. It is more than a remote possibility that they are at the very least just watching things for him."

"At the most, they have been told to do something. But what and when?" Richard had begun to pace before her.

"I think that will depend on how long it takes him to find the Dark Knight," Vanessa said matter-of-factly.

"What makes you think that is who he is looking for?" Richard focused hard on her face, but could see little as the clouds covered the moon once more.

"I am not stupid. It does not take much thought to determine that the man following the Dark Knight's men is after the Dark Knight." Her voice was tight and high pitched. It cracked as she spoke.

He thought there was more to it than she was saying, but knew there was nothing to be done about it right now. He needed to get her to say what she needed to say and return to her bed. It would be disastrous if the wrong person saw them speaking. "What will he do when the Dark Knight doesn't show up?"

"Take someone or do something so he will not have a choice but to show himself." The moon peeked from behind her floating veils and shone across Vanessa's dark eyes. He met her gaze and held it. He knew her.

Every time his heart tried to tell him who it was, his mind refused to listen, saying it was impossible, leaving him with an unsettled feeling, like knowing a word that is on the tip of your tongue, but not being able to get it out.

"Take who? You?" This worried Richard, he might not remember who she was but he had come to care a great deal for her in the short time that she had been here.

She gave a short snort of laughter. "I do not think so. I do not think it will come to that. It would be funny if he did."

"Funny, I think not." Richard shook his head. Only she could think it funny.

Van just shook her head in return. "He would only want me if his intention was to get to Peter."

Richard realized this was true, but still did not understand the humor in it. It was not funny in his opinion for Eolian to kidnap her to get the Dark Knight to rescue her. Eolian of all people knew Van had a tendency to rescue women in peril.

"I want an extra watch put on the boys. I believe they are up to something. They have changed too drastically from what the others reported on the march here, for it to be a coincidence." She reached across and gently touched his arm. "I fear for you."

"Me?" he asked in surprise.

"You are the closest to the Dark Knight and unless something else happens, you are the only pawn he has." She let her hand fall away and took a step back.

"What do you mean, if something else happens?" He felt that familiar tickle of recognition tease him and disappear.

She only took another step away.

"I will keep a close watch on the boys and do not worry about me. I can take care of myself." Knowing he would get nothing more from her this night, he just smiled and shook his head in wonder. "I will speak with Peter in the morning."

With a quick nod she disappeared into the darkness toward the castle.

Richard stood for several moments until he was sure she was safe inside without incidence and then turned to head back to the barracks. He approached the dark building and slowed cautiously as a dark figure stepped from the shadows.

"Have a nice chat with the lady?" Sneering at him was Ryan Deumount, his deep brown eyes almost black in the moon lit night.

"What are you doing out here? You are not on the night guard tonight." He had met Ryan the first night his men arrived. He was new to Peter's men, had only been with him for about six months. Every one said he seemed to be loyal, but no one admitted to trusting him. He was a cruel man, a warrior through and through. Richard did not like or trust him.

"I do not have to answer to you," Ryan said. "You are not the man in charge of me. As far as I am concerned you are no better than I. You may have been second to the Dark Knight, but he is not here, is he?" Ryan stepped closer to him, breathing deeply upon him. "Where did he hide away, anyway? Everyone wants to know."

Anger flashed through Richard like a hot tendril of flame and his fist clinched around his sword hilt. "Hiding is not something the Dark Knight would do."

Ryan's eyes flicked nervously to Richard's sword and then back to his eyes. He held his ground.

"He is a man of honor, which is more than I can say I have seen from you." Richard grinned as anger lit in Ryan's eyes and his lips snarled. "And aye, you do answer to me, I may have been the second to the Dark Knight, but what a lot of men around here seem to have forgotten was that I was third to the Dragon Knight long before that." Richard took a deep breath and let his hand fall from his sword as the anger slipped from him. "I may have lost some standing over the years, but I still stand beside him. I may no longer be second, but I am a far cry above you."

Ryan raised his fists as if he was going to strike him.

Richard just smiled. "Go ahead. It will be the last thing you do." His voice was calm even though his body thrummed with anticipation. He would be reprimanded he knew, but that would not stop him from killing Ryan if given the chance.

Ryan stepped away from him and Richard walked back to the barracks.

He understood why Ryan and the other men acted like he was of lower status than they were. They slept in the castle and he in the barracks with the lower men. He had been offered a bed in the castle, but he refused. He would sleep with his men. He could not bed down where his men were not. It was not right and Van would not have approved.

♕ ♕ ♕

The sun rose that next morning and for once Van was not with it. She lay on her back as she had when she returned to the bed. Peter slipped carefully from the bed, but Van felt him move. She lay with her eyes closed, not ready to face him.

She waited until she heard the door click before pulling herself from the bed. She walked naked to the small window and looked out across the stables. The men were already saddling their mounts and her heart sank as she watched her men.

A large lump lodged painfully in her throat and she turned away. She dressed quickly and went to the large warm kitchen. Anna, Amy, and Joseph were huddled around a table. Their faces all lit up with smiles as she walked into the room.

They ate slowly, talking of the day to come. They made plans to visit Anna's secret place, but were in no hurry to go. Van enjoyed her time with her young friends, but the only place she really wanted to be was out with her men. She knew those days were gone. She could no longer afford the luxury of seeing her men. There were too many people now at risk because of her.

"Milady."

They all turned toward the door at the soft sound.

"Yes, Buckley," she said with a smile. In the very short time that she had been there, she had grown very fond of the short, round man who served as a day man for the castle. He was always open and friendly with her.

"There is a man who would like to meet you, milady." He had an odd smile to his face.

"I can meet him in the library." She hesitated when Franc Buckley didn't move. Smiling at him she raised a questioning brow.

"Milady, he asked if you could meet him at the bench in the garden. I have already taken the liberty of sending the grounds men out for a while. I shall accompany you there." When her three friends started with her, Buckley shook his head. "Just the lady. She will be only a moment," he said and started off toward the garden, not looking back.

"I will meet you at the spot," she said and smiled sweetly. Then she followed Buckley.

Buckley stopped at the edge of the garden. "Shall I await you here, milady?"

"No Buckley, if you trusted him enough to arrange this meeting, I am sure I will be fine." She waited for him to walk away and then stepped into the dark shadows of the trees.

The flowers were beginning to come to light, to look as she remembered them from so long ago. She stopped for a moment. Closing her eyes, she took deep breaths of the sweet and moist smells around her.

"You are very beautiful." She opened her eyes to see Devon walking toward her. His smiling face held a nervous tilt to it.

"Thank you, my boy." Vanessa said in her high pitched squeal. He had noticed over the last few days that it had softened from when she had first arrived. It was becoming less irritating. Either that, he thought with a smile, or he had gotten used to it.

"Boy? That is funny, seeing as I am older than you, my lady." He kissed her hands gently. "I am glad you came. I need to speak with you about something." He took a deep breath. His whole body seemed to be shaking with heart pounding nervousness. What was he doing here? He was talking to the wrong person. He should be asking Peter.

Not only was it proper, he found he was less afraid of Peter.

"What is it? Here sit." She dropped, unceremoniously to the bench, patting beside her. He sat heavily. "Relax." She said. She looked him in the eye and he had a quick flash of recognition before it disappeared like fog as she glanced away.

"Relax? That is easy for you to say, I am sure I do not scare you the way you do everyone around you." He looked startled at his open confession.

She looked back at him with a smile, a proud looking smile. "Just tell me."

"I want to talk to you about Amy, my lady." He took another deep breath and the rest came out in one long exhale. "I want to marry her."

"And you are coming to me?"

He was glad he had as the smile warmed her entire being. She took a deep breath and Devon was certain she was going to say no.

He looked down at his boots and thought he should have at least cleaned them before he came to speak with her.

She touched his shoulder briefly. "I like you very much, Devon. You are very important to me and I know that Amy feels the same way. You have my permission. "

He jerked his gaze from his dirty boot into her black eyes. "I do, my lady?"

"Of course you do. I believe you are honest, caring, and loyal and you will take all those qualities into the marriage with you. You will be as good a husband as you are a soldier." She stood with a smile. "You should get back to training, I have a feeling that no one knows you are here."

She waved it off when he started to answer. Shaking her head, she walked away. He watched her with a mingling of admiration and worry. He was concerned about her. Her relationship with Peter was turbulent and it was causing friction between them. It was also causing some discord in the men.

It was unsettling to see the lord and lady at war and that seemed to the men and to Devon what had happened. A war had been declared and until a cease fire was announced, all the men were on edge when around them.

Van smiled as she walked away from Devon. She had been surprised he had come to her. A grin spread as she realized that Amy must have insisted on it.

Van made her way across the courtyard to meet her friends when a small voice stopped her. "Milady."

She turned toward the trembling voice and found a young boy from the village. She could not place his name. "Yes, my child?"

He looked around carefully and then thrust a small section of parchment at her. He smiled shyly and walked away.

Van's brow wrinkled in confusion and wonder. She watched him begin to run across the dusty yard in front of the stables and shook her head. She turned her attention to the parchment.

In Verges familiar scrawl was simply, *Here for you.*

Those three small words lifted her heart and spirit more than she would ever have imagined. She knew he was here already, but his small shaky script told her firmly that she was not alone.

Smiling widely, she nearly ran to Anna's secret hiding place. She pushed the branches out of her way and ducked into the hiding. "Where is everyone?" She asked Anna who appeared to be the only one there.

"Joseph wanted to go for a swim at the lake, Amy took him." Anna pulled at the long grass she sat in. Her face down, a shy look, but it had changed since she had first met the girl. It was different in a way she couldn't put her finger on.

She sat beside her young friend. "You did not want to swim?"

"Oh I did, I just..." She giggled nervously.

Van smiled and touched her lightly on the arm. "What is it?" The love that had grown for Anna scared Van. She wished to go back to the beginning, to the day she arrived here. To do the right thing and not put the ones she now loved in danger because of her selfish behavior.

A bright smile shone on Anna's small round face when she looked up at her. "I think I am in love, milady."

"Love, with whom?" Van took the small trembling hands in hers and held them tightly.

"Douglas Sheire." The name was nothing more than a deep sigh. "Do you know Douglas?" The girl squirmed slightly and looked at her hopefully.

"Aye, I do," Van said squeezing the girl's hands. "He is very handsome with his black hair and bright green eyes. He is a big man." She thought of the comparison between the young girl and the big warrior. "Does he know you like him? I mean, have you talked to him at all."

"Aye." Anna's eyes widened and her face turned a dark shade of red. "Oh, milady, not aye, that he knows I like him. I meant aye we have talked."

"I understand." Van laughed gently. She was concerned about Anna's feelings for Douglas. Her main concern was that Douglas wasn't interested in Anna and she would get hurt.

Anna seemed to relax slightly, but her face was still a glowing shade of red.

"Last night I went for a walk." She looked down at her kid slippers. Her ears turned pink. "Not far," she added quickly. "Just around the courtyard, but he walked with me." Anna's pleading gaze jerked up to Van's face. "Oh please, milady, do not get mad. He was very nice and he did not try to touch me." She dropped her eyes quickly.

Van stiffened. Her heart thudded deeply in her chest. She was sure Anna was lying. She did not believe that Douglas would take advantage of the child, and she would hate to have to kill him if he did. "Anna?"

Anna took a deep breath and then whispered. "He held my hand, milady." Her face blushed so deeply, it turned the roots of her hair to a deep pink. "Are you mad, milady?"

Van relaxed. "No Anna. That is fine. I know how you feel. Even that soft touch of another's hand is enough." Her heart fluttered as she thought of Peter's soft caresses after they made love. She pushed Peter from her thoughts and concentrated on the subject at hand. "If it is to go farther than that—"

Anna sucked in a deep breath. "Lady Vanessa," she hissed in embarrassment. "I am not ready to think of that. I am only fifteen."

Van shook her head, relieved. "Are you going to stay here for a little while?" At the nod of her brown hair, Van kissed her on top of the head and left her to her daydreams of Douglas.

She walked to the lake to see if Amy and Joseph were still swimming. As she drew close she heard voices. They were not Amy or Joseph's.

It was Peter and Richard. Van dropped into the prickly bushes and crept forward. Careful not to rustle the branches, she pulled her dress around her knees.

She peered from her hiding space and her heart once again fluttered as she saw Peter standing beside the lake. The sunlight sparkled off the rolling surface of the water.

"Do you really believe he followed you here?" Peter had considered over the last couple of days that Eolian was here because of Richard and his men. He had also considered the fact that he was an enemy of Eolian as well. It was a possibility that he was here for Peter. "He could be after something else, not the Dark Knight."

"Their arrival shortly after ours says aye. Also, my lord, he was reported as being seen in Junket. It was not long after we were there that he was seen." Richard looked out over the water and squinted at something in the distance. He looked back as Peter began to speak.

"Junket?"

Vanessa had been there as well. Richard and the Dark Knight's men were there. She was there, and Eolian had followed someone from there. Since they had arrived within days of each other it did not set well with him.

He felt an unaccustomed fear. What if she were in danger? She knew of Eolian and Verges. That was impossible, right? Of course she couldn't have anything to do with them. She was a woman of good breeding. No, she was a woman born to good breeding, he told himself. He had no idea what life she led before she came here.

He shifted from foot to foot to relieve some tension. She was born to it, but he had no idea how she was raised. It was obvious that she was not raised the way she should have been.

"Aye, Junket. That is where we left Van. I just thought I should let you know…my feeling on it."

Peter just shook his head. "It is good you did. Return to the men, I shall be along soon." He turned to the water and let his mind wander. When he had serious decisions to make or questions to answer, he always found it easiest to let his mind drift. It seemed easier to overlook the answers when you were searching too hard for them.

He reached down and picked up a smooth round rock. Bouncing it in his hand, he gauged the weight and balance. He found a happy position and pulled his arm back. He tossed it across the top of the water.

The water splashed in several places as the rock skimmed across the gentle waves. He reached down and found another. He skipped it as well. He smiled as he watched the sixth ripple appear in the line before the rock sank.

He picked up another stone and threw it. It skipped along the water making five small ripples. His mind, as it did so often lately, moved to his new wife. She was something of an enigma to him. Just when he thought he had her, she surprised him.

As he wandered from thoughts of her temperament to holding her down and making her obey him in every way, he began to smile. As he reached for another stone, a heavy body hit him, knocking him to the ground.

He issued a loud grunt and began to grapple with the large and strong form that lay on his back, keeping his face pinned to the ground. His mind went to Eolian and was sure he had sent a man for him after all.

Fighting fiercely, Peter struggled to get off his stomach. He pressed his knees beneath him, brought one arm under him, and balanced on his elbow. The other elbow he swung backwards and felt the satisfying crunch as it connected with his attacker.

The weight shifted and he spun over, knocking his assailant to the ground. Peter instantly rolled on top and shoved his heavy forearm into his attacker's throat to keep him pinned to the ground.

Vanessa looked up at him calmly. She had a grin on her face and part of the powder had been removed in the struggle. He tried to suck in a breath, but it refused to go through the clenched muscles in his throat. "Vanessa?" His voice came out in a painful croak.

He could not comprehend it to be her. It could not be his wife lying beneath him with blood running from her lips, cutting a thin line in the powder on her jaw. He took a shallow breath and pulled his arm from her throat.

Forcing the breath into his lungs he tried to make himself relax. He could not. "Vanessa, what are you doing here?"

"Surprising you." There was no crying, no concern as to the blood she was losing. Instead, she pulled him down, pressing her lips onto his. He could taste the metallic flavor as he tried to pull away from her, to take control of the situation.

Soon all control was lost and he allowed her to slide her hands between them. She first ran her hand along the length of his hard shaft and then released it.

He pulled her dress up over her head as she caressed his hardness. He began to pull his clothing off and she leaned forward and frantically tugged at them in an effort to help.

Once they were both naked she wrapped her legs around him. He plunged into her depths and all was lost as he rocked against her.

Gulls cried and scattered as they cried out in mixed pleasure some time later. Peter pulled off her and began to rearrange his clothing. He turned and watched her slide into her dress. "What do you think you were doing out here? I could have hurt you."

Adjusting her dress, she ignored him.

"I would like an answer and I want it now." He took a threatening step toward her, but could not manage to make the anger come forward. He had felt surprise, then worry and guilt when he saw what he had done to her, but not anger.

She smiled sweetly at him as he began to slide into his boot. As he began to tug it on she said, "You could not have hurt me, you tried. It was not good enough. My mouth does not even hurt, even with all the kisses." With that she turned and ran, bare feet flying along the grass.

She had a head start by the time he got on his other boot. It was either that or take one off, and either way it meant lost time. He raced around a bend and she was gone.

He slid to a stop looking around him. She was gone. Walking slowly forward, he saw a small stand of boulders. There was a small path in between those boulders and the lake. There was no choice, but to go through the center. A perfect ambush site.

He grinned, knowing that he had guessed her plan. He crouched low and stalked toward the rocks. He planned to go over them as silently as he could and jump her from the top.

Van smiled as she stalked along behind him, walking between the small shrubs and trees. She had only run a short way and as he turned to find his other boot she had slid beneath a small bush covered with small white berries.

Now she stalked the man who thought her stupid enough to pick so obvious a place. He underestimated her, and that was the first rule in war—never underestimate your opponent. Hiding in a small prickly bush, which when she moved jabbed her incessantly, she watched him climb the boulders. She was impressed at the silence and speed with which he did it.

She rushed to the rocks as he disappeared over the top of them, made it to the top, and peered over the edge. Peter looked around carefully. He looked left, right, and down, but not up.

He began to look discouraged and a little concerned. A loud grunt issued from him as Van jumped on him from the boulder above, throwing him to the ground.

Instead of fighting to get loose, he caught her leg in his hand, running his fingers up her dress. There he began to tickle her inner thigh.

"Stop, that's not fair, you cannot…stop." Her breath came heavily as she squealed and screamed with laughter. Easily flipping her over, he took control. "Stop."

"Nay, I will not. You will learn the folly of your ways." Peter panted and his grip on her slipped, but he regained control quickly. "When will you learn that you cannot beat me?" He tickled her relentlessly, until tears began to slide down her temples, her head and body thrashing to get loose.

"I c–c–can," she stuttered. Knowing only one thing to distract him, she pushed toward him, instead of pulling away. The moment her bare body, warm and moist from excitement and the remainder of his seed, hit his hand, he was through. Pleasure filled her at how quickly he responded to her.

The chase had been exhilarating and he didn't bother with her dress. Shoving her roughly to the ground, he pushed it above her hips. She laughed with pleasure as she watched him fight with the laces he had just tied, tearing them in his frenzy to release himself.

Free, he drove into her and kissed her passionately. He wrapped his fingers through her hair and forced the kiss deeper. Painful swirls of pleasure pulsed through her and begged to be set free.

She wrapped her legs around him and moved her lips to his ear. "Harder," she whispered boldly.

He responded with a burst of speed and power that she had not known he possessed. Pushing up onto his arms, he pounded into her with wild abandon. Her screams of passion echoed through the trees as she felt him spasm deep inside her.

He rolled off her, thinking if she was going to run now there would be no stopping her. He had done well to roll over, let alone run. But she apparently had no intention of running. Pulling her dress down around her, she watched him with an amused look on her face as he struggled to get his belt fastened once more. Moving his hands, she finished buckling it for him, and then kissed him gently. First on the nose, then the mouth. A tender kiss that had nothing to with passion, but set every nerve in his body afire.

Van deepened the kiss, making his mind numb with the gentleness of it. The love he felt in that one soft kiss tore at his heart. It swelled, hurting his chest and clogging his throat. Wrapping his arm around her sun warmed shoulders, he pulled her away and looked deep into her eyes.

It was not the first time he had stared at her eyes, so black they seemed bottomless. They were so right, so full of life and so familiar to him. He felt as if he had known her all his life or at least a lot longer than the short time since he had met her.

Deciding that now was not the time to ponder the questions of where he knew her from, he pulled her down into the crock of his shoulder. She laid her head against his bare chest and wrapped her arm around his waist.

They lay like that for several hours, staring out over the ripples in the lake and talking of the land and the castle, the people around it and children.

"Will you be all right with me going to see my father?" Peter was surprised by the comment and more, by his gut wrenching reaction to it.

He still harbored a fear that her father was the thing she needed to take care of before she could leave. He took a shallow breath and hoped his voice came out smoother than his nerves were feeling. "Aye. I must say that I will be upset that you are gone, but it will be fine. Do you plan to go soon?" He hoped the answer was no.

"Aye. On the morrow."

"Will you be gone long?" What he really wanted to ask was if she was going to come back if she got things worked out with her father.

She tightened her grip on him and snuggled closer. "Maybe two days, maybe less if things do not go as planned."

He smiled.

Silence fell over them as the sun began to set, throwing magnificent colors across the surface of the secluded lake. It was a peaceful silence and Peter wondered how many people he could just sit with and do nothing, and still be comfortable. He could think of none.

The sun had set and he turned to tell his bride they should go before it got too dark, just to find her eyes closed, head still supported by his shoulder. "Vanessa, my love." No response. He moved slightly and her head rocked, still she did not wake. It was unusual, she was a light sleeper. "Vanessa," this time a little louder.

"Huh?" She blinked several times and then smiled up at him. "What?"

"It is getting dark. We should go. I had a hard time waking you." He said it with a smile, but it sent a panicked look onto her face. "What?"

Van just shook her head with an unsettled feeling growing in the pit of her stomach. He got to his feet, pulling her along. She allowed the assistance, feeling a little dazed and unsure. How could he have tried to wake her and her not known it. That was impossible. She had never slept through anything.

Then she knew. The last thing she remembered was thinking she had never felt more secure, more safe. She had always known she had loved him, but it was more, she realized…She turned to him in wonder. "I trust you."

He just looked at her for a long moment. "I am glad. It helps in a marriage if there is trust."

"Nay, you don't understand." How was she to tell him? She had only trusted one person enough to let herself fall into a deep sleep. Only Verges. She trusted him with her life, her heart, and every secret that she had.

She trusted Richard as well, but was never comfortable to sleep around him. She had always been afraid that she would talk in her sleep.

Looking deep into Peter's questioning eyes, she wondered, should she tell him the truth, show her trust in him. Opening her mouth to tell him, she changed her mind. She tried once more, only to shake her head in confusion.

Now was not the time and Peter seemed to realize it. He smiled and shook his head. "Let's get back to the castle and when you are ready you can tell me."

She was surprised to feel tears threatening as she threw herself into his embrace. "Let's go home."

A comforting tenderness seemed to swim through her veins, warming her soul as she thought of that word. Home. It was a wonderful word she decided. She had never missed not having a home, until she had one.

In the massive dining chamber, the smells of the roasted meats overcame Van as she sat beside her husband. She rubbed her leg against his beneath the table and smiled at the small shivers of heat that exploded from the contact.

"Lord Grayweist, may I ask you a question?" Richard asked. At Peter's nod he continued. "Have you heard anything about the Dark Knight?"

Van choked on the meat she had just swallowed, the soft spicy taste of the roasted pork turning to dust in her mouth.

Peter tapped her back and handed her the goblet of ale. "Are you all right, now?"

She refused to meet his eyes. "Fine, I just swallowed wrong, I guess."

Turning back to Richard, he shook his head. "I have heard not. You would think we would have heard something by now. I am beginning to wonder if something may have happened to that arrogant little snot."

Van had no control of her tongue as the words just tumbled out. "What do you mean arrogant little snot?" Realizing what she had said, she stuttered "I–I mean, that does–that does not seem to be the way you should talk about a knight."

The men laughed. "You have no idea who he was." Peter turned to the others at the table, waving to the men who had come with Richard. "Ask any of them, they will know."

She declined, but sat back out of the conversation. Then wondered how to get out of the room when the talk went in the direction of her temperament, well that of the Dark Knight's.

Laughter came easily as they swapped stories of him. Peter leaned back with a fond grin. "I remember when he first came to me, asking to be my personal squire. I had one already or I would have taken him. He had shown no fear as he had stood before me."

Van remembered the day well. She had been terrified and had been sure that she was turned down because of that fear. She was delighted to know that he had thought her brave.

Her face heated up with embarrassment and she fiddled with her goblet of ale. She had gone to him for two reasons. One was because he was the king's champion and two because she was in love and wanted to be closer to him.

Peter's voice drew her attention. "He was young to be a squire and I was sure he would not go far, end up dead or quit. I was sure it would be one or the other." He gave a humorless laugh. "If I had known how he would risk his life to save me I would have had taken him. Not like the one I had. Ran at the first show of real trouble."

Grant slapped Peter on the back laughing. "You remember that boy, standing up to the doctor. He had seemed so noble. From what I hear, he had quite the reputation with the ladies."

Van slouched, trying to avoid anyone's attention. All she wanted was to escape from this room. No, she thought sadly—all she wanted was to join in as the Dark Knight.

From the side table Devon put his word in as well. "He had so many mistresses I think that was the only reason we did the tournaments, to get money to send to the ladies." This brought rank laughter and yells from the entire room.

Van smiled. She missed the way the men were together. Even here, in her presence, they were restrained, as if she were a delicate thing that would be damaged if the wrong words were said. She hated it.

They were not like that with the maids. No, with them they were rough and loud, like she had been when she was around the maids. Hitting their rear ends and acting just as lewd as the other men. She missed it. The stories of Van the knight were rolling around, until she could take it no more.

How was she so far away from who she was supposed to be? Could she not just be the person she was happiest being?

She wondered as she kissed Peter's cheek and mounted the stairs who that was. She thought she was a knight. That was who life had made her because there were no options. But what if her mom was wrong? What if she had lied?

Even as Peter came in the room a few moments later, she was still in an upheaval about her identity.

Soon he had her thoughts on nothing but the pleasures of him.

Falling asleep sometime later, well sated, she wondered if her father could answer any questions or if he would just add more confusion to her already weary mind.

CHAPTER 20

Van walked toward the carriage with the small army bag she had carried since she had first became a squire hanging limply from her left hand. She slid her right hand through the arm of her husband.

Peter looked questioningly at the small bag, but said nothing. The bag carried what little clothes she believed were needed for a couple of days. Van glanced over at Peter, down to the bag, and then back to the awaiting carriage. She was not about to divulge anything without being questioned. If he asked, she would say it was a gift, which was not a lie. Richard had given it to her when she became his squire.

She nodded to the driver as he opened the door and stepped back. Peter took her elbow and pulled her around to face him, causing her to gasp softly.

Looking up into his face, she was surprised to see the concern and worry etched into his handsome features. His brow was tightly knitted with lines and his jaw was tight. He tried a smile that must have felt as awkward as it looked because he let it fall quickly away.

She turned long enough to lay her bag on the hard seat and then she allowed him to pull her into his arms. The hug was quick, but he had held her tightly. His arms gripped her almost painfully and she could feel him trembling.

She wanted to ask him what was wrong, but she could not seem to make the words come out. She wanted to know why he looked worried. She was only going to see her father.

The horses snorted loudly and pawed at the dusty ground, making the buckles of the harnesses jingle. Van noticed that the driver had disappeared, probably to give the two newlyweds a moment alone.

She smiled up at Peter and kissed him gently. He helped her into the carriage, shut the door almost reluctantly, and hit it to signal to the driver they were ready.

The carriage lurched forward and the horses whinnied anxiously. She leaned back against the seat and closed her eyes. Her decision to go had not been an easy one. Knowing she owed Matthew the courtesy of at least hearing him out, and wanting to give him the opportunity, were not the same thing.

She wanted to keep believing what she had known all her life, but as a leader and a knight she was obligated to consider all sides of an argument before making the final decisions.

She shuddered and realized she was frightened, scared of what knowledge he might bring to her. As confused as she was, now she knew it could get worse.

If she believed her mother, then there was a valid reason she had ended up as a knight. But if her mother lied, then all of it was for nothing. Van did not want to think that her life was for nothing.

As much as she was scared, she was also curious. Curious about Matthew, a man who might not be as he was portrayed, and surprisingly, about her mother as well. She had never stopped to think of it before, but she realized she did not know her mother very well.

Van had been sent to Grayweist when she was only ten to live and train. Her mother had refused to come see her at the castle and Van had not seen her again until she was seventeen and a knight. By then Van had been able to come and go as she pleased.

At least she now understood why her mother had been unwilling to see her at the castle. With Van's father living right down the road, her mother would have been recognized.

The carriage jolted as Van slipped into the past and she could see her mother, vibrant and alive striding around the small home in Junket.

"Remember, it is very important no one finds out you are a girl." Patricia's voice was strained and ragged. "Your father is searching for you and his men were close to finding you. They were in the village yesterday." She looked panicked, packing Van's things into a small case in jerky motions.

"Aye, Mother, I understand." And she did. She had been drilled on it daily as she grew. Now ten years of age, she was well aware of the dangers she faced. "What I don't understand is why I have to leave. Why I have to become a page."

"You have the potential. It has been remarked upon by many of the men that I should have already sent you to page training. They have seen you with the other boys." Patricia pulled open a drawer and pulled several shirts from it. She tossed them into the small satchel.

Van watched her mother's rapid actions with worry eating at her innards. Her stomach clenched and she sent up a prayer that she could handle the new challenge. She clenched her fists behind her back to keep herself from grasping her mother's hands and begging her to stop.

Her mother turned back toward the dresser and pulled open another drawer. "Thompson has even commented that you are already better than the others, faster and stronger, and although as the son of a surgeon you will not be eligible for knighthood, you will still enjoy being a squire." She glanced at her with a nervous smile. "I just know you will."

"I am not a boy though, Mother. How am I to do these things?" Standing in the center of the room, she could only watch as her only possessions went into the case. She looked around the small meager room with a pang of sadness. She did not have much, and they were always struggling to make a decent living, but she had never gone without food or shoes.

She did not want to leave her home and her mother. It was not an easy life there in the small village. She'd had to work hard to help out. But she did not want to leave it for something that she was unsure she could even do.

"You will be fine."

Unconvinced, Van watched her mother's frantic packing. Suddenly, Patricia stopped, turning on Van with wide eyes. "You enjoy those things, the sword practice, the horse riding, the daggers?"

Van sucked in a breath. Dagger practice was forbidden to children under twelve by the elders of the village. She tried to give her mother a shocked and innocent look. She was sure it looked as wrong as it felt.

"Do not look at me like that," Patricia said. "Everyone knows that you boys do those things, forbidden or not." Her mother put her hands on her hips and pinned Van with an intense look. "My question is, do you like them?"

"Aye, Mother. Very much so. I am only scared that I cannot do them. The boys will be better than me. They will not be like the boys around here. They will be well trained and…well, just better." Van threw her hands up in frustration. She felt unable to express her concerns. "I am only a girl, no matter what you want me to be, just a girl." She could feel the pressure of tears behind her eyes and she blinked quickly several times to ward off the onslaught of the unwanted emotions.

Her mother relaxed and pulled her into an embrace. Van wrapped her arms around her mother's waist and clung to her. She knew her life would be changing and she felt unsure of herself.

Her mother's words were kind and gentle. "You are who you are and no one can change that. It is not what I want you to be, it is what you are. I can tell you to pretend to be a boy, but I cannot make you enjoy it and excel at it." She pulled away and cradled Van's face in cold and trembling hands. "You are Van, strong and proud, and you are capable of achieving anything you set your heart to. If you tell me you do not like these things and this is not what you want with your life, we will figure something else out."

"I am scared." Shivers ran through Van. She hated being afraid.

"There is no shame in being scared. Fear is a good thing. Fear listened to makes you cautious. If you take that fear and overcome it you are its master, not its slave."

The carriage jolted to a rough halt and Van's head bounced against the back of the seat. Her eyes flew open and she gasped as she was drawn back into the present.

Sighing deeply, she looked at the closed door and took several deep breaths as she waited for the driver to pull it open. She heard the latch click and squinted as the bright sunlight invaded the cool, safe dimness of the coach's interior.

"Vanessa, my dear. I am glad you decided to come." Matthew stood with his hand extended, staring up at her. "Lord Peter did not have a problem with you coming?"

She ignored the offered hand and jumped from the carriage. Turning back, she grasped her small satchel. "Peter has little to say over what I do. I am not in the habit of asking permission before I act."

She looked past his anxious face to the home she would have grown up in had things been different. There would have been vast differences when compared to the life she had led.

Sleeping in the cold, cramped halls the pages had inhabited, instead of the thick, plush pallets that she knew to be inside the castle, were just the beginnings of the differences.

"Can I look around?" It was out of her mouth before she could censor it.

"Of course." Turning to the young man who had driven her, he smiled. "Take the bags in before you leave."

"I do not have any bags, just this."

Matthew jerked his head around at her, a look of surprise crossing his face before he controlled it.

Van raised the small bag. "I am not accustomed to packing before I go somewhere."

"We can drop it off as we look around," he said carefully and dismissed the driver. He looked closely at the small brown bag, but like Peter he chose not to ask, for which Van was grateful.

She said nothing as she followed him from room to room, dropping off her bag in the chamber she would use for the night, and listening to his commentary about each of the rooms. On the walls of the Great Hall, she saw the portraits of her ancestors. Her heart fluttered with excitement as she saw the resemblance of each of them.

All the men had the same look, the same black eyes and restless image. One side of the hall held just the males and across from them on the opposite wall were their wives.

Before the picture of her great-great grandfather, Van stopped and stared. In his hand was a dagger, beautifully crafted. The long-handled blade shone with a life of its own. Her breath caught in her throat. It took a moment for her to force the air into her tight lungs.

The emeralds and rubies glittered as the artist caught the magnificence of the gems. Van's breath came in soft ragged gasps as she stared at the family heirloom. It was identical to the one she had strapped around her thigh at that very moment.

Van caressed it through the fabric of her gown as she tried imagining a childhood here. That proved impossible. Every time she tried, the image would shift to her life in Grayweist Manor, the training and abuse she endured.

"Can we sit down and talk now?" Matthew asked softly, touching her arm.

She looked down at his hand and forced herself not to jerk it away. She glanced up at him and nodded.

Leading her to the library, he motioned her to the chairs by the cold fireplace. Along two walls were more portraits. These were of cousins, aunts, and uncles, as well as all of their wives and husbands. She gazed at them, unsure of what to say and how to begin.

After several moments of silence he said, "I am sure you have questions."

She looked at him confidently, although she felt "anything but" as she considered this. The truth was, now that she was here, she was uncertain. More and more, she thought her life had been easier as a knight. Battle and death were easier by far than facing her life.

"Aye, I suppose I do. That is why I am here." She took a deep, shaky breath and looked around the well lit room. Two walls were filled from floor to ceiling with books of all different sizes and colors. She wondered if he had read them all.

She had never had much need in her life to read. She knew how, but barely. It was not something that was a necessity for a soldier.

The candles lit the room around them, showing the details in the large portraits that covered the rough stone walls. The windowless room was large, but comfortable. "Where is your new wife and kids?" This was not what she wanted to ask but it was a good beginning she supposed.

"They are still seeing her parents. They will be here in a few days. If you are still here, you will meet them. If not, we can come there to see you." His voice shook slightly.

Van turned her attention fully to him. His hands were trembling slightly and his eyes crinkled at the corners. He appeared as nervous and unsure as she felt.

"Tell me about my mother. What was she like when you met her?" she asked. His nervousness seemed to relax her. Made her feel like she had the advantage, a feeling she much preferred and always had.

His eyes widened and his brow wrinkled as his eyebrows rose in surprise. He narrowed his eyes and seemed to consider the question. "I suppose she was much like she was while you were growing up. She had not changed much as she grew older." He looked at her questioningly apparently unsure of what she was really asking.

Van leaned back in the big chair and crossed her leg under the wide skirt of her dress. The cool material of the silk slid across her legs and sent a shiver up her spine. She took a deep breath and forced herself to relax. "I–I did not see my mother much." She struggled to explain to him why she needed to know about her mother without giving him any real details. She found it impossible so she finally said, "I left home when I was only ten and did not see her again until I was seventeen and not many times after that. I do not know her well. I would like to."

"Ten? Where did you go? Where did she send you?" He leaned toward her, his knuckles whitening as he gripped the arms of the chair. His face lit in anger and turned a dangerous shade of red.

She stared at him calmly and tilted her head, smiling patiently.

He waited a few moments in that ready to pounce posture and then took several deep breaths. He released the arm, flexed his hands, and sat back, but the red tint of anger still flushed his features. Features that looked too much like her own to be comforting.

She grinned, thinking that if she looked like that when the Dark Knight was angry, it explained why there were few people who would argue with her when she was him. She laughed lightly, remembering Devon's words. '*I probably do not scare you the way you do everyone around you.*' Perhaps it wasn't just the Dark Knight who looked like Matthew.

Matthew took another calming breath, that appeared to do no good, and then continued. "I met your mother when she was only seventeen. I married her even though I knew she was in love with someone else, but I loved her so much." A look of sadness replaced the anger. "I thought I could make her love me."

Van forced herself to hold his gaze, but she much preferred the anger to this look of loss and pain. "Who was she in love with?" she asked, but was sure she already knew the answer.

"Paul Burgess. She went to find him when she left me. It took me awhile to track her down, but I eventually found him. When I found him, I found her." He closed his eyes and leaned his head back against the chair. "I was told she never had you there. They said it was just a boy, Dr. Burgess's son. I was told that he was about two years younger than you." He opened his eyes suddenly and looked at her suspiciously. "You were with your mother until you were ten."

She nodded her head carefully. She was sure now that she should not have come. She had been worried about what she would learn from him and realized a little too late that she should have been more concerned about what he could learn from her.

"Why then did no one at the village know about you?" His dark black eyes peered at her intently and she fought a compulsion to tell him everything.

She took a deep breath and answered calmly. "They did, they just did not think I was her daughter."

That was the truth. It was also the only thing she would say on the subject, no matter what else he asked. Surprisingly though, he asked nothing further, just gave a quick nod. She was sure he didn't believe her and wanted to know why he dropped it, but asking would only draw out a subject that she could not afford to dwell on.

"When I met her she was sweet and stubborn," he said, relaxing back into the story once again. He continued talking, but did not take his piercing eyes from her face. "I loved her dearly and wanted nothing more than her love in return." His intent gaze clouded over as his mind slipped away into the past. He smiled. "I loved to hear her sweet tinkling voice and to watch the sway of her hair as she danced. I wanted her."

Van let her eyes wander across the room and tried to picture her mother happy in this home, laughing, and dancing. It was an image that came easily.

Matthew's voice soothed her as he spoke lovingly of her mother. "The sound of her laughter could lighten any burden I may have had and I was determined to marry her even though she was not a—" He jerked his head up and clamped his lips together.

Her eyes swung back to him in shock. "Mother was not a virgin when you married?" She cringed, not really wanting to hear any more about the woman she had looked up to.

"Do not think badly about your mother," he said quickly. "It is not her fault what happened."

"How can you say that?" If it was true that her mother had stolen away his beloved daughter when she was a year old and hidden her away from him, then how was it possible that he could defend her now? If he was the monster that his mother portrayed him to be all these years, he would not be defending her at all.

"I say it because it is true and you are here for the truth, not for what I wish for you to hear." He smiled sadly. "There are things I would rather not tell you, but they are things you need to know."

He fell silent and she studied him. A sharp and persistent pain began to throb in the center of her mind. She nodded for him to continue and waited.

He took a few moments to gather his thoughts or perhaps to control his emotions before he resumed his tale. "She was in love with him when I met her. I was just too pig headed to care." He stared down at the trembling hands in his lap.

Van wanted to go to him. To lay her arm across his shoulders in support as Richard had done for her so many nights as she grew up. But she could not bring herself to do so. She kept her seat and allowed him to continue at his own pace.

"I wanted her and I did things that I regret now. I bribed her father to get his blessing." He laughed cynically. "I was a lord and Paul just a surgeon. It was not hard, and she was forced into a wedding with the wrong man."

Van's heart pulled for Matthew's pain, but the ache in her mind confused her and she struggled to know who to believe.

"Dr. Burgess left the area and she rightfully blamed me. I still loved her. There was nothing I could do to get her to love me." His eyes shimmered with unshed tears. He did not look up, but continued studying his weathered and sun-darkened hands.

He fell silent for a time as he clenched and unclenched his fists. The sound of creaking knuckles sounded loudly in the overpowering silence of the large room. Van took in his hunched shoulders and deep ragged breath. He appeared to be weighed down by some invisible force that he could not shrug from his wide shoulders.

"Matthew?" she asked softly after several minutes had spun out.

His shoulders twitched and he stopped flexing his fingers, but did not look up. "I forced her nightly into a physical relationship. She fought me all the way. When she got pregnant with you I left her alone, but it took over a year for you to be conceived."

A silent tear slid down his cheek and tore at Van's heart. Then his face darkened.

"I was so happy that she was to have a baby. I had desperately hoped that it would bring us closer together, but it drove her farther from me."

"She did not want you to be my father," Van said almost silently.

He looked up at her, but not in surprise, and then looked back at his hands. He slid them across the knees of his leggings. Sweat from his palms darkened the blue material.

"No, she did not like the fact that I was your father. She told me on many occasions that I did not deserve you. Even though she was right, it pushed me from her. I refused to take her unwillingly, again, after you were born." He smiled a weak smile. "I did not have her again and the nights were hard. It had been over a year and a half since you were conceived and since I had taken her."

His face tightened in a mixture of guilt and regret. "I begged her to love me, to lie with me. She refused and finally one drunken night I took one of the maids. Your mother caught me and went berserk. She hit me with the chamber pot."

"You only cheated on her the once?" she asked in a tight quiet voice. She had been told many times that he had been with lovers throughout their entire marriage.

"Aye, just the once." His eyes seemed to plead with her when he drew his haunted gaze to her face. "She did not want me, but she did not want anyone else to have me either. I was well into my cups, angry, and lost. I hit her." His gaze wandered over her shoulder and he stared off into the empty space behind her. "The next thing I knew was she had packed you up and left. I was surprised. Not that she had left, but that she had taken you."

"What do you mean not take me?" Van could hear the angry crack in her voice. Pain filled her with the knowledge that her mother might have not wanted her. Pain and anger, because she was not sure she was surprised.

Matthew caught her gaze and held it.

She could feel her face growing red with frustration. It was a mistake to have come here and now her fragile world was on the verge of falling completely apart. There were only a few options available to her in this. One, her father had changed drastically over the years, two he was lying, or three…her mother had lied to her all her life.

"I am sorry. Truly I am, for I know that all this is not easy for you." He stood quickly and walked around to the back of his chair. He stared at her over the top of it and clenched his fingers onto the tall back.

She waved away his words. "What do you mean surprised?"

"I was surprised because she was never interested in you. Not because of you, but because of me. Because you were mine." He began to pace.

Van wanted to scream at him to stop. The pain in her head was swelling and she was beginning to see small white flashes. The pacing was making it worse as she tried to concentrate on his movements.

Every word he spoke drew her farther away from her mother. If her mother's lies had not caused such a big difference in her life, it would not be so hard now. But those lies had created a whole new person—a person who did not want to go away.

"After you were born she refused to spend any time with me, at night or in the day. When I would search her out, we would fight. So I turned all my attention to you. I spent all the time with you while she was off on her own." He stopped and turned his full attention to her. "I resented it at first, but my love for you took over my feelings for her. When she took you, she took my life," he said, his voice shaking.

Her mind reeled at the thought that her mother may not have loved her. That she was only a pawn in her mother's revenge. She tried to push the thoughts away.

"How did you remarry when you and mother were still married?"

"I learned that your mother had had the marriage annulled about four years after she had left me."

Van's mouth dropped open slightly and she snapped it shut.

Matthew looked at her in confusion. "Surely you knew that, since she had remarried Burgess."

She nodded. She wanted to be spiteful and tell him the truth, that her mother had never remarried nor had she gotten the marriage annulled. She wanted to hurt him for the hurt he was bringing to her, but she could not. It did not matter now that her mother was gone and it would serve no purpose to hurt the children or his new wife.

"Tell me about your wife and children, my brothers." She thought of the boys and found she was anxious to meet them, even though her father said they were nothing like her…or him.

As Matthew told her about his new wife, marriage, and the two boys, ages seven and three, she let her mind wander. She thought back to the first years she remembered. Not only did her mother want her to be a boy, the woman told her to say she was Dr. Burgess' son. The times that Van had baulked at the idea she remembered her mother getting very angry. What was it she had told her?

'*You should have been his son. You should be grateful. There is no reason for you to be curious of that other man. He is not your father anymore. Paul is.*'

Could all Matthew said be true? Could her mother have only loved her after she had convinced herself Van was Paul's child? That she didn't love Matthew's daughter, but she loved Paul's son?

She realized Matthew had stopped talking and was looking expectantly at her, but she could think of nothing to say. "You looked for me." It was not a question, because although she didn't want to admit it, she already knew the answer.

"Aye, for nineteen years. I never went back to see your mother, although I had people keeping an eye on her, hoping you would show up. The only one that ever came to see her was a knight." He watched her face closely. "If you were with her until you were ten, you must have known their son, the Dark Knight?"

"Did you know Dr. Burgess?" she asked in response, unwilling to discuss the Dark Knight. It was too much of a risk. She could not allow anyone to find out who she truly was.

He grunted in irritation. "You are stubborn."

She grinned and ran her hand along the smooth fabric of the well-worn chair. "I have been told I take after you." It was hard for her to admit that, but the grin that slipped across his lips was worth it.

"Aye." His smile slipped away and he shook his head. "He was a nice man. I liked him, even though I tried hard not to." He sat heavily back into his chair. "He was good to your mother, even when she had tantrums. He gave into her needs and let her have her way. Paul was the kind of man she needed."

"I am not sure of that," Van replied reluctantly. "Always getting what you want makes you soft and spoiled."

He shrugged thoughtfully. "Perhaps, but it was the only type of man she would settle for and I was never that type of man. It was my way, no options." His lips twitched and he sighed. "I am sad to say, I have not changed. My wife now is malleable. She does as she is told and she loves me."

Something in his eyes and his voice caused her to start. "Do you not love her?" She saw the answer in the pain in his black eyes. He didn't, he still loved Patricia. "You still love Mother?"

"Aye, I still love her very much and I love you, too." He smiled sadly when she stiffened. "I know that things are not good between us and I will not push you. I will give you all the time you need, but I want you to know I want a relationship with you."

Her thoughts of forgiveness were drawn short as she focused on one thing he had said. "If you did not go to see my mother again, how did you plan for the marriage?"

"Patricia sent a messenger," he said simply. "She said to get a marriage together and to come and get you. That she would send a message when you were there."

Van heart began to race and air caught in the tightness of her throat, burning painfully with each ragged breath.

Matthew's face grew concerned and he stood, taking a step toward her. "One of my men went to see her and then I came to get you. I had thought she knew that my standing and influence could get you a better husband than she could arrange for."

Van jumped to her feet, pacing the large room. She couldn't fathom it. "She told me, you came to her, telling her you were sorry for wanting to kill me and that you had changed."

"Kill you? What the hell are you talking about?" He reached for her as she paced by him, but she jerked her arm from his grasp. "Stop and talk to me. I don't understand." His arms dropped to his sides. Confusion and pain swam in his eyes. Eyes so much like hers. "I could never want to hurt you."

His words had wormed their way into her heart and mind and had softened her against him. His sweet words and touching stories had taken their toll on her hatred and anger, but it was the pain and confusion that now screamed in his quiet voice that made her positive that he was not lying.

"I cannot stay here." She turned and ran from the room, making her way up the winding staircase without seeing the stairs beneath her.

In her chambers, Van tried to get herself under control. How could her mother have done this to her?

She heard a light knocking on the door, but she ignored it. It was more than likely her father and she could not face him right now. The knock came once more and then heavy footsteps disappeared down the corridor.

She slumped down onto the bed and closed her eyes.

Everyone had the same story, the same story of a man distraught over the loss of his beloved daughter, a man who searched for her for nineteen years.

Thoughts spun through her mind, the same thoughts that had crossed her mind when she was younger and it was late in the night. She would lay awake thinking of the man who had sired her. She would try to imagine why a man would search for so long just to kill his daughter. She had pushed those thoughts away when she was a child, but now she let them run freely.

Why would it be so important to him to have his daughter dead? No one could care that much if he had a daughter. Once the daughter was out of sight, she should be out of mind as well.

Out of mind if he had wanted to kill her, but not if he only wanted to be her father.

The castle seemed to creak around her as if the walls were trying to put in their opinions, too. The wind began to blow branches against the outside walls as if hands were reaching for her, in comfort or something else, she was unsure.

She lay back onto the pillows and shuddered lightly. Her head throbbed as restless thoughts whirled through it like dirt in the whipping wind.

Forcing her breathing to slow, she tried to concentrate on something besides the headache that had taken hold of her.

She thought of the man who had acted as her father. She liked Dr. Burgess, but Matthew was right, he was the kind of man who did whatever Patricia had wanted. Even when he had disagreed with her about the way she was raising Vanessa, he would let her do what she wanted. Not only was Van her daughter and not his, but even if she had been his, Van really doubted he would have stood up to Patricia.

She had never felt a bond with Paul, who had tried mostly to just stay out of the way. Sadly, there had been no deep bond between her and her mother either. Paul and her mother seemed to keep her at a distance—perhaps just because of her father.

She tossed and turned until late in the night and still she could not find sleep. Unable to bear facing Matthew in the morning, she grabbed her bag and silently left the manor.

It was not a far walk and the night was clear and not too cold. She had been in colder weather and had walked farther in her life, so she set off toward her new home on foot.

The entire way to Grayweist she suffered fresh pain. What she wanted more than anything was to get on her horse and run, to just disappear, but she knew she could not do that.

She was not supposed to be the Dark Knight. She was not supposed to be a warrior. Those were things she should never have been.

She knew now that she should have grown up in the comfort that Matthew would have provided and been the kind of wife Peter deserved.

The soft breeze caressed her cheeks and eased her mind. Perhaps she should just tell Peter the truth. She trusted him and his judgments. She had no doubts that he would help her.

She had seen the way he had changed toward her, the way he looked at her now. She was beginning to think that he loved her. She hoped it was not just her hopeful imagination that saw these things in his eyes and his actions.

When she got back, she would explain it all to him. Tell him everything and then try to become the kind of woman she should be.

She was supposed to be a woman. She could be a woman. She would have to wear the right clothes and stay away from the men, but it was the way it should have been in the beginning. She would work it out with Matthew and life would be as it was meant to be before her mother used her as a pawn.

CHAPTER 21

A s soon as Vanessa's carriage had disappeared from his sight, Peter let out a troubled sigh. Worry tickled the back of his mind. He could not forget what the stable master had overheard when she was speaking to her horse.

She had told him that she could not yet leave. She still had something to take care of.

A constant barrage of questions ran over and over again through Peter's dark thoughts.

What if she deals with her father and then disappears? What if that is all she needs to do before she can mount her horse and ride away? Would she really just leave? Could she?

He tried to push the concern away, but it still buzzed incessantly in his ear like a coven of gnats.

He did his best to ignore it and set to completing his tasks for the day. Knowing he would get no sleep without her warmth against him, he decided it would be the best time to stake out Marcus Teredo's sheep.

He kept his mind occupied that entire day with preparations for the evening. He would take the men early and set up a camp. They could stay hidden in the tall grasses that surrounded Teredo's pasture and in the thin line of trees that flanked the grass to the west.

He would have a few days before Vanessa returned and he hoped that in that time more sheep were taken and they could catch the thieves. More, he hoped he could find enough to keep him busy so he would not dwell on her absence and what it might mean for him in the end.

👑👑👑

Ryan tugged on the sleeve of Gregory Penchiot as the men trudged along in the growing darkness on their way to their destination. Penchiot was a tall man, thick as a barrel and about as pretty. His brown hair was dull and lifeless and his green eyes were dim. He gave off the impression of a stupid man. He was cruel and mean and had few ideas of his own. No, he did what others told him.

That suited Ryan just fine.

He liked men around him who did what they were told. Men like Christopher Dalton who had yelled out for the entertainment at the wedding feast. Everyone seemed to believe it was Peter's little whore that had coerced him into yelling, but it had been Ryan who had told him what to say and when.

He nodded to Christopher and the three men began to slow.

They slipped through the marching men until they were off to the side and out of hearing range. Ryan smiled snidely. "I have a small job for you, Penchiot."

Ryan had noticed the jealousy that Peter showed when he saw his bride with other men. He planned to take advantage of that.

The jealousy was not bad yet. It was just a glimmer, but with the correct seeds sown it could grow into an infestation. One that could make Ryan's last few days here entertaining if nothing else.

It would serve the overly large woman right to have her marriage fall apart for what she had done to him, he thought spitefully. His loins still ached at the missed opportunity with the enticing little minx, Amy.

"I want you to go to Lord Lawston and make some small comments for me. Nothing bad, just some friendly advice." Ryan grinned as the smile spread across Gregory's face.

He leaned forward and whispered quietly what he wanted said and then the grin widened into a full-toothed smile. As he watched Gregory hurry away to catch up with their fearless leader he thought of his actual task for the night.

He had to stop this ambush from happening and he knew a simple way to do so. He planned to throw a rock at the head of that big stupid beast of a man, Verges. He grunted as Gregory touched Peter's arm. He could only hope that Verges was smart enough to know it for the sign that it was.

♚ ♚ ♚

Peter was lost in thought of where Vanessa was and what she was doing when he started at a soft touch to his elbow. He turned to look into the face of Gregory Penchiot.

Gregory had joined him almost a year before and Peter still did not trust him. He had considered letting him go several times, but the man did nothing he could point to with conviction. It was just a feeling, one he could not shake.

"My lord, may I talk to you?" he asked as he sidled up next to him. "It is quiet important."

"Aye, Penchiot, what is it?" Not in the mood for any problems, Peter only listened with half an ear, his mind on his bride. He was not looking forward to the nights without her. More than likely, he thought, he would spend every night with the men.

"I am not the only one who has noticed..." He fell silent and soon Peter was drawn from his thoughts.

He turned his attention to Gregory. He came to a stop and waited. The men behind him stopped as well. He glanced at them and then back to Gregory.

Gregory smiled lightly and continued. "I mean, I would not say anything against Lady Vanessa…"

Peter scowled at him. "Just tell me. I do not have time for riddles this night."

Gregory cleared his throat and leaned closer to him. "She has been seen in the garden in the middle of the night and not alone."

"What do you mean, not alone? Who was she with?" Peter took a step back, not wanting to here Richard's name mentioned, but he knew that was what he would hear.

"One was Richard—"

"*One*?" Peter could not hide his anger.

"Devon has also been seen in the garden alone with her, Gary as well." His voice was consolatory, but his eyes gleamed nastily. Peter barely noticed either.

Soft waves of doubt had caressed Peter ever since he had first seen Vanessa with the men. He knew he was jealous, but he had thought it under control. Now as those soft waves began to violently crash against him he knew it was not.

He'd had doubts about her loyalty many times, seeing her with the men and the comfort she seemed to feel around them—comfort she should not feel.

Peter told himself firmly that she would not betray him. He reminded himself it was fear left behind by his mother, but the doubt lingered persistently.

"I do not think it your place to tell me of my wife and her goings and comings. I think you should concern yourself with what you do from now on." With that Peter turned and walked away.

He took his place in the tall grass as the last of the daylight faded from the sky and watched the growing shadows closely for movement, but his mind wandered.

Vanessa was forced into a marriage with him and she was unhappy. These things he knew without a doubt. *What loyalty did she owe him?*

Images of Vanessa in the arms of other men danced before him in the darkness. He closed his eyes tightly, but her writhing body taunted him behind his closed lids.

How could she do that? "That would explain why the men were so close to her." His frustrated whisper disappeared into the darkness. And why they seemed so loyal, he thought.

He opened his eyes and tried to concentrate on the task at hand but doubts and jealousy tore at him. Pain stabbed his heart and a tight lump clogged his throat.

How many other men had she gone to? How many others knew her intimately? He could not bear to think of it. What was he to do? There had to be something he could do that would tell him if his suspicions were accurate.

Suddenly he saw several dark shadows moving among the sheep and thoughts of his betraying wife were lost.

The plan of attack was already set forth and no signal was needed. All the men knew what was expected of them and they moved quickly but silently. Peter's heart began to race with adrenaline as they closed in on the intruders.

Peter was close enough to reach out and grab one of the dark figures when the peaceful night broke into chaos.

A deep grunt of pain and surprise was heard. Then a shout, then screams, and men began running. Peter heard the sounds of fighting and the thuds of blows connecting.

Eolian's men broke away and began a steady retreat. Peter took chase. He barely registered the sounds of pounding feet behind him.

He felt a hand on his arm and slid to a stop as he was jerked around. He drew his fist back, but took an unsteady breath as his eyes focused on Grant's face.

"Peter, stop. What are you doing? We do not know how many men they have out there." Grant gave Peter a gentle shake and gestured around the darkened trees. "Look how far we have already followed them."

Grant dropped his hand from Peter's arm and Richard stopped behind him as he looked around. He focused his gaze on the accusing face on the moon and realized his mind had not been on the chase. He did not know where he was.

Turning, he almost told that Grant he was right, almost, until he saw Richard standing alongside him. Then he felt his face redden and a scowl pulled at his lips.

His wife may have betrayed him, and he would find a way to discover the truth, but for his friend to have done it was something else. Anger shook his voice as he spoke. "What did you do?"

The men, breathing hard from the fast chase through the trees, had begun to gather around.

"My lord?" Richard's act at confusion enraged Peter.

He attacked the man he had thought of as a friend. Both men slammed to the ground. Peter got in several hits before he felt hands tugging at him.

Grant's voice was almost panicked in the confusion. "Whatever it is, my lord, I would suggest we take it back to the castle."

Peter was pulled to his feet and yanked back. Grant refused to release his arm when Peter twisted at it.

"This is not the safest place to be distracted." Grant pulled Peter along with him, taking the lead. The men followed.

Peter kept looking back at the men, each glancing at one another for some clue as to what had happened. Like they don't know, Peter thought.

Back at the castle the men were led to the dining hall. Peter grumbled and said he was not going, but Grant tightened his grip on his arm and dragged him along.

Peter was confused by his thoughts. He could not pull himself from the past, from the pain of his mother's abandonment.

Richard turned toward him with his fists clenched. "Now, shall we talk about why the men took off, or about what happened between us?" he stood facing his friend, his face red with anger or embarrassment.

Perhaps both, Peter thought as he took a deep breath to try and control the violent shaking that overtook his limbs. "They were somehow tipped off. Someone was seen, that is all. As to the other, I will talk to you in private."

His voice rose as he bellowed across the room, "Horacio, Puelo, come." His voice lowered. "Grant, you and Devenroe will stay as well."

Again his voice boomed as he addressed the entire hall. "The rest of you may retire."

He waited until the room was empty, save for the five of them, before turning on Richard again. "I trusted you, all of you and this is how you repay me. This is how you repay me for taking you in after the Dark Knight abandoned you."

He ignored the look of sudden and dangerous outrage on Richard's face and turned to Gary. "And you, this is your thanks for me taking in you and your sister."

"My lord—Peter, what is this about?" Grant asked.

"They know. How many times have you taken my wife, Richard?"

Peter did not give him time for an answer. Ignoring the shocked and confused look on Richard's face, he threw himself at his traitorous friend. They both hit the floor with a deep grunt of pain and Peter drove his fist into Richard's face.

The men standing around tried to break it up, Peter just shrugged them off. What stopped him, when it finally registered, was Richard's refusal to defend himself. He just lay there trying his best to protect his face from Peter's blows. He did not throw a single punch.

Dark and poisonous jealousy rampaged through Peter's system as he pulled himself off Richard. With his head hanging low, he sucked in deep and painful gasps of air. "Why do you not even fight back? You could at least have the decency to do that."

Richard, blood spiraling down his thick whiskers from cracked and broken lips, just shook his head. "You are my friend. I will not hit you. When you are through and we can talk about this, then I will talk to you."

Peter snorted loudly. "My friend, indeed." He fought the urge to once more attack him. He had exhausted enough of his anger that he would not attack a man who would not even defend himself.

Richard shook his head sadly. "I do not know why you think I would betray you, but if I have done something that was offensive to you." He took a deep breath and bowed his head in what looked like shame. "And I know I have."

Peter's heart plummeted into the pit of his stomach and rolled around, making him want to throw up. He did not want to hear more. It was his mother all over again.

Richard cleared his throat. He took a step closer to Peter and looked him in the eye, catching his gaze and holding it. "I have spent time with your wife. I have been with her alone and done things that I should not, with the Lady of the castle." He lifted his hand when Peter moved to speak. "I do not know how to explain it. I am drawn to her, and although she is attractive, my attraction is not sexual."

Peter's breath began to slow and he clenched his fist tightly at his sides.

"I look at her and think I know her, think I have seen her somewhere and then she talks to me." Richard smiled in wonder and Peter wanted to punch him once again. "She treats me like I am her second-in-command and the men that came with me, hers."

"I have seen," Peter growled, but his anger was calming and in its wake was more confusion. He did not want to believe his friends or his wife would betray him, but he could not stop the doubts.

Richard reached for his arm and Peter pulled away. "I should have put a stop to it. I just did not know how." Richard said quietly and shrugged. "Honestly, I did not want to. I feel like she is my friend."

Peter began to really listen and more, he could understand. He looked at the men who shuffled uneasily. He could see on their faces that they too felt the same. He felt the same recognition, the same familiar tugs at his conscious when he looked at her as they all did. This was not the first time it had been spoken of.

Richard looked back at the other men and then focused on Peter again. "I felt out of place here until she came along. It feels right that I stand at her side, and that I give her my loyalty, but above all else I am your friend."

This time when Richard reached for his arm, he stood his ground and allowed Richard to grasp his elbow firmly. "I am loyal to you as I have only been to one other, the Dark Knight." He shook his head. "I do not know why he felt he had to go, but I am grateful you took me in. I would not risk our friendship for even a woman as amazing as your wife."

"How am I to believe that?" Peter could hear the pathetic whine in his own voice and he cringed.

The doubts were deep seeded by his insecurities and jealousy. The confirmations by his loyal men had made those seeds sprout and take firm hold, reaching through his soul like weeds and strangling out the flowers of love that had begun to bloom there.

He wanted to believe that his friend of so many years would not betray him, but the evidence seemed overwhelming.

Turning to Gary, he asked him. "What of you, have you been alone with my wife as well?" He was sure he would get a denial.

"Aye, my lord," he said softly, keeping his gaze firmly on Peter's face.

Peter clenched his teeth and hissed softly with a sharp intake of breath. Before he could speak Gary continued.

"I went to see her in the garden to speak to her of Anna. She is close to my sister. Anna has been seen with Douglas Sheire."

Peter relaxed his jaw and waited.

"Since our mother is gone and Anna seems to look up to Lady Vanessa, calling her what has seemed to have stuck from the day she saved Joseph, the Dark Lady, I went to speak to her." Gary smiled softly. "I did not want anyone to overhear my conversation so I spoke to her in the garden one day before supper."

Peter watched him shrug and forced himself to relax. Peter was an only child, but he understood the love of family and the concern for those you are responsible for.

"She promised to look after Anna, to protect my sister and to talk to her about things a mother should tell her. Things a brother cannot." His face tinged in pink and he cleared his throat. "Things I would not even know where to start with."

Having nothing to say to argue with that, Peter just looked to Devon, what would be his innocent excuse. "And you?"

Devon took a deep breath and cringed. His face darkened and he looked at his boots as he ran them back and forth across the floor. Peter saw the guilt wash over him but waited, anger blossoming behind his eyes, making him see spots of red. "Well?" He finally asked when Devon remained silent.

Devon looked up, his eyes twitched from side to side and he would not meet Peter's gaze. "I am sorry, my lord."

The blood pounded in Peter's ears. His teeth bit into his bottom lip so hard he tasted blood. He was right, she had betrayed him. He stepped forward with clenched fists. "Tell me now."

Devon's face turned white, but he did not drop his eyes. "I went to see Lady Vanessa about Amy." His words came fast and low. "It was Amy who told me to and—" He shook his head. "—nay, I will not involve her, I could have told her no, I just…" He took a deep breath. "I went to her to ask for permission to marry Amy."

Peter's mouth dropped open, and he slammed it shut so fast he hurt his teeth. "Why would you ask her? I am the one you should have come to?" Peter's brow furrowed with surprise and distrust. He was sure he had caught the young man in a lie.

"I told Amy that. That it was my duty to come to you since you were my liege lord." He grunted and shook his head. "She told me you shouldn't be."

Peter sucked in a deep breath. Anger blossomed and his voice echoed through the large and mostly empty room. "She said what?"

Grant laid his hand on his shoulder and Peter shrugged it off. The men beside him shifted nervously.

Devon went on. His words now came out in a rush, growing faster and faster until he didn't seem to breathe. "She said I had to ask her. Lady Vanessa is responsible for Amy, and I would have asked you, but Amy said she would not marry me if I did not ask Lady Vanessa." His breathing had gotten ragged and his face was almost purple. "She said Lady Vanessa would think it her place as the one in charge of Amy and—"

It was concern for him that caused Peter to touch his arm. "Calm down. Breathe."

Taking a long breath, he held it until Peter thought he may pass out, his face going from almost purple to a deep red.

He let it out in a whoosh. "I cry your pardon. I should have come to you." Devon grasped his hand tightly and bowed over it. "Please my lord, I love Amy and would do nothing to hurt her." He straightened this time, holding Peter's gaze without guilt. "You have my loyalty."

Peter pulled his hand away. "All of you leave me be."

He turned his back on them as they shuffled from the room, but he could hear their soft mumblings. They were probably discussing his insanity, he thought bitterly.

He had to find a way of putting his doubts to rest one way or the other. He considered his choices as he made his way to his chambers and his big empty bed.

The only one of the men that he was sure was not lying was Devon. Not because he trusted him more, but simply because going to her as if she was the liege lord was as much a betrayal to Peter as if he had lain with her. He knew the boy well enough to know if he was going to lie, he would have chosen a safer one.

Options for discovering the truth flew threw his mind and were immediately dismissed as useless. The only one that kept resurfacing was to find someone that Vanessa had showed particular interest in and see if she would betray him.

It had to be someone he could trust to tell him the truth. His first thought had been Hestlay, but he did not think Vanessa showed any signs of being interested in him. She showed him respect, but that was all.

He went through the list of those she appeared close to. Some of which, like Gary and Richard were dismissed for obvious reasons. One name crossed his mind and stuck—Telpher Constaire—and he was a man Peter trusted. He had been with Peter for many years and was loyal without fault.

Telpher had also spent much time with Vanessa. Peter had seen them on several occasions. Vanessa acted like she knew the young man, asking him questions of his family, his life and the changes in it over the last few years.

Peter had been jealous of the time they spent together, but Telpher was happily married and had turned down many women because he would not betray his wife. So Peter had pushed the unwanted emotion away easily.

Peter tossed and turned that night, pain and confusion, stealing sleep from his grasp. An empty side to his bed was not the only thing on his mind as sleep eluded him. Every time he closed his eyes he saw the men and his wife.

Long before morning, he gave up the pretense and left his bed.

Sitting with the brandy in his library, he tried to keep his mind blank and as the sun was beginning to come through the trees he searched out Telpher.

Once found, Peter led him to the servants' entrance at the rear of the castle. The candle in Peter's hands threw trembling light across the wooden beams that ran through the stonework of the thick walls. The cobwebs he had seen so many times before had been washed clean, probably from his nice little, well, big wife. She could not be construed in any way as little. Not in stature or in attitude, he thought with a snort.

He turned his attention to the man who followed silently behind him. "I need to ask you something. Can I trust you?"

"Of course, my lord," Telpher said, an arched brow marring his high forehead with wrinkles.

Peter sat the candle in a crook in the wall and turned back to him.

"You can still say nay." He began but Telpher shook his head. "Don't shake your head until you hear it. I have heard several people tell me Vanessa is not faithful—"

Telpher's questioning look turned angry. "My lord, Lady Vanessa would not—"

"I know. I have heard that also. What I need is peace of mind. I want you to seduce my wife." Peter ignored the shocked look that rippled through Telpher's chocolate brown eyes and pushed onward before he could talk himself out of it. "I know she likes you and if anyone can get her you can."

Telpher arched his brows and smirked. "I don't think that is—"

Peter continued without waiting for him to finish. "I also trust you to tell me the truth and not take her all the way. Just far enough to know that she will."

"I do not think this is a good idea, my lord. I know she will not be happy…" His features took on a worried almost frightened look.

Peter felt anger spread through his features, heating his face.

Telpher looked at him and then sighed. "I will do whatever it is you need of me, my lord. I pledged to give my life for you." He shuddered. "Even if it is to the lady of the castle when I anger her."

"You will be fine. She is not violent."

Telpher gave a snort of laughter at this and a quick vision of the bloody mess she had made of the guards posted outside her door flashed before Peter. He pushed it away. If she hit Telpher, Peter would make it up to him.

"She should be home any day now. Just find her alone. See her in the garden. That seems to be where she likes to take the men." Painful anger tightened his throat, leaving a lump behind. He cleared his throat and tried to speak around it. "Tell her whatever you need to, to get her to betray me. Then let me know how it goes. I want to know, no matter what." Peter really did not really want to know, but he needed to. "Do you understand me?"

"Aye. I understand." Telpher looked as though he wished to say more, but held his tongue.

"Good," Peter said. It would be settled one way or the other soon and he would know the truth.

They turned away from the door and toward the dining hall where breakfast would soon be served. They had just rounded the corner into the shadows when the servants' door burst open.

Peter glanced back to see Vanessa pushing it closed. He stepped into the shadows and pushed Telpher toward her. Only after he had done so did he wonder what she was doing home so soon and why had he not heard a carriage. He pushed away the worry that things had not gone well with her father. One problem to solve at a time, he thought as Telpher approached her.

CHAPTER 22

S tartled at the noise of scraping feet behind her, Van's breath caught. She turned, putting her back against the wall. "Telpher, what are you doing here?" As she relaxed her breath became even but shallow. Dust from the road wafted off of her and tickled at her nose.

He stepped close to her. "I saw you coming. I want to speak with you."

"What is it that you want?" Her voice trembled. She only wanted to go to bed, maybe stay there till next spring.

"I want you. I know you have been with some of the other men." He ran his hands up her sweat moistened arms.

She looked down at his trailing hand and then stared up at him. Her weary mind was unable to understand what he meant. "What are you talking about? Get away from me." She pushed him, only to have him grab her arms tightly and pull her close to him.

"I know you are with the others. I only want to get in on the fun. Give me what you give them."

He pressed into her trying to kiss her. She jerked her head to the side.

Anger began to peak through the confines of exhaustion. "I have never betrayed my husband and I am not about to start now. How can you say these things? Let me go." She tried to push past him, tried to remove his tight grip, but she could find no will to fight. "I thought you were my friend," she said weakly as she pushed at his arms and hands.

It seemed all her strength was gone, drained from her slowly ever since her mother had died and her life had been torn apart. All she wanted was to get to Peter, tell him the truth, and to go to bed wrapped in his arms with no secrets between them.

Telpher pushed her up against the wall. "You should not give Peter much thought. What loyalty do you owe him? He is not someone you chose to marry. Everyone knows you are unhappy."

The anger burst through the clouds in her mind, shining brightness across her thoughts. Her mind cleared. Her long night was forgotten, her body no longer weary. She pushed against Telpher's chest, but he leaned against her using his full weight to pin her to the wall.

Surprise and weariness had allowed him an advantage, but it was not one she planned to let him keep for long. She ran her hand across the slit in her skirt toward her dagger.

Telpher pulled at her skirt. It billowed around her legs and made the dagger slit bunch and become useless to her. He lifted it farther up her legs. She could feel the coolness of the castle across her bare knees.

Her eyes narrowed at the man who had claimed to be her friend. "You should be ashamed. How can you do this to me, to Peter, or to your wife?" He had claimed to lcve his wife fully and faithfully. How could she have misjudged him so bad?

Telpher cringed at the mention of his wife, but continued to rub at her arm and raise her skirt. She twisted trying to get loose, or at least get the skirt lowered to where she could use her dagger.

She felt disappointed in herself for trusting him. She used to be a better judge of people than that. She shook her head angrily. She used to be a lot of things she no longer was.

Mostly she felt anger for Peter as his friend and loyal man pushed her skirts up to her thighs. Peter was the one most betrayed and it was an affront to her husband she would not allow.

She slipped her hand toward the bottom of her skirt which was almost to the point that she could reach her weapon. Almost to the point where she would make him regret his decision to betray Peter.

Telpher then stopped raising her skirt. He looked up at her and opened his mouth as if to speak.

Van did not want to hear anything come out of his mouth. No more sweet talk or pleading for her to lie with him.

Van forced herself to relax and stop fighting. She ran her left hand up his arm and smiled. "You want me that bad?" she asked in what she hoped was a seductive voice.

Telpher looked bewildered for a moment as she wrapped her left foot intimately around his ankle. She ran her foot up and down his calf, caressed his neck, and threaded her fingers into his hair. She pulled his head close to hers. She spoke directly against his lips, feeling his tremble as she spoke. "Tell me what you want to do to me?"

He only groaned.

She pulled his face close to her shoulder and ran her nose along the length of his neck. She pulled the skirt higher with her right hand. He began to pull away from her as her hand closed around the jeweled hilt of the dagger.

Relief had washed over Peter as she had denied Telpher's advances. Now he watched with mounting rage as her foot massaged the back of his leg and her hand pushed through his dark brown hair.

As she pressed her face closer to his, a knot started in the pit of Peter's stomach and wormed its way to his throat. Angry that she had actually betrayed him, he stepped out of the shadows and opened his mouth, but the words froze.

Vanessa suddenly balled Telpher's hair into her clenched fist and jerked his head back. At the same time she hooked her foot around his ankle, jerking his leg forward. Off balanced Telpher fell hard onto his back. Vanessa kept her hand firmly planted in his hair and landed with a thud on top of him, a dagger held firmly against his throat.

Peter's heart lurched. His breath stopped short and he gasped sound-lessly.

Vanessa pulled tightly on Telpher's hair and pressed the tip of the dagger into the delicate skin beneath his chin.

"Wait," Telpher pleaded.

The sight of the small trickle of blood running down Telpher's throat as the steel tip broke skin tore through Peter's shock. He stepped closer to them, but neither seemed to notice.

"You are wrong. I do have a reason to show him my loyalty. I may only have one, but it is a good reason." Vanessa's voice shook with out-rage and Peter feared for Telpher's safety. "I do it because I love him."

Peter's heart stopped, all doubts of her virtue dissipated.

"You on the other hand, one who is supposed to be his friend? You have lots of reasons to give him yours. I should just kill you now for the betrayal that you have committed."

Peter's heart seemed to lurch back to life and he lunged forward. "Vanessa, stop."

Van looked up into her husband's wide eyes and wanted to collapse into his arms. It was not a feeling she had ever had before, but she did not dislike it.

She had spent the night walking through the cold darkness, thinking of all the things she was, more importantly, everything she wasn't. She was more confused and angry by the time she had arrived home than she had ever been. Looking up into his blue eyes, she was sure of three things: her love for him, her trust in him, and his trust in her.

"Stop, do not hurt him. He was following my orders." Peter held his hands out to her. "Please." His voice sounded strange, tight.

"What do you mean? Why?" She stared at him in total confusion. She was sure she had heard him wrong.

"Let him up and I will tell you," he said softly. "Do not hurt him."

She stared at him for a moment, feeling lost, and then looked down at Telpher.

"I am sorry," he whispered softly. His jaw moved slightly against the dagger and more blood oozed from beneath its tip.

Without a word to him, she pulled it away. She stood, ignoring him completely as Telpher pulled himself out of the way. "Now, tell me."

"I was told you were betraying me and…"

She sucked in a shocked breath that burned at her throat and seemed to shrivel her heart. "And you thought you would turn some of your men loose on me instead of just asking me?" So much for his trust, she thought. She took another shaky breath.

"Vanessa, just give me the dagger before you hurt yourself with it. You could injure someone by not knowing how to use it." His voice was patronizing, like he was speaking to a young child. A young stupid child.

Her black eyes turned to slits as she stared at him. Anger pulsed through her veins, warming her like a fire in the bowels of the castle warms the walls. "How is it that you think I know nothing? Do you not even realize all that I have done? What do you think? I am to sit and do nothing but have your babies?"

"Give me the dagger," he said, holding his hand out.

"Aye, my lord. You want it? Here." Flipping the knife into the air, she caught it deftly by the blade. The cold shimmering metal was only in her fingers for half a heartbeat as she threw it at the wooden beam right beside his head.

Telpher let out a tight yell. The blade stuck into the wall not an inch from the dumbfounded look on Peter's face.

Peter's heart lurched into his throat, and he was sure it was going to come out as he let out a soft grunt of surprise. She had actually thrown it at him.

"Thank God, you missed, my lady." Telpher had jumped to his feet, rushing toward her, thinking to subdue her, just to have Peter wave him back.

Peter stared at the jeweled hilt of the blade and felt his breath catch. Her throwing it at him no longer seemed important. How had she gotten it? It was the Dark Knight's blade. Emeralds and rubies flared in the candlelight.

It was unmistakably the gift he had given to the Dark Knight as reward for saving his life.

Vanessa stalked toward Peter, her face red with anger. Most of the powder was gone. He could see her tanned face beneath the thin layer and in parts there was no powder at all. Some he was sure had been lost in the tussle with Telpher and some on the long walk home.

She stopped long enough to pull the dagger from the wall. "I never miss. Next time it will be at your big stubborn skull instead of the wooden beam." With that she walked back out the door into the cloudy morning, the dagger disappearing into her dress.

Peter turned and looked at the smooth, straight entry hole in the wood. It was a small section of wood completely surrounded by stone.

He jumped as Telpher's voice sounded in his ear. "You think she really aimed for that? It does seem a little odd that the knife hit the only part of the wall it could stick in, especially after that toss."

"Aye." He pushed the door open and went after her.

He was afraid for her. Eolian had been in Junket the same time as she and the Dark Knight. If she was involved with them in some way, Eolian may just as well be after her. He had not mentioned his worries to Richard that day by the lake, but he had thought of little else since then. If she was in danger, he would do his best to protect her. She just had to tell him what was going on.

He caught her on the way to the stables. Grabbing her arm, he spun her around. "Damn it. Stop and talk to me. Just where do you think you are going?"

Vanessa yanked hard. She stumbled backwards as she pulled her arm free, barely catching herself before she fell. "Leaving, that is where I am going. Now move out of my way." She tried to go around him toward the stables.

He stepped in front of her. "You are going to talk to me. There are things I want to know about."

She glared at him and turned, stomping off toward the men getting ready to go to the training fields.

Peter caught sight of all the men stopping to watch them, but ignored them. He needed answers and she was the only one to give them to him.

"Are you all right?" Richard asked as she walked close to him.

Before she could answer a frantic shout came from toward the castle. Peter turned. Gary ran toward them.

"Lady Vanessa! Lady Vanessa! Thank goodness you are here." Gary slid to a stop before her. "Have you seen Anna?"

Worry seized Van's mind and made her forget about Peter and his ploys to catch her in a betrayal. "Nay, I just got here. What has happened?" She placed her hand on his trembling shoulder and gave it a gentle squeeze.

Taking a deep breath, Gary started in a shaky voice. "Anna is always here in the morning to have breakfast with me, my lady." He looked up and stopped, a look of hopeful anticipation crossing his face.

Van turned to see Amy approaching, followed closely by Joseph and Devon. When Amy shook her head, he continued. "I had them look as well. When she did not come down for breakfast, I went to find her."

Van looked back at him and grasped his trembling hand.

"Oh, Vanessa, she is all I have." His voice was thick with unshed tears and a deep fear that trembled through his words.

"We will find her, but you have to tell us everything." Peter's voice sounded calm as he stepped up to them, but his eyes betrayed his concern.

"I went to her chambers and I found a mess." Gary began. "It looked as if there was a battle in there. I found a torn piece of her night robe and blood on the bed. I am afraid someone has ra—" His voice broke into a soft sob as he could not continue.

"If she is hurt or afraid, maybe I know where she is hiding." Van looked at Amy. "Did you look there?"

Amy looked confused for just a moment before realization set in, and then she gasped. "Nay, God, I did not even think to."

Van shook her head. Releasing Gary's trembling hand, she began to walk to the high wall that separated the woods, and Anna's secret place, from the castle grounds.

Peter grasped her arm. "Wait, you cannot go by yourself. What if she is hurt? Will you carry her the entire way back? I will go."

Peter began to follow, Gary right on his heels. Van turned on them. "Nay, if what you think has happened, did happen—" Her heart slammed against her chest as she prayed that it had not. "—then do you think she wants men to barge in on her. I will go myself."

Peter did not fight when she pulled her arm free and began to walk once again. "And if she is hurt, can you get to her fast and get her back quickly, on your own?"

"Nay." She looked back at the great distance to the stables and thought of the arguments she was going to face to get there and shook her head. "Nay," she repeated.

She turned and began walking toward the back wall once more. She could see the open gate, left open more than likely by Anna as she had fled.

It was almost a complete U-shaped path to get from where she stood to the gate and all the way back to Anna's secret hiding place. It would take too much time to go the long way.

The fence was only about five foot high. She could go over it, but getting Anna back over it if she were hurt would be something else. Plus she needed to be fast. She only had one option.

Peter watched her walk away, head high and determined. He was about to go after her, despite her objections when she placed two fingers into her mouth. The deafening whistle that issued forth stopped him in his tracks.

He registered the answering scream of a horse from the stables and the crash of wood that could only have been the stall gate. Not looking back at the screams of the stable hands, he kept his eyes glued to the tall woman as she grasped the hole where he now knew her dagger was kept.

Vanessa grasped the material and pulled. Peter heard the long tear as the skirt fell open completely on the side, baring her leg from thigh to ankle. During it all, she never broke her stride.

Peter called out as her huge destrier thundered past him, screamed for her to watch out. Beast began to slow until Vanessa whistled again. He regained his speed, tearing straight for her. Peter's breath caught in his throat as he knew he would not be able to save her.

Vanessa reached out a long arm, gripping the coarse waving mane as the animal thundered past, and smoothly swung herself onto his massive back.

Peter felt a jolt of fear as she wobbled slightly on the racing stallion, one creamy white leg glistening in the dim sunlight. Shadows played off the thick muscles as they rippled in her effort to stay on the unsaddled mount.

The men all stood with their mouths agape as their Lady rode toward the wall. For once Peter did not feel a twinge of jealousy. He fully understood their awe.

Vanessa leaned forward and ducked her head as if to avoid the wind. Her stallion rode straight for the wall. He did not slow or turn and then, to Peter's horror, he was too close to change course.

"She would not." Peter did not even realize he had spoken aloud until he felt a small hand on his. He looked down to see Amy's smile.

"Milord, she would, but she will be all right." She spoke with confidence.

Peter wished he could be as sure, but he wasn't.

He thought his heart would stop as Vanessa did what he had feared she would. He held in a scream as the massive animal bundled its legs underneath it, taking the jump smoothly. Leaning forward, she seemed one with the animal.

Peter held his breath as they disappeared behind the wall. It seemed forever that the two were out of sight.

He had time to imagine her broken and bloody body lying beneath the horse, both dying.

He released his breath in a relieved rush when he saw them, both horse and rider, safe and still moving fast.

The fear that clogged his throat still remained as he watched them pounding toward the woods. It was in that moment of fear, those few seconds that seemed like eternity, that he realized he loved her. How had he not seen that before he wondered?

He loved her, and she loved him. And as soon as she returned he would beat her senseless for terrifying him the way she had. Then he would hold her and love her and never let her out of his sight again.

Van broke the tree line, sweat trickling through the powder on her face. She slid from Damien's broad back before he had even come to a complete stop.

"Easy, boy. Stay right here." She spoke, to calm the animal, as well as to let Anna know she was there, not wanting to frighten her.

"Anna, it's only me. It's Van. I am coming in, alone." She stopped dead as she took in the terrified girl.

Anger and a vicious blinding hatred awakened within her. Her breath whistled through her heaving chest and her whole body shook.

Anna's face was swollen and bruised, blood coming from her nose and lips. The soft white gown Amy had made for her was torn and streaked with blood. Her delicate feet enraged Van beyond words. They were bare and bleeding, stained green from her long run in the grass and thorns.

"Vanessa, I am so sorry..." Heartbreaking tears broke the paralysis that had held Van. She ran to her, pulling her into her arms. Violent sobs wracked at the fragile child she held.

"Do not say that. You did nothing wrong. You have nothing to be sorry for." She buried her face in her hair, kissing her softly on the neck. Van pulled her head up and noticed powder streaked across the girl's hair, but it did not register that it had come from her face.

"I did. I tried to do what Gary told me to." Her breath hitched as another string of sobs burst forth.

"What did Gary tell you to do?" Van asked, confused as to what her brother had to do with any of this.

"He said, if I was ever attacked, *raped*—" The word came out as a bare whisper. "I was to fight, but if I was going to be hurt, I was to stop fighting, just let them take me." Shudders wracked her small frame. "He said my life was more important to him than my...my..."

Van agreed with him, she would have told her the same thing. "Shhhh, I understand. Tell me what happened."

"I tried, but the more I tried not to fight, the more he would hit me. He became furious with me, said it was my fault it didn't work, then he would hit me harder." Anna's sobs became almost deafening, her words barely understandable. "The more I tried to let him...then he, he made me fight him. Made it hurt until I couldn't stand it. Then he, then...he..." She buried her face into Van's chest and began to wail. "Don't let Ryan hurt me again. He said he would be back."

Blood drained from Van's face as she understood what had happened. The young girl was hard to understand through the sobs and the hiccups, but as she finished in a whisper, Van understood.

Understood who had done this and why he had become more violent, instead of less, as she cooperated. The men may be on good behavior around Van, but she still heard things. Ryan liked fear. Some of the stories that went around also said that without the fear and the fighting, he could not get his member to stand firm. She had paid little mind to these rumors, but now she was sure they were true.

A white hot fire was beginning to burn its way through her—the anger and confusion she had felt at her father's home, Peter's betrayal, and everything she had tried to be and tried not to be.

Everything collided, turning to a raging thunderstorm inside her, and yet her voice was calm. "Easy, I will take you to Gary and I will take care of it. I never should have left you."

Her body had begun to take over, her mind awaiting the results. She had promised Anna's brother to take care of her and she had failed.

Standing before the cowering child, Van brushed her fingers through her thick black hair. Pulling it all into three sections she quickly braided it before tearing a strip of cloth from her already ruined dress. Folding the braid together until it was a thick, short braid, like the one she was used to wearing, she wrapped the cloth around it to keep it in place, out of her way.

Van gathered Anna up into her arms, putting her arm underneath her trembling legs to carry her. She could feel the cold and congealed blood on the back of her gown. It stuck to her arm as she made her way to the fallen log where she had left Damien.

Anna threw her arms around Van's hot and sweaty neck and burrowed deep into her embrace. Her hot tears ran across Van's neck and slid down her chest.

The anger she'd harbored, the pain and the confusion Van had felt since her mother's death fell upon her at once. The guilt, at allowing this child to be hurt, at all the ones she loved that she was lying to, consumed her. The terror she felt, when she thought of all those she had put in danger by just being here, combined together and buried her.

She lost all conscious thought patterns as her swirling emotions gathered together into a black, encompassing rage. Van did not remember mounting Damien and was only vaguely aware of the small frame she protectively held against her chest.

Holding both arms around the girl, she allowed the huge animal beneath her to gallop. His stride was smooth and she had no difficulties keeping her balance with her thighs.

They went the long way, through the gate and back around. Her anger continued to boil over, spilling the hatred and rage into every thought and breath she had.

Every man had gathered in the courtyard awaiting her return. The Dark Knight, released from all restraints, freed as she had never been free before, spotted Ryan Deumount in the center of the men.

CHAPTER 23

Van tightened her thighs against Damien's heaving sides and urged him to a stop several feet away from the standing crowd of onlookers. The men stared, shifting back at forth and darting nervous glances at her.

She nodded to Gary to come get his sister before she swung her leg over the neck of the panting horse. She slid to the ground with the frightened girl still in her steady arms. She sensed, rather than heard, the collective gasp as she dropped Anna gently to her bare feet, her blood covered arm sliding from beneath the young girl.

"Easy, Damien," she muttered as the animal's ears quivered and his nostrils flared. Her voice came out in a calmness that did nothing to betray the rampaging anger that was racking her entire system.

She steadied Anna against him and turned away.

She held her head straight ahead and didn't even look at Gary as he approached her. She kept her gait smooth and deliberate.

Her mind contained only one thing, the death of Ryan Deumount. Her mind whirled with options on how to accomplish what needed to be done.

She was in need of a weapon and knew that no one would willingly give one over to her. She watched the bright sunlight glitter off Gary's sword as it swung from his hip as he hurried toward his sister.

Gary's eyes were distracted and hollow as he stared at Anna. Van grinned. His distraction would be all she needed.

When Gary was directly across from her, she side stepped, her shoulder slamming into his. He fought for balance. She swiftly pulled the sword from his scabbard. Her gait increased and she strode quickly toward the men.

She took in Gary's shout behind her, but the words did not reach through the anger and guilt that swirled through her, clouding out everything like a dust storm. She saw the looks of astonished surprise on the men's faces before her, but ignored them. Somewhere deep inside she knew she was making a mistake. Her conscious screamed at her from the depths of the Dark Knight, but this too she pushed away.

The Dark Knight's deep graveled voice screamed for Deumount to show his cowardly face.

The men parted before her, leaving Ryan to face her alone. Wasting no time and allowing no chance for anyone to interfere she swung the heavy sword at him.

Ryan's face dropped in shock. He leapt back and barely had time to pull his sword free and bring it up to protect himself.

Steel clanged against steel, its echo rippling through the silent crowd. The shock of the blow raced up the muscles in her arms and through her shoulder. Her face tightened as a vicious grin crept across her lips. Her chest heaved as she gasped for breath and her heart raced.

Exhilaration filled her in bright flashes of power and desire. The need to humiliate this man ached deep within her. She wanted more than to see his death. She wanted to weaken him. To not only kill him but to destroy him.

She would kill him slowly. Tease him first before she pounced on him and slaughtered him. She laughed silently inside.

She tried lifting the sword and feigned a need to struggle with it. Ryan watched her closely and a knowing look crossed his face.

The first rule of war was never to underestimate your opponent, and he had just broken that rule. She began to circle around him. Her lips spread wide in a smile of pure joy.

Peter rushed forward, but a hand on his arm jerked him to a stop. "Let me go." He spun on the man, a snarl fixed on his face.

"My lord, I cannot do that." Grant held his arm tightly. "He will not hurt her but if you interfere, you might."

"I will not hurt her, now let me go." He jerked his arm free and took a step forward. His heart plunged into the dirt below him, and the pain shot up through him as it ground beneath his feet. Fear for his wife fought with the common sense that told him that Grant had spoken the truth.

Vanessa struggled to lift the weapon. Her arms shook as she swung again, the heavy sword wobbling in her grip. Peter's breath stopped as the clang of weapons drilled painfully into his head.

"He will only protect himself," Grant said calmly at his ear. "If you distract her she may hurt herself."

Peter took a half step forward and forced himself to stop, knowing in his heart that his friend was right.

"Let her wear herself out. It will not take long. I am surprised she can even lift that thing." Grant gestured at the two people who circled each other. One was in full armor and the other in a thin dress that was covered in blood and torn from hip to ankle.

Vanessa struggled with another swing and the report of connecting metal rang across the silent courtyard.

Grant shook his hand at them. "See he only stops her blows."

Peter grunted at him in anger. Grant stepped away. Peter knew he would have given the same advice, but that made it no easier to stand aside while the woman he loved was in danger.

Van circled slowly, her heart racing in anticipation of the work to come. She fought to raise the sword, giving him plenty of time to prepare for her blow. She swung the heavy blade, one that was much like the one that lay hidden in her large wardrobe trunk.

The sun peeked from behind the clouds, spilling its light across the warriors who bunched together. She kept her focus on the smug-looking man before her.

He smiled. His arms and legs appeared relaxed and unprepared. His responses would be slow and jerky.

Sweat began to trickle down the small of her back and down her temples starting to sting her eyes. She ignored it all and never looked away from the enemy.

"What did you do to that poor girl?" Van asked with a deep gasp of unsteady breath and took another halfhearted swing.

"I did nothing to her. Whatever she told you is a lie," Ryan said louder than necessary.

She assumed it was for the benefit of the others watching.

Van took another swing, this time putting more of her weight behind it. Unprepared for the extra strength she put into it, Ryan's grip on the sword slipped and it almost fell from his hand. One more hard blow right on top of the first and he was forced to swing at her. His swing pushed her back long enough for him to secure his grip on his sword once again.

"Do not lie. I know what you did," Van yelled, also for the benefit of the crowd. "Taking a woman against her will, forcing her, the way only a cowardly man would do." She smiled at the look of outrage that crossed his face.

She forced him into another partial turn, until he was almost facing the men, maneuvering him, like a puppet in a dance. She knew she could make him do whatever she wanted him to do, move him wherever she needed him. It was much too easy and she was disappointed.

She had hoped for more of a fight than she was getting, something to relieve the anger and pain that pricked at her. "Are you a coward?"

Calling a man a coward was one of the worst insults you could deliver and very few men would allow it. Not from a man, and certainly not from a woman.

Van smiled as he shouted directly into her face, "I did not force her. She was willing. She wanted it."

This bought a cry of outrage from Anna.

Van heard the pain in Anna's voice, but tried to ignore it, to not let it distract her from her goal. She swung Gary's sword at him with enough force that the vibrations from the impact trembled down her arms and into her spine.

Van swung again, dancing him around as she went, until he was facing directly into the mass of the men. Her voice trembled with anger when she spoke. "Willing? Does a woman look like that if she is willing?" She jerked her head toward Anna but did not take her eyes off of

Ryan, who was now tense and prepared. "A woman does not end up bloody and bruised from willing and wanting."

She swung hard at him, a full blow, and smiled at the shock on his rage-twisted face. He took a step toward her. Good, she thought. She wanted him angry, wanted him to fight back.

Peter's heart seemed to bounce between his stomach and his throat and he felt nauseous. He wanted to go to her, but Grant once more grabbed his arm, holding him back. "She is going to be hurt, let me go."

Peter could see the joy in her eyes as Ryan lost control of his temper. He seemed to forget who he was fighting and of all the people who stood watching.

A quick flash of memory crossed Peter's mind. He clearly saw Vanessa panting heavy and apparently lost in anger pulling at his leg as he sat astride Jackal. It had been an act to distract him until the cinch came loose.

All an act and he knew now that she was doing it again.

He looked quickly to Grant. "She is baiting him. She wants him to fight back and she is going to die." His voice was tight with panic and his whole body seemed to shudder.

Grant shook his head and held him tightly. Peter looked back to the grisly scene before him.

Vanessa continued her verbal bombardment, as she swung the sword harder and faster at him. "Besides, from what I hear you cannot rise to pleasure a woman unless you are hurting her. Even then it only works some of the time."

The men behind Peter gasped at this and Ryan growled in a deep, deadly warning.

Vanessa seemed to ignore the threat and laughed. Peter's was amazed at her gall and then his face froze. His mind tried to take him somewhere else at the sound of that laugh, but he could not decide where or to what. He knew that laugh and he had the feeling he had seen all this before. He stared at the back of her, the muscles rippling beneath the dress, now sweat drenched and clinging to her back.

Vanessa's voice drew him back to the deadly reality before him. "Perhaps it doesn't work for women. Do you like something other than women?"

Peter watched his eyes as Ryan looked up into the faces of all the men. Anger and embarrassment washed the color from his face. Two dark red splotches appeared high on his cheeks as the rage enveloped him. "You damned bitch."

Light reflected off his broadsword as Ryan attacked.

Vanessa moved, but not fast enough and his sword raked across her bicep, blood spilling onto her decimated dress, she didn't seem to notice.

Peter screamed for her and lunged forward. He was pulled to a stop by Grant on one side and Richard on the other. They dragged him back to his place, if not to his senses. He struggled to get to her, even though he could see she was defending herself well.

One blow fell after another from Ryan's sword, silencing her mouth.

She fought back blow for blow. No one moved or spoke as the battle went on. Peter knew they all feared that interference would result in injury to her.

Her weak and wobbly strokes from before were replaced with hard, fast, and confident blows. Blood drained down her arm, mixing with the innocent blood that had started it all.

Peter yanked his arms free from his captors but stood as he was. He watched with a mixture of pride and fear as she battled. Her face was pale from lack of blood and she was beginning to look exhausted. Sweat ran down her face in small rivulets.

One hard blow drove her leg back behind her. Peter gasped and put a hand to his heaving chest.

Vanessa appeared about to fall. She had one leg out straight and the other curled beneath her. Her bare leg glistened with blood and sweat in the shimmering heat of the day.

She fought for balance and Peter stepped forward.

Richard grasped his arm. "Stop, Peter. You must not interfere. It is an act...and I helped perfect it." His voice was soft with wonder.

Peter glanced at Richard's confused face, but took no time to ask any questions. He looked back at the fight in to time to see the gleam of victory in Ryan's eyes.

Ryan stepped quickly into the space beside her outstretched leg. He raised his sword for the winning blow, but Vanessa stood quickly with her sword before her. Standing straight, she was face to face with him, her sword close to his throat and he had no choice, but to step back.

He stepped right into the outstretched foot behind him. His arms flailed for balance and as he went down Vanessa caught the hilt of his sword with the length of hers. It flung out of his hand with a vibrating ring. It slid toward the men spraying dirt and torn chunks of grass with it and Ryan hit the ground with a loud grunt.

Van's mind screamed in victory, blocking off all other sights and sounds. She stepped over him before he could regain his feet and slid the tip of her sword against the delicate hollow of his throat. One of the few spots unprotected from his thick chain mail.

Van's breath came in hard gasps that hurt her chest with each deep inhale. Pain surged through her arm and she felt about to tumble to the ground. The loss of blood, lack of sleep, and emotional stress were catching up to her, dragging her into a pit of darkness.

Ryan swam in and out of focus before her. "Now you will die for what you have done to her."

Before she could carry out her threat she felt a small body collide with her.

"Please, don't kill him," Anna pleaded clinging to her. "Please." Her voice was thick and her body racked with sobs.

"Anna, he hurt you." Van could not stand to see the tears, could not stand to think her friend was hurting.

"Please, I cannot have a death because of me." Anna shuddered and tightened her grip around her waist. "Promise me."

"Go stand by your brother." How could this day get any worse? She wanted nothing more than to separate his head from his worthless body. Her anger had not been satisfied and her body begged to have the freedom to kill him.

"Promise me." Anna looked up at her with tear filled and trusting eyes.

Van pushed the sword deeper into his soft flesh. She felt a moment of joy as it pierced the skin and blood began to ooze slowly out. She pushed harder.

"Please." Anna's voice was soft and she laid her small hand on Van's blood soaked arm.

Van nuzzled the top of the girl's head with her face leaving a streak of powder that Van grunted at. She felt a moment of worry, seeing that powder, and knew without a doubt that her face held none. Too late to worry about it now, she thought. Her conscience tried to tell her I told you so, but she pushed it away. "I promise he will not die today because of you, now go."

Anna reluctantly walked away and Van forced herself to move back. "You should be grateful to her, for she has given you a gift today that you do not deserve…your life."

She heard shouts from behind her. Screams of warning and she felt feet vibrating the ground as they rushed toward her. Peter screamed at her to watch out, but she only waited. She was aware of the men rushing forth to her aid.

Van waited until the footfalls were right on top of her, until she could hear the raspy breathing of the man, and then she spun on him. Sword held flat, she used all the strength her anger gave her.

There was a moment in which she saw Christopher Dalton, sword held high and a look of rage contorting his face. Then his face disappeared.

She heard feminine screams even before she heard the wet, soft sound of a head rolling across the earth, followed by the thick thud of a heavy body that followed it down.

She heard Ryan jump to his feet and spun back on him, sword held out straight toward his chest. Now she was the one facing the men. They had all stopped. She could see the wonder on their faces. She could see the confusion and the questions.

She heard the soft murmured words that started to mill around, words that worried her for the sake of her loved ones. Words like, "Dark Knight" and "it cannot be him."

Van stood proudly, fighting the nausea that swam through her dizzy head. Her arm straight and accusing as the sword pointed unwavering at Ryan. "You will leave these grounds." Blood dripped into the dry ground, but her arm remained steady and still.

"You have no authority to tell me to leave. I am not one of your men, Dark Knight," Ryan snarled at her.

Her thick voice, deepened with arrogance, growled at him, rumbling through the crowd. "You are right. You are not one of my men. Go ahead and ask Peter what he thinks." She grinned an arrogant halfcocked grin. "Go ahead, because I would like to see if you can finish the question with your head lying over by your friend's." She saw the hesitation in his deep brown eyes. "Please, ask him."

"You will not kill me. You promised." Ryan said with a smug grin. The grin fell away when she laughed.

The amused laugh was the first thing that had caused her rock steady arm to move, vibrating with the deepness of it. The Dark Knight said in his deep and graveled voice. "Nay, I did not. You have to be careful what you get as a promise. I promised that you would not die today because of her."

She smiled and tried her best to ignore all the shocked stares of the men and all the mumblings rolling around among them. "This would not be because of her. It would be purely for my enjoyment and my pleasure. I would like to see how far I can get your head to roll."

She noticed the men's eyes dart from her to the decapitated body behind her and back to her. She twisted her arm so that the sword lay flat, making it easier to slice through the tough tendons and bone of the neck. As she pivoted her wrist, the muscles in her bicep convulsed as they worked hard to hold the heavy sword. The gash in her arm opened farther and fresh blood dripped to the ground.

"I need a horse and my things," Ryan said angrily.

"Aye, I need a lot of things as well. Add it to your prayers. Now get out of my sight." As she watched Ryan, followed closely by Gregory Penchiot, who ran to catch up with him, she knew she had made a mistake. Her anger was not yet satisfied and as the two men went through the rear gate and disappeared into the woods, she had to force herself not to go after them.

She turned back to the men and grumbled, "Damned insolent women and their promises. Mothers who want you to promise to wed." She looked up at the pale face of Amy. "You and your meddling. I should have killed Ryan the night he touched you." Her anger was starting to fade as she turned at last to Anna.

"And you. I should have killed him now, when I had another chance." She took a step toward her, painfully aware that Gary pulled her protectively against him. She felt a twinge of regret but kept her face calm. She ran her now trembling hand down the girl's arm. "Are you all right?"

Anna nodded her head. "I am, but your face. You have such a bad scar. How did you get it? "

Blurs of double vision dizzied Van and she struggled to keep her feet under her. A wave of blackness passed before her. She ran her hand along the scar and smiled.

Peter watched her closely and his mind was whisked away to a time long ago. He lay in the tent, his shoulder demolished and a woman with a sweet laugh and a hypnotizing voice hovered above him. Her black eyes shimmering with worry.

A twinge in Peter's shoulder seemed to remember the night as well. He stared at Vanessa…Van, he thought shaking his head. Van.

Peter looked around the men and saw the same confusion on their faces as he felt himself. "Go to the lists, now." His voice sounded strangled. "Two of you take care of the body."

Most of the men turned and walked away, without a backward glance. Van stared after them longingly, and Peter finally understood her need to see the men.

Gary had stayed with his arms wrapped around Anna. Grant, Richard, and Devon, his arm around Amy, had stayed as well.

"My lord." Van turned her head back at the sound of Gary's voice. Peter did not even glance at Gary. He could not take his eyes of his wife.

"Take care of your sister," Peter told him.

Peter stared at Vanessa intently. He could not seem to make his mind understand what had happened. The soft musical voice of his phantom woman swirled around him, confusing him more.

He had berated himself for years as he had the same dream over and over again of the woman leaning over him. Of him running his hand along her smooth cheek. That the dream was of a woman did not stop his disgust with himself because he knew the truth.

But he hadn't known the truth, he thought. Or perhaps somewhere in the back of his mind he had known, he told himself optimistically. Confusion darkened his thoughts and he scowled.

How could she do this to him? He had just discovered that he loved her and now she did this.

Peter groaned. He could not think of it now. His mind was too befuddled with swirling questions that seemed to lead not to answers, but only to more questions. For now he decided he would go to the lists with the men and try to escape at least temporarily into sparring and sword play.

Peter motioned for the remaining men to join him. Richard and Grant walked past her, but as Devon stepped past, Van swayed heavily and would have fallen if Devon had not grabbed her.

Her head rolled and Gary's sword fell with a clang to the ground.

"Van!" Devon's panicked yell made Peter take a step toward them. Amy rushed to her side and Anna broke free from her brother's arms and joined her.

Van waved the girls away and pushed Devon's arms from her. She stood on unsteady feet and swayed. Devon moved to take her into his arms once again, but she slapped his hands.

"I am fine." Her voice trembled in a weak whisper. She swayed again and Peter knew she was not fine.

He longed to go to her, but found himself unable. He stood his ground and stared at her, unsure of what to think or to do.

She swayed against Devon and looked at Peter sadly. "I am fine," she said again. "Just take care of Damien. He trusts you."

Peter started at the sound of the horse's name. He mentally kicked himself for not recognizing the stallion given by the king to the newly knighted boy. There were many things that were beginning to stand out in his mind, now that he saw the truth. Things that now seemed obvious, but at the time had only been a tickle at his deepest thoughts.

She held Devon's arm for a moment until her legs steadied then she released him. "Make sure he did not hurt himself."

Peter watched her sway and held his breath. He released it when she regained her balance and spoke again.

"See that he did not injure anything either coming out of the stall or over that wall. We hit hard." Her voice was steady, but low.

Gary took Anna into his arms again and spoke to Devon. "You take care of the horse. Amy and I will see to these two." He turned toward Peter with a questioning look.

Peter looked at Richard, lost in misery. Then turned and walked away.

Richard stared closely at Van, his breath coming in shallow gasps. All the things his mind had been trying to tell him over the past week all came rushing at him until he could hardly get any air in his lungs.

Van looked over to him and smiled weakly.

"Are you truly..." he asked wanting her to tell him no, that he was mistaken. He could not even ask the question for he already knew the answer.

"I—" She took a deep breath and shook her head. "I am sorry."

Richard's head spun with confusion and he took a step back, feeling an almost physical blow.

His swirling thoughts took him back to all the things they had done together. He could clearly see the times he had hit her and allowed her to do dangerous things.

He had treated her like a man, not a delicate woman like she should have been treated. He had taken her to taverns and left her in the midst of dangerous men while he took women upstairs. He talked to her of things that no young woman should ever hear.

His heart stopped and his breath lodged beneath the lump that grew suddenly in his throat. He had beaten her.

He could not face what he had done to her, a mere woman, and he stared at the ground. The drops of her blood and the headless body did nothing to soothe his frayed nerves.

He saw her reach for him. He looked up into the pleading eyes that shimmered with unshed tears and his heart broke. Unable to forgive himself, he turned and walked away.

Van stared after the man who she had thought of as a father all her young life. She stood, wavering with the hot sun beating down on her and did not care if she bled to death standing right where she was.

The air seemed to be sucked from around her and she gasped.

"Van, come on." Amy's voice sounded as if it were from the other side of the moon. She tried to focus on it, but it fluttered out of her grasp.

"If not for you, than for Anna," Amy said. She wrapped her arms around Van and tugged gently. "She needs you now, Gary needs you."

Without a word, Van followed them into Anna's bed chamber.

Inside the chambers, they got Anna laid onto the bed. Amy turned and spoke softly to Gary. "You should wait outside."

"I do not know." He looked closely at Van with an untrusting gaze.

Van felt as if she had been crushed beneath his suspicious gaze. She understood it though. The Dark Knight had an awful reputation and she had worked hard to get it. Now that hard work was coming around to bite her like a serpent that had been raised and nurtured to a massive and powerful creature.

She opened her mouth to speak, but the words were stopped as the door burst open. Douglas came rushing into the room. "I am sorry, my lady. I could not stay away. I made it part way to the lists and had to return."

He dropped beside Anna's bed and grasped her hand. Anna smiled weakly and began to cry.

He looked up at Van with widened eyes. "Did I hurt her?" He tried to let go of her hand, but Anna held on tight.

"No, but you both must wait out in the hall." She gestured to Gary. "Take him."

Douglas reluctantly released her hand and put his hand on Gary's arm.

"I am staying. I do not want to leave my sister with..." He stopped, but he looked at Van.

Anna smiled up at him. "I love you and I trust her."

Gary looked at her and then at Van. He took a deep breath and held it for a moment, then released it. "I know of the Dark Knight...of you." He began, but then shook his head. "You hid it well, and revealed yourself in order to avenge my sister. I know you love her and I trust you as well." With that he walked out and Douglas shut the door behind them.

They washed and cleaned the young girl up, her sobs soon slowing and then stopping altogether. There was tearing but nothing that needed stitches and for that Van was grateful, but she knew she would not be so lucky.

Van sat in one of the chairs by the small window where the light was best to allow Amy to examine her arm. Anna pulled herself from the bed and sat silently beside the chair Van perched on and held her hand.

"Van, it's deep." Amy sounded a lot like she might lose what little breakfast she had eaten.

"I know." Van said calmly. She looked down at the wide scared eyes of the young girl at her feet. "Anna, will you be all right in here, or would you like to leave?"

She shook her head. She would stay.

Turning to her little day maid, Van smiled, a weak try at one. "Get Gary and your sewing kit."

Carrying a small sewing kit Gary walked into the room, followed closely by Douglas. Van sat, one sleeve torn completely off her dress, still as a stone.

Gary said nothing as he walked to her. He glanced toward the bloody water in the night basin beside the bed. His eyes clouded, but he remained silent.

Amy walked in with a fresh basin full of hot water. Gary took it carefully and cleansed the cut on Van's arm. "I have to clean it well or it will become infected."

He refused to look at her face, at anything except the wound.

"Do it then." She sat still as he splashed a liberal amount of brandy onto the wound. She felt him wince as she took a quick intake of breath and tightened in pain. She clenched her teeth until her jaw popped audibly. Anna jumped at the sound.

Van closed her eyes and let her mind wander as he quickly began to stitch her arm. Her mind took her to the last time she had been stitched. To the nights she had held Peter's hand in the privacy of the tent. To the way she had caressed his hair and his face and kissed his cheek gently as he lay unconscious. She had confessed her love to him late into one of those nights and he had moaned lightly in response.

"I'll bandage it up, and then you should get some sleep."

She looked over at Gary's pale face and felt a moment of concern. "Are you all right?" She asked, and then was startled when he laughed.

"Aye, it is you who are not," he said with a shake of his head.

"Will you stay in here, please, milady?" Anna asked quietly as Gary helped her to her feet.

Van was reluctant to leave her side and, knowing that Peter was still in the lists with the men, she agreed to stay. She crawled into the small bed beside her.

Van watched the small group of people that looked to one another nervously. Gary smiled at his sister as he settled into a chair at the foot of the bed. Douglas sat gently on floor and took Anna's foot in his massive hand. Van smiled as Amy crawled into the bed on the other side of Anna.

Van slipped into a restless sleep with Anna's head lying on her shoulder, Van's good arm wrapped protectively around her.

CHAPTER 24

R yan clung to the rocking neck of a stolen horse and tried his best to ignore his rolling stomach and pounding head. Gregory rode slightly behind him after having been yelled at earlier to leave him alone.

They were making their way to where Ryan hoped Eolian still remained. Silence, broken only by the steady thrum of the hooves pounding into the soft ground, followed them through the clear, cool night.

They had spent the day at the Doveslane Inn, to rest and acquire the horses. Gregory had taken a serving wench, a round yet willing red head, Annette, up the stairs. Ryan had been too absorbed in thought for such a distraction.

He had sat drinking and nursing his demolished pride with the sour brandy that they served. He had stayed at the dirty table until night had fallen.

Now he held tightly to his pilfered ride and knew he had drank much too heavily. He hoped to stay seated through this short trip, but he thought his chances slim as his head reeled.

As he rode, feeling every dip and swerve the animal made, he became lost in his own mind and memories.

He could see Anna, the soft spoken girl, too manageable. Too cooperative, he thought sourly. He had not really wanted her.

What he wanted was that fiery little thing Devon was always around. Amy had spirit and would always put up a fight.

When they had first arrived he had wanted Lady Vanessa, but he knew he could never attain her. Then as he had watched her with her husband he knew she had too much spirit for his liking.

He loved them to fight, but what he enjoyed more was the fear.

Lady Vanessa would never show fear, and now he understood why. He growled deeply in his throat as he thought of the humiliation she had put him through.

He pushed her from his clouded mind and drew his thoughts back to Amy. Vanessa may not show fear, but Amy did. She had fight and a spirit that would take a long time to break, but she was afraid of him.

He smiled when he thought of the night he had pinned Amy to the wall. Her well-endowed breasts pressing into his chest. He had hardened painfully at the terror in her eyes as she had fought him.

His smile fell away.

Vanessa had shown up then, pulling him off. He had thought he would die there, but Amy had saved him, just as that twit of a child, Anna, had done a short time ago.

Amy had begged for her to stop, telling her it wasn't worth it. He replayed the look of anguish in the coal black eyes. Whoever she was, Vanessa, the lady, or Van, the knight, one thing was sure, she loved Amy. He had known it without a doubt when she had said, "If you are all right and you will not cry anymore."

He had heard the concern and the caring in her soft voice.

His distracted mind registered movement among the shadows, but his drunken reflexes were nonexistent. The large bay mare he rode was pulled to a stop as a massive chunk of the surrounding shadows detached itself from the trees, grasping the reins.

Gregory's horse bumped into the rump of his and she reared up. He gasped loudly and almost tumbled from the horse. He looked around him dazed and then looked down at the man holding his reins.

"Damn, Verges. You scared me, and it was more than your looks this time." He laughed at his own wit, but the big man didn't smile, didn't even acknowledge he had spoken. Ryan's laugh turned to a deep scowl.

"What are you doing here? We heard there was some commotion at the castle." Verges did not wait for a response, just began leading the horse away.

Ryan snarled at him. He hated Verges. He did not trust him and he feared him. What he feared the most was that he knew Verges hated him as well.

Verges led them deep into the surrounding woods through twists and turns that soon had Ryan lost and confused.

Ryan asked where they were. There was no answer. He asked if Verges was sure he knew where they were in the dark. No answer. Verges did not respond to any of his questions, just continued to lead them farther into the darkness.

Blackness was all Ryan could see. He put his hand in front of him, bumping his dirty fingers into his nose before realizing they were there.

Taking a deep breath, Ryan forced himself to keep silent, letting his eyes drift shut. He felt the horse rocking beneath him and could hear the soft crunching of leaves from beneath the horse's hooves. Then everything faded as blackness took him.

"Get down, you lush, and get in there." Ryan's eyes snapped open and he grabbed the horse's mane to keep from tumbling off backwards.

They had stopped next to a small shanty. The door stood open throwing light onto the horses and the riders.

Ryan took a deep breath to steady himself. The cool air rumbled through his stomach and threatened to expel what little contents it contained. He dropped shakily to the ground and trembled. It was not from the chill of the night.

He was terrified of Eolian Montgomery, had been since long before actually coming into his service. Not one to allow even the slightest slip, it was said that the Knight of Fear would behead you as soon as look at you. It was proven several times in front of Ryan and he was beginning to wonder if it was a bad idea to drink first.

He shook his head gently to clear it, but it only blurred his vision further. He swayed. A large hand shoved into the center of his back, propelling him toward the waiting, open door.

Ryan's feet stumbled across branches and sticks and he almost fell. He swung his arms and to his amazement kept his feet beneath him. Fear began to swim frantically through his veins, pushing the brandy from his pores in a sour smelling sweat.

His mind began to focus as a deep rumbling of dread sobered him. He stepped through the door with Gregory right on his heels. He could hear Gregory's heavy breathing and feel the trembles that ran through his body when he brushed against him.

Eolian sat calmly in a chair in the center of the room. It was the only chair in the room Ryan saw as he looked around. He stood before him nervously and waited.

"Why are you here?" Eolian asked him in a soft soothing voice that Ryan knew never portrayed his actual emotions. He sounded calm when he was raging with anger. The calmer he sounded, Ryan knew, the worse it was.

Ryan took a deep breath and told in detail the fight and Christopher's death. The telling of it was difficult, especially with the rank breath of another who terrified him running across his neck. The room was small, but made smaller by the unearthly bulk that Verges possessed.

Ryan took another deep breath and smiled shakily. "She is more than just a good swordswoman. From the day she arrived, she wore her face thick with powder and has treated Richard and his men like they were her own." He paused, but Eolian did not speak.

Ryan trembled with worry as he continued. "The battle washed the powder away." He felt Verges shift behind him. "Her face is scarred deeply across the cheek, in the same place as the Dark Knight."

Eolian had sat patiently waiting for Ryan to have his say and was sure it would be useless. He had thought he knew what this was about. Ryan was a dangerous man who had little brains to keep him out of trouble. Eolian was sure the stupid man had raped someone or killed someone and had been sent away.

That it was the lady of the castle who had sent him away was interesting but Eolian still planned to kill him when he was finished speaking.

Now that had changed. Now he was unsure if Ryan had brought him useful information or if Ryan's imagination was running wild and making connections where there were none.

He looked down at his feet momentarily. The dirt floor beneath them was packed hard from years of use and even more years of sitting unused before that.

He glanced up past the sniveling man who trembled before him. The walls were twisted with age and weather, giving a slightly skewed vision, making one want to cock the head to the side to look at them. He fought the urge to do so.

His mind whirled with the possibilities. Could it be possible?

He went over what he knew of the Dark Knight. He was the son of a surgeon whom he looked nothing like. Although, he did look like the last husband of his mother. Exactly like Matthew Fordella. But Matthew had only had a daughter. A daughter who had mysteriously disappeared, Eolian thought sullenly.

His mind fought with the idea that the Dark Knight, the man who had defeated his armies and been a thorn in his ass since the brat had still been a squire, could possibly be a woman. His first thought had been self-serving and he had not allowed it to grow. He could not dwell on all the times he had been beaten by some mere girl.

He pushed those thoughts away knowing they would get him nowhere.

Instead, he went quickly through his dealings with the Dark Knight and, as they always did, his thoughts stopped on one small child: the small boy that Melinda Dawson had given birth to. He had searched for the boy, wanting nothing more to kill the child he had believed to be the Dark Knight's.

His thoughts stuck on the fourteen year old girl he had wanted so badly. He had tried to buy Melinda from her father, but the stubborn man had refused. Eolian had threatened to kill him and had taken her anyway. Her father was unhappy, but he had not gone after her.

He had taken her every night until Van had stolen her from him. Van had claimed the child as his own, and Eolian had searched for years for Melinda and her child to enact his revenge on them both.

Someone had seen the child before they had hidden it away from him. It was said to look like Eolian. That had infuriated him more. He could not allow someone else's child to live, especially not one that might resemble him.

The Dark Knight had claimed the child and it was said that he had fathered many. The men around Eolian in the cramped room jumped when he barked out a bray of laughter.

A father of many…he was a woman. His laughter continued until he was gasping for breath.

When he got control of himself, he looked at Ryan, as the nervous man cleared his throat.

"You want to say something else?" Eolian asked still unsure if he now wanted to kill him. Ryan might come to some use, he mused.

Ryan took a deep breath and nodded. "That information was free, but I have more. I would like a reward for the rest, my lord."

"Well, what is it and what do you want?" He assumed the man wanted money, he always did, money and power, like every other short sighted man.

"Lady Vanessa is very attached to her small day maid, my lord." Ryan shifted uneasily and glanced over his shoulder at Verges.

Eolian enjoyed having Verges around, he loved the fear the giant man bestowed on people. It made it easier to accomplish a lot more.

Ryan drew his gaze back to Eolian's and continued. His voice shook. "Amy Devant. Vanessa loves her and would be devastated should anything happen to her." He grinned. "Would do anything to get her back."

Eolian was surprised he offered the information without agreeing on the price. He could smell the brandy on him, but thought it more than the liquor.

"I would like Amy after you have the Dark Knight, my lord." A lustful grin spread across his thin lips. "I would have already had her, but Lady Vanessa stopped me from taking her."

Eolian smiled at the venom spewing from the angry words. He knew it was more than the girl. It was the fact that Van had nearly killed him, humiliating him in front of all the men.

He decided he would allow Ryan his revenge. He grinned widely and wondered what Ryan saw in that grin as the man cringed.

Aye, he would allow Ryan to have whatever was left of the girl after he had persuaded Van to tell him where Melinda and his child were.

Eolian knew now without a doubt that it was his son. He had wondered over the years if the child was a result of their nights together, before she was stolen from him. He truly loved her, or at least he thought he did.

Now it did not matter. He would have his child and when he was through with Melinda Dawson she would wish she was dead.

He laughed and waved the men away.

When the door was shut behind them, he smiled into the dark corner. "Did you hear that, my dear?"

Rebeka stepped from the shadows, feeling an excitement thrum through her, and walked to his side. Running her fingers though his dirty, black hair she smiled. "Aye, my lord, I could almost feel sorry for Peter." She began to laugh. "Can you imagine how devastated he must be to have married a knight?"

"You will help me, will you not?" He pulled her onto his lap, tearing open the front of her dress, buttons flying as he exposed the milky white smoothness of her large breasts. She gasped lightly and let her head fall back.

Her breasts and ribs were marred by bruises, both old and fading, and new and painful.

"Aye, my lord." She enjoyed the gentle pain he inflicted on her more than the controlled love making Peter had shown her.

Peter was too gentle, always in full control of himself, too boring as a lover. He always seemed to be so worried he would offend her or hurt her, that it wasn't fun. She pitied his wife, who if he ever made love to her again, would endure the silent and gentle love making he provided.

"I need you to go back to him. Nay, don't look at me like that." His fingers dug deep into her tender flesh, releasing a hiss of pleasure, her nipples rising in response. "I need a distraction. He will keep his distance from her as he tries to sort things out, I would guarantee it."

He took the hard little pebble into his teeth, biting gently at first, to tease. Then harder, leaving teeth imprints on the reddened flesh. She could think of nothing but the sweet jolts of pain that surged through her breasts and settled deep between her thighs.

He spoke to her between lips that rubbed across her tight hard nipple. "Things will be in upheaval for a while and, to make sure of that, you will be there."

He threw her to the ground. She landed with a cry of pain on the hard cold dirt floor. He rose slowly from his chair and walked toward her. Her heart thumped painfully in her chest. He opened his braies as he stepped over her. Her eyes widened and she cringed in a mixture of fear and delight.

"You will not go tonight, for they will be too upset now. Plus I have need of you." His voice was thick, his eyes wide, wild, and dangerous.

She shivered in anticipation. Not just from the thought of the love making, but of the devilish revenge she would bestow on both of the ones who had humiliated her. Especially that giant woman warrior.

She began to laugh. Soon her laughter turned to screams.

Verges reined in his horse as soon as he was out of sight of the camp. His mind whirled. He knew if he sent a warning to Van she would prevent them from taking Amy.

He could not allow that to happen. This might be the only chance they would have at defeating Eolian. Verges could use the distractions to his advantage and if they worked it right they had a good chance.

He would be the one to retrieve Amy, even if Eolian had other plans. He would make sure nothing happened to the young woman. If he could get her here safely, and keep her safe, everything else would hopefully fall into place.

He would send a message to Van after they had taken Amy. He trusted her to make plans on her end. He would have to make some on his. All they would need is a distraction long enough to allow Peter and his men to arrive.

He snorted. She would have to get away without Peter following right behind, because if they could not take Eolian by surprise, it would not work. There was a lot riding on luck and Verges knew their chances were slim.

In the distance he could hear the violent love making coming from the shelter. He hardened and closed his eyes.

It had been too long since he was with a woman. He grunted and reeled his horse around galloping back toward the camp. In the midst of the men were always women—slaves taken from their homes to be cooks and harlots to the men.

He spotted one small woman and pulled alongside her. She looked up at him with a mixture of revulsion and fear. That look went straight through his heart.

Anger swirled through him. He reached down and yanked her onto his horse.

"Please, leave me be." She began to fight him. He pressed her face into his thigh and turned back toward the trees.

He had never taken one of these women, not wanting to anger Eolian. He was too large in all ways and he would hurt them. Now he no longer cared if he angered Eolian or not. No matter how things worked out, he did not believe he would be under the hand of Eolian much longer.

"Let me loose." Her muffled screams sounded against his leg, her hot breath seeping through his rough sewn pants.

"I will when I am through with you." He yanked hard on the reins and his stallion reared as he slid to a stop.

Verges slid to the ground with her in his arms. He laid her gently to the ground and dropped on top of her bracing himself on his arms so as not to hurt her badly.

She began to struggle. He forced her tattered gown up and spread her trembling thighs with his knees. "Don't fight me and I will try not to hurt you."

She fell still, but as he freed himself and his large shaft fell hard against her she stiffened.

He slid inside her as carefully as he could, caressing her breast as he did so. She began to squirm, her face clouding with pain. He slid in and out gently and controlled, but knew he was hurting her. It pained him to do so, but it had been so long.

Tears slid down her face and she began to fight.

He increased his speed to get it over with for her as quickly as possible and wished he could give her pleasure.

She struggled but did not truly being to fight until he tried to kiss her.

She gagged and turned her head away to keep his kisses from finding her lips. She pressed her hands against his face to shove him away and began to scream. She called him a monster, a vile deformed pig, and an evil disgusting ogre. She begged him not to soil her.

It angered him, and more, it hurt.

Hurt because this woman gave herself to the vile men that made up this army and yet he was not good enough for her.

He knew who and what he was, but he didn't know how to change it. He was who he was because of the circumstances of his birth. He had been ridiculed and abused all his life and he was not about to allow it from this whore.

Wrapping his hand around her long and delicate throat, he gave enough pressure to stop her screams while leaving just enough slack to allow some breath. Her face began to turn a dark shade of pink.

Her mouth opened in a gasp to get air and he clamped his lips onto hers, shoving his tongue into her mouth.

Closing his eyes to the pain of who he had become, he rammed into her harder and faster. He knew he was too large for her, knew he was damaging her, but he closed his mind to anything but the pleasure that ran through his loins.

Someday he hoped things might be different for him, but for now, he just felt lost.

CHAPTER 25

P eter stood off to the side and watched as the men threw themselves into the mock battles, swords slamming hard into others. Practice was more violent than usual, but Peter understood why. The men's minds were not on their training.

The second time that blood was unnecessarily drawn, Peter called a halt, screaming at the men to go home. He watched the men walk despondently back toward the castle. They looked weary and confused and he felt the same.

Peter mounted Jackal. When Grant moved toward him, he waved him off and made his way to the thick woods.

He paid no attention to the direction he went. Head down and hands loose, he gave the massive stallion his head.

Confused by the lack of direction, and absent of the controlling grip that always led him, Jackal balked, momentarily stopping in the dark, coolness of the woods. Peter allowed him to stand as he wished and then lost himself in confused thoughts.

He could feel the rhythmic movements when Jackal once more began to walk. Peter paid no attention to where his stallion's slow gait took him.

All he could see in his troubled heart was that young boy who leaned over him. He could almost feel his hand running along Van's smooth, warm cheek. Over and over Peter's voice sounded deep in his consciousness. "You are beautiful."

Then the soft laugh that had haunted him for three long years echoed through his mind.

"Lord Lawston?"

The deep voice drew him out of his misery. He looked around confused at his surroundings.

"Peter?" He glanced down and was taken aback to see Van's father.

Sending a scathing look at his mount, he muttered. "Thanks, just what I need today."

"Excuse me, my boy?" Matthew took the reins as Peter dismounted and handed them to a tall redheaded groom.

"Nothing." It was probably a good thing that he had arrived here. Somehow Matthew would find out about his daughter. Peter did not want to be the one to tell him, but it would be better coming from him than someone else. "I need to talk to you. It is important." He looked up at the castle. "The wife and kids are not here yet, are they?"

"Nay, but I am glad you are here." Matthew grasped his forearm and shook it in greeting. "I wanted to ask you about Vanessa. I sent up for her not long ago and she had already left. On foot." He dropped his hand, a look of eager hopefulness crossing his face.

"She made it home early this morning." Peter cringed at the thought of her homecoming.

"Very good." Matthew's face relaxed and he waved his hand dismissively at a waiting groom. "I was preparing to send a message to make sure she had arrived safely."

Peter watched the groom lead Jackal toward the stall and asked, without turning to face Van's father, "Can we talk inside, maybe over a large brandy, or perhaps three?"

Matthew chuckled without amusement and when Peter glanced at him he noted that his face looked drawn and worried once again.

Matthew felt a tightness in his gut as they mounted the stairs. It increased at the pained and turbulent look on the rugged face of his son-in-law. Whatever he wanted to tell him would not be good and Matthew was not sure he wanted to hear it.

In the library, with a stout brandy in hand, Peter led him to the two chairs the farthest away from the window. Matthew took it as a bad omen, as if the young man did not want to expose whatever he held in his heart to the brightness of the day. Perhaps afraid it would bring it to life.

"So, what is it son?" he asked cautiously, but Peter remained silent.

Matthew took a deep drink of his warmed brandy and watched Peter do the same. He had always had a connection to the young man. He knew he owed his sanity to Peter. If not for him, even if he had only been thirteen at the time, Matthew would have gone mad over the loss of his daughter.

Peter had stayed with him, talking to him all night for as long as Matthew had needed him, though the time now was a blur. He did not know how long he had been lost in misery, but he knew every clear memory held Peter at his side.

Matthew had told Vanessa that it was the closeness of the two properties that had been the reason for the marriage. It was that, but it was also more.

It was a debt of gratitude. Peter had helped him search for her when she was first missing and for many years after she was taken. They had never given up on finding her and had searched until he had received the missive from Patricia.

No, Matthew thought, it was more than just repaying a debt owed. He watched Peter, who seem to gather his thoughts or mayhap his courage to speak.

He had wanted his daughter to marry Peter because he remembered well how Peter had been the only one with the ability to quiet his little girl. There had been many a night when no one could calm her, and Matthew had resorted to sending for the young lad, many times in the middle of night.

The minute Peter held her and talked to her, she would smile and laugh, reaching for his face. Even as young as he was, with his own interests to see to, never did he fail to come to her aid.

More than anything, that had been what Matthew wanted in a husband for her, one to stand by her side.

"I need to talk to you about your daughter."

Peter's voice drew Matthew from his memories. He looked up at him and forced himself to wait.

Peter stared down at the brandy he slowly swirled and shook his head. "It will not be easy to say, but I think it best if it came from me."

Panic began to set in as Peter took a long drink. Holding his peace, Matthew tried to calm himself. He just wanted her to be all right. Had something happened to her?

Peter had sat struggling with how to say what needed to be said. With where to begin. He took a deep breath, but could not think of an easy way to start. So in lieu of any ideas, he opened his mouth and just blurted it out. "Vanessa is the Dark Knight."

"What?" Matthew's surprised shout brought his short and portly butler rushing into the room, but both men waved him away. "Why would you think that?"

Tremors gripped Peter's muscles and he forced himself to look at Matthew. He could see the confusion and the doubt in his eyes. "There are several things."

A flash of candlelight shimmering off a dagger thrown at his head sparked in his mind. "A dagger," he said simply.

"A dagger?" Matthew asked uncertainly, his brows arched.

"The dagger you gave me." He took a deep breath and saw no way to get around telling him the whole story.

Peter quickly told him of the confrontation when Van had arrived home. He told him of his part in it and laughed bitterly. "I had planned to have him seduce her and tell me about it, but I am glad I was there when it happened. If not, I do not doubt she would have killed him there in the servants' hall."

Matthew didn't say anything, but the shocked look on his face and the small shake of his head spoke loudly of his displeasure in Peter's actions.

Peter ignored the guilt and the disappointment he felt in himself and pushed forward. "After I told her what I had done she threw the knife at my head." He chuckled. He was now sure she had hit exactly where she had aimed. "Well, at a beam beside my head. It was undoubtedly the dagger I gave to the Dark Knight, the one you gave to me."

Peter took another drink and Matthew nodded. "Aye, you told me you gave it to him. There are ways that she may have gotten the dagger."

"Aye, but there is more." Taking a deep breath and watching the growing horror in his companion's dark black eyes, he told the story of the sword fight that had ended in one man's beheading and two others being sent away. "With the end of the fight all that thick powder was gone. On her cheek is a thick scar."

"Many people have scars. That does not mean they are one and the same," Matthew argued, but did not look as sure as he sounded.

"I know that scar. That face has haunted my dreams for three years. I can still see him…her…" Peter grunted. "I can still see *Van* standing before that doctor with the side of her face stitched and brutal. I know the scar."

Matthew stood, taking Peter's goblet without asking and refilled the both.

Peter waited until the man was reseated before he continued. "I also spoke briefly with Richard Devenroe. Vanessa made him her second-in-command from the moment she arrived."

"This is not possible," Matthew said without much conviction. "I have been keeping an eye on the Dark Knight for years. He has many mistresses. Many and there are several children that the man has."

Peter knew all about his mistresses and his alleged children, but he was more concerned with something else. "Why were you keeping an eye on the Dark Knight?"

Matthew stood abruptly and started pacing. "I never told anyone, but I found Patricia."

Peter rose to his feet, but remained by his chair. "You found her?"

"Aye, many years ago, but Vanessa was not with her. She was with Paul Burgess, Van Burgess' father. At least that was what I was told."

"Aye, he was said to be the Dark Knight's father, but I had never known who his—" Peter grunted and corrected himself irritably. "—her mother was."

"When I found Patricia in Junket—" Matthew stopped when Peter looked up sharply at him. "Do you know the place?"

"Aye." But Peter decided to say no more. He knew now why Van had such a connection with the Dark Knight and Eolian. He did not want to tell Matthew his concerns for her safety. For now it was enough to convince him she was who he said she was.

After a moment, Matthew nodded and continued both his tale and his pacing. "I asked throughout the village. No one had ever seen her. I thought that if I kept an eye on all of them, eventually I would be able to find my little girl." He gave a shaky laugh. "I saw her."

"When?" Peter walked slowly to the table that held the brandy. He refilled his cup and turned to watch Matthew's steady strides back and forth across the library.

Matthew laughed unsteadily. "When I first found Patricia, Vanessa was ten. I saw her with a group of boys in the forest." He smiled, his pacing stopped and his eyes took on a faraway look. "They were practicing with daggers and swords. I learned that it is not allowed that young boys do it without supervision, so they were hiding in the woods."

Peter laughed. "Imagine that, she was disobeying the rules even then."

Matthew laughed as well. This time his laugh sounded slightly less troubled. "Aye, that is my girl." His face glowed with pride. "I saw a tall boy, the image of me when I was a child. I remember thinking that would be what my son would look like if I had had one. When I asked after him, I was told he was Burgess's son and that he was only eight. I could have taken her then." He looked up at the young man with a sudden grin. "I guess it is good that I did not. She never would have been there to save your life."

"What do you know about the Dark Knight, about Van?" Peter didn't want to know anything and he wanted to know it all. "I know of rumors only. If you have watched him, perhaps you can lay rest to some of them."

"Perhaps aye, perhaps nay," Matthew said with a sly grin.

Peter cringed.

"I will tell you what I do know, as facts," Matthew continued. "There are several children who have his name. He has six mistresses at the moment, although at times he has had more."

Peter groaned and shook his head. He had heard stories of lots of mistresses, but did not believe it. He did not want to believe it especially now that his wife was the one who had them.

Matthew smiled at him gently. "Money is sent by a messenger that no one has ever seen. Van did go to see the mistresses and is brutal when it comes to women." He shook his head his face clouding, his high smooth brow marred with tight wrinkles. "I know for fact that he uses force as well as threats of rape to intimidate them."

Peter remembered well the confrontation with Rebeka and Vanessa sliding her hand down the front of her shirt. He had been too appalled at the time to think of the implications of it then, but now it seemed obvious.

Matthew was quiet for a moment and then cleared his throat. "There is more, but I am not sure you want to hear it."

"I do not." Peter sat heavily in the chair beside the table and refilled his cup once again. He realized he had lost count of how many times it had been filled already. "But tell me anyway."

"He beat a woman to death."

Peter jerked his head up to stare at him in disbelief, spilling his drink across his lap.

"I do not know the circumstances involved, but I know the story to be true." Matthew walked heavily to the chair that faced Peter and sat despondently. "I know with my mind that things are falling into place...but my heart? I cannot see a woman acting that way."

"I can. At least her." Peter reluctantly told of the encounter with his mistress in the stairwell and then again at the dining hall. "You cannot imagine the surprise to see your wife slide her fingers into the gown of your mistress, and when she said 'if I was in the market for a mistress,' I had the strangest thought that it sounded as if she already had a mistress at the time."

Matthew nodded his head. "Not one...six."

Peter rolled his eyes and then laid his head against the tall back of the chair. "Funny."

"It does explain much."

Matthew's voice echoed through Peter's head like a hammer against an anvil. Pain swirled through his overworked senses and settled into the beginnings of a throbbing headache.

"When I went to pick her up, I asked her about daily life in Junket and she would not tell me. I thought at first it was because she was angry with me, but I think it was because she had not been there in so long."

Peter heard the legs of his chair drag against the stone floor and flinched.

"I just cannot see my little girl that left as the one that did all those terrible things that man has been accused of." There was a pause and then Matthew's face appeared above him.

Peter straightened his head and blinked groggily. The brandy weighed heavy on him, dragging him into a deep darkness that he did not want to fight against. He welcomed the coming of the black void that sleep would take him to.

"You look exhausted; let me send you to a room. After some sleep we can talk."

Peter nodded his cumbersome head and allowed the servant to lead him to a bed.

👑👑👑

Van awoke in the morning, weary and sore in every muscle she had. Her arm was throbbing incessantly. She opened her eyes and stared at the ceiling above her, vaguely recalling leaving Anna's bed and making her way to Peter's.

She remembered clearly the disappointment that had left her clutching her pillow tightly when Peter had not come to bed by the time the sun was well set. She had finally fallen into an uneasy sleep.

She turned her head and flinched when she saw the smooth covers on his side of the bed. The coverlet seemed to glare accusingly at her as if to say it was all her fault that he had slept elsewhere.

Amy opened the door quietly. Van debated on sending her away, but pushed herself to her feet instead. She allowed Amy to cleanse her wound and change the bandages.

Van sighed in relief when there was no sign of infection and no hints of fever. At least as of yet, but what tomorrow would bring she was even afraid to guess at.

Amy tried to talk to her and she listened halfheartedly. Finally she shooed her away, telling her to check on Anna.

Van dressed in her gown and sat before the mirror to douse her face with powder. It was unnecessary now, but she did not want to remind them of who she really was. She made her way through the large estate. Peter was nowhere to be found and there was no one to ask.

When a servant saw her they would go the other way.

She watched them walk away with a mixture of calm acceptance and guilt. She could not find any anger for these people. They had taken to her, shown her loyalty, and she had betrayed them.

They were scared of her now and she could not blame them.

They were treating her as the Dark Knight was treated when he visited other castles. His reputation, nay her reputation, was one that bestowed fear in their hearts.

The reputation was all deserved and again she wondered what it was all for. Her mother had lied to her and the person she loved being was only a lie.

She should be the sweet demure woman she was supposed to be. Taking a deep breath, she decided that it was what she needed to be now.

Honesty with herself was not something she could allow right now, not if she was going to make herself into a true woman. She could not allow thoughts of the Dark Knight. She could not think of the things she would miss as him, or the past life she had once loved.

It had all changed the moment she had married Peter. It was not fair to him that his wife was not the woman he wanted her to be. Her heart clenched tightly and swelled into her throat, threatening to push tears ahead of it. She swallowed hard and shoved them away.

She wandered for some time before finding her way back to her bed.

Amy awoke her sometime later, changed her bandages, and assisted her to dress. She instructed Amy to turn her into a lady. Amy just looked at her dumbfounded. When she nodded at her, Amy set to work without another word until she had finished.

Van stepped in front of the mirror and Amy stood beside her. "You look elegant, my lady."

Van's hair was coiled high upon her head, instead of hanging down her back with only a brushing to prepare it for the day as she usually wore it. She was gowned in a soft blue silky dress that slid across her skin with a cool slithery feel that made her think of a snake wrapping around her body.

She had suffered through the lacy chemise that itched at her body and the uncomfortable kid slippers, now without the leather sole as was proper. She stared at the woman staring back at her and wondered who she was.

Her mind was empty and her soul had curled into a tight ball in her stomach, causing it to cramp and ache.

Amy questioned her mood and her health. Van shook her head to both without speaking. Amy walked with her to the dining hall, but Van ignored her presence the best she could.

She only wanted to sleep and hope that all this would all be gone when she awoke.

Several whispers made it to her ears as she stopped outside the dining hall doors. They spoke of Peter going to see his mistress and that Rebeka had not stayed where Van had sent her.

The room fell silent as she walked in. She walked to her seat and hoped she did not look too disappointed that Peter's seat was empty.

She had been terrified of what she would have to endure when she arrived in the hall, but the silence was more than she could handle.

She forced her head up and walked to the head table. She heard a soft gasp and turned toward the door.

Peter stood staring at her. He was dressed in rumpled clothing and appeared to have just gotten off a fast moving horse, his hair standing on end in places and wind whipped in others.

He continued into the room, stopping beside her. He kept his gaze fixed on the table and waited silently for her to take her seat.

She wanted to scream. Scream for him to acknowledge that she was there, for him to speak to her. She gracefully took her seat without a word. Her numb mind knew it was what she deserved for betraying him the way she had, but it still hurt.

Head hanging and shoulders slouched to hide her height, she sat beside her husband and ignored his constant looks at her face, hair, and dress. She probably should not be wearing the makeup, as he had asked her not to, but that was before. Now she thought it was best to hide the last of the knight.

She tried to shove him from her heart, but without the knight, she felt empty and lost.

Supper was awkward and silent. Van knew it would stay that way as long as she was there.

She hated the way everyone was looking at her, the way they talked behind their hands as if she did not know they were speaking of her.

Tears clogged in her throat and she fought with the guilt of knowing it was her fault that the men were uncomfortable.

Looking up at Richard, she thought to begin a conversation that might break some of the tension.

Before she could speak Richard looked pained and broke eye contact.

Richard could not bring himself to look at her. It tore at his heart. All he could see when he did were the things he had done to her.

He had been cruel and treated her like no woman should have been treated. He did not understand what had brought her to be who she was, but more, he could not understand how she could not be disgusted with him. He was disgusted with himself.

She should hate him, yet she didn't. The speech she had given him before going to her mother had spoken in volumes of love and caring. Even after what he had done to her.

Her love was too much for his self-hatred to endure.

He looked up to tell her how sorry he was for all he had put her through, but all he saw was her retreating form as she walked from the hall. He looked down and the food from her side of the trencher she shared with Peter had been left untouched.

♛ ♛ ♛

Amy watched Van's slouched form retreat from her table and got up to follow. She entered Peter's chambers to see Van standing in the center of the room, staring at the large bed. "Why are you doing this?" When Van did not answer her Amy tried again. "Van—"

"Vanessa. Lady Vanessa." It was a tired and empty voice.

"Vanessa?" Amy knew she hated that name. She had been adamant about it. "I am worried about you, milady. You do not seem the same today."

"I am not. I am who I am supposed to be now. I should never have been the other." Her back trembled as she took in a deep breath. She walked to the bed and stopped at the foot of it. Her hand reached out to smooth a wrinkle on Peter's side. "I cannot be him anymore. Now I am just me."

"Just you? If this is who you are supposed to be, than why is it so easy for you to be the knight and so hard for you to be the lady?" Amy drew away from the empty look that Van turned on her.

She looked lost. Depression and hopelessness pained her dark eyes. It was a look Amy had never seen on her. She seemed to have given up.

Instead of the arrogance and pride that usually filled her, she seemed dispirited.

Van looked back at the bed.

"You cannot be something you are not," Amy declared. "If you were not supposed to be him, you would not have taken to it so well. You would not have enjoyed all the things you did." She jumped as Van slammed her fist into the foot board. Her blow shook the bed and ran through the room.

"Take Joseph and put him in with you or in the nursery, and tell Peter that I have moved back into my chambers. He can come to his."

Before Amy could say anything Van disappeared into her chambers and the door between the two rooms closed. She rushed out to find Peter.

When she found him lying asleep in a chair in the library she began to cry.

Opening his eyes he looked confused at first as to where he was. "Aye?"

"I did not mean to wake you, milord, but Lady Vanessa sent me to tell you she has retired to her own chambers so that you do not have to hide in the library. Or to wherever it is that you went all of last night." Without waiting, for a response she fled from the room. Van had not said those things and she should not have either, but they had slipped out. Angry and powerless to help her friend, she didn't know what else to do.

Peter stared, jaw slacked as she turned and fled the room. The door slammed, ringing through his head.

He shook his head, trying to bring his sleep and brandy laced mind around what it was she had told him.

Hiding?

He was not hiding. Not now and not last night.

Was he?

CHAPTER 26

Morning came as it always did, but Van found it difficult to rise with it. Her face felt flushed and her arm throbbed more than it had the day it was injured. She closed her eyes and considered going back to sleep.

She did not want to rise, did not want to face the people of Grayweist, but mostly she did not want to face herself.

She opened her eyes and groaned as Amy crossed her mind. She didn't want to worry her, and more she did not want to listen to a lecture or to answer any questions.

She swung her legs over the side of the bed and a wave of nausea washed over her. She had a momentary fear that her stomach would relieve itself onto the floor between her feet.

When her stomach stopped rolling, she pushed herself to a standing position, her injured arm nearly giving out on her. She grunted in pain and cradled it across her stomach.

She dreaded changing the dressing, knowing it would be infected. She wobbled slowly to the night table and peeled her bandage off. The wound beneath was red and angry, the flesh around the cut was puffy and clear liquid seeped from between the stitches.

She hadn't anticipated this complication on top of everything else. It had been two days since the injury and it had been kept clean. Of course she had eaten nothing since then and her sleep had been anything but restful.

She hurriedly dressed, fixed her hair, and her face. She walked to the door, opening it just as Amy reached for it.

Amy looked up startled. "My lady, I was coming to help you prepare for your day." She looked at the injured arm and reached her hand toward it.

Van stepped back. "I am fine." She ignored the worried look Amy gave her and walked away.

She made her way to the garden where she sat on a long marble bench and stared absently at all the work she had accomplished. The gardens were once more as beautiful as they had been when she was a page here.

Her stomach rolled in protest when her mind tried to dredge up memories of her time here. She pushed them away quickly knowing they would only lead to memories of her time as a knight.

"Dark Lady, can I talk to you?" Joseph's small, cautious voice pulled her from the past and from dangerous thoughts that would only lead to more heartache.

"Of course. Sit by me." She patted the bench beside her. She had come to love the young boy in the short time she had known him, and she did not like the concern she saw in his face, or the fear.

He looked at her expectantly. "Are you truly the one they call the Dark Knight?"

"Not anymore, but aye once I was. Are you scared of me?" She knew she would fall apart if he said yes. It was something she could not take. She was holding on to her sanity by the barest of threads and was sure it would send her over the edge.

"Scared for you, but not of you." He shrugged and looked up at her timidly. "I want to know if you will go back to battle." Tears began to stream down his face. "Will you leave me like my mother did? You are all I have now, milady."

She pulled his trembling frame into her arms, ignoring the shooting pain that went through her. "Nay, I will no longer be a knight. Now I am just…" She took a deep breath, feeling the pain and loss. "I am just Lady Vanessa."

"You are not happy about that." His voice was sure. "Why?"

"You head back to the castle and find Amy." She was fighting lethargy as her mind began to numb. It was the only way she found she could deal with her new personality. What did regular women think about? What did they fill their day with?

He grasped her hand and held tight. "Are you going to be all right?"

She pulled her hand away. "Just go." It came out as a gruff whisper, more icily than she had intended, but she did not look up as he left.

Not knowing what else to do with her time, she went back to her room. Too tired to do anything else, she fell atop the covers and allowed sleep to take her into its serene darkness.

The cool peace of sleep that she longed for did not take her. She fell into a pit of dark dreams, images of silks and laces smothering her, strangling the life from her. She fought against the confines of the silky materials, but they soon consumed her.

♚♚♚

Amy sat with Anna and the two of them discussed the fragile mental health of their lady. Amy looked up startled as Joseph, tears running down his dirt-streaked face, came bursting into the room.

He did not wait for anyone to speak to him but began to blurt out the conversation he had had with Van and of the sadness on her face. "She would hardly look at me. Is she mad at me?"

"Nay, honey bear," Amy told him. "She is just having a hard time right now. She will be all right." She wasn't so sure, however, she was relieved that her voice sounded more confident that she did. At least it made him stop crying.

"Are you sure?" Anna asked, her voice weak and troubled. "She did not even come to see me this morning. I saw her before bed last night. She did not look good, but at least she was speaking to us."

Amy tried to smile in reassurance, but it sat wrong on her face and she allowed it to slip away. She was worried about Van as well. "You two stay here and I will go get her. She will be fine." She patted Anna's arm and Joseph lightly on the head and rushed from the room.

Not finding her in the garden, Amy rushed up the stairs to her chambers. The door was locked. She knocked lightly not sure if she would get an answer.

"I need my rest. I will be fine." Van's voice trembled and Amy had to lean against the door to hear her. "Just let me be."

Tears slipped down her cheeks and she resisted the urge to bang on the door until Van let her in. She could feel Van slipping away and knew if something was not done and soon it would be too late.

She slipped from the castle and raced for the training fields where she knew she would find the help she needed.

She slid to a stop far enough away to be out of danger, but close enough for the men to see her. She heaved for breath and pressed her hand into the stitch that had started in her side.

She tried to smile at Devon as he rushed over to her, but when his hand touched hers she burst into tears.

"Amy, what are you doing here? It is not safe for you to be here." He pulled her into his arms holding her until her sobs had slowed to the occasional hiccup.

"I am worried about Van. She is not herself," she said into his sweaty chest. She sighed and pressed herself farther into his warm embrace. She had felt scared and alone as she had raced toward the lists, but the warmth and comfort of his strong arms drove those feeling away.

He wrapped his hands around her arms and held her away from him. He looked into her eyes and she was lost in the love she saw there. "What happened?"

"You saw her last night at dinner, but today it is worse." She began to cry again as she told him Joseph's story.

"Perhaps she just needs time. We all do." He spoke for all of them but he looked specifically at Peter as he spoke.

She glanced at Peter and saw the lost look on his face. It disappeared as he grimaced and joined a mock battle. She looked back at Devon and shook her head. "I am worried she is doing harm to herself. She did not eat last night, nor breakfast this morning, and I am not sure she has eaten anything since returning from her father's."

Devon's brow furrowed in concern. "That is a problem."

She relaxed knowing that he was listening and starting to understand the danger Van was in. "She has shut herself in her chambers and will not talk to me. She will not even let me close to her."

"What can we do for her?" Devon asked.

"She has had so much pain and loss lately that it is all catching up with her. I was with her when her mother died. She has not cried for her. I know she has always hid her emotions, but even if she were a man she would still need to grieve." Tears came to her again and he wrapped an arm around her, leading her back to the castle.

Devon kissed Amy gently, telling her that he would see to things and left her in her chambers. He, too, had been concerned for Van since dinner the night before. He just did not know how to express the fears he was feeling.

Devon stopped by Van's chamber door and knocked. Nothing from the other side. He tried the handle only to find it still locked. He walked around going through Peter's room and tried that door. It held firm, locked as well.

Back at the lists, he approached Peter, feeling closer to him than he had in the beginning when they had shown up on his doorstep, asking to be taken in. A lot had happened since then.

"Lord Grayweist, may I speak to you for a moment?" His voice trembled, making him sound as unsure of himself as he felt.

Richard and Grant had turned to leave, but Devon raised his hand to stop them. "Can you both stay as well? I would like as many opinions as I can get."

Devon led them to the far side of the lists away from the other men before he turned to them. "I want to pass on a concern of Amy's…and mine." He caught Peter's gaze and he shook his head.

"About Lady Vanessa?" Peter didn't need an answer to know he was correct. It was on everyone's minds. "Is she all right?" He had worried about her the night before. She looked so helpless when she had retired. Yet he could not bring himself to approach her. He felt guilt swarm him and a sense of failure as he realized that Amy's accusations were correct. He had been hiding.

"Nay, I do not think she is. She will not eat, nor will she talk to anyone." Devon leaned closer and lowered his voice. "Joseph said she would hardly talk to him, or look at him for that matter, and she will hardly talk to Amy either."

Peter looked at Richard's guilt ridden face, cringed, then glanced quickly away.

"Amy says she was there when Van's mother died and she has not cried for her. She thinks Van is on the edge of a breakdown." Devon's voice shook and Peter had to look away from him.

Peter was at a loss at what to say or what to do to help her. The silence strung out between them for several long moments. Peter stared down at his hands and realized with a start that they were trembling.

His heart was heavy. Van was not his only concern, though she was his most important. He also had to figure out a way to help the men deal with this new development. Van's men were lost and confused and needed guidance that he was unsure how to provide.

How was he to help them when he could not even help himself? he wondered bitterly.

"I was there when her mother died as well," Richard said into the silence. His eyes were glazed over as if he was lost in the past.

Devon raised his brows and Peter glanced at him. Devon nodded and his eyes brightened. "That is right, you were in the cabin. We were all at the funeral."

Peter thought for a moment over what Amy had told Devon. "If Amy was there when Vanessa's—" He took a deep breath. "—Van's mother died and you were there as well, why did you not recognize her?"

Richard laughed. "All I saw of her was a pitchfork and hair thrown over her face."

Peter shook his head not sure if he had understood. "What?"

Richard's eyes cleared slightly and his gaze met Peter's. He smiled. "She ran from us when we arrived at the cottage. Van pounded on the door and she opened it brandishing a pitchfork, but I could not see her around him...her." He groaned and shook his head. "This is going to take some getting used to."

"Aye it is," Peter agreed.

"Van had pulled her against him and she passed out. When he—" He groaned again but didn't bother to correct himself. "—threw her onto the pallet in the room, in *her* mother's room. Amy's hair was covering her face."

Devon shook his head. "We all saw her, but at the funeral she had a thick black veil. We never saw her face and she never spoke."

Richard nodded in agreement. "I was in there while the doctor talked to Van. He tried to get her to show some emotions, telling her that even a man had to cry."

The men in the lists had begun to mill around instead of practicing. Peter watched them momentarily while Richard spoke. They kept casting furtive glances toward his small huddled group.

"The doctor told her then that she could not keep it all inside or it would cause a breakdown." Richard looked down at his hands, clenching them at his sides. "She just shook her head, saying there was no time for a breakdown. She told him she would do it later. I guess later has not come yet."

Grant drew Peter's attention when he spoke. His voice was soft and low. "She has had much more to deal with since then. I do not know exactly what is going on with her father for it is not my business, but I know it is straining her."

Peter nodded when Grant looked to him for confirmation. The problems with her father were tearing her apart inside. Peter had seen it in her face when she had left for her father's home. Even though she tried to hide it, Peter had felt the pain swirling within her.

Grant nodded. "If she has stopped talking to anyone, she may be hiding inside herself. Changing from a man the scope of the Dark Knight to a dainty lady, cannot be easy."

"I know. I know." Peter did know, but this was not helping him any. He understood the problem already. What he needed was a solution. He was afraid that those answers would not come and he would lose her. "We all saw her last night. She is finally dressing like I want and trying to act the meek little wife, but it is not her." He hung his head shamefully. "I just do not know how to face her or what to say to her."

He closed his eyes and prayed for some answers to be bestowed upon him, but no one spoke. He sighed deeply, a black streak of dread winding its way around his mind, darkening his thoughts and eating away his hopes of a brighter future.

A sad smile crossed his lips and they trembled when he spoke. "I have wondered at the things Van told the king that night she became the Dark Knight." He looked up at them. Their faces held the same lost fearful look that he imagined his own face held. "She said I had faced adversity for her. I thought at the time she meant the boys, but nay, she meant her."

"The boys, my lord?" Richard asked him gently.

"I saved her from a group of six boys when she was still a page here." His mind drifted back to that day long ago. "They had her down and she was losing dreadfully. When I saved her, she was mad. Mad at me." He shook his head in wonder. "Yelled at me, said she had it all under control. The next time it was only four boys and she looked to be losing then as well. I almost did nothing with the last gratitude I had gotten."

Richard laughed. Devon and Grant both shook their heads. Peter noticed the men had ceased even the pretense of practice and were now standing around, watching curiously. He said nothing to them, but returned to his tale.

"When I saved her, I received the same reception. She was angry at me again. She took a swing at me. Telling me to mind my own business." He rubbed his knuckles against his palm.

Richard shifted from foot to foot and the men began to move closer to them.

"She hit me. I..." Peter was not sure how to continue. He closed his eyes against the wave of guilt that crashed against him. "Now that is all I see. The bloody lip that I left her with."

Things obviously had not changed, he thought, cringing as he recalled the bloody lip he had given her by the lake.

"I understand." Richard's voice shook with emotion.

Peter opened his eyes and stared at the Dark Knight's second-in-command.

"I see the same things, but more." Richard looked at them all, from one to another, and then focused on the dirt between his boots. "I left her with broken ribs one time. I gave her more than one beating. Treated her like..." A deep breath trembled through his shoulders. "I cannot bear to think of the delicate lady she should be, would have been, had it not been for me."

Peter watched a tear slide down his cheek. His throat clogged with emotion itself. He swallowed hard and looked at the other two men who now studied their own boots.

Richard ignored the tear and continued, his voice husky. "When we got the missive from her mother, she stopped me before we headed out. Told me that everything she had become was to my credit." He sucked in a deep breath that wheezed slightly. He smiled at Peter.

Peter thought it looked forced and slightly painful.

"I can tell you though why she was so mad when you saved her." Richard glanced at the men, who had advanced another step or two toward them. He looked back to Peter. "When she first arrived, she was not as good as some of the boys who were already here, not as strong. She was young for a page."

Peter shook his head. He already knew that. He had seen the way they taunted her. His stomach lurched when he thought of the way the boys had tormented her and Peter had done nothing about it.

"She fought hard to become the best, but they were cruel to her." Richard continued. "She fought dirty. Anything she had to do to win. Soon they knew that, one–on-one, they were no match for her."

Grant laughed disgustedly and added to Richards words. "They would torment her if there was two or three. I saw her lose at first to a group, but soon she got to where she could win against them as well."

"Aye," Richard agreed, smiling as he remembered. "In order to get better, to learn, and get practice she would seek out groups."

Peter sighed. "She would torment them, lose or not, just so she got the practice?"

"Aye," Richard said. "She got good enough. No matter the group, they would no longer take the bait. She may lose in the end, but there were many injuries to the boys before she let up. No one was willing to risk it."

"I do not know what to do with her. After supper I will talk to her." Peter gestured to the men and led them all toward the castle, his mind in a turmoil every step back.

How was he to face her? How could he ever apologize for all the things that had happened to her? How did he help her become a woman, a wife? How could he get her to let go of all she was before? *Could* she let go?

Did he really want her to?

♔ ♔ ♔

Van was feeling stronger, but she knew most likely it was from the large amount of brandy she had drank. Not used to drinking, the alcohol went quickly to her brain, making her feel lightheaded.

She was not one of those silly drunks. That much she understood quickly. The anger that had disappeared over the last days had returned full force. It clouded her mind as much or more than the brandy and she was in a foul mood.

Her life was falling apart and the master of all situations found herself in control of nothing. She could not do anything. She did not even know who she was anymore.

She had been better before the brandy. She had felt numb, felt absolutely nothing. Now the anger was beginning to swell. She felt trapped and didn't know what to do to fix it. It was too late to turn back now. Everyone knew who she was. She closed her eyes and considered mounting Damien and just riding off and losing herself.

"Milady, I brought you food." Amy stood in the doorway.

Van threw back another mouthful of brandy and turned to glare at her.

"Milady?" Amy knew that Van did not drink. *This cannot be a good sign*, she thought sadly.

"Just leave." The command was bitter and angry.

Amy took a deep shaky breath. "Milady, Van, Please. You have to eat."

She took a step into the room and knew instantly that it had been a mistake. Standing in the center of the room, Van had looked much like a cornered animal protecting her den. Trespassing into her safety zone set her off.

Her black eyes glittered dangerously. They were the eyes of the menacing knight, who had stood before her pitchfork. Fear shot through Amy and her first thought was to run, but she was too late. The tray fell to the floor and she threw her hands over her mouth to hold in a scream.

"*Get the hell out*!"

Peter jerked his head up as Van's thundering voice, and the crashing of a table, was heard all the way to the overly quiet dining hall.

Peter looked up as Amy fled into the room. Not taking her regular spot she fled to Devon at the side table. Close enough for Peter to hear her sobs, she clung to her soon–to-be-husband as he pulled her onto his lap.

Standing so quickly he almost fell, Peter heard the surprised gasps around him. He ignored them all. He nearly ran from the room and took the stairs two at a time.

He looked into his wife's chambers. She stood with her back to him, silent and rigid by the window. She held a brandy in her hand. He had never seen her drink.

Across the threshold were the remnants of the bedside table. Someone had obviously thrown it at the door. Anger flushed through him anew. She had thrown it at her friend who was only trying to help her.

He stepped into the room, avoiding the tray of food that lay splattered across the rushes.

That was the last straw. As his rage boiled it became easier to see her getting a beating, whether knight or lady, she needed to get one now.

"What in the hell do you think you are doing?" He had planned to talk to her calmly, to explain everyone's position, and to get her to answer some questions. To hold her if need be, to let her cry on his shoulder as the woman she had been the last two days would do.

That had all changed when he had seen the splintered table.

Van turned toward him, her color high. Her eyes held black smudges beneath them. She had apparently not slept well in several days. He did not know how to help her and that was what scared him the most.

What was it they said, she needed to cry? How to make this woman cry? He did not think it possible.

She was a rock. The only emotion he had seen was anger, anger that was more than apparent now. It was no doubt intensified by the unaccustomed drink, but that didn't make it any less volatile.

The image of the guards she had brutalized, the man she had beheaded, and the scraps of wood that were once a beautiful oak table, showed him he had seen nothing of her anger. She had always kept herself in check with him.

No matter how he had pushed her, her love for him had let her keep control. Was that true? Did she love him?

His heart lightened. She had told Telpher that she did.

Even if he had felt her affection for him in the ways they had made love, that wasn't the same as him hearing the words. Even if she did really love him, would she hold control with the effects of the alcohol?

His mind raced with more questions that had no answers. He was tired and weary. He wanted his calm life back.

She stared belligerently at him and took a long drink.

"I asked you a question." Peter kept control of his anger the best he could and thought a good start would be to get her to talk.

"Aye, I heard." Her voice was tight, controlled, and thick with gravel.

A voice he knew well now. He could almost feel the anger that boiled beneath the surface. That grin that he had grown to love and hate at the same time was back full force. Pride and arrogance glorified.

"What do you want to know? You'll have to be more specific." Her words were slurred and her frame trembled as she struggled to hold her balance.

He had never met the Dark Knight. He had met the boy, girl, who would become him. But he had not had anything but rumors to go on as to the knight himself.

Now, he thought, he was meeting that knight. He had a glimpse of the conversation with her father fly through his mind. A mention of a woman beaten to death. "I want to know first about that." He gestured to the table, to the gouge in the door.

"I needed an incentive for someone not wanting to listen." Her voice was tight.

"And about the dress and the hair?"

For a moment she looked confused, and then she looked down. Her dress was rumpled and appeared that she had slept in it, but still looked very proper with a thick lacy chemise underneath hiding her form.

"I am trying to be the wife and woman I am supposed to be, my lord. It is what you want, is it not?" Her voice had changed to one he had never heard.

It was somewhere between the gravel and the high pitched squawk she had been using. He realized it was the first time she had used her real voice, but now it sounded sad and lost. The anger had disappeared.

He didn't answer her question because it was what he *should* want. But knowing how she had been the last couple of days, he had actually missed the woman she was before. Was that even who she really was? Nay. She had held herself in check. He mused about what she was really like and knew he wanted to find out.

But first he had to help her. He needed to get back to the anger. With that at least she was allowing herself to feel something. This hiding from herself would just not do.

"Fine, you want to be my wife and the woman I want? First, you will always dress properly."

If she actually did that, he would miss seeing her slender form draped in the soft cloth.

"Aye, my lord." It had been a long time since she had called him that. It was an emotionless agreement.

"You will not ride. As a woman you are not an able horsemen, and as such you will not even be allowed the sidesaddle on your mare I gave you." He saw the hint of anger in her eyes, but she quickly hid it. Hid it but not gotten rid of it completely. He could see the glint still lingering there. It was a start.

"Aye, my lord." She nearly spat the words out at him.

"You will not be allowed any contact with the men." That one was a mistake. It only brought a deep look of pain to her face.

He thought it was from not being able to see them until he caught a mutter under her breath that sounded suspiciously like, "They will like that." Then she added, "Aye, my lord." The anger had been replaced with a sense of dissolution.

He was beginning to get frustrated. He hated that look of emptiness that surrounded her. He wanted back the fiery woman he had married.

Perhaps, he thought, he would have to use drastic measures. "You will allow my mistress to return and stay in the castle."

Her body was racked with a terrible shudder. "Aye, my lord."

He could not explain the pain and anger that ripped through him when she agreed. "How dare you say aye to that?" he screamed at her, forgetting all his well laid plans.

She didn't answer. She grinned that deep arrogant grin and arched one black brow.

"You put that damned brow down and start talking to me. You will tell me what the hell your problem is." Anger blurred his reasoning. "You have mistreated the only one who has stood beside you through all of this, hurting her, and assaulting her." He gestured frantically at the pile of wood behind him.

Van's gaze dropped to her feet and she stood motionless.

"Have you no honor? Perhaps you would like her to join the other woman you killed. Is that what you want?" Peter's breath came in harsh gasps.

He saw anger spring forth in her eyes as he had talked and he realized that in his ranting he had accidently hit her one sore spot, one that would always work—her pride and her honor.

He should have thought of it before. He had already seen the results and Devenroe had told him of the same.

A heavy hand knocked on the door.

Peter growled. He wanted to ignore it now that she was finally beginning to respond with something besides that look of lost compliance.

He opened his mouth to tell them to go away when Grant opened the door and waved frantically for him to come.

Peter looked back at his wife, but the moment had passed. The opportunity was gone. She no longer held anger. She was once again lost as she sank to the edge of the bed.

He watched her features ripple as she disappeared into what appeared to be painful memories. He thought he knew what they were and cursed himself for bringing up the woman she had killed.

"Damn it, woman, trust me. Trust me. I can help you through this." He didn't know if she heard him for she gave no sign that she had.

Van had, she just didn't know if she could put her trust in him once more. She questioned her honor for the first time in her life. She had been enraged when he had asked her of her honor, when he had questioned it as she was doing now.

She would have fought to defend herself had he not mentioned the woman she had killed. She had killed her out of necessity, but it still haunted her. It was war and everyone was defending themselves.

The lady had been one of them. Van had done what she had to do to save Richard and she had done it with honor. At least she thought she had. Now as the pain swirled through her and her mind fogged, she was unsure.

It had been a year before she became a knight. The blonde woman, not much more than a child, had seduced Richard. When he was well in his cups, she had tried and almost succeeded in killing him.

Van shuddered as the memories swamped her.

Richard had called out in pain and Van rushed to his side. The woman was struggling with him. Richard had then lost consciousness and she plunged the dagger into his side. She had raised it to do it again when Van attacked her, throwing her across the room.

The woman had huddled in the corner as Van had shook Richard, pleading with him to live. That she would do anything for him to live. She had been terrified he would die and she had turned on the woman.

Van wondered at her honor now, knowing she had not had to kill her. She had done it out of anger. Out of fear that the man she looked to as a father was dead. Out of lethal revenge.

She had beaten her long past the time her breath had stopped. Richard had pulled her off the dead woman. Blood had covered her hands as she stood shaking in his arms.

Peter watched as she raised her hands, looking at them as if there was something on them. Van took a deep breath that shook her entire frame.

Peter turned to Grant, who ushered him into the hall.

"What is it?" Peter tried to hide his irritation at the man who had interrupted.

Grant shuffled his large feet. "I am sorry, my lord. I would not have bothered you, but…you have a visitor. I said I would come for you."

"Tell them to wait." Peter turned to go back to his wife.

"I tried but she is making a scene and I did not want Lady Vanessa to hear her, my lord." Grant glanced toward the closed door as if making sure it was still shut and Van had not come out to listen.

"Who?" Peter was afraid he knew.

Grant's answer was a mere whisper. "Miss Constance, my lord."

"Bloody hell!" Peter started for the stairs. He would have to get rid of her quick, before Vanessa found her here. Not in the condition she was in. He would have a dead woman on his hands. "Where?"

"The library."

Peter stomped unhappily down the stairs. This was just what he needed after telling Vanessa she would have to allow this very woman to live here.

He had not meant it. He didn't want any woman but the damned one up the stairs.

CHAPTER 27

V an looked up at the sound of the door clicking shut. Her face tightened in surprise to find herself in an empty room. She had been lost in painful memories and had not even been aware Peter had left.

She took a deep breath and closed her eyes. What had he asked of her? For her to trust him.

She was unsure if she could put her trust in him once again. She had once and she had been rewarded with Peter sending Telpher to accost her.

Her heart pleaded with her that he had only acted out of jealousy, that he had been scared to lose her.

Her mind scoffed saying that even if that were true it did not excuse his actions.

She shuddered, tired of feeling torn in two.

Perhaps he had been jealous and he did care for her. At least some, she thought sadly. She shook her head.

She agreed with her mind—it was no excuse—but she agreed with her heart as well. It may not be reason enough to excuse his actions, but mayhap it was enough to earn her forgiveness.

She opened her eyes and peered at the door. She heard voices, but they were too low to understand. She did not know what she was supposed to do, but she knew she could not do it alone.

She nodded determinedly and decided that she would once more put her trust in Peter. She needed to trust someone and if they were going to make their marriage work it had to be him.

The voices quieted and Van tightened her shoulders. She pulled the door open to an empty hall. Her brow furrowed in irritation.

She knew he had disappeared into the library the night before so she thought that would be the most likely place to start searching. She would find him. Tell him everything and then she would throw herself at his mercy to help her get through it all. To become a wife that he deserved.

She walked carefully down the stairs and stopped at the bottom. Light spilled from around the cracked library door. There were voices behind it, but they were too low to hear. She hesitated. It would not do to start out her new life as a proper wife by bursting in on a meeting.

She stared at the door and fought the urge to peer into the crack. Concern wormed through her that it had something to do with the men. She tightened her grip on her resolve and tried to be patient.

♔ ♔ ♔

Rebeka leaned against the desk in the library and looked up at what had once been her calm and dignified lord. He was now red faced with rage and looked like a madman. It excited her, though she wished he had acted thusly when she was in his life. What had that woman done to him?

"What do you want?" he asked, looking quickly at the door and then back at her.

"I just want you, my lord. I heard you were having problems with your new wife. I heard who she is and I came to help you." With a seductive smile she allowed the silky cloak to slither slowly down her body, the coolness of the library bringing gooseflesh to her bare skin. The cloak pooled at her feet.

Peter moved to step away from her but she threw her arms around his neck and pressed her nude body up against him.

Peter growled, "Do not do this. I am not interested in anyone but my wife. I have enough going wrong right now without need of you to help it along." He placed his hands on her waist and tried to move her off him.

Rebeka tightened her arms around his thick corded neck, feeling the pulse thundering beneath the surface.

I know what you need." She pressed her belly into his manhood. Her pride itched in irritation when she realized the only thing she was managing to get a rise out of was his temper.

He pushed back harder on her this time and she fell onto the desk, but refused to release his neck. The oak was cold against her flesh, but she ignored it as she wrapped her pale white legs around his hips, clasping her ankles together.

Anger was beginning to boil beneath her hurt pride. How dare he turn her down, especially in favor of that behemoth?

Peter sneered at her and reached behind her grasping an ankle. She clenched her thighs tightly around him.

Rebeka's glance shifted to the door as it swung open. There, peering in with wide, dismayed eyes, was the lady of the castle. Oh, this could not get any better, Rebeka thought joyfully.

Rebeka looked back at Peter and moaned seductively. She pressed her breasts into him and caught his lips with hers.

She knew he would break the kiss and ruin the image she was working hard to portray, so she broke it herself before he could.

Looking directly at Vanessa, she gasped in a fair imitation of surprise, "Oh my."

Rebeka pulled quickly away from him, yet still clung to his neck. She only wanted to move far enough to make sure her audience saw her nakedness.

Peter turned to follow her gaze and his heart stilled, his hands frozen on the legs still around him. There in the door stood a shell of the woman he loved.

A single tear, one that threatened to tear out his very heart, welled up and slid silently down Van's cheek, cutting through the paleness of the face powder. She turned and fled.

He fought to free himself from the woman who held him tightly with her arms and thighs. "Vanessa!"

"You do not want her. She cannot be what you need," she shouted as he tore her entrapping limbs from around his trembling body. She let out a scream as he threw her to the ground.

"Get out of our home!" He raced from the room and toward the front door sure that Van would run to the stables.

His heart lurched and he slid to a stop when he heard the slamming of a heavy door from the direction of the sleeping chambers.

He took the stairs two at a time and almost fell several times. He fought for balance but did not slow.

What the hell was he going to do now?

As he pounded on her chamber door, he heard the inner door between the two rooms slam. "Damn!" He would make this right for her if it was the last thing he managed to do.

He would hold her and never let her go. He would tell her he didn't care what or who she had been and that he loved her. Pain and guilt swirled through him.

He pounded twice more and then shook himself. The key, he thought as he berated himself for not thinking of it before he had hurt his fists. He just needed to get the key and then he could make everything right.

Running to his bedside table, he rummaged through the drawers. His struggled to draw breath through the tight band that cinched around him. Pain shot through his chest every time he forced air into his lungs.

He cursed loudly when he found no key. His spirit sank. She had outsmarted him. She must have gone through here while he was pounding on her door and she had taken it.

Without thought he began to pound on the center door. He screamed at her to let him in.

He did not care who heard or what they thought of it. His only thoughts were on removing that horrible look of agony he had seen on her beautiful face.

"Open this door or I will get an axe and break it down." He was tempted and he might have if he had not thought the moment a hole was in the door she would throw that dagger through his head.

She had promised the next time it would be through his stubborn skull. He didn't doubt it, not now.

A thick lump wedged firmly in his throat and he swallowed hard around it. His fists ached from the power he had put behind the blows, but still there was no answer.

He ignored the pain and continued to pound on the door until he realized he could hear sounds from the other side. His fists stilled as he listened.

From the other side of door, muffled as if buried in pillows he could hear her painful sobs. They were raw, ugly, terrifying sounds. He could feel her pain deep inside him. His heart ached for her. His stomach twisted as he attacked the door once more.

"Vanessa, let me in. Do not do this." He waited, but there was nothing but more of those hoarse sobs. "Vanessa, it is not what you think."

No response. Tears pressed painfully against his the back of his eyes. He blinked hard several times.

"Vanessa." His voice was harsh and painful.

He turned his back to the door and sank pitifully to the floor.

He dropped his head against the door and whispered, "I am sorry." He knew it was not loud enough for her to hear, but he could not tell her through a door.

He would wait until they were face to face. He brought his hands up before him. They stung painfully and, turning them from side to side, he was shocked to see the blood that marred them.

Dropping them into his lap, he closed his eyes and listened to the never ending sobs that seemed to be wrenched from a body unaccustomed to such emotion.

He fought the tears that pressed unrelentingly at him, but he felt several slid down his taunt cheeks despite his efforts to stop them.

This was the breakdown they had all feared. It had come to pass because of him. How was he to face her now? Now that he had betrayed her, even unintentionally, once again.

The night slipped by as her tears chased him into sleep. His head turned in slumber, his ear pressed gently to the door, listening to her sadness even in his dreams.

Dreams that were now changed.

The same lovely face, the same dark black eyes, dagger cut still fresh, hung over him as it always had. The same sweet haunting voice.

But now the deep black hair hung loose around her beautiful face. It brushed against his bare chest erotically.

The drips that hit his injured shoulder were no longer blood as they had once been. They were now her tears. Tears so hot they seemed to burn him.

He reached to stroke the perfect cheek, as he had almost every night since it had happened, but she now was gone.

Verges sat in a carriage below Van's chambers, her sobs drifting down to him. His heart clenched with each tortured cry. He was unsure what Rebeka had done, but he would take his revenge on her. He smiled savagely at the thought of her death.

Edward and Harry Hurtado cringed away from him. Harry sat as far into the wall of the carriage as he could make himself go, as far away from Verges as he could get. Edward sat in the seat facing them.

Both boys avoided eye contact and shuddered every time he moved. Verges smiled about this. His heart drummed with excitement, and the hope that this would soon be over. He wanted Eolian out of Van's life, wanted her to live happy and free.

He glanced from one brother to next with disgust. He hated boys like this, bullies and tyrants, but they had done their job. The Hurtado brothers had carried out their part of the plan without a hitch. While Rebeka was distracting the household, they had absconded with the little day maid Amy.

Wrapped in a white sheet, Amy writhed on the floor of the carriage between Verges feet. The abduction had gone unnoticed as far as Verges could tell and now they only awaited Rebeka's return.

The door opened and Verges tensed in caution. It was Rebeka. She slid into the seat across from him with a look of disgust on her face.

"What are you doing here? You were not part of the plan. I made sure of that." Her voice was full of venom and anger, and he wondered momentarily if things had not gone as well as she had hoped inside the castle. He was sure it hadn't and that pleased him.

"I know you tried to make sure, but things are not always in the control of a whore." He smiled at her sharp intake of breath.

The carriage jerked to an unsteady start and she gripped the side of the seat. "How dare you."

Verges ignored her outrage. He did not like her in the least and it was more than just her mistreatment of the woman to whom he had pledged his life and loyalty. He could feel the evil that seemed to wisp from her very being.

He relaxed back against the seat and forced himself to remain patient. He would enjoy her death, but it had to come at the right time and now, unfortunately, would not do.

Verges tensed again as they approached the guard house. His muscles and nerves tingling with readiness. The carriage stopped momentarily, but the guards let them go through without incident. He grinned, one more step toward victory.

He turned his attention back to Rebeka. Her look of fear had disappeared since she had come under the protection of Eolian, but he thought he could change that.

"You did not tell me why you are here. I do not need you," she snarled at him, but the arrogant look fell away when he smiled. She recoiled and he could see the fear brimming right beneath the surface of her calm façade.

"I am here to make sure that you do as you were instructed and to make sure this—" He pushed his foot gently against the, now still, form on the floor. "—is delivered unharmed. I will not allow your hatred of that man and woman in there—" He jerked his thumb back toward the castle. "—to affect what the Knight of Fear wants done."

Rebeka spun toward him, anger dripping thickly from her words. "How dare you?"

Edward and Harry tried to disappear into the shadowy corners of the carriage. They both stared at the clasped hands that lay trembling in their laps.

Hatred dug at Verges, and he snarled at her.

She flinched away, but did not stop speaking. "Eolian will let me do as I will with this little piece of baggage" She kicked the sheet sharply.

Amy's muffled cry was barely heard. Verges relaxed some. She had lain still and silent for too long and he was beginning to worry that these two worthless boys had tied her gag too tight and she had smothered.

Rebeka waved her hand dismissively at him. "There is nothing you can do about it. She will die at my hands, just as that meddlesome Dark Knight will die at the hands of my master and lord."

Verges could feel a cold anger chilling his blood. His chest tightened and he clenched his fists.

Rebeka began to laugh. "That woman is just worthless trash and will die without honor as she should."

A hot white flash of rage burst across Verges's thoughts. He lunged across the seat. Agile for his size and massive bulk, it took him half a breath to pin her beneath him.

Her laughter died even before his hand wrapped tightly around her throat. There was a scream from one of the boys, but he did not know, nor care, which.

His anger was barely harnessed as he tightened his fingers. The tips disappeared into her soft skin. "There are a lot of things Van may not have, but honor is not one of them." He watched in rapture as her eyes began to glaze over.

Leaning himself tighter against her, he pressed his face to hers. The terror in her eyes as she struggled against him made him smile.

This evil woman had caused much hurt to Van. Rebeka was not the first to fall for inflicting pain on the Dark Knight and she would not be the last. If all went well, many would fall over the next few days.

He smiled a deadly grin up at the boys as the last of her breath caressed his cheek. They could not take their eyes from him now.

Without a word, or any warning, and careful not to step on the struggling woman beneath his legs, he shot his massive paws out. Sausage-like fingers gripped the sun reddened neck of each boy. To keep them from calling out or struggling, he slammed the hard heads together, smiling as the blood ran down their smooth cheeks.

Keeping pressure for a few heartbeats after he could no longer feel the pulse thudding beneath his palms, he tossed them against the side of the carriage without a second glance.

Carefully he pulled the small bundle off the floor and onto his lap and removed the sheet.

Her eyes were wide with fear as she looked into the liquid brown eyes, recognition filling them. She stopped struggling. A soft joy tickled at Verges's heart when she lay calmly in his arms. He was still amazed that this small girl trusted him.

Pulling the gag from her mouth, he smiled at her. "I will not hurt you." He held her gently, not undoing any of her bindings. Not yet. He still had to use her as a pawn to get to Eolian and he could not free her now. Not after so much had been risked to get her.

"I know. I am one of Van's girls, right?" She jumped at his laugh.

"Nay, not exactly, but it amounts to the same thing. Her girls are mistresses. You are her friend. Are you hurt?" He held her tightly to keep her from seeing the three bodies behind her. He didn't want her any more frightened than she was.

"Mistresses? But Van is a woman?" she gasped in shock.

He smiled and shook his head. "I will let her explain that to you. Now I need you to trust me. Can you do that?" He watched her eyes darken. "Van trusts me."

"I do also." She looked him square in the eye, unwavering, to show her faith and trust in him. What do you want me to do?"

"Do not act as if you know me. Show fear of me. It is important for you to do that." He did not want to hurt her, but he had a sinking feeling that he would have to. "I hate to do this, but if you cannot pretend fear, you will fear me for real." He tightened his grip painfully as her breath caught, just to make a point. He saw the fear linger in her eyes.

He released her and she gasped for breath.

"I will not hurt you if you are a good actress, but your life, mine, and Van's all depend on your performance. Do you understand?"

She nodded. Her eyes showed fear, but not nearly as much as he had hoped. He prayed for her sake she would not make him demonstrate his power. He did not want to hurt one of the few people that trusted him, that made him feel like…less of a freak.

"You have to stay tied. Do as I tell you and I will help get you out of here unharmed."

The carriage came to a stop. Quickly he replaced the gag and wrapped her tightly again. Stepping out of the conveyance, he tossed her roughly over his shoulder.

"Aye, I will send word for you and the boys at the Inn," he said to the dead woman who lay with her neck bruised and swollen.

He slammed the door and turned to the driver. "Take them directly to Doveslane Inn. You are to see a woman there by the name of Annette. Bring her out to the carriage and she will see to Miss Constance's safety."

He began walking to the small cabin, listening to the rumble of wheels disappear into the distance.

He thought back to the trip he had made to see Annette before meeting Rebeka at the castle. He had taken her upstairs, but not for what most men did. He had never used her in that way.

He needed her from time to time and considered their relationship one of necessity, which meant she was off limits to his rampages.

She had agreed to dispose of the driver, and the bodies. She would do as he said, not because of the gold he had given her, but because she was terrified for her life and that of her family. She was loyal to him because of fear and fear alone.

He had always thought fear was the ultimate power, but now he wasn't so sure. If someone better came along to protect them, the fear would vanish, then no power.

Van had done much to convince him that fear was not the biggest power. He laughed gently and adjusted Amy across his shoulder. The Dark Knight's reputation was built mostly on fear, but she had been the one to make him realize that friendship and a loyalty based on respect and caring was better than fear.

That was a bond worth dying for and one that no one bigger or stronger could take away. The only way to lose one's loyalty was due to your own actions, not those of someone else.

Verges pushed everything from his mind when the broken down shelter came into view. He stepped through the door and pushed it closed behind him.

"Verges, where are the others?"

He felt his unwilling passenger tighten at Eolian's deep voice.

"Miss Constance was afraid of what would happen here and took the boys to the Inn to protect her. I said we would get her when it was all done." Verges, none too softly tossed his bundle onto the floor in the corner of the shelter. He did it as a show for all watching as well as a reminder of what she was supposed to do. He only hoped she listened.

Eolian shook his head with a look of pitiful disgust on his usually calm face. "I thought she might want to watch. That is the problem with women. They are weak. Weak of body and of mind." He snorted. "I had thought she was different."

Verges said nothing.

"Did they retrieve the right one?" Eolian didn't wait for an answer before unwrapping the small woman. She looked frightened and Verges forced himself to calm. "Aye, it is the right one. I checked her myself when they got into the carriage."

"My dear, did this beast hurt you?" Eolian's voice was calm and slightly soothing.

It had always given Verges the chills, because he knew what lie beneath that façade.

Without an answer she scooted away from him.

"You had best answer my questions, my dear, or I shall have to make you…uncomfortable," he informed her, but she still said nothing. "What is your name?" Nothing. "Verges, pray help me."

With a deep breath, he walked past the knight to Amy's trembling frame. There were too many men standing in the small room to do much of anything. He so wanted just to throttle the man before him. He could not, and besides, that would only be a temporary solution.

He had thought of it often, but knew that another would just step in and take his place. There were too many warriors just waiting for their opportunity. Nay, they had to destroy him as well as a large number of his followers.

The only options he had available to him now was to send a message. That and that alone was all he could do until help arrived.

He walked toward Amy. She feigned fear, but while her body seemed frightened her eyes showed trust.

That would not do and he had warned her. He grabbed her by the hair and roughly pulled her to her feet.

Pulling her tightly against him he slid his massive hand across her breasts, giving a hard squeeze. One that he only released when he saw the fear and she began to fight in earnest, her body and her eyes now reflecting the same terror.

Eolian walked up behind him and Verges tensed when he felt his warm breath against his cheek as he leaned close to Amy's face. "Now I asked you your name."

"Amy…Amy Devant," she nearly yelled.

"Now, that was not that hard was it?" He caressed her cheek. "I have only one other question for you and then you will go with Verges here." He patted him on the back companionably and Verges fought a shudder of revulsion. "You will spend the night with him. I think I shall give him this honor. He has worked hard for me."

Amy's frightened eyes widened and the color drained from her face.

Eolian smiled. "Now my last question. Do you think the Dark Knight will come to rescue you? Are you important to her?"

She spit at his feet.

Verges cursed silently and lifted her off the ground by her hair. She screamed, her hands flying up to grasp his wrists. His mouth crashed down onto hers.

She kicked against him and tried to close her mouth, but he slid his tongue into it before she could. Regret swam through painfully and he once again prayed, to no one in particular, that this would soon be over.

He grasped her round bottom and pressed her tight against him, holding her there until the laughing men had walked from the cabin.

The instant the door clicked shut Verges released her. She wiped at her mouth and then opened it to scream. He knew she meant to accuse him of lying and betraying her. He wrapped his fingers around her throat cutting off her air supply. Whatever words she was going to throw at him died beneath his grasp.

"Be careful what you accuse me of if you want to live. I still mean to help you." He let his grip soften, then fall away, when she made no move to scream. "I warned you about what would happen. Now, I hope I will not have to make any more examples, but I must play my part as well as you."

"You could at least say you are sorry," she whispered through her tears.

"I am sorry." He grinned. "Though I did enjoy the kiss. Devon Horacio is a lucky man to be getting you." He laughed at the shocked look on her face.

"How did you know, did Van...Nay. She would not tell anyone." She pulled away from him.

"I know much. Now get some sleep. There is no telling when he may be back. I will keep watch and awake you if they are coming this way."

Verges jumped in surprise, but did not turn to face her, when her low voice sounded. "If this is how you treat someone who is under her protection—" She took a deep breath. "What would you have done if I did not have that protection?"

He did not answer.

V an awoke slowly and tried to open her eyes. They were swollen and sticky from the long night of tears that had besieged her. She scrubbed at her face and could feel the heat baking off her. The fever was worse. "Well, hell," she said softly to the empty room.

She moved her arm. It hurt, but she thought the infection seemed somewhat better, though she didn't take time to look. She pulled herself from the bed, every muscle screaming at her to lay back down and go back to sleep.

She ignored them and dragged herself to the night basin. Washing her face, she stretched.

Amy had not come in to awaken her yet, so Van thought she had some time to pull herself together before she showed up. If she shows up, Van thought bitterly. After throwing the table at her last night, she might decide that avoidance would be a good option until things calmed down.

Van decided brandy was the first order. Drinking heavily, she felt stronger, able to ignore both the physical and emotional pain.

She pulled on the hated undergarments and covered them with a proper and frilly dress. Then, feeling numb inside, she sat before the large mirror to apply the thick and itchy powder that she had come to hate.

Smearing it along the unscathed side of her face, along the center of her nose, and down her chin, she sighed. What was she going to do? She had agreed to allow that woman stay in the castle and apparently Peter had taken her up on it.

She had not planned on it being so soon. Well, she would cope somehow. There was no choice. She tried to ignore the small pricks of anger and pride that jabbed at her. They refused to be ignored so she closed her eyes to will them away.

When she believed she had them silenced, she opened her eyes and looked into the mirror. What she saw staring back at her was startling.

The sun darkened, scarred side of her face was in vast contradiction to the ladylike appearance of the other side. With the makeup splitting up the sides of her face she clearly saw the two warriors that were battling for her life and for her sanity. Slowly she turned her head.

One way, then the other.

Who was she supposed to be?

One way, then the other.

She could see plainly who she was, who she had always been.

One way, then the other.

Did it matter what had made her what she was?

Was there no middle ground?

Looking straight in the mirror, she could see the truth of herself. Truth she had tried to hide as of late.

She could not stand to be the meek little wife. It made her stomach curdle to do so. She could not stand the primping and pampering it would take to be a proper wife, and more, she would never accept a mistress. Never!

The needling anger began to dig at her again, this time she let it.

She could not find sadness or depression. All that had escaped with the release of the tears last night. She had cried for everything—for the loss of her men, for the loss of her mother, and for the loss of herself.

As anger turned to rage, she decided she had not lost herself. She was who she was, who she always had been and always would be.

Aye, there was a middle ground, she told herself and slammed her fist against the dressing table. She might no longer be the Dark Knight and she would never be the lady, but somewhere in the middle was…

The Dark Lady began to roughly scrub the makeup from her face with the hem of her dress.

Finished, except for a thin line of powder down the center of her nose, she rose. Her fists clenched around one of the powder tubs. She picked it up and smelled the light floral fragrance.

The muscles in her arms jumped and she allowed the fury to flow through her. She relished the feeling. She had been numb for too long and her body flourished under the passions of emotion that caressed her.

With sudden fervor, she flung the tubs of powder against the far door. She felt free, free for the first time since that dreadful message. No, free for the first time in her life, she corrected.

No matter what happened from here on out, she promised herself, she would just be who she truly was.

She knew she was not wanted here. Her men had felt betrayed and she didn't blame them. They had turned their backs on her and Peter…well, Peter had made his choice obvious last night in the library.

She would disappear. She raced into the hall and ignored the pounding that was coming from the middle door.

Peter hammered his fists into it. He had heard the horrendous crashes coming from his wife's chamber and was in a panic. The sounds had awoken him, stiff and uncomfortable from sleeping the entire night propped up against her door.

"My lady, are you all right?" He heard Grant's voice, slightly panicked, coming from the hall.

Tearing open his door, he almost collided with his trusted friend. He could hear her footsteps disappearing down the stairs. The urgency to go after her was curtailed by the curiosity of the crashes and the dust that hung around her door.

He took a deep breath and tried to still his rapidly beating heart and harsh breathing. Pushing her door open all the way he looked at the thick powder that smothered the air, drifting down covering everything.

He nudged the broken chunks of pottery, heavy with the face powder. It was obvious what had happened, but why?

Peter looked up at Grant. "Is this a good sign or bad?"

"That all depends," Grant said, a smile crossing his face.

"On?" He cocked a questioning brow, his lips tightened with worry.

Grant gave a soft laugh. "On whether, you want to be married to a gentle lady or a mischievous knight, my lord."

What did he want? Peter wasn't even sure he knew. "I guess it will not matter if she gets that horse saddled before I get there." With that he set off at a run, dread pushing his feet to move faster.

He stopped only long enough to ask the groom if she was there. When he nodded, Peter told him they were not to be disturbed and then he entered the dark enclosure.

In the stable, past lines of already saddled steeds, he found her about to mount Damien, his saddle already in place. Obviously, Peter thought with a smile, she saddled them almost as fast as she could unsaddle them.

She let out a scream as he pulled her from the stirrup, throwing her to the ground. He fell atop her and pinned her to the hay. He was so relieved she had not escaped him that he began to kiss her. Hot, possessive and desperate kisses.

Soon she stopped struggling and his heart twirled ecstatically when she returned his kisses.

Finally, he reluctantly broke the kiss and looked down at her. Her eyes showed the strain that she was under. They were swollen and red, with dark circles beneath.

He could feel her hot skin beneath his hands, but the taste of brandy on her tongue made him think the warm flushed skin was from drink.

"You missed some." He ignored her confused look and lifted his hand, wiping off the streak of powder that lined her nose.

"Could you get off of me, my lord?" She shoved at him and he willingly rolled off.

Her eyes flashed with anger and he knew he could not force her to stay. She had to stay because she wanted to, because she loved him.

She got to her feet and wavered. He reached for her, but she pushed his hands away when they tried to assist her.

"Please, talk to me." His voice was low and pleading as she reached again for the bridle. Her hands stilled.

"I need to go."

She didn't look back, but she didn't mount up either. He felt hope begin to blossom.

"Where?" No answer. "Will you come back?" That was what he really wanted to know.

Turning back to him, she smiled. It was that grin he had come to hate and look forward to at the same time. That arrogant smile he had missed. "I do not know."

That pained him to hear, but he understood.

"Will you talk to me first?" He wasn't sure what he was going to say or how was he going to convince her that last night had not been as it appeared?

When she didn't answer, he stepped toward her. "Please."

Her dark eyes were full of suspicion as she looked at him. "What?" Van said wearily, her voice strained and low.

That was enough for him, even though she didn't let the reins loose. It was enough to know she would stay to listen. Now all he had to do was figure out what to say.

"I would like some answers." The answers he got might tell him what he could do to help her, to make her want to stay with him, to get her to forgive him. He sighed deeply.

"Fine. Ask away, my lord." Her voice was cold, all the earlier passion gone.

"Why did you lie to me? To all of us?" He could not hide the pain from his voice as he looked at her accusing eyes. He knew she was seeing the night before with his arms around a naked Rebeka in the library.

He would tell her how sorry he was and give her the explanation that she deserved, but first he wanted to help her. And for that he needed to know what had brought her here, to this life.

"How many enemies do you have, my lord?" she asked simply.

He shook his head. "Many, I suppose, at least at one time. Now, I do not know. Why?"

"The Dark Knight has many as well. Some in particular would do anything to see him in the ground...to see me in the ground." She smiled and patted Damien. He snorted lightly. "Now if you were a woman, would your enemies fear you? If they knew you had lied and you were weak, would they still tremble before you?" She sat on a large bale of sweet smelling hay and allowed the reins to slide through her fingers.

He noticed her hands were trembling. He wanted to take her in his arms, but he held off knowing she was not ready.

"If they discovered I was a woman, they would still fear the warrior that I was." He puffed his chest out in pride, but he understood what she meant.

She shook her head. "Did you fear me, as you would have the Dark Knight? If he had shown up at your door, would you not have treated him with more respect?"

He did not respond. He was not able to bring himself to tell her yes.

She smiled and nodded as if he had agreed. "If you found one of your enemies to have a weak spot, would you take advantage of that?"

He watched her lay her hands across her lap and pick straw off her dress.

"I did not fear you, but I did not fear that arrogant knight, either."

She looked up at his words and held his gaze. The horses around them pawed restlessly at the ground. Damien nickered, some responded in kind.

Peter walked to her side and looked down into her eyes. "And there are many who still fear you." He sat beside her, not touching for now. "But I know what you are saying, and aye, I would take any advantage I could, and being a woman is a disadvantage. No offense."

"I do not take offense to the truth, for you are right, my lord." She twisted her neck first one way then the other. It emanated a loud pop. "I could not tell anyone. Not and put someone in danger. I could not tell my men—" She took a deep breath and looked at him apologetically. "—*your* men that I was a woman."

He slid his arm around her shoulders and pulled her into him. She resisted at first and then relaxed against him. He could feel the heat of her through her dress and the first wisps of doubt began to cloud his mind. He looked at her closely and wondered if it were more than the drink.

"I did not tell them, because I feared what it would do, and I was right. They see it as a betrayal and they will no longer even look at me." Her voice broke and she cleared her throat. "If I had spoken the truth in the beginning, I would never have gotten to where I am, to who I am."

"Why did you not tell me? You should have trusted me." He jumped at the strangled laugh that erupted from her.

"Tell me when it is that you earned my trust, my lord? Then tell me what you did on the two occasions I approached you to give it to you anyway?" She dropped her eyes to her bare feet. "Once with Telpher and then in the library last night."

He followed her gaze and groaned. She had not even bothered to put on her slippers. He pushed the irritation away. "How did you get to be…" He didn't know how to finish, but there was no need for she answered anyway.

"To be what? The Dark Knight? Through a lie, my lord." She stiffened against his arm and when she shuddered, he tightened his grip on her being careful to avoid the thick bandage he could feel beneath her dress.

"From what I have figured out my mother was trapped in a marriage she did not want and sought to punish the man who forced her there."

He watched her face cloud over, her eyes drawing tight with pain. He wanted to heal her, to make her whole, to keep her safe.

"When my father found us, she sent me here to enter page training. I always thought it was to protect me." She shook her head. "But it seems I was not in need of protection."

Peter looked at her in confusion. He was sure he had not understood her correctly. "To protect you, she sent her little girl to be a knight? That is far from safe." He was enraged that a mother could treat her child in such a manner.

He started at her chuckle.

"You do not understand, my lord," she said with a growing smile.

He was going to scream if she called him my lord one more time. He was sure she was doing it just to anger him.

"I have never been a little girl. I have always been a boy. From the moment I could understand, I was told to say I was Dr. Burgess's son." She fiddled with the reins in her hand and shrugged. "I took to it like a fish to water, a bird to the sky, or so the sayings go. I was the best at everything in Junket and I was the one picked to come train, my lord."

Peter still did not agree, but he thought he understood. "Once you were here, you were no longer the best?"

"Nay, I was not." Her nose wrinkled in apparent disgust. "They would taunt me. It did not matter that I was younger by far than the majority of the boys. If I did something wrong, I would hear from them."

"I remember and I should have done something to stop it." Guilt pushed at him and rebuked him for his lack of actions.

She looked up at him with questioning eyes. "Why, my lord? You would not have for any other boy."

He had no answer and could only shake his head. "You were...a girl."

"What I was, was the best in Junket, and I was soon the best here as well. That is what I was and all I was." She spoke with a quiet dignity and pride that shook Peter to the core.

He thought about it and she was right. He had been beating himself over and over for not protecting the little girl she should have been, but he was forgetting the strong page that she actually was. It mattered not if she was boy or girl. She was strong and had been well able to take care of herself without Peter's intrusions, as she had proven many times.

"So they tormented you. That is why you hate the name?" It fell into place now and he could remember, on at least one occasion, hearing them taunting her with the name Vanessa.

She nodded her head and looked back at her hands. "I was never to be considered for knighthood since I was not a nobleman's son. I would forever be a squire and they were always there to remind me." Her voice dropped to almost a whisper of breath, the words tight with pain. "The others would chant at me, aye. 'Vanessa, Vanessa.'" Her voice took on the taunting sing-song tone of little children who are mean and spiteful "You ride like a girl, Vanessa. Van-es-sa, you throw like a girl.'"

He could not help but tighten his grip on her when she looked into his eyes. Hers were dark and haunted.

"I grew to hate that name and every weak thing it stood for. As I made myself known among the others, and they realized that I was indeed the best, they held respect for me." She smiled sadly. "You see, Vanessa represented everything I was not."

"Everything that you are still not?" He was sure he understood now. She hated being Vanessa because she was not the weak woman, not the meek little wife. He had been scared of her independence and her pride, afraid she would leave him. She would not. She was proud and strong, but she was loyal.

She nodded. "I was the best here, and I got that way fast. I earned the right to be a squire and you know the rest." She leaned her head back against his arm and closed her eyes.

Peter could see the pain and weariness in her face and wanted to take her back to her bed. Before he could do that there were a couple of things he wanted to know and he thought it best to get the answers while she was in the mood to talk. He did not know how long it would last before she shut herself back up and he did not want to miss the opportunity.

He took a deep breath. "I want to know of the woman you killed and I want to know why Richard took orders from you like you were the one in charge on the night you saved my life." It was an odd sensation to owe his life to his wife. He was the one who supposed to be keeping her protected…the one to save her, if need be. Not the other way around.

She tensed against him.

"I also want to know about your mistresses." He wanted to know more than those things, but he did not want to tire her too much. When he had the answers to those, he could tell her the things he needed to say. Things that started with I love you and I am sorry.

"Aye." She kept her eyes closed and leaned her head against his arm. She shuddered. "The woman I killed and the fact that Richard took orders from me are one and the same." Without ever opening her eyes, she quickly told of the woman and the reasons she had beaten her. Peter's heart went out to the scared young girl she had been and understood. He could not say he would not have done the same.

Her voice quivered as she continued. "I was not proud of it—am not proud of it and it haunts me to this day. I have questioned my honor, and you were right last night. I did not do it out of honor, but I would do it again."

She opened her eyes and looked at him, moving out of the circle of his arm. He tried to hold her, but she pushed his arm away.

"As to my mistresses—" She looked angry and her face was flushed. "Do I ask you about yours?"

His heart ached. He would make it up to her, for all his mistakes since she had arrived. "If you will tell me of them, I will answer anything you want to know." He would be honest with her. She was right, he had done nothing to earn her trust and it was about time that he did.

She looked at him for a moment, either measuring his honestly or debating on if it was worth it to trust him again. Either way, she must have decided in his favor because she relaxed and continued.

"They are women that have been abused, raped, or deserted. I take them in. I help them, give them money, and the protection of my name. In all ways they are my girls." She glared at him. "I just do not have sex with them in the library of my home."

Peter cringed at the snide comment and decided that it was his turn to talk, to tell her what needed to be told, for both her sake and his. He could not risk losing her, not now that he had comes to terms with who she was. He wanted to get to know the real her, not the knight, nor the fake lady. She needed to discover who she was as well, and he looked forward to the journey together.

He opened his mouth, but the long awaited explanation was cut short by shouts outside. Van pulled herself to her feet as Richard's deep voice boomed through the stable. "I do not give a damn what he said. I will see the Dark Knight, and I will see her now. Over you, around you, or through you, it makes no difference to me."

Van gasped and raced for the door. Peter followed right behind her. Her breath came in heaving gasps as she stopped at his side. "Devenroe, what is it?"

Peter waved off James Rothman, the quiet young groom, who had been stupid enough to try to stop him. Peter was just glad that he hadn't been hurt for his trouble.

He looked from Richard to a red faced and agitated Devon. "What is going on?"

"Amy is gone, my lord." Devon turned his attention to Van. "We had the men searching the castle and the grounds for her, but with no luck."

Devon looked to be on the verge of tears. Peter could see them swimming in his liquid green eyes. Looking back at the stable, it had not occurred to Peter that all the horses were saddled and ready for the training fields, but there were no warriors.

"We were on the way to get you…maybe you know where she is?" Devon asked before his voice broke completely.

Placing a comforting hand on the young man's trembling shoulder, Richard looked at her. His face held a look of worry that ripped at Peter. Richard never took his eyes off Van as he spoke "On our way to you, a boy from the village gave me this."

Van looked from Richard's reluctant gaze to the rolled parchment dangling in his hand. She took it without a word, and Peter watched her face tighten as she read the contents.

She growled thickly. "I may have been joking before, but I may just kill the next messenger."

Peter looked at her questioningly, curious of what she meant, but she did not look up from her reading.

"Who brought this?" she asked staring down at the message.

"He is just a small boy from the village. He could not know anything—"

Richard broke off as she waved off his words without looking up. The intent look on her face reminded him much of the Dark Knight that had rescued him. He could not understand how he had not seen it before.

"What did he say?" Van asked in a deep gravelly voice.

"He said, that the Dark Knight and only the Dark Knight was to get this message. He said…" He looked at Peter and then spoke carefully, guarded. "He said that the drowning man said to give it only to you."

Peter noticed her start, but she did not look up from the missive. Curious of whom the drowning man was, he forced himself to hold off on more questioning until he knew what was going on.

Van finally looked up and caught Richard's gaze. "Where is he?"

Peter wondered at the determined look on her face. She stared at Richard who shifted uncomfortably.

"Vanessa…Van, what is going on?" Peter touched her arm, the skin hot through the sleeves of her dark blue silk dress. He wondered once again, concern tightening his chest, if it was perhaps the cut on her arm that caused the fever, and the fire within her was not caused by the brandy.

"Eolian has Amy," she said simply.

Devon sucked in a painful breath and a tear escaped to slither down his reddened cheeks.

Van shot a sad smile at Devon and grasped his arm. "She is alive and well, for now."

"Why does he have her?" Peter wanted to wrap his arm around Van, but she stepped toward Richard. Peter felt no jealousy, only concern.

Van shoved the parchment into Richard's chest. "Mellie."

Richard's face paled as he opened the missive with shaking hands.

"Explain it to them while I *question* our small messenger," she said as she walked away.

"He is just a boy," Richard reminded her, but she did not respond. He read the message aloud.

        "Lady Dark Knight,

"You took something of mine, now I have done the same.

"I will not harm your new lady as long as you do as I say

"Bring me her and *my* son, and bring her alone. If I see anyone else with you, Amy will die. You know where to go."

Richard looked up and shook his head. He stared at Van's disappearing back and took a deep breath. "Melinda was only fourteen. She was pregnant, though no one knew it at the time." He looked back at Peter. "Van stole her from Eolian, put her up in a home, and took care of her and her son. Like most of her mistresses' children, the boy has Van Burgess's name."

Peter still could not fathom the amount of mistresses and children the Dark Knight had. He had always thought they were wild exaggerations.

"It was always assumed, by all but me and one other, that the child was indeed Van's." Richard continued. "Now Eolian knows it is not, that the child is his, and he wants revenge." Richard looked at the paper again.

"If the woman is in danger, that will be dealt with first." Peter waited until Richard looked back up. He caught his gaze and held it. "Send someone to get the woman and her child, and we will make a plan. Do you know where he wants her to come?" Peter tried desperately to still his thundering heart. He felt for Devon, knowing he must be terrified.

"Nay. I would say it is to the place she rescued Mellie from, but I do not know where that is." Richard's face tensed, his forehead marred with wrinkles as he thought deeply. "It was on one of the many trips that Van took alone. When she returned she had her."

"Vanessa will know. Send for Melinda and her son. Let's get the men rounded up." Peter turned to go, but Richard grasped his arm.

He shrugged regretfully. "I cannot do that, my lord."

Peter turned slowly toward him, anger peeking through the worry in his mind. "You mean you cannot or you will not?" Peter asked, trying to keep the aggravation out of his voice, but knowing he failed.

"I do not know where she is. I know where some of the others are, but I do not believe even Van knows where she is at the moment."

A few men were starting to gather near the saddled horses. They milled around unsure of what to do next. The rest of the men, Peter was certain, were still searching the grounds and the castle.

"Eolian almost found her and Van had her moved. Van was unable to get away from the armies, and the move was done through messenger. Only one person knows where she is." Richard looked around the yard and then back at Peter.

"Who?" Peter asked.

Richard just shook his head.

Peter scowled deeply. Richard set his lips in a stubborn line and shook his head again. Peter could see that he knew, but was unwilling to say. Anger sparked inside him and tried to catch hold.

He opened his mouth to speak, but shut it again as James Rothman ran from the stables yelling for his lordship.

Gripping tightly onto his narrow shoulders he gave a slight shake. "What is it my boy?"

His eyes were wide, his breath coming in dragging gasps. "That big black stallion of your wife's is gone."

Peter shook his head, trying to fight the panic that tried to swallow him whole. He closed his eyes and took a deep breath, trying to convince himself that the stallion had just wandered off. They had left him unattended, he told himself rationally. "Leave us, James."

When he opened his eyes again, James had disappeared.

A look of panic crossed Richard's face and he sucked in a deep breath. "She would not…Hell and Damnation." His face flushed of color and he turned and ran from the stables.

Peter stared for a moment and then quickly fell into step behind him. Devon followed as they ran toward the castle.

Bursting into the kitchen through the servants' entrance, Richard slid to a stop and Peter almost ran into him. "Where is the boy?"

The cook turned to him. "He has eaten and gone, sir."

"Before or after Lady Vanessa came to talk to him?" Richard asked, his breath coming in hard sharp gasps.

"Lady Vanessa has not come by, sir," she said looking at the men in confusion.

Peter turned to Richard. "What is going—"

"Outside," Richard said interrupting him and Peter did not argue. He ushered them all out the door in a rush.

Once they were away from the door, Peter pulled Richard to a stop. "What is going on?" He spoke quietly, not wanting anyone to overhear.

Richard hesitated. Peter grasped the front of his tunic and gave it a hard yank. "Start speaking, now."

Richard looked at him for a moment and then nodded.

Peter dropped his hand from his shirt. His body trembled and he could not stop it no matter how much he concentrated his will on it.

"Van will probably have my head for this," Richard said reluctantly. "There is only one man who knows where every mistress is and that includes Melinda. He is the one who gets the money to them when Van is unable to." He took a deep breath, held it, and then released it in a great whoosh.

Peter knew of this man from Van's father. He had said no one knew who the man was. Obviously Matthew was mistaken. He eyed Richard carefully and forced himself to wait.

"This is not going to be as bad as it sounds, so please listen until I am done before you lose your temper." Even with saying that, Richard took a step back.

Peter's insides rolled and he wondered how much worse this day could get. "What makes you think I am going to lose my temper?"

"The man is...Verges," Richard said carefully.

"*What*?" Peter noticed several heads turn at his shout and Grant came running toward them. He forced himself to calm.

"I said to wait. Please let me finish, my lord."

Grant stopped beside them and Peter held up his hand to forestall any comments.

Richard took a shaky breath. "Verges is the man that knows it all. She saved his life when he was drowning. He has been spying on Eolian for her ever since. He is the drowning man and he has a plan to overcome Eolian."

"How do you know this? And why have you not bloody damn well said anything before now?" Peter snapped. He was angry because Richard had come to him asking to be taken in, but he had not given him his full loyalty. He had kept things from him, important things.

Richard rubbed his temple as if a deep pain had started there. He dropped his hand and held Peter's gaze. His eyes were apologetic. "Van told me of him, in case something was to happen to her. She said if I were ever to get a message from the drowning man I was to do whatever he said." He shook his head. "I did not tell you of Verges because I made a promise to Van that I would tell no one of him."

"Why did you not tell us when you got that message?" Devon asked quietly.

Richard dropped his eyes. "I wanted to leave that to Van, but with her gone it is now left to me. I can only hope I am doing the right thing."

Peter nodded in understanding and grasped his friend's arm. Richard looked up at him and smiled weakly.

Peter did not like it. It still felt like a betrayal, but he reminded himself that he had known from the very beginning that Richard, and the men who came with him, were still loyal to the Dark Knight. The fact that *he* was now a *she* had not changed that. "Tell me what you know."

"Verges is high in the ranks of Eolian's army and he will be the one in charge of Amy. Do not fear, Devon, he will not hurt her," Richard assured him.

"Not hurt her?" Peter exploded in disbelief. "How can you say that? I know what that man has done—the rapes and the murders. He cannot be trusted—" His words were cut short as he watched the color drain from Devon's horrified face and he regretted his rash comments.

"Nay. Listen to me." Richard turned his gaze to Devon and grasped his arm. "Hear me well. He will not hurt her. Aye, he is violent and capable of all those things, but not with her." Richard dropped his hand and his gaze moved from Peter to Devon and then back again. "Verges takes care of Van's mistresses. He will not harm anyone who has her protection and aye, he can be trusted when it comes to Van and her wishes."

Devon leaned forward. "How do you know?" he demanded, his voice a hopeful whisper.

"I know because he has never hurt anyone whom she cares for. He would not betray her. He pledged his loyalty and his life to her when she risked herself to save him."

Peter could understand the feeling. He knew what it was like to owe his life to her.

Richard turned his full attention to Peter and Peter saw the determination in his gaze, the forcefulness in his stance. "I understand your position, my lord. I have questioned his intentions, and his loyalties, from the beginning. Even though Van has always trusted him, I have not," Richard said, with a growing smile. "But now I know his loyalty can be counted upon. He can be trusted."

"What makes you so sure now?" Peter asked carefully. He had seen the confidence on Richard's face and that was enough for him. He trusted Richard's judgment, but he was curious as to what had convinced him.

"He knew." Richard snorted a short bark of laughter. "He knew the whole time that she was a woman."

Peter stared at him incomprehensively.

Richard smiled. "When she saved him she was hit by a log in the water and knocked unconscious. Van told me that when she regained her senses she was by a fire—without her clothes."

Peter nodded. "If he was going to betray her, Eolian would have known she was a woman long before now."

Richard nodded.

"So we now have the problem of where Van has gone off to," Peter said. His mind whirled with possibilities, but no answers came to him.

"Do you think she left alone?" Grant asked.

Peter knew she would and that made his heart stop. He gasped for breath and felt a sharp pain as his heart lurched to a start again.

"If she does not show with Melinda and the child, what will happen?" Devon asked, his voice was weak and lost. His eyes shimmered with tears that were held by the thinnest of threads of will power.

Richard sighed. "She will not go unprepared, she will have a plan. We just need to figure out where she went."

Peter gestured for the men who had gathered to mount their steeds. He turned to tell Grant to gather the rest of the men when a movement caught his eye.

Joseph walked toward him with confidence, holding a black helm with a silver stallion emblazoned on its side.

CHAPTER 29

Van's mind spun with excitement and worry as she walked away. When she heard Richard begin to read the parchment, she quickened her pace.

She had no intention of going to see the messenger as she had claimed. She knew who it would be, the same young boy who had brought the last message, and she knew he would know nothing beyond what he had told Richard.

Instead, she took the steps into the castle and headed for her chambers. She knew she had to get herself together as quickly as she could. She would not have much time before they realized she was gone and she needed a good sized lead before Peter followed.

The cabin where she had rescued Melinda was set in the midst of a wide meadow, in the center of a box canyon. It would be impossible to get in without being seen. The cliffs to the rear of the cabin were too steep to transverse and the meadow was too flat to hide anyone approaching from the front.

The only way she had gotten Melinda out was with the help of Verges. Eolian and his men were out to loot and plunder and Verges had brought her into the woods that hid the opening of the canyon. He had killed the two men who were keeping watch with him and told Eolian that Van's men had come upon them in numbers too great to defeat.

Van had spread the word that she had come upon the cabin by accident and had not realized that it was occupied. Eolian seemed to believe it or at least had not suspected Verges, for he still continued to trust him.

Her arm throbbed painfully with each deep thrumming beat of her heart and her labored breathing was becoming bothersome. She cursed her weak body and tried to push the pain away so she could concentrate on the problems at hand.

She knew Eolian would be watching for her, but he would also have scouts out watching her back trail as well. He would assume she would have the men following her and she could only hope that Eolian's scouts would give up and return with the news of a clear trail by the time Peter came through.

She moved silently through the castle, keeping her ears and eyes open she was prepared to hide quickly if need be. The halls were teeming with servants and soldiers and she could not risk being caught.

She knew there would be no way her overbearing husband would allow her to go on her own, and she would not put Amy at risk by sending someone in her place.

Eolian's message played over and over in her mind. He had been specific that she came with just Mellie and the boy, who would now be two.

So she herself would go. That much was easy. How she was going to manage Mellie and her son she was still unsure, but she would worry about that when the time came.

She could not take Mellie even if she wanted to. She had no idea where Verges had hidden her and she would not put her in danger even if she did.

She clenched her fists tightly and pain shot up her arm. She thought of the last time she had seen Melinda's young son. He had barely been walking. Her face tightened and she swore to herself that she would never allow that innocent boy to be corrupted by the man who had sired him.

Van heard footfalls of several men echoing along the hall not far ahead. She looked carefully behind her, and then ducked into a darkened alcove.

She held herself tight against the wall and peered around the corner. There were five men walking slowly. They stopped and knocked on a door. When there was no answer they entered. Soon they stepped out and began their walk again.

At the head of the group was Marshall VanDyke, the young boy who had been terrified of horses when he had first arrived. She watched him carefully taking in his slight frame, long blonde hair and almost delicate features. From a distance he might just pass for Melinda, she thought and smiled. Though she was not looking forward to telling him that.

She had heard good things about him. He was progressing nicely on horseback and his skill with the sword was unmatched among the boys the king had sent. According to Richard, he would soon be surpassing some of the men at arms.

Marshall might be just what she needed. She was just unsure of how to get him without arousing suspicion.

She tensed and waited. The men entered the next room. She held her breath. The ache in her arm had intensified and she could feel the heat baking off of her skin.

Closing her eyes, she released her breath in a small whistle then opened her eyes at the clicking of a door. She stole a look around the corner and sighed in relief. Marshall was now in the rear. He walked slightly behind the others.

She sent up a prayer that they would not see her and pressed herself as far into the shadows as she could. They passed by her.

Leaning out as Marshall walked past, she shot her hand out, clamping it around his mouth, and yanked him into the alcove.

He fought against her and she slammed him into the wall. "Shhhh," she whispered.

He stopped struggling and stood silent.

She left her hand on his mouth and looked out. The men did not notice that Marshall was gone. They rounded a corner and disappeared from sight.

She released his mouth and waved him along. He followed silently and without question. She was relieved she did not have to make any explanations here in the hall.

She led him quickly to her chambers. The room still hung with powder and she had to step around broken shards of pottery.

"Milady?" he said in a confused voice looking around at the mess of shattered jars and the thick layer of powder that covered everything.

She ignored him, pushing the door shut and wincing as shards crunched under it. She walked toward the dressing table.

"Milady, is there something you—"

She began to unbutton the thick gown that swirled around her hips and Marshall's voice stopped in a small screech.

Van dropped the gown and when she looked up it was to the young man's back. She set her jaw obstinately and growled. "I do not have time for this, VanDyke." She glanced around the room, quickly taking stock of what she would need. "There is a trunk in the corner. At the bottom are hose, tunic and boots."

He started toward the trunk without question, but did not look at her.

"There is a sword and a long black band of leather as well. Get them for me." Van continued to remove her clothing without shame.

Hearing his gasp, she thought he had turned back to her nakedness, but when she looked at him he was still leaned over the trunk. There were dresses strung out across the floor and he had pulled the heavy chest plate out and laid it behind him.

She watched him as he stood. He turned toward her and held up the black helm with the silver destrier on it. He looked from it to her and this time did not seem to take notice the extent of her undress.

His face was bright with wonder and amazement. "You really are the Dark Knight, milady?" He looked confused and slightly alarmed. "Sir?"

"Either is fine," she said with a smile. "Just bring my clothing, then the sword and only the mail." She took a deep breath. She would like to take the armor, but knew that it would just get in the way. "There is a blade in a short leather scabbard, get it for me as well."

He approached cautiously and, with his eyes averted, held her clothing out to her. When she took them he turned back to the trunk.

Van found herself grateful for his respect, or his shyness. Whichever it might it be, it kept him from noticing the bright redness and the swelling in her arm.

She slid into her clothing and winced when it scraped painfully against her wound, but kept in the deep groan that begged to be released.

She took several deep breaths as she pulled on the long leather boots. She felt winded even dressing herself and began to question her ability to carry out her mission. She knew if she did not ride soon, she would not be able to.

Marshall returned with the heavy chain mail.

"Put it on." She was pleased when he did so quickly and without question. It made her mission easier without having to fight or explain her actions. She strapped the dagger scabbard around her thigh and pulled her dagger free. She looked at the glittering jewels in its hilt and shook her head.

She laid it on the dressing table. She did not want to risk losing it. She went through to Peter's chambers and took one of his extra daggers from the drawer where he kept the key to her door.

When she returned, Marshall was standing waiting, with her sword held out to her.

She pushed her doubts away and strapped the sword's scabbard around her waist cinching it tight across the tunic. Without the bindings she usually wore her breasts pressed against the tunic, stretching the material taunt. She no longer felt exposed and vulnerable as she had when her father had come to pick her up in Junket. She now felt a cool wave of freedom crash over her.

She beckoned him closer. "You cannot question me on this. What I say goes if we want to get Amy back."

He watched her intently. "You know who has her, milady?"

His inspection of her made her nervous, but he did not argue and that was all she could ask for. "Aye, but I will tell you on the way. Now we need to go."

He held a short leather scabbard out to her. She took it and stared at it momentarily.

She gently pulled the short dagger from it. The dagger was without a hilt, instead only having a smooth dip where the thumb and forefinger could grasp. It was only efficient as a thrown weapon.

Generally she wore the dagger in her hair but it was awkward to get in, requiring her to braid her hair around it. She didn't have the luxury of time on her hands to accomplish that.

She scowled for a moment and looked down at her booted feet. She was happy to be wearing the boots again. With each piece of clothing she donned she felt more and more like her old self.

Only there was a difference, she felt free. She didn't have to worry about who knew, didn't have to be concerned and always on guard that someone would find out her secret.

She took a deep cleansing breath and said goodbye to both the Dark Knight and the meek lady.

It felt good to be free. She could be herself, as soon as she discovered who that was exactly.

Her gaze caught on her thick cleavage, bound tight by the tunic and belt, just a small amount of flesh peeking through the V-cut neck and she thought she might have another option besides her hair.

The dagger glittered in the sunlight peering through the window behind her as she checked its condition. It was well sharpened and had been cleaned before being put in the trunk.

Marshall stared raptly at the strange weapon. "Where did you get such a thing, milady?"

"I had it commissioned by a smith when I saved his daughter." It had been Melinda's father's show of gratitude. Her father would be happy to have her back, and not hidden away. "It has always ridden beneath the helm of the Dark Knight, hidden in my wide braid, but I have come up with something better." She slipped it back into its sheath and grinned.

Marshall sucked in an audible breath as she slid the weapon into the dark cleft between her breasts. Its tip stopped at the belt cinched around her narrow waist.

She ignored his look and walked to the door, pushing at pottery jars with the tip of her boot as she went. She shoved one over and smiled. It was busted down the side but it still contained much powder.

She picked it up and looked over her shoulder at him and guessed him to be about the size of Amy. She walked to the trunk and retrieved her helm.

She nodded to him and led him quickly to Amy's chambers.

They met no one along the way for which she was relieved. She ducked into Amy's room and waved for him to follow, closing the door firmly behind her. Walking to the small window, she looked out over the courtyard.

Richard still stood beside Peter and Devon and they appeared to be deep in conversation. Heaviness bore down on her as she wondered if she could ever make Richard understand why she had done what she did. She pushed away the unpleasant thoughts and concentrated only on the tasks at hand.

Pleased that things were going so quickly, she walked back to the center of the room, laid the powder jar and her helm on Amy's bed, and opened the small trunk at the end of it.

She dug through the clothing in it until she found what she hoped would fit him. "Put this on."

It was the first time he had baulked at her instructions, and anger pricked at her at the disobedience. Marshall just looked at the dress she held out to him. "Milady?"

She shook it at him. He still did not take it. "Now."

This is what she had feared would happen. That people would look at her and forget who they were dealing with. That they would forget that the Dark Knight was a deadly and dangerous creature. It would be easy for them to think of her as just a woman now, but that thinking would get them killed.

She had once dreaded that ignorant attitude, but now she found herself wishing for it. She sent a quick prayer to the gods that Eolian would make the same mistake.

For her enemies to doubt her was one thing, but for her men to do so was not acceptable. She arched her brow and scowled and allowed the anger to sweep through her. She stepped up to him and held the dress under his nose. "I do not like to repeat myself," she growled fiercely.

He looked into her face and swallowed hard. Stepping back quickly, he took the dress and slid into it without further hesitation

Van helped him to fasten the buttons. "Sit." She pushed him down on the trunk.

He grimaced and leaned back when she dipped her hand into the tub of powder.

She raised her brow, but relaxed when he did not argue. She applied it thickly to his face. Then she quickly braided her hair, her arm throbbing painfully. She wrapped it in the thick leather band. "Is Ebro saddled and ready?"

"Aye, milady. He is saddled."

"I need to see to someone. There is something I need done. Meet me in the stairwell." She ignored the panicked look on the lad's makeup covered face. Whether it was for her safety or worry that he might be seen dressed as a day maid, she didn't know nor did she have time to care.

As he went one way, throwing a hooded cape over his shoulders, she made her way to the nursery. She prayed the one she wanted was in there.

Pushing open the door she let out a sigh of relief when Joseph jumped to his feet. Before he could let out the scream, she shushed him. "Quiet."

"Milady, did they find Miss Amy?" His voice was tight and he looked at his feet as he spoke.

She quickly walked to him and dropped to her knee beside him.

Her head spun and her breathing was labored. The pain was ravaging her now and it was making her thoughts hard to process.

She knew she had to hurry before the fever made it impossible to function. They still had to get free of the castle, and then it was at least half a day's hard ride to the cabin.

"I want to tell you I am sorry, my lad. It was uncalled for to treat you as I did. If you forgive me, I shall require your help." She smiled sweetly at him when he looked up.

"Will it get Amy back?" At her nod he jumped to his feet. "I will help you, milady."

"I want you to talk to Peter as soon as they realize I am gone." She waited for his nod. "I need you to tell them where I am going. You have to remember this. It has to be exact. Can you remember it?"

When he said aye, she told him the directions to the cabin and made him repeat it back to her, twice.

"Tell him I am fine and I know what I am doing, but I needed to get there alone first. Give him this." She handed him, what she hoped would remind Peter that she would be fine.

With one more repetition of the directions and a run through of what he was supposed to tell Peter, Van left him with the Dark Knight's helm and went to meet Marshall.

At the stables, Marshall drew Van into the stall with Ebro. "Milady, you are ill." He looked at her in concern. "Wherever we are going, it is not a good idea for you to travel."

"Silence." She looked out the door and watched the men milling around. Richard. Peter, and Devon had stepped closer together and Richard was shaking his head stubbornly.

She was sure he was at the end of his tale and her time was almost up. Stalking around the stables, she tried to get her foggy mind to focus on the problem.

Van walked first one way and then back, suddenly coming to a stop. She smiled. "Get me two swords from the smithy." Marshall left at a run.

A large, yet soft horse blanket was draped across bags of grain. The sturdy burlap bag of grain was just the size of a small child and once she had it wrapped in the colorful blanket she thought it could work.

At least, as long as no one looked closely. She pushed that negative thought away and focused on the things she had to accomplish.

When Marshall came running in with two freshly made swords, she pushed them into the sack. He mounted and with some difficulty she managed to hand him the heavy grain sack that would be his "child," swords ensconced inside, and settled his skirts around him. Leading his horse, as well as Damien, out the rear entrance she mounted.

During the hard push through the woods and into the surrounding area, she explained her plan. She needed a woman and a child. He now fit that image. "When we get to the cabin, there will be a big and not-so-nice-looking man, more than likely in a hooded cloak. He is on our side, do not kill him."

Marshall nodded, but said nothing. He kept looking at her closely. She felt like screaming at him that she was fine, but she held her tongue and her temper.

"If all goes well, he will be the one to come to us. When we get there, just follow his lead and mine." And hopefully we will get out alive, she thought, but did not add.

The ride was hard and tiring and she allowed Damien to have his head. Cooped up in the stall for so long, he was excited to be out and free. He tossed his head and whinnied. As he raced across the plains, the pounding of his hooves on the hard packed ground tore through her.

Her head was beginning to throb unmercifully. Double vision swam before her eyes. She looked with weary disillusion at the gathering clouds off in the distance. Black and threatening, they matched her mood. She repressed a shudder of worry, concerned for herself and the raging fever that gripped her.

Having no room in her mind for self-analysis, she pushed the doubts away. She had to stay focused on Amy.

She prayed for strength. The life of a knight was deeply spiritual and through it all a true knight held to the code of honor and the belief of God. She prayed now as she never had before.

Prayed for the safety of her loved ones, prayed that the soldiers would find her in time, and prayed that she would not die until Amy was safe.

Van caught a small movement off to her left. A scout was hidden, not quite deep enough to be missed by her experienced eye. She slowed the horses.

They were close. They had made good time, but it would do no good to get too far in front of the rescuing army. That was if everything had gone well at the castle and there was a rescuing army on the way. *Please let Joseph remember it all.*

"There is one scout, keep your eye out for more," she whispered over to him. Then in a louder voice she added, "I am sorry Mellie. I know it is a hard pace. Is he all right?"

Taking her cue, Marshall peered under the edge of the blanket and made a response in a quiet whisper. "There is another scout off to the right, up on the hill, milady."

She barely glanced that way. "It will not be much longer. I am sorry about this, but I will get you out of it," she said for the benefit of those listening.

The trees were starting to thin. The thick underbrush swept down to the soft, waving grass that surrounded the small cabin. From where they were, Van could hear the rumbling of the water crashing to the rocks beneath the awesome falls at the back of the cabin. She could feel the mist cooling the air.

It felt good on her overheated skin.

When the cabin came into view, Van felt the earth drop from beneath her. In all directions she saw men. There must have been at least a hundred. Verges had told her there were forty at last count, but that Eolian had more men wanting to join him.

Evidently they had done so. "Whatever you do, boy, keep your wits about you. If you lose your head over this, you will indeed lose it. Do you understand?"

"Aye, milady," he whispered.

Van saw Verges standing in the doorway of the small building. Beside him was Eolian. Her blood chilled.

"The big man in the door is the friend I spoke of." Van glanced again at Verges and then turned her gaze to the knight that had been a thorn in her side ever since she had become the Dark Knight.

"Halt. Stay where you are, *my lady*." Eolian's voice echoed across the waving grasses of the meadow. "It definitely is my lady, is it not? I was told, but to see you…" He moved down the two small steps and swaggered toward her.

"Aye, it is," she said proudly and held her head high.

"There is not much difference, I must say. Except I am sure I would have remembered a chest of that magnitude." Eolian turned his smiling face at Marshall.

Van held her breath. He looked right to be Melinda and the bundle looked to be the size of a two year old. Their success all depended on Eolian's belief that Marshall was Melinda.

"My lady, drop your weapons," Eolian shouted.

She released her breath. So far the plan seemed to be working.

"Show me Amy first," she growled back at him.

"You always were the arrogant little brat." He shook his head, but he gestured to Verges.

Verges stepped inside the cabin and returned with Amy. She tried to run, but Verges yanked her back into his chest and held her tight.

"Now as you can plainly see, I have kept to my end of the bargain. She is alive. Minus a few bruises, she is well." He laughed good-naturedly. "Not that she did not find enjoyment here, aye, Verges?"

"She had better not be hurt. If you have let your demon defile her, I will see your head on the end of a spike." Knowing Verges would not touch her mattered not. She needed to act as Eolian would expect her to. And anyone knowing her, as a man or a woman, knew that her temper was never on a very sturdy leash.

"Now, my lady, dismount and drop your weapons."

Van dropped to the ground, her mind now on what needed to be done. She could feel the fever and pain rushing through her, but it felt as if it was happening to someone else.

She hardly registered the ripple of pain that ran through her infected arm as she hit the ground.

"Dismount my future bride as well, Vanessa." He spit the name out like it was a bitter root.

She drew her sword, spinning to face him. This time her anger was very real.

"Vanessa, do you plan to take on my entire army with just a whore and a bastard child? Do you, Vanessa?"

Taking a deep breath, she tried to focus on what was important: Amy and her safe return. That was all. Reluctantly, she dropped the sword to the ground.

Van helped Marshall from the horse. He cradled the heavy sack to his chest. His dismount was awkward with the heavy weight of the grain and he had to adjust the blanket. It made the charade more believable.

"Drop your dagger as well, Vanessa." Eolian's sing-song chant tore through her. He gestured to Verges who then pushed Amy into another soldier's arms and began to lumber toward her.

Cringing at the name, Van pulled the dagger from its home at her thigh and dropped it to the ground.

Seeing several men rush forward, Van scooped the dagger back up quickly and grabbed Marshall, pulling him in front of her. Wrapping her forearm around his throat she pushed the dagger to the blanket he cradled before him.

He tucked his hand inside the brilliantly colored throw, his arm trembling. She tightened her grip on him, shaking her head against his. She did not want him to rush into anything.

"One man will come, one only, if you wish to even see your child." She sent what she hoped were nervous looks at Verges, who had stopped not far from her.

"That man there can come." She pointed to a small, less threatening man off to the left. "Then you will send Amy down and we will exchange women."

As she spoke, she saw the two scouts ride past her. She released a nervous breath. It appeared she had wasted enough time.

Eolian listened carefully to the scouts and began to smile.

He looked at her. "You really came alone. I knew you would. You were never smart enough to fool me."

She tensed and felt Marshall shake his head lightly. She struggled against the anger that rushed through her. She wanted this man dead and she wanted to be the one to kill him.

"One man is fine, but it will be the man I chose." He glanced at Verges. "Verges, check them."

Saying nothing, Van allowed him to check under the blanket. He ran his hand across the two sword hilts and smiled. Then he checked under the brown woolen hood Marshall wore.

"Good," he said and stepped away.

No one moved as Verges stopped beside Eolian and spoke quietly.

Van waited patiently. Verges stepped away and wrapped his arm around Amy.

Eolian began to smile. It was a deadly smile. Marshall shuddered and Van could only hope that he would hold it together during his first battle.

CHAPTER 30

V an watched with growing concern as Verges led Amy closer to her. His grip was tight on her arm and he pulled her back when she tried to yank away from him.

Van took in the ghastly paleness of Amy's face, her torn and soiled dress, and clenched her fists so tightly her arms began to tremble. Amy looked at her with fearful eyes that were puffy and red from tears. Guilt hit Van so hard that it nearly knocked her over.

It was her fault that Amy was hurt. Tears clogged her own throat as she struggled to remain still.

Van cringed at the dark marks across Amy's face. She wanted to believe that they were not strike marks. Yet having seen enough of them in her life, she knew them for what they were.

There were bruises on Amy's arms and on her neck and her hair was in tangled disarray.

Anger made it hard for Van to hold her place. Pain trembled through her, and she fought her first instinct which was to draw her sword and start swinging. She could not lose it now. *Oh, Peter, please be on your way*, she pleaded silently.

As Verges led Amy toward her, Van watched the men inch their way forward. Eolian was not going to allow the trade, but she had already known that and was prepared.

She tightened her arm around Marshall, wrapped her fingers tightly into the blanket, and tensed. "Get ready." It was just a breath against Marshall's ear, but his body grew taut in response.

A bare nod of his head indicated that he was. She could feel the pent up energy quivering through him.

Never taking her gaze off of Verges, she waited. She slowed her breathing and closed her mind to anything except the men coming closer to her as she watched them from the corner of her eye.

Verges looked quickly at the three men that were coming forward. He smiled and flicked back his hood.

When Verges was two strides from the horses, the men rushed them. Verges pushed Amy into the arms of a tall and lanky warrior with bright blonde hair. Then he leapt for Van.

He moved quickly, but not quick enough to stop her attack.

Van flung the dagger into the retreating back of the blonde, his body falling to the ground as Amy jerked free of his loosening grasp.

Marshall stepped away from Van. The blanket whirled in a colorful blur as Van yanked it free of the cumbersome grain sack. She grasped the hilt of a sword and in one fluid movement both Van and Marshall pulled the weapons free. The sharp blades sliced through the thick burlap. Grain exploded into the air in a spray of kernels and dust. It thickened the air clouding their vision and invading their nostrils.

Amy rushed toward Van, weaving around the men that reached for her. Verges lunged at her, his hand closing around her dress. But let his fingers slide over the soft wool and cursed dramatically as she rushed past him.

Van turned to see Marshall pushing his sword through the protruding stomach of a man swinging a mace at him.

Van shoved Amy toward Marshall and screamed, "Get her out of here."

He turned in time to catch her. "Milady." He tossed his charge onto Ebro's back. Her hands turned white as she grasped the coarse mane of the snorting stallion. Then he turned back to Van.

She swung her sword at one of the men.

"Milady," Marshall said, taking a step toward her and raising his sword to assist her.

"Damn it, get her the hell out of here." She swung her sword again at fierce looking warrior who came at her relentlessly. Her strikes were weak and pathetic compared to her normal blows. The vibrations of the impacts caused her to moan loudly as they ripped through her infected arm.

Anger stabbed at her like a stray thrust of a sword. Rage at her own illness and at Marshall for his stubborn insistence on remaining. She opened her mouth to scream at him once again, but nothing came out.

A grateful pride soothed her as Verges charged at Marshall. Marshall finally flung himself onto Ebro's back behind Amy and kicked him into motion. Van would remember to discipline him later if she lived to get the chance.

She ignored Amy's scream of terror as Marshall raced to safety.

Van's sword found its mark and the man before her finally fell. Another man rushed her. Verges grabbed her. He wrestled the heavy weapon from her. She struggled against his strength, and felt hers leaving her rapidly. She tried to put up a good show for Eolian's benefit, but could do little more than lean heavily into Verges's massive chest.

With Amy now safe, the throbbing pain threatened to drag her into darkness. Men came at her from all sides, with weapons drawn, and she gave up the pretense of fighting.

"Amy." Verges's panicked word cut through the gathering fogs like a bolt of lightning.

She forced her mind to focus and looked up. Her breath caught. Marshall was fighting with a man on one side. A redheaded soldier rushed them from the other, his hands outstretched to rip Amy from the protective arms of the young man who fought valiantly for her life.

"Let me loose for a moment." Her voice trembled and she hoped she had the strength left to help them. She began to struggle with all the power she could muster.

Verges allowed his grip to loosen and then he lost his hold on her completely just as the man's hands grasped Amy's arm.

Amy screamed, struggling frantically. Van drew the small handleless blade from between her breasts. The cold steel glittered in the sunlight, light spinning off of it as it sailed across the still air. The man fell to the ground, the blade buried completely into his chest.

Marshall's sword found its mark on the second man and they were free. He spurred Ebro heavily in the sides. The horse lunged forward, disappearing into the tree line.

Verges grasped her tightly against him once again. She smiled, hearing Eolian's enraged scream, as the destrier bearing its two passengers disappeared into the woods.

"Get them!"

Warriors jumped onto steeds and fell into pursuit.

Van slumped against Verges, her head lolling listlessly.

"What do we do now?" His whisper caressed the top of her head.

"Wait." Her voice was weak and trembling. It was the thing she hated the most, but they had nothing else to do but wait. "And pray."

Peter led his army through the trees carefully following the directions given to him by Joseph. He had recited his lines carefully and handed Peter the helm. Peter's heart had dropped.

Now as they went through endless trees, he was beginning to fear that Joseph had gotten it wrong.

He turned to speak his concerns to Richard and Grant when a heavy crashing came through the underbrush not far ahead of them. He shot his hand up, calling for a halt.

Ebro burst through the shadows and Peter gasped. Upon his back was what looked like Marshall VanDyke, but he was dressed in a bright floral gown and his face was thick with powder. Peter's shock was short lived as he realized why the young squire must be dressed as he was.

Van had found her Melinda. He wondered quickly what they had used for her son, but the sight of Amy clinging desperately to Marshall and hiding her face in the ruffles of his dress pulled his mind to more important issues.

Marshall glanced at Peter, but barreled straight for Devon. Before anyone even had the thought to speak, Marshall shoved Amy away from him and threw her into Devon. He caught her and pulled her onto his lap. His arms flew around her and she began to cry.

"Get her out of here. Take her home, *now!*" Marshall screamed and, without awaiting a response, wheeled his horse around. The young man who had been so backwards and shy only a week ago screamed at Peter as he rode past. "Lady Van is weak with fever. She is ill."

The last words floated back at Peter, his fears coming to life. His heart fluttered and threatened to stop, but Peter ignored it. He kicked Jackal hard and took chase after the fleeing Marshall. He heard the thundering horse beats of the steeds, the snorting of excited horses telling him that his men followed close behind him.

Peter watched with pride as Marshall slid his sword into the saddle scabbard. Standing in the stirrups, urging his mount to race even faster, he pulled the gown and cloak over his head.

There was a moment of concern when he almost unseated himself in the process, but then the soft material disappeared beneath the pounding hooves of his horse and Marshall was seated once more.

The young lad, brave beyond what anyone had given him credit for, pulled his weapon free once more and led the charge through the trees. No hesitation was now evident and Peter was sure he was well on his way to becoming a great leader.

He saw a large group of horses racing toward them. The riders saw his approaching army and wrenched hard on the reins, wheeling their mounts around and racing back the way they had come.

Peter felt as if his life was violently ripped from his still conscious body as his horse broke the tree line. Standing in the center of a hundred soldiers was his wife, dressed as a man and trapped in the unswerving embrace of Verges with Eolian standing at his side.

A multitude of doubts swam through Peter's mind. What if they were wrong about Verges? What if the man was not as trustworthy as Richard believed? How would he live his life without the woman he loved?

As he watched his wife and tried to push away doubts, Van slumped in the big man's arms. Peter's mind froze and his body went numb. Every nerve felt set aflame, as if a small ember had caught in the dry grasses of his emotions, as he took in the flush of her face. He urged more speed from Jackal.

Jackal snorted and tossed his head and, extending his neck and lengthening his stride, gave over the extra speed that Peter asked of him.

Verges's arms tightened around Van as she collapsed against him. "She is ill." He had never felt panic before, and as the strange emotion rampaged his system, he shuddered. He did not know what he would do without her.

Eolian looked carefully at her and then back at the approaching army. Swords began to clang loudly echoing off the steep walls of the canyon behind them.

Eolian screamed for a retreat and turned to Verges. "Bring her," he said and fled in the direction of his horse.

"What do I do?" Verges looked to her for orders, alarmed to see the glazed pain in her eyes. He could feel the heat of her smooth skin burning through his clothing and she hung heavily. He was afraid she would not answer and looked at Peter.

"Take me. We cannot risk him getting away." Her breath came in deep gasps and her voice was a bare whisper. "Take Damien, with me along he will allow it."

"Van, you are not well," he said, his voice catching in his tight throat.

"Nay, and if I die and he gets away, it will all be for naught."

He knew she should not be moved, but he also knew she was right. He carried her to Damien's side and mounted. He kicked him into motion and pushed the horse hard to catch up to Eolian.

He leaned forward urging her mount to even greater speed.

Her voice whispered against his cheek. "It is our job to slow them. No matter what happens..." Her voice was becoming almost too low for him to hear over the pounding of the horses' hooves and the screaming of men and swords.

Verges came up beside Eolian as she spoke again. "No matter what happens...slow them long enough for Peter to catch..." Her body fell limp and her head jerked erratically with each jolting stride of the destrier.

"Van!" The word came out as a terrified plea as the warrior he held was lost to him. A deep sense of pain and loss gripped him and his mind crumpled. He held her tightly against him and blinked back tears that had not threatened him since he was a child.

Eolian looked at Van's now limp form, her head jolting with each deep plunge Damien made. "Is she dead?" he screamed over the pounding of the hooves, over the shouts of the men.

Rage filled Verges at the sound of Eolian's voice. He was the cause of all of this. Verges fought the urge to fling himself off the horse and throw the man to the ground. But that would help no one, so he forced himself to keep his saddle beneath him.

He felt her fever-heated neck but was unsure, with the jolting ride, if he felt anything or not. His heart constricted with something he had never felt before. It was not a pleasant feeling, not something he wanted to feel again.

Verges was terrified. He could not bear to think of what that rending feeling in his throat and chest would become if she were actually dead. "I do not know." The words sounded lost, pitiful, even to his own ears.

He tried desperately to keep her dead weight against him. Her lolling body whipped around and slowed Damien as he fought against the unsteady weight on his back. He bumped into Eolian's horse several times, hindering the progress they were making.

Verges was happy with the slowing pace, but Eolian was not. "This cannot go on. I have no need of her now." Without a word of warning he grasped the thick black braid, and tore her from Verges's grip.

Verges barely held in a scream of horror as she was ripped from his arms. He tried to catch her, but the off-balanced weight nearly pulled him from the saddle. Verges's mind screamed as pain tore through his head. He could do nothing but watch as her body hit the hard ground. Kicked once by a following mare, she rolled over the side of a long wet embankment.

A burning hatred ate its way through all of Verges's good intentions. He cared no more for anything but revenge. His hands itched to be around the throat of the man who had caused all of this.

Peter and his army were lost from Verges' thoughts as was the need to defeat Eolian's army.

Leaning toward Eolian, seeing nothing but the burning white rage before him, he reached for the man's throat, but the image of Van disappearing over the edge of the ravine stayed his hands.

Pain and fear brushed away the deadly webs that rage had spun, clouding his mind. Van still needed him. He sent up a desperate prayer to a God he had never believed in, that she had not hit the water, and tried to think of a way to quickly stop Eolian, without getting himself killed.

That would do nothing to help his lady. If they got away or if he was killed, Peter might look for days before he found her. With the fever that already raged her system, she would be dead before then.

Damien, the Damned Beast, true to his name solved Verges's dilemma of how to slow Eolian's army. Suddenly bereft of his mistress's comforting scent, of her sudden loss to him, he panicked.

Fighting desperately against the reins, Damien took the bit into his teeth and refused to release it. He tried to turn back and slammed into Eolian's steed, throwing them both off balance.

Then Damien staggered in the other direction, slamming into the horse that flanked him on that side. That horse stumbled and fell into the dense underbrush. Damien struggled to keep his footing, screamed in frustration, and began to buck.

Verges held tight and smiled when he heard the screams of panic begin to sound among the thundering horses behind him. They picked up Damien's terrified scent and herd mentality hit the animals. They began to fight amongst themselves, biting and kicking, throwing more than one rider to the dirt.

Verges battled for control of Damien, throwing him once more into Eolian. Both men hit the ground, rolling hard.

Peter had watched as Verges yanked on Damien's reins and threw himself into Eolian's steed.

He yelled for his men to hurry as Verges and Eolian hit the ground. Excitement and fear fought for control of his senses and boiled in his blood as they battled.

Eolian was on his feet instantly and began to run. Damien slid to a stop. His chest heaved and his thick neck was slick with sweat from the hard run. He turned sharply and nearly lost his footing on the loose rocks.

Peter fought a deep sense of dread as Damien thundered past him. Peter looked around quickly for Van, but did not see her. Peter had seen Verges pull Van onto the horse and now there was no sign of her. He forced himself to go forward and tried his best to push her and the panicked stallion from his thoughts to concentrate on the battle at hand.

He led his men into the swarming mass of confused and terrified horses and took advantage of the panic that swirled through them. Metal clanged loudly as swords were drawn and thrust.

Relief touched Peter as Verges drew his sword against Eolian's men and began to fight.

Screams rent the late afternoon air. Blood-curdling cries raged as men fell beneath heavy steel.

Warriors fell around him, but Peter focused on Eolian, turning his fear for Van into rage and concentrating all his strength on capturing him. He relentlessly hounded him until finally, with Peter's contingent of men on one side and the tall jagged walls of the canyon on the other, Eolian had no choice but to turn and fight.

With a deep throated battle cry, Eolian lunged at him. Peter swung his sword in return, parrying the swift and hard thrusts.

His blows fell hard, his anger and pain giving him strength he did not know he possessed. His thoughts returned to Van, and he knew time was precious. He had to find her, and he had to find her soon. She was ill and now she was lost somewhere.

He threw caution to the wind and attacked ruthlessly, not giving quarter until Eolian faltered from exhaustion. Peter swung his sword hard once more. Eolian's feet slipped in the loose rocks that littered the ground at the bottom of the walls. He fell to the ground with a defeated groan, and Peter propped his sword against the man's heaving chest.

Peter's arms shook from the battering they had taken. His legs felt weak and useless below him.

He heaved in painful gasps of air. Looking around, he noticed that the battles nearby were slowing. There were several of Peter's men still in hand to hand combat, but with others joining them, Eolian's men were surrendering quickly.

He looked down at Eolian and shuddered. "Where is my wife?"

Eolian laughed weakly.

Peter pushed the sword firmly against his chest and Eolian's laughter died.

"Kill me and you will never find her," he wheezed, his breathless laughter turning to gasps.

Several men had surrounded Peter. He glanced at them. Their faces, smeared with sweat, dirt, and blood, held the look of joyful exhilaration of victory. He wanted to feel that same elation, but could not. Not until he had his wife in his arms and had convinced himself that she was fine.

"Take him, secure him tightly. And if he moves, or tries to escape, cut off something."

"What, my lord?" Richard's voice echoed with seriousness.

"Anything that dangles."

Eolian's face drained of color, and his breathless laughter seemed to choke him. Peter smiled at him and walked away.

Looking around at the men taken as prisoners and at the dead on the ground, Peter shuddered. He had hoped his days of war were over, that he had seen the last of the senseless killing.

Relief surged through him when he noted that none of the dead were his. He looked through his men taking measure of the wounded.

His heart ached for Van as his mind took stock off his surroundings. He needed to find her. He looked carefully through his men for the uninjured and the injured that were still able to ride. He counted the men who were able to start searching and was pleased with the high number.

Sounds of a struggle pulled him from his thoughts. He turned and his gaze quickly found Verges holding a struggling man in his arms.

Peter did not recognize the man at first and rushed forward. He was jerked to a stop. He spun around raising his sword as he went.

Gary Puelo raised his hands in front of him. "My lord," he said, his voice shaky.

Peter relaxed and dropped the tip of his sword to the ground.

"That is Ryan Deumount. Pray, wait."

Peter turned back to the two struggling men and waited. He could feel the pain and anger that radiated from Gary. He knew in his heart he should stop Verges, knowing full well he meant to kill Ryan, but instead he placed a comforting hand on Gary's shoulder.

Many of Peter's men gathered around to watch the final clash of might. Verges appeared not to notice.

His thick hand wrapped around Ryan's neck. "Verges," Ryan whispered in a ragged and pained voice. "Stop, help me get away and we will free the other—"

Peter grinned as his words were cut off. His face turned an angry red color as Verges leaned closer to him. "You hurt my lady, my Van. No one will get away with that." His voice was thick with rage. He shook

Ryan in his hands like a rag doll. "You should suffer severely, but since I do not have the time I shall have to make due."

With a quick thrust of his broadsword he gutted the man from groin to neck Blood spilled onto his leather boots, soaking his cloak. "No one lays a hand on my Van."

His growl was so threatening that Peter stepped back. He realized as he glanced around that he was not the only one. All his men had stepped away.

Peter took a deep breath and walked toward him, Richard and Grant at his side. Their boots crunched in the small pebbles. Verges dropped Ryan's decimated body and spun on them. His sword came up defensively.

He held the dripping sword toward them, but did not make an aggressive move. He simply waited.

Peter stepped forward until his chest was almost touching the blood stained tip of the wavering sword. "Where is Vanessa?"

Color drained from Verges features, and he slammed his sword into his scabbard. "I do not know where she fell." He raced for the closest horse to him, lunged for his reins, and jerked the stallion around even as he mounted.

Peter's mind flooded with fear. What would he do if they did not find her? Not waiting to see which of his men would follow, he mounted Jackal and trailed behind Verges as he rushed back the way they had come.

Peter glanced behind him and saw at least a dozen men in tow. He sent up a prayer that they would find his precious wife.

Damien was pacing at the edge of a deep embankment. He stopped, looked over the edge, and whinnied loudly. Peter sighed in relief.

Verges nearly threw himself from his mount's back even before the steed had fully stopped. Then he half fell, half slid over the edge of the embankment and disappeared.

Peter jumped from Jackal and raced to the edge, his heart beating so hard it vibrated through his ears, drowning out every other sound.

He looked over the side and his stomach clenched. Fighting nausea, he watched Verges at the bottom, pulling Van out of the freezing river.

Peter started down the bank as Verges lifted her into his arms and begin to rock from side to side.

Peter slid to a stop at his side and reached for her neck. He pressed hard into it, his eyes filling with tears when he felt nothing. A deep aching pain wrenched at his heart.

A deep wail of agony began to well within him and then suddenly he felt something beneath his trembling fingers. His heart stopped and he held his breath.

A tear slid down his cheek and he pressed his fingers harder against her. He waited. Then there it was. Another small jump under his finger. His breath released in sighed of relief so strong he started to cry.

He looked up into Verges's pained brown eyes, so filled with love and fear that he placed a hand on the man's massive forearm. "Her pulse is weak, but it is there." He ran his hand over and over across her cheek as he had three years ago, but what was once warm and smooth skin was now cold and clammy. "She is just so cold, deathly cold."

Verges stood with her in his arms and cradled her to his chest. He turned to look up the steep embankment, his face setting in a tight line of determination.

Peter followed his gaze up the muddy wall before them. He took a deep breath, losing himself in an overwhelming sense of dread and failure.

Peter looked back at Van and resisted the urge to take her, even though he wanted nothing more than to wrap his arms around her and never let go. He knew if he did, he would sink to the ground and never move. And that would not help her.

He pushed the tears away and tried to concentrate on getting her out of the ravine. Falling apart in self-pity was the worst thing he could do.

He reached across, touched her cold face one more time, and turned away. The mud of the high wall was steep and slippery. It had taken skill to make it down. He would never make it up with her, no one would.

Richard slid down the bank. He laid his hand upon her face.

It scared Peter how pale she was. Paler than that dreaded powder had made her he thought.

"How do we get her up?" Richard asked dropping his hand to his side.

Peter shook his head. He did not know and that terrified him. He watched as Verges handed her limp body to Richard.

Peter looked up at his men. There were at least a dozen standing looking down into the deep pit. One man would not be able to get her up, but many might.

Verges pulled off his cloak, draped it across her, and began to tuck it under her.

Peter took some of her weight in his arms and between the three of them they soon had her wrapped tightly in the woolen cloak that was still warm from Verges's body heat.

She began shivering so badly that Peter was beginning to think his idea of rescue was too late.

"I want all the men to take a position on the embankment. It is slippery and unstable, but we are going to pass her up." His trembling voice sent the men into action.

He could see his pain and fear reflected in their faces as they took unstable footholds down the bank.

He turned to Richard and smiled, or tried to. "She will be fine, she cannot be otherwise." His eyes stung with tears that threaten to fall once more. "The Dark Knight is an irritating brat and is too stubborn to be anything but fine."

With the men in place, Peter and Verges made their way up the ladder of men, hand after hand assisting them to the grassy bank above. "Hand her up."

Carefully, from arm to arm, they handed her up. Peter's heart slipped into his stomach every time one of the men would slip in the thick sludge. Hands would grab and stabilize, but Peter did not draw an easy breath until Van made it to safety.

Verges took her at the top. Peter mounted Jackal, who pawed restlessly at the grass. Verges handed her to Peter and quickly mounted Damien.

Peter let out a tight breath, not knowing he had been holding it until she was safe in his arms.

He spurred homeward. Peter had never been more afraid in his life. Her shivers became more violent as the day raged on.

He wanted nothing more than to stop and just hold her, but he kept on. He had to get her to the doctor.

The hours passed until he was finally at home. With Van in his arms he mounted the stairs to their chambers, unmindful of the thick slimy trail of mud he left across the clean rushes.

He took her to the bed that he had not shared with her the last few days, all because of his pride and stupidity.

CHAPTER 31

The surgeon quietly examined Van as Peter watched over her with a growing sense of dread. The doctor said nothing as he listened to her chest and her back. Said nothing as he smelt her breath and then began to scrub her arm.

He pulled the stitches from the angry red gash and cleansed it well.

Peter watched all this and barely contained the need to yell at the doctor, to grasp him by the hair, and scream at him to say something, anything. He held back, knowing the doctor didn't even want him in the room, but Peter had refused to leave.

Finally, when Peter was sure he was at the end of his patience, the doctor turned to him. "I scrubbed her arm. It is still draining infection, so it must be kept clean and as dry as possible. I will replace the stitches when it stops draining."

Peter opened his mouth to speak, but a lump of tears suddenly clogged his throat. He swallowed hard and tried again, the words came out, but they were weak and terrified. "Is she going to be well?" He did not think he wanted to hear the answer and the doctor's sudden look of pity made him cringe.

"She has a lung inflammation, the infection from her arm has weakened her body, and the dunking in the cold river pushed her over the brink." He shook his head sadly and continued with that incessant look of pity that Peter wanted to pummel off of his face. "I want you to be prepared for the worst. I have seldom seen someone this far advanced pull through."

A scream welled up inside Peter, but he held it in. A tear was all that escaped. It slid down his cheek, but he ignored it.

"If she makes it through the night it will be a good omen, but…" The doctor let his voice trail off, saying clearly there was not much hope.

Peter shook his head and sat beside her on the bed. He did not look up when the doctor left. Taking her trembling hands, he kissed them gently. She did not move.

Peter slid in beside her silent body and as night fell Van began to speak. She talked in her delirium to men and women from her past. Peter wondered how much of it was delusion or how many of the wild tales were true.

He sent up a prayer that he would get the chance to find out. He held her close until sleep finally took him.

Morning came and with it the first of the visitors. Matthew arrived at the castle not long after the sun had risen. Peter sat beside Van when Matthew came in to talk to her.

His talks with his daughter had been painful to listen to even though he had been with him through much of it and already knew the tale. Peter watched his face range from pained to ashamed and knew the telling of it was just as painful to say as it was to listen to.

He told her of his life and of the pain of losing her. Of how he regretted it all. He kissed her gently, telling her he would repeat it all to her when she was well.

Peter shuddered and hoped he got the opportunity.

Matthew turned to Peter with a weak smile and a shrug. "Perhaps it will be easier the second time it is told, eh, my boy?"

Peter grasped his trembling shoulder, thinking again how alike the two were. It was more than looks. Matthew may not have raised his daughter, but her temperament was all his.

Matthew took Van's chambers, telling Amy she could move a pallet into the room if she liked. She accepted gratefully and Devon took his place at her side. No one mentioned they were not yet married, and Peter would have had someone's head if they had. They only wanted to be close to Van while she was ill and he would do everything he could to allow it.

The men came and went throughout the day, most only staying for a few moments to check her progress.

It was late afternoon when Peter closed his eyes. He had just begun to doze off when Margaret stopped in with a smile. Peter opened his eyes, but barely registered her asking if she could put a pallet in the hall for that large scary man because he slept on the floor the night before and refused to leave the doorway.

Peter was weary and exhausted. His mind was beyond rational thought. He nodded. She leaned over, kissed Van on the forehead, and Peter slipped into darkness.

When he opened his eyes, the sunlight had faded and Margaret was gone. He lay there for a moment and tried to decide if she had ever been there. He slowly pulled his arm from under Van and slid from the bed.

He tried to remember what Margaret had said, something about the big man sleeping out in the hall? He quietly opened the door and indeed Verges was on a pallet right outside. To Peter's surprise Richard lay sleeping beside him.

Verges opened his eyes. "She all right?" His voice was weary and tired.

Peter shook his head. He wished he knew. "You did not come to see her."

Verges looked down and then back up at him. "It was hard not to, but I did not know if I was welcome."

"Always," Peter said with a smile and walked back into the room.

Peter slid into the bed with her, but sleep eluded him. He kissed her gently and closed his eyes, pulling her overly warm body against his. He did not know how long he laid there before he heard the door open. He opened his eyes only a slit and saw Verges slowly walking toward the bed.

Peter closed his eyes again. He did not want to intrude, but as he was also curious of what the man might say, he feigned sleep. The bed shifted, not enough to indicate that Verges had sat on it, but Peter thought he might have knelt on the floor and rested his arms upon it.

It was silent for long enough for Peter to wonder if perhaps he would not speak. Then his deep voice started in a thick whisper.

He spoke to her of past times and things they had done together. Peter again was surprised as he had been when her men had come to speak to her. They too spoke to her of the past and he was amazed that many of the stories of the young upstart knight had not been embellished.

It was more than the stories they told, it was the concern and love that Peter heard in their voices, as he now heard it in Verges's, and that affected Peter the most.

When Peter opened his eyes again it was to the burning heat against him. Her body twitched as she kicked at the covers. Her high fever scared him and he prayed again that it would soon break.

He looked for Verges, but he was gone. Peter wondered how long he had slept and when he had drifted off.

He got up quickly and brought the night basin over beside the bed. He dipped a soft cloth in the cold water and began to wash her body, trying desperately to cool the burning inside her.

♛ ♛ ♛

The days passed in slow agony for the Grayweist household. Days that Peter did not leave her side, alternating between cold sponge baths to cool her when her fever raged at its highest and laying naked against her, clasping her tightly in a desperate effort to share his warmth when the chills gripped her in their deadly clutches.

It was the same routine over and again all through the long and tedious hours, hours that turned to days. Days that threatened to steal what little sanity Peter had managed to hold on to.

It had gone on for a sennight. Peter's patience and his temper were running thin. He sat watching Verges pace in tight circles like a caged beast until he could stand it no longer. He threw his hands in the air and slapped them against his thighs. "Stop pacing," he said, his voice coming out gruffer than he had intended.

Verges stopped suddenly. "I just feel so useless. What can I do, my lord?" He looked for the world like a lost child.

A distraction was in order before he drove Peter mad. "You can help me with something that I think Vanessa—" He took a deep breath. "Van will approve of."

Verges listened intently to his instructions. A wide smile spread across his face as Peter told him to retrieve her mistresses and their children.

Peter smiled back, but thought Verges's smile just as gruesome as his scowl.

He breathed a sigh of relief when Verges walked out of the room. Turning to look at his wife, he cocked his head. For the first time since he had returned home with her, she lay easy, her breathing calm.

He walked to the large chair he had pulled next to the bed and sat carefully, never taking his gaze from her. He ran his large and calloused fingers along her cool skin, the other hand grasping her limp fingers.

It only took moments to realize her fever had broken and joy bubbled up inside him like a geyser. He had to clamp his lips together tightly to keep from crying out in relief.

It must have happened during the early morning hours. He caressed her cool face and thought back to the night before. Peter realized he had been drenched in her sweat as she embraced him tightly, lost in the grips of a dream. It had been a horrid nightmare and Peter had been terrified.

He closed his eyes against the pain and shuddered as once more he could feel Van writhing in his arms, her body burning with fever. He had not known what else to do but hold her. So that is what he did.

She screamed for Richard to live, her desperate cry cutting through Peter like a dagger. Clinging to him desperately, she told Richard she was sorry. She pleaded with him, telling him that if he would only live she would be the perfect squire, obedient, and calm.

Peter raised a brow at this, but said nothing, only held her tighter. He knew she had lied—obedient and calm did not come easily to his wife— and he found he was glad.

Suddenly the nightmare changed and she began to strike him, her hands reaching for his neck before he could get hold of her wrists. He did not know what to do. He was frightened she would hurt herself as she wrenched at her wrists to free them.

"You will die for what you have done," she whispered in an agonized groan. Then she began to weep, once more talking to Richard. "I have shamed you. She should not have died." Peter was startled that his strong wife was still haunted by the death of the woman she had slain and he felt guilt for ever having brought it up to her.

A small cold hand, tightening in his grip, pulled him from his dark thoughts. He opened his eyes to clear and vibrant black ones. "Van, you are awake. How do you feel?" His voice cracked with relief.

At first she could just shake her head, her voice so tight she could do no more than croak.

Jumping to his feet, he grasped a tankard of ale from the side table and pressed it to her almost white lips, while he carefully supported her head. She drank slowly and he smiled remembering when it had been she who had held the drink for him when he had been injured so long ago. "Better, my love?" he asked when she leaned her head back.

"Aye, my lord," she said and tried to sit up.

He supported her weight and put several pillows behind her so she could prop herself up. The bed swayed under his weight as he sat beside her, clasping her hands. "How do you feel?"

"Tired, thirsty, and confused. How long have I been in bed?" She looked around his chambers and shook her head. "I am sorry, my lord."

Crushing her in his embrace, he took in the welcoming coolness as her arms snaked hesitantly around his neck. Kissing her deeply, possessively, he sighed.

As she gently lay against him he told her first of what had happened in the library with Rebeka, and then of her fall, of the results of the battle, and how long she had worried them all.

"All?" She leaned away from his embrace and collapsed against the pillows. "Who is all?"

"Devon, Gary, Douglas, and every man out there have been by to sit and talk to you. Amy, Joseph, and Anna have been just beside themselves with worry."

A small half grin spread across her ever reddening lips as health flushed back into them.

He grasped her hands and smiled. "Your father," he said, pointing to the adjoining room, "has not left your side. He is also beside himself and would like to talk to you."

"I do not need him to talk to me. I just need to tell him that I understand." Her breathing was low and still labored, but it came easier to her and for that he was delighted.

"Verges and Richard are the ones who have been most concerned, with the exception of me." He pulled her fingers to his lips and kissed them. "I have slept here beside you, never leaving your side. Verges and Richard have slept out in the hall, guarding your door."

Her laugh was like a balm to his soul. Its soothing sound reminded him of the phantom woman that he had dreamed of for so long. It was a relief to know that the woman was not a young boy as he had feared all this time.

"Verges is staying here?" Her black eyes sparkled with gratitude. "Thank you, Peter."

"I need to talk to you about Verges if you are up to it?" The seriousness of his voice caused her smile to disappear and he regretted it.

The gratitude in her eyes faded to concern. She nodded cautiously.

"I have some concerns. He has attacked a woman in the village. She was unhurt and though I think she embellished, he admitted to approaching her with lust on his mind." Van did not look shocked as he had expected, but then he did not know why he had thought she would be. She had known the big man for a long time. "That, I see, does not surprise you, my lady?"

"Nay, I know Verges well. Is that the only trouble?" she asked with a look on her face saying she knew it was not.

"Nay, he has attacked several of the men. Both times it had been one of mine. He is respectful of the men at arms of the Dark Knight, but mine seem to be fair game." He shook his head slowly. Then he smiled. "He broke one man's arm over Miss Violet."

"*Violet*? She is here?" Her hands gripped the edge of the soft down filled blanket as she sat up too quickly and collapsed against him. "*How*?"

Panic set in and Peter clung to her, his heart pounding painfully in his throat. "I will tell you if you promise to lie down and relax."

He waited until her back was sinking into the soft pillows and the color was slowly coming back into her hollowed cheeks.

The scar, like a beacon shining on the tanned skin, called to him. He reached for her cheek and had a momentary fear that she would disappear as she had in his dream.

He knew it was a ridiculous notion, but he had had the same dream every night since she had been hurt. She was always gone before he could touch her.

He sighed in relief at her smooth skin, real and warm, beneath his loving administrations.

"Aye, Violet is here. Violet, Mellie and her son, as well as three other of your ladies. You will have to ask Verges which ones, for I cannot remember the names of all your paramours. The last should arrive later today with Verges." He gave a soft laugh.

"What is so funny?" Her lashes were nearly touching her cheeks as sleep seemed to drag at her.

"I was just thinking it strange, I sent Verges—Verges—to see to the ladies. I sent him so they would not be frightened."

She answered as her eyes closed completely. "That makes sense, Peter. They are comfortable with him. They know him and that he is gentle when he should..." Her eyes flew open. "How is Amy? Did he hurt her badly?"

"Nay, she had not been able to act scared and Verges had to play his part. He played the marauder the way they expected him to."

"I will talk to him, let him know..." Her eyes drifted shut.

After several moments of silence he thought she had fallen asleep.

Then her voice began again as if it had never stopped. "…that the village and your men are as well under my protection. Then everything will be fine." She smiled sleepily, her eyes still shut. "I would tell your men, Violet is special to Verges. He cares for the big woman. Have you seen her, she is bigger than me."

"Aye, she is." Peter had seen her. Violet was thicker than Van and taller. Her figure was like that of a bear, stout and wide. The man, now laid up with a broken arm, called her a giant of a beast.

She was massive and not attractive. Her limp brown hair fell around a face too hawkish for a woman. Her beautiful violet eyes were her best feature, also giving her the name she went by.

He had asked Verges her real name, but he would not divulge it. He thought to ask Van but had a feeling she would say the same.

"I would like to see him cleaned up. She likes him as well." Her voice was now just a whisper.

Peter had spoken to Verges about her after the incident. He had admitted to caring for her, but he did not believe she liked him. "Sturdy, a woman who might be able to accommodate my needs, not that she would ever consider it," Verges had confided.

"Clean him up?" Peter asked carefully.

No answer. Believing she must finally be asleep, he gently pushed himself away from the bed. He walked toward the door, thinking to inform the others of her improvement.

His hand on the door, her voice stilled him. "Aye, he will never get the courage to ask for her love as he is. He needs help."

He turned back and looked at her.

Her eyes pleaded with him. "Help him." Without awaiting an answer, she curled into a ball, sleep finding her quickly.

Days had passed with increasing boredom for Van. She stood staring out the window toward the lists as she thought back over the last two days.

Much to her irritation, the men had not come to see her, none of them. She was distressed and hurt that they had not. She was sure they still held a grudge against her for her deception.

She had held her tongue about her misery and doubts but somehow she thought Peter had known.

He had told her that they were busy. While she had been sick the king had come for his men and now they were trying to get the barracks and the castle ready for the first set of pages that should arrive within days. He had told her not to blame the men, for they were trying to give her the rest she needed.

She was still unsure if that was true She looked out at the lists and wondered why there were no sounds coming from the training grounds or the barracks if they were so busy.

Her heart clenched in pain. She was sure they were avoiding her as they had before she had fallen ill.

She pushed those thoughts away and tried to think of happier ones. Her mind lit on her father. She shook her head in wonder that after so many long years of thinking of him with hatred he was now one of the first places her mind took her when she tried to think of something better.

Her father had finally gone home after a long talk between them. He had laughed, saying he should be insulted that the only way he could get her to listen was when she too weak to fight back or to run.

She had forgiven him, promising to work on a relationship as the years passed. It was something she found she was looking forward to.

She shook her head in wonder again and spoke to the garden below her. "Poor Amy."

Amy, Anna, and Joseph had come to see her yesterday. All her girls had been gathered around the room. Her friends had stood, mouth agape, while Van introduced them to one doxy after another.

Soon all the women would have a home of their own, or husband if one was desired. Peter had told her last night that he already had several warriors asking to be considered for husbands for some of the girls, Melinda included.

Van's smile widened.

Verges had been the biggest surprise. She grinned, rubbing her hand across the back of her neck and stretching.

Verges had seen the doctor on Peter's insistence and his teeth, while still discolored, no longer hurt him. A comfortable bed in the keep, his own chambers with a massive tub, specially made as a gift to him for all he had done had gone far to make him look almost unrecognizable.

"How dare you come into my chambers, a stranger?" she had ribbed him when he had first come in. He had looked surprised at first but then he grinned.

"I take it you approve, my lady?" He stood before her in breeches and tunic. His hooded cloak had been discarded days before. His long black hair hung loose around the disfigurement of his face. It was a face she loved.

"Does Violet approve?" she had asked him. His excited look had told her everything she needed to know.

"I do not hurt her." He had then dropped his voice shyly. "She has agreed to be my wife."

That had gotten her out of bed, flying into his arms. "Verges, I am so happy for you. You mean so much to me. You will stay with us, will you not?"

"Peter has asked me to stay, to help with the training of the new lads. Although the ones who arrived yesterday seemed less than thrilled to see me." His voice dropped to a proud whisper. "One screamed."

Even clean he was a gruesome sight.

She had told him of the village and Peter's men and that they were under her charge. His only response had been to say that some of Peter's men were undisciplined and he aimed to see that changed.

Peter had told her that the men were beginning to mingle. Both sides were reluctant, but compromising. Ranks were the hardest thing to determine, and that what was giving them the most problems.

She grinned, thinking how nice it was that Peter was keeping her informed of the comings and goings of the men. It was a big change from the way their marriage had started out.

Peter walked, unbidden, into the room. He smiled as she turned from the window, drawn out of her reverie as the door closed behind him.

She opened her mouth to speak but he waved her words away. "I have waited for this day for some time now, for you to be well. I need you to come outside with me for a moment."

Curiosity and excitement swirled together and her heart began to race. She was delighted to be out of this room for any reason. She hated being cooped up like a caged animal, it made her hair stand on end and left her nerves frayed.

As she walked toward him he stared at her and seemed to change his mind. "I think it can wait for a moment."

He stepped up to her with a heart so full that he thought it would burst. Reaching for her, he wrapped his arms lovingly around her.

She opened her thick robe and wrapped her arms around his neck. Reveling in her nakedness, he began to kiss her gently as he cupped a full breast, rubbing his calloused thumb across her nipple. He kept his lust under control, not wanting to take her too soon. She was still weak from her illness and he was afraid to hurt her.

Her kisses became desperate and her body arched against his. She wrapped her hands through his hair and held him close as her tongue slid into his wanting mouth.

He kissed her neck and held her tight.

"I love you. I need you." Her words were a soft plea so full of fear— fear of rejection, fear of loss—and yet so heavy with hope that he wanted to cry.

He whispered against her ear as he caressed her, "I love you, my sweet. You are my life."

She began to cry, openly before him, her face glowing with happiness and he smiled. There were now no walls between them, no secrets. Only love and passion.

He pulled away from her, pushing her hair from her face. A beautiful face that he prayed he would see smiling up at him for the rest of his life.

"I did not know what to do when you were so sick. I was so scared I would lose you. If you had died, you would have taken the best of me with you." Peter clung to her as if he were drowning, afraid that if he let go she would somehow disappear.

She clung to him just as vehemently as if she felt the same.

"Please do not leave me, ever," he pleaded.

Her tear-choked voice made his heart swell. "Never."

A knock on the door interrupted them, reminding Peter of why he had come to her in the first place. "We will be right down."

Van looked at him curiously and smiled. She was anxious to see what surprise he had in store for her. She went quickly to her dressing table and did not complain when he assisted her.

Soon he had her dressed, kissing her several times as he helped her into her gown, not bothering with the lacy underclothing she hated so much.

She laughed, feeling happier than she ever had as he swung her into his arms and carried her out into the hall. She clung to his neck and kissed his ear gently. He groaned as he carried her down the wide stairs and out the front doors.

She looked up into the bright sunlight and her breath caught as she looked out over the mass of bodies that swarmed the bailey of the castle.

As Peter stood her on the ground before Richard, she fought against hopeful tears that tickled her throat.

"I apologize that we have not come to see you in the last few days, my lady. I hope you know you were in our prayers and our thoughts." His voice was thick with respect and he looked at her lovingly, as he had when she was still the Dark Knight.

"Richard." The tearful word was all she could say.

Behind Richard were her men, Verges included, and flanking them were Peter's men. All stood at attention. Then as if on cue all her men dropped to one knee before her.

Her hand flew to her throat, her breath caught, and she would have fallen had Peter not grasped her waist. His encouragement meant everything to her, as did his love.

Her eyes met Richard's deep green ones as he spoke. "My liege, we have made a grievous error. We swore our fealty to you and when you needed us the most, we turned away." His voice shook with passion and her heart stilled. "We would reaffirm our pledge to you. Our fealty and honor is yours, if you will but accept it and our humblest apologies."

Richard dropped to his knees before her, his hand outstretched above his bowed head to await her answer.

She looked out at all her men with their heads bowed in a pledge of fealty to her and she was transported back in time to the first time they had made the gesture.

With a lump in her throat she stepped away from her husband and on shaky legs approached her men.

She raised her bare foot and laid it gently in Richard's waiting hand, his fingers curled around it possessively.

Peter stepped up beside her and wrapped a loving arm around her waist. A tear streamed down her face as Peter's men took to one knee.

They were finally as one.

EPILOGUE

England 1161:

Peter paced before two new squires who had been sent from the manor of Lord Johanson. He watched carefully as Daniel Reeres, and Raymond Donlay struggled against their captors.

Daniel cursed as Richard's arms tightened around his kicking and screaming form, while Grant did his best to contain the other irate lad.

Peter knew that things had been coming to a boil between the two arrogant young men for two weeks now. Raymond was a bully, treating the smaller and younger Daniel with malice and disrespect since long before they had arrived.

Their disobedience was the reason they had been sent to Grayweist. Lord Johanson had hoped Peter would be able to turn the boys around. They were at constant war with each other and had been since Daniel had come to be a page under Hardy Johanson.

While Raymond stood at least six foot and was burly as an ox, Daniel was at least a good six inches shorter and thin.

Peter saw great potential in the younger Daniel. His size was not a deterrent to his strength or his skill with a sword. Peter had seen him practicing after the others had gone to sleep. He was good and getting better.

Peter paced back and forth before them and scowled deeply. The men around them waited patiently for the situation to be settled.

Peter had contrived every way to get through to Raymond the importance of judgment. It was not safe to ever assume anything in battle, especially not to underestimate the abilities of another. Appearance meant nothing.

He had tried everything he could think of to get across to the arrogant young know-it-all that appearance meant nothing. Peter did not know how he was going to get him to understand.

His last resort was to give them both a sword and let them deal with it. But until Raymond no longer believed himself impervious to the smaller boy that would not be possible.

Peter knew that if Raymond went into it unprepared and too cocky, one or both of them would be hurt. He had never dealt with a more stubborn fool...Well, yes, there was one, even cockier than any of the boys he had encountered so far, including Raymond. In fact he had spoken to that very arrogant and pigheaded woman about his options concerning the boys.

He smiled as he thought about his beautiful wife. He had missed her in the lists these last seven months, even though he was surprised that she had followed his instructions for once and stayed away.

In the beginning he had fought Van tooth and nail for as long as he could before admitting defeat. When the first pages had arrived three years ago, it had been an everyday battle to keep her away from them.

Peter had absolutely and adamantly refused to let her come to the lists. That had all changed, in a big way, a little more than a year after they had been married.

The boys and the men faded from his mind as he was swept back to that warm day two years ago...

Peter returned to the lists after seeing to his tenants. Anger swirled through him when he saw his wife standing nose to nose with one of his new men, Mavis Bowers. He shook his head. She was not even supposed to be at the lists.

He dismounted several paces away, but neither seemed to take notice of him as they shouted at each other.

Mavis loudly told her to take herself back to the kitchen where she belonged and Peter cringed as she threatened to cut off the place where his brains were dangling.

Peter rushed toward them, hoping to stop the confrontation before it got any further out of hand. The men and the new pages were all milling around, unsure of what to do.

Peter stopped at Van's side just as Bowers drew his sword. Peter had a quick vision of her, sick and fevered in bed, as she had been after the battle with Eolian and fear quickly turned to rage.

He pulled Van behind him and advanced on Mavis. "If you would like to live, I would suggest you never insult my wife again." His voice boomed with the darkness of a thunderstorm.

The color drained from Mavis's face and he dropped his sword.

Peter turned to Van, surprised to see her calmly waiting for him to finish. She mounted her horse willingly and said nothing when he mounted Jackal and reined in beside her.

Unease began to set in his mind, but he pushed it away, telling himself that she was acting this way because he was finally getting through to her. She rode silently to the castle, a slight smile on her face the entire way.

At the castle he kissed her gently.

She kissed him back, but the grin she gave him sent chills down his spine, he just wasn't sure why.

He dismounted again at the lists and Richard and Devon, as well as several others of the men who had ridden with Van before their marriage, stared at him with concern and misgivings. "What is that look for?" he asked Richard.

Richard smiled a little uneasily. "I just have not seen the Dark Knight in a while, my lord."

"You see her every day," Peter said surprised.

"Aye, I see her every day, but it has been a long time since I have seen him," Richard said. When Peter had only stared at him, Richard shook his head. "You interrupted at the wrong time. He has been tormenting her since his arrival six months ago, saying he has heard of the reputation of the Dark Knight."

Peter sucked in a deep breath and shook his head. Her silence had not been acquiescence, but anger. He shuddered to think of what her devious mind was planning to get even with him.

Richard sighed and looked across at Mavis who smiled arrogantly as he spoke to some of the men. "He thinks it is all exaggerated or else she is lying about being him, and he had told her so. She had decided enough was enough, and when you pulled her away she had just put her hand on the hilt of her sword."

"Hell," Peter said quietly. He looked in the direction of the castle and considered going to her before she did anything rash.

"You embarrassed her. Now he thinks he was right to call her just a woman and not to respect her." Richard shrugged apologetically. "When you pulled her behind you like she needed protection, I saw the Dark Knight come forward."

Peter laughed and it was an uneasy sound that made him shudder. "That explains the grin. I did not understand why it had made me nervous when I dropped her off, now I do. I will—"

Thundering horse beats cut his words off. Turning, he blanched.

Riding toward him, in full armor, was the Dark Knight. She rode with her black helm resting on her thick thigh, and an arm slung carelessly over the top of it.

"She is beyond enraged, my lord." Richard gave a groan. "She has the helm off so you will see it."

She took both hands off the reins and slipped the helm over her thick black braid. Damien skidded to a shaky halt before the men. Before he had come to full stop, she had landed on the ground, sword in hand.

"I would suggest you draw your sword." At Devon's warning to Bowers, Peter looked at the unprepared man as Van approached.

Mavis laughed, proclaiming loudly, "Putting on a costume changes nothing. You will always be just a girl, *Vanessa*."

Peter looked at her, thinking of the strength she possessed and fearing for Mavis's safety.

Van twisted her hand and rotated the sword until it pointed out behind her like a dagger ready to plunge into the man's heart. She swaggered toward him lowering her head until all that showed in the shadows beneath the helm was the arrogant grin.

Richard shoved Peter forward. "God, she will kill him."

Even as Peter began to move, the Dark Knight's deep, graveled growl, full of arrogance and pride, proved Richard was right about her intent. "This *girl* has killed better men than you."

With no more warning than that, she swung her sword in an overhand arch and almost took off Mavis's head before he got his sword free to stop her. She rotated her calloused hand once more and the sword swung back into the proper position.

The ensuing battle was short, but violent as she hacked at him with the same ferocity she had possessed in her encounter with Ryan Deumount. The only difference being, Bowers was not the swordsman he thought he was.

Mavis lost his sword to a heavy blow and was dropped to his knees by the crushing impact to his ribs that followed. The flat of her sword had knocked the wind from him and he held up his hands in surrender.

Peter saw the battle lust still raging in her eyes and was prepared when she swung her blade in for the killing blow. The ring of steel echoed across the field as Peter stepped in front of the downed man.

Horror spread through Peter when instead of giving up as he had expected her to, her grin spread and she swung on him. On him, her husband. He could not believe it, and he barely had the wits about him to raise his weapon to defend himself.

"Stop. What are you doing?" he asked in a panic.

His wife advanced on him as he stepped back. She didn't answer his question, just thrust at him once more.

He deflected the soft blow with a growl. "Stop. Now." He was starting to lose his temper, which with her it seemed to happen all too often.

"Why?" She parried and thrust without the fervor she had used only moments ago. "Are you afraid to face me?"

Peter didn't believe it for a moment. Her deep ebony eyes still smoldered with the fires of her unsatisfied anger.

At first he only tried to block her blows, but his temper was getting the best of him. When she swung several hard, true hits against him, he stepped away stunned by the strength behind them.

She had been his wife for over a year. When did she practice to stay in such shape?

Her ringing voice put him quickly on the offensive. "Men, what is your lord's first rule of battle."

The men all spoke in unison, their voice clearly ringing though the lists. "Never underestimate your enemy."

He attacked.

The men circled them unsure of what to do. The battle raged until both combatants were slick with sweat.

Van sliced through his chain mail with a slow sweep of her sharpened sword and Peter returned the blow with a bruising shot to her ribs.

With a grunt of pain she doubled over. Peter knew she would not surrender to him, and he caught the hilt of her sword, ripping it from her hands. It skidded across the meadow tearing a swatch through the grass. He lifted the sword to her throat to show he had won.

His heart fell into his stomach as Van spun toward him and the deadly sharp edge of his sword scratched the skin of her throat, a trickle of blood ran down her dark, tanned skin.

Horrified he thought to withdraw his sword and beg her forgiveness. That was until he felt a sharp pain in his abdomen. Looking down his eyes widened in disbelief.

Through the rent in his mail she had slipped her dagger, the very one he had given her, its jeweled hilt sparkling in the warm sunlight. The cold steel had pierced his skin, not enough to be lethal, but enough to know it was there.

She smiled, no, she grinned that same devil-may-care grin that still tormented him. "Shall we call it a draw, my lord husband?"

Unfortunately, it was then that he noticed more blood than the small trickle on her exposed neck. The shot to her ribs had torn through her mail, and was now bleeding.

He dropped his sword tip to the ground and took a step toward her with a question on his lips.

Her soft whisper stopped him more than the dagger that had somehow found its way from his waist to his neck. "You were not about to ask me if I was all right in front of your men, now would you have been, Dragon Knight?"

When he shook his head no, she smiled up at him with such love and adoration that it took all the control he had not to sweep her into his arms and kiss her—and be damned who saw it.

His control may not have been enough to keep him from her arms, but her arrogant words were. "You do know, my lord, that the only reason I did not take your head on the many occasions you gave me was because you are my husband and I love you, right?"

His laughter rang out across the lists. "And you know that the only reason you got those occasions was because I went easy on you, because I love you, my lady wife."

He watched her retrieve her sword, but instead of sheathing it she pointed it to the assemblage. Her smile was gone, the knight back.

The growl was directed to Mavis, who now stood looking at her with awe. "Anytime you want to lose that wagging tongue of yours to my blade, just call me Vanessa once again." Her eyes swept the men. "That goes for anyone."

He watched in pride as she sheathed her weapon and mounted Damien, who had stood calmly while steel rang around him. She faltered slightly and Peter forced himself not to help her.

He had to see to her wound, but he would not embarrass her again. He smiled, walking to his horse.

"I shall return soon, I need to take care of something," he said ignoring the warning scowl she sent at him. "I do have one sword she will not fight if I use it on her."

Her face flushed red with embarrassment and she kicked Damien into a gallop.

She had made it to the castle and her bed chambers before he arrived. Miceal met him at the door. "She says you are not allowed to enter in your armor."

"Why? So she has a better shot with that bloody dagger?" Even as he grumbled he quickly allowed Miceal to assist him. Telling him to bring some hot water and fresh bandages, he entered her room.

She stood naked before him, her back to him. The first thing he noticed was the gash across her ribs she was dabbing at with a linen cloth. He had done this to her.

He tried to ignore her naked breasts and backside as well as his painful arousal and tried to push her onto the bed. "Sit, I need to clean you, to see if you need stitching. It may hurt. I am so sorry. Can you forgive me for—"

Her lips stopped his words as she wrapped her arms around him pulling him onto the bed. He fell between her spread legs.

"What are you doing? You are bleeding. I have to see to you. We cannot—" He groaned deeply as her swift hands released him from his braies.

♚ ♚ ♚

Peter quickly pulled himself from his memories before he hardened and embarrassed himself before his men. He looked at them and shook his head, pacing before them.

They had stopped their struggling and now stood watching him, a look of growing concern spreading across their faces. He smiled and thought to make them sweat a little longer.

Peter remembered scolding Van for her stupidity, had scolded her with zeal with every stitch he put in her side. But from that day on she was at the lists, in full gear. She not only watched the men but fully participated in the training of the boys, as well as practicing with the men.

When the men at arms had left her wanting more and bored, she would seek out her husband. She did so in such a charming way that he had never turned her down.

She would sway her hips up to him, look up through her long lashes, and smile so sweetly it almost made him forget himself. She would wink at him and say, unfortunately loud enough for all to hear. "I will go easy on you, my love, as not to tire you for when you want to sheath your sword later."

He blushed now as he thought about it.

When she could not draw him to the lists to practice because he had other things to do, she would wait along his route to ambush him. Leaping onto him, or knocking him from his horse. He had bloodied her nose more than once. He had growled at her once. "You cannot keep doing this. I am going to hurt you. I have to assume you are an enemy, I cannot let my guard down."

Her response, spoken with a slight pouting of her lips, was, "If you ever let it down, I would be disappointed, and no longer feel the challenge of besting you."

He didn't try to dissuade her again, but he got his own revenge on the few occasions he could outsmart her.

Things had changed much for him in the three years he had been married. He had gone from thinking a woman didn't have a decent opinion, to relying heavily on his sometimes sweet, sometimes angry, but always volatile wife's suggestions.

Now he went to her first when he had a dilemma. She was clever, stubborn and extremely intelligent.

His thoughts were drawn back to the problem before him as Grant cursed the arrogant and stubborn Raymond who had once again began to struggle. Peter had moved to intercede when Raymond stopped struggling and all the men stared.

He cursed loudly as he saw what they were seeing.

Coming awkwardly toward them, stopping every few steps to grab her swollen and massive stomach, was his beautiful wife. Her pregnancy, the reason she had been forbidden to come to the lists, was well into its final stages. "Speaking of stubborn," he said irritably as he started toward her.

The boys were released as the two knights that had held them stepped toward their lady, concern thick in their eyes. The men, pages, and squires watched as Lady Van leaned heavily on the massive frame of Verges.

Peter paused and watched as Verges shook his head vigorously, once, and then twice. Whatever it was, she seemed to be insisting on obedience.

It did not look good and, if Peter knew his wife, more than likely it would be worse for him.

Verges supported her, her trembling frame leaning heavily in his embrace. Panic set in as Peter took in the pain contorting her face. Labor had begun. "Verges, what is the meaning of this? She should not be here in her condition." His voice was edged with anger and fear.

"I am so sorry, my lord. This was not my idea." Verges released her, pulling Peter into a massive and painful bear hug. As the men came forward, the big warrior called a halt to the rescue by placing his dagger to Peter's throat.

All swords drew forth with an ear ringing chime, steel slipping from the tight leather scabbards. A deep sigh came from Verges.

"I am sorry, my lord," he repeated.

Van, taking first Verges's sword and then Peter's, walked toward Raymond, no sign of the pain or the labor that had plagued her only moments ago. It had been a trick, Peter thought.

"So sorry, my lord," Verges repeated.

"Stop saying that and let me loose. She will be hurt." He struggled in vain, helpless to do anything but watch. "What is she doing?" he asked, but he already knew.

Van had told him that Raymond would always think himself above everyone until someone showed him differently, but she had agreed he could not just throw Daniel at him.

He cursed himself for not realizing she had told him last night of her plans. She had said, "He needs to be beaten by someone unexpected, not one he would think a challenge, but it has to be someone of experience."

He had just laughed, saying Raymond would be well prepared for anyone with skill. He remembered her knowing smile. When suspicion had started to bud in his mind, she had kissed it away.

He had been wrong. And he was angry at her for her distracting him, for her ability to do so. "Verges, she will be hurt. What if he hurts the baby?"

"She, at least, has chain mail under her gown. It is long and is some protection for the child." His voice was a mere whisper. "I am sorry, my lord, I must do as she says. I do not believe she will be hurt." His voice shook with uncertainty. He then added with conviction. "Besides, if it looks as if she may be even slightly fatigued, I will release you, no matter her anger at me for doing so."

"I know," Peter said and ceased his struggles. "I also know I am going to beat her as soon as she has that baby. It cannot protect her much longer. Yes, as soon as she has the child, I will blister her sweet little bottom till she cannot sit. This is too much. She is taking years off my life."

Van looked across the boys and recognized Raymond on sight. She had dealt with his kind often enough to know the look.

She threw Peter's sword to the sixteen year old boy. He reached up and grabbed it. She smiled. "You are Donlay. I have heard about you."

"I am. Who are you?" he snarled at her. "Are you the wife of that menacing giant who hit me within an hour of meeting me?" He sent a scathing scowl toward Verges. "I am the son of the Duke of Blightly and you do not know who you are messing with."

There was a look of surprise as the heavy sword came down at him without a word. His reflexes brought his up, steel sparking against steel.

Much to her disappointment, there would be no playing with this mouse as she would have liked to. That would risk the baby, and she would not do that. She knew she had to end it quickly.

She swung hard against him. He was quick with his returning thrusts, but not quick enough. She watched with a growing grin as he began to take on a panicked, harried look.

Less than a dozen swift swings on her part left him struggling for breath and looking confused at how he could possibly be losing. One more swing took the sword out of his hand, flinging it to the grass beyond them.

Van lunged toward him quickly bringing the deadly tip of the long blade to his throat. Off balance, Raymond fell.

Van smiled.

With a bewildered Raymond lying on the ground, sword still at his throat, Van looked around the group of awe-eyed boys. She ignored the angry looks from the men-at-arms and the knights.

They all looked ready to take a switch to her, Verges included. There was nothing she could do about that now. She had to finish it.

She cringed, thinking of Verges' anger when he found out that her pains of labor had not been falsified for show as she had claimed.

Her deep, graveled growl echoed as she shouted, pointing the sword at the assembled company. "What is the first rule of battle?" She fought nausea and a quickly passing light-headedness.

Everyone responded. "Never underestimate your opponent."

Turning the sword back to the embarrassed boy sprawled on the ground, she posed the same question to him. She got the same answer.

"Never underestimate your opponent," she repeated, her voice loud and strong, the pain hidden for now, but not for long.

She motioned for Raymond to rise. He swiftly complied. Pointing her weapon at the assembly her voice faltered as her abdomen rippled, pain driving through it.

"Never! Whether it be a known enemy."

Her sword swung to Verges. "A loyal friend."

Her searching sword found Daniel. "A smaller combatant."

She thrust the sword into the soft earth, the hilt quivering. "Or a very pregnant woman."

A soft wave of her delicate hand and Verges released his prisoner. Peter was to her side in a moment. "Are you stupid, or do you just not care about our child?" Despite the anger in his voice his hands were gentle as he caressed her stomach. The roughness of the chain mail caught at his fingers.

"I told him you would be all right. That you were just acting," Verges said.

She dropped her head guiltily.

"Van?" Verges growled out the question with quiet anger. "You said…" He gave a sharp laugh. "Careful wording and you can say anything and get away with it." His voice was tight, strained.

"Van, you were acting, were you not?" Peter, his hands still on her, already knew the answer as her stomach heaved beneath his fingers. It infuriated him. "You went against another blade when you were in labor. You are stupid." He sucked in a tight breath. "I am lucky although, you will not be pregnant much longer. With the baby coming, it will not be long now."

"What will not be long?" Her voice was a shadow of itself and fear enveloped Peter as the contractions came once again.

He cringed at the pain that rippled through her features. "Nothing, but I am sure Verges will help me with it." His threats were forgotten as she suddenly clung to him, collapsing fully into his embrace.

Her arms wrapped her stomach, her teeth cut into her lip, blood oozing, as her stomach heaved in another contraction.

She shuddered in his arms. "Please, do not let me scream here."

His heart wrenched as a tear slipped from her tightly closed lids.

"Did you walk here?" Was that his voice, so thin and full of terror and uncertainty?

"Nay, we have the wagon just on the other side of the trees," Verges said and before anyone could speak Raymond ran in the direction Verges and Van had come from.

Peter watched him race away and smiled. He figured the boy had to do something instead of standing there with the realization that a pregnant lady of the castle had beaten him in sword play.

In moments the carriage, Raymond driving it, was racing toward them.

Peter quickly got her into the carriage and Verges took charge of the reins. The carriage lurched and soon were flying back to the manor.

Peter heard the sounds of horses behind the carriage. Then a contraction ripped through Van, and he was aware of nothing but the terrible pain his beloved wife was in.

"Hold on, we will be there in a moment. We will get a midwife, you will be fine—"

His breath caught and his heart stopped at the quick shake of her head. Her hands clung desperately to him, drawing him close. "Nay."

"Aye, you will be f–fine." He stumbled on the words. His tongue seemed big enough for two people.

"Aye, I will be fine with you by my side. I meant, that we will not get to a midwife. I will not make it to the castle." Her voice strained with pain and she clenched her eyes tightly shut. "I have to lie down. It is coming now." Her voice was starting to pick up a slight slur.

"You will make it fine. It will only be a minute. Labor I am told takes all day." He told himself that she could not have the baby in a rolling carriage. No, that was impossible. They would make it.

She began to struggle off the seat and he saw two options, try to stop her or help her. He helped her onto the floor of the carriage. She lay back and refused to meet his eyes.

"It has been all day. Do not be ma—" A quick cry was ripped from her as she bore down, the contraction the worst yet. "Please, it is coming." His face drained of color and his breath felt ripped from his lungs.

Her moans grew closer together as the contractions came one on top of another. Peter's stomach clenched as he saw a thick gush of fluid spread beneath Van.

Frantically she scooted against the wall of the rocking conveyance, drawing her knees up and apart to allow room on the floor for Peter. Not an easy task for two large people, but Peter thought nothing of the cramped space as she ripped the long skirt of her kirtle up and out of the way.

Peter groaned, feeling faint at the sight of the red tinged liquid pooling beneath her quivering bottom.

He could see her fighting a scream, her lip bleeding in several places where she had bitten into it. Small crescents cut into her palms, the blood seeping in rivulets.

He shook his head, knowing her reasoning. She felt it was not honorable to scream, to show weakness, and she would not as long as she could possible hold it off.

"Hold on." Peter crammed himself between her knees, gently rubbing her thighs. He pushed the chain mail up her rippling stomach and shuddered. He had only been this frightened once before, when she was so sick with fever. And that had been years ago.

"Peter, help me, it's coming." Her soft gasping whisper scared him far more than the screams he had heard when other women gave birth.

As a man he had never occupied a room when the process took place. He didn't know anything about delivery. Questions swirled in his addled brain.

Should there be blood? Was she supposed to be this pale? What was all the water from? Was it a bad sign?

"Please, Van. Hold on. I cannot live without you. Please do not leave me. I love you." He massaged her heaving belly gently, clutching at her trembling thighs as contraction after contraction slammed through her.

He was the one to scream when he realized the strain on her face, the tightness in her muscles. She was pushing, God help him. "Verges, hurry." They had to be almost there, they seemed to have traveled for hours, not just the few minutes they had.

Peter felt relief as the carriage came to a jerky stop. It swayed precariously to the side as Verges jumped hard to the ground, screaming orders for hot water, clean linens and a midwife.

His relief was short lived as the rounded belly under his hands tightened, harder than a rock. A ripple roved just below the skin. A head appeared, a soft cry of pain escaping Van's pale lips. Her hair was plastered to her head with sweat and tears. One more swift push and she collapsed back. The baby came in a gush of blood and fluids.

Peter barely registered when the door was ripped open behind him, barely took note of Verges' curse, followed by a call for the midwife to come to the carriage.

All Peter could see was the perfect miracle that rested in his arms. His son, a small version of himself, began screaming at the intrusion of cold air against the warm wet skin. His healthy cries were wondrous to hear.

"Van. We have a son." His voice was full of wonder.

She smiled at him through weary eyes. "Father will be pleased when he knows he has a grandson."

Peter laughed. "Even more so when he learns you have named the boy after him." Peter laid the child on her chest and wrapped his arms around her to hold his family to him.

He had never been happier or more loved.

About the Author

Dawn Chandler was born in Coffeyville, Kansas but doesn't remember much about it. Though she recently had the opportunity to visit there with her husband, and she very much enjoyed the Dalton Museum. She always thought she should have been born in the Wild West. She moved to Idaho when she was 6 and grew up on Murtaugh Lake, where her father was the dam keeper and the ditch rider. She spent her days in the lake, swimming, catching fish and tadpoles, from sunup to sundown most days. Not hard to imagine that her first full length novel was about a mermaid. At nights she would spend her time watching football with her dad or cooking with her mom. In 8th grade she had a teacher, Mrs. Smith, who wanted her to publish one of her short stories. Looking back on it she says she should have done so. If she had, she would have been an author before now, but she was not ready to be published back then. When she first started writing in school she hated it. She had to write their way and only their way—in the correct process, outline, rough draft, and so on. Chandler has learned in the progressing years that she is a seat-of-the-pants author, but in the beginning she just thought that writing was not for her. She could not, no matter how she tried, get the outline done. She could not sit and sketch out a whole story from beginning to end. She found quickly that if she just sat and wrote, she could get the first draft out without a problem, but the teachers didn't want her to do it that way. She really began to love writing when she met Mrs. Smith and she told Chandler that she could write it in whichever order she wanted. She understood her as a writer and didn't push her to be something she wasn't. She has been writing ever since.

She is grateful to have the support of her husband and children. Together they have 7, Charles, Cynthia, Kara, Mary, Tina, Pam, and Richie. She loves them all dearly and is happy to have them in her life. Now that her kids are all grown up, she likes to spend time on the semi-truck with my husband, Rod, seeing the country. She loves visiting all the small towns and is grateful to all the nice people she has met. She enjoys swimming, camping, four wheeling with her 4 X 4 group, spending time with family and friends, hiking, writing (of course), drawing, painting, reading (a vastly wide list of authors, her favorite though is Stephen King), and she loves taking pictures as she travels the countryside (if she is lucky and they are not in a big hurry and can even stop to take them). Today she is busily writing her novels, *The Dark Lady*, released in 2013, through Black Opal Books, *The Infamous A.H.* to follow shortly (fingers crossed), and about 50 more started in the computer that will be released as time and her muse allows.

Visit Dawn at her website: http://www.dawnchandler.net.

www.ingramcontent.com/pod-product-compliance
Lightning Source LLC
Chambersburg PA
CBHW060150260626
47160CB00001B/201